UNICORN BOY

DAVE ROMAN

COLOR BY HEATHER MANN

:01

First Second
NEW YORK

Special thanks to Jessica and Jacinta Wibowo (JesnCin) for coloring pages 1, 3, 8, 20, 25, 26, and 27. And John Patrick Green for his help with fonts and typography.

First Second

Published by First Second
First Second is an imprint of Roaring Brook Press,
a division of Holtzbrinck Publishing Holdings Limited Partnership
120 Broadway, New York, NY 10271
firstsecondbooks.com
mackids.com

Library of Congress Cataloging-in-Publication Data is available.

Our books may be purchased in bulk for promotional, educational, or business use. Please contact your local bookseller or the Macmillan Corporate and Premium Sales Department at (800) 221-7945 ext. 5442 or by email at MacmillanSpecialMarkets@macmillan.com.

FIRST
EDITION

First edition, 2024
Edited by Calista Brill, Kiara Valdez and Steve Foxe
Cover design by Molly Johanson
Interior book design by Molly Johanson and Casper Manning
Production editing by Helen Seachrist
Authenticity read by Jackson Bird
Color by Heather Mann

Drawn with Papermate sharpwriter pencils on Strathmore Bristol paper.
Inked using a combination of Windsor Newton Series 7 sable brushes, Speedball India ink, Pentel Brush pens, and the Procreate and Astropad Studio apps for iPad.
Lettered (mostly) with Yaytime font.

No cats or muffins were harmed in the making of this book.

Printed in China by 1010 Printing International Limited, Kwun Tong, Hong Kong

ISBN 978-1-250-83026-5 (paperback)
1 3 5 7 9 10 8 6 4 2

ISBN 978-1-250-83027-2 (hardcover)
1 3 5 7 9 10 8 6 4 2

Don't miss your next favorite book from First Second!
For the latest updates go to firstsecondnewsletter.com and sign up for our enewsletter.

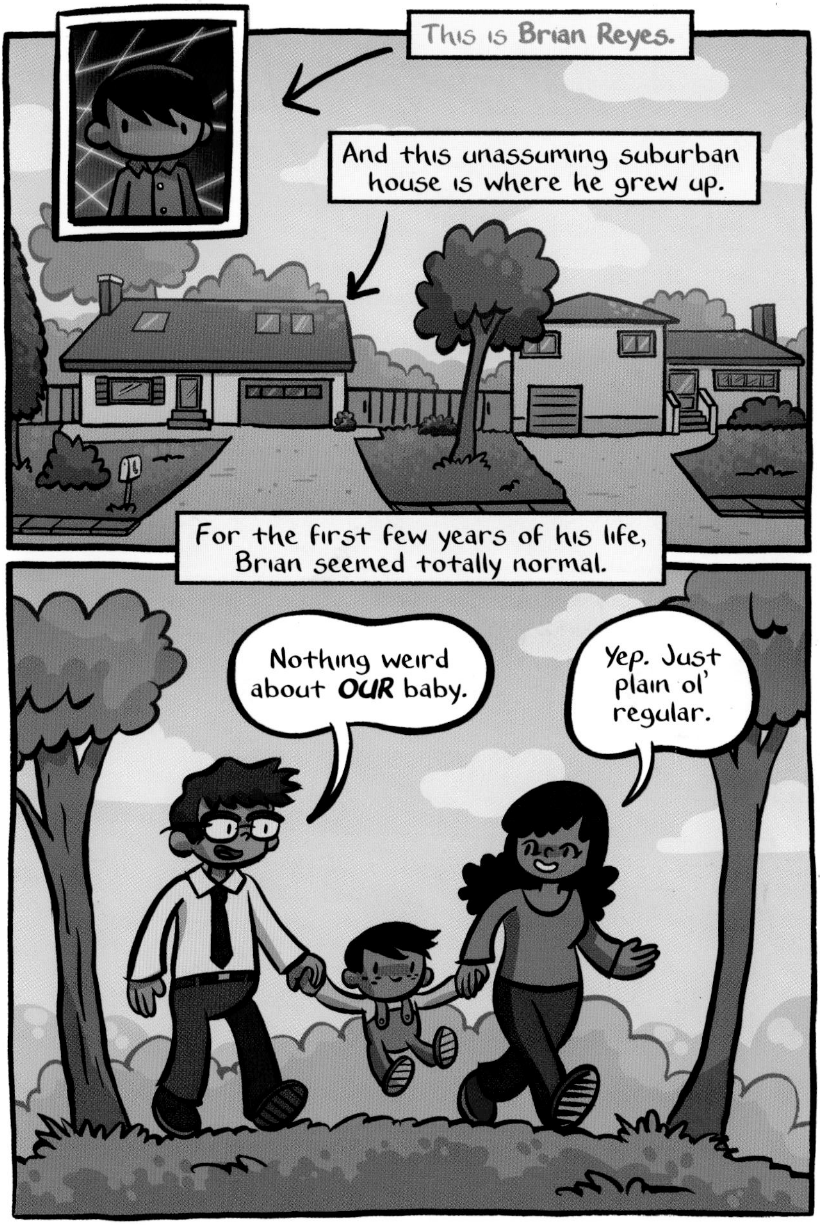
This is Brian Reyes.
And this unassuming suburban house is where he grew up.
For the first few years of his life, Brian seemed totally normal.
Nothing weird about OUR baby.
Yep. Just plain ol' regular.

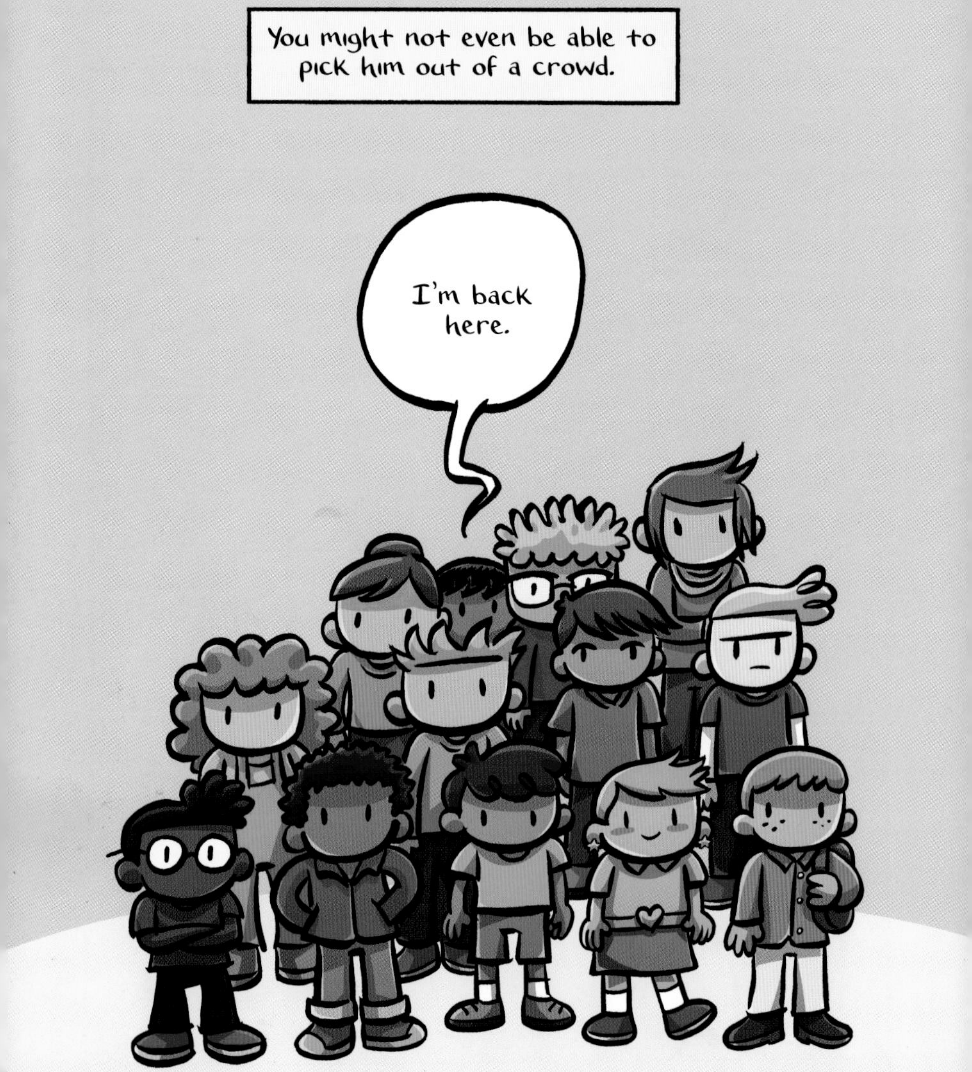
You might not even be able to pick him out of a crowd.
I'm back here.

But one average Tuesday afternoon, Brian found a new bump he'd never noticed before.
That's **DIFFERENT.**
OUCH!
And sharp!

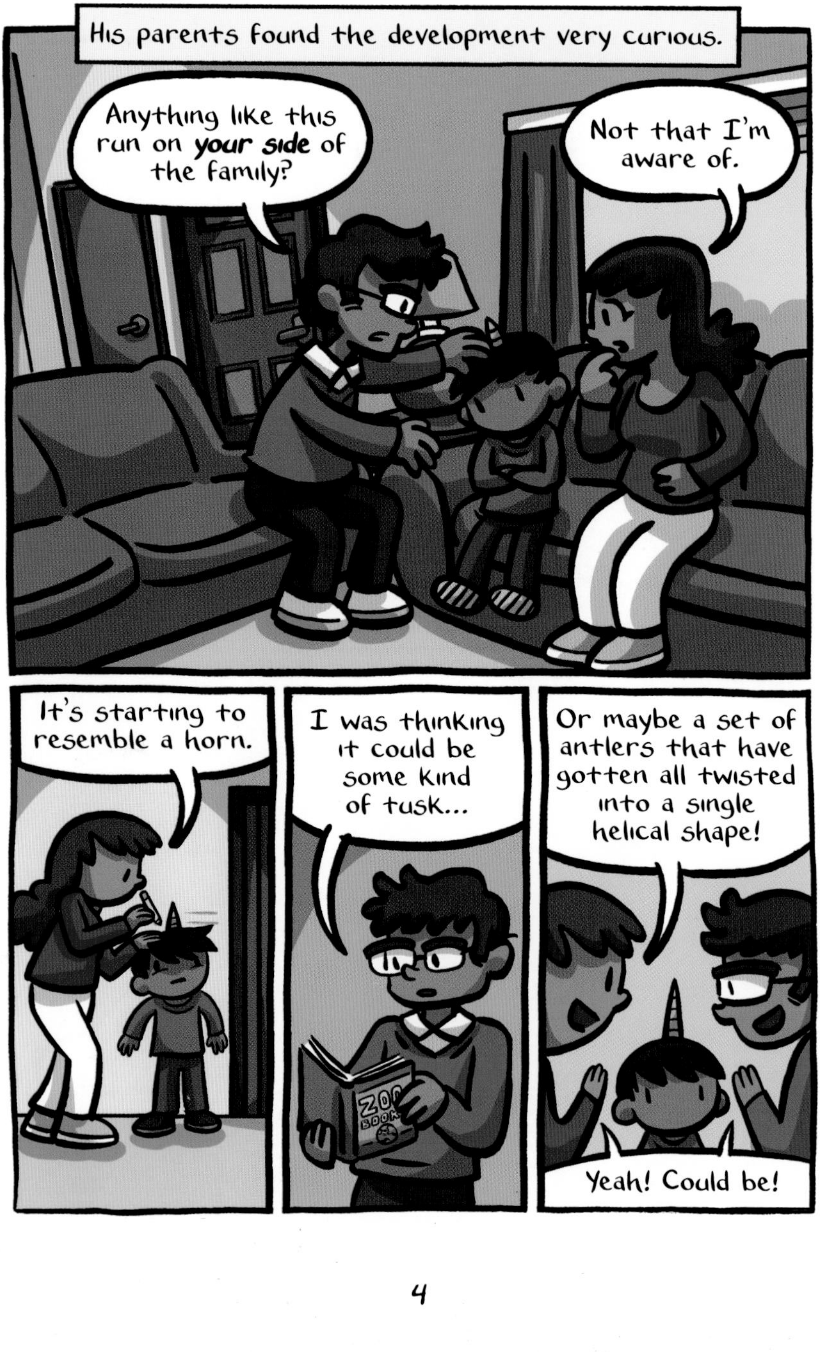
His parents found the development very curious.
Anything like this run on **your side** of the family?
Not that I'm aware of.
It's starting to resemble a horn.
I was thinking it could be some kind of tusk...
Or maybe a set of antlers that have gotten all twisted into a single helical shape!
Yeah! Could be!
ZOO BOOK

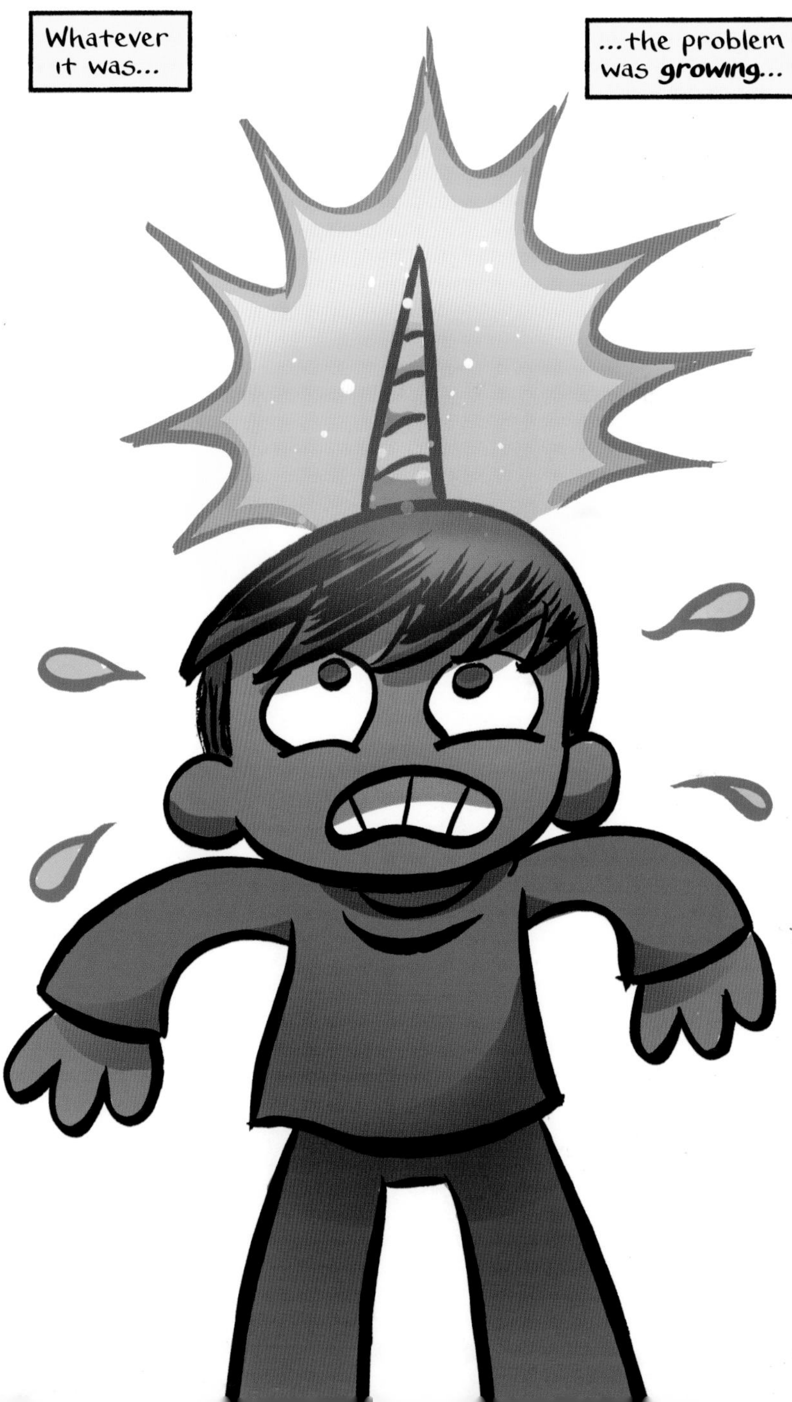
Whatever it was...
...the problem was **growing**...

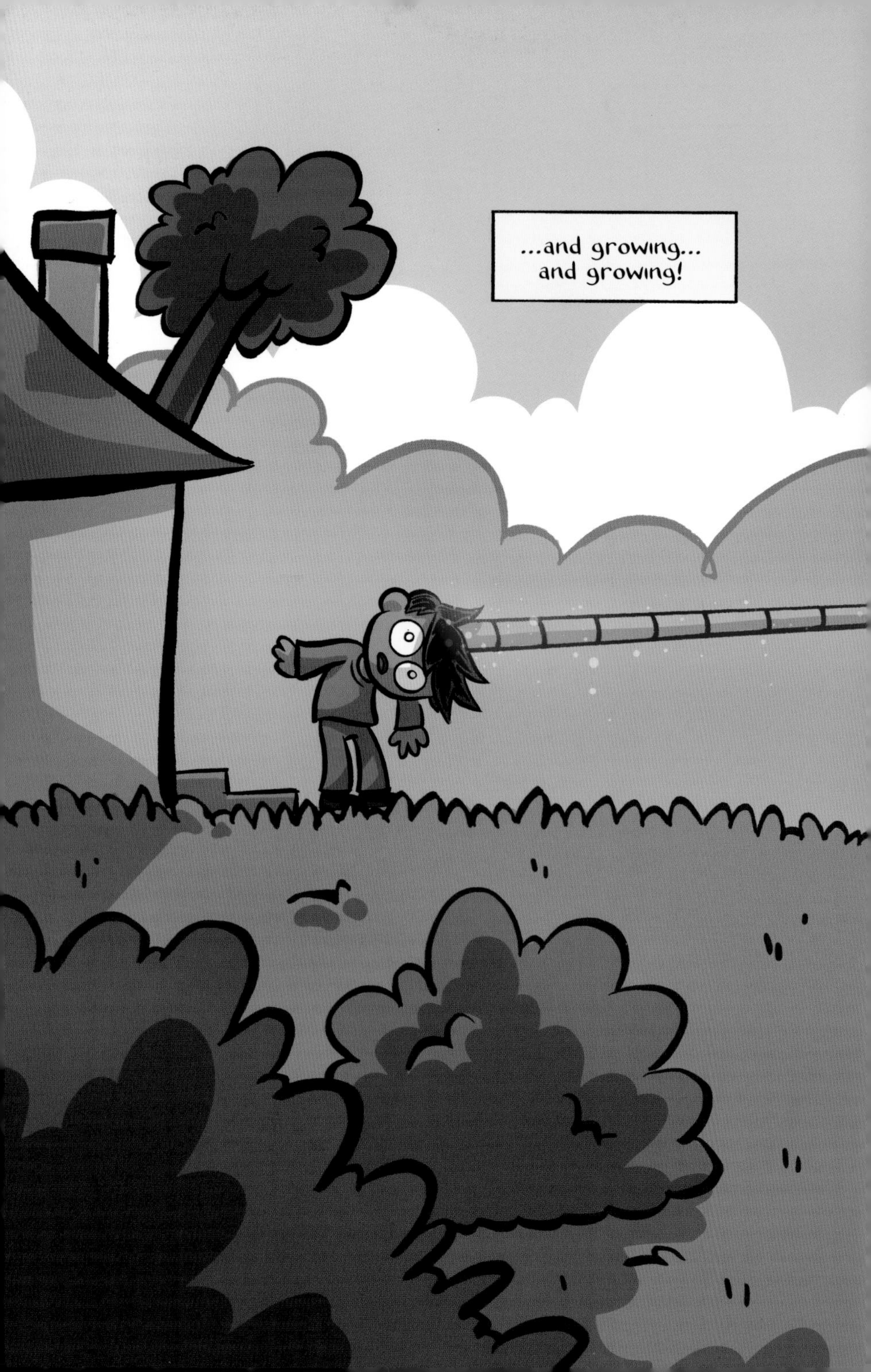
...and growing...
and growing!

Okay, maybe not **that** big...
...but it certainly felt like things were **spiraling out of control.**
MAIL

Was it magic? **Probably.**
FIZZ
POP
BOOM
HUZZAH
It was certainly unpredictable.

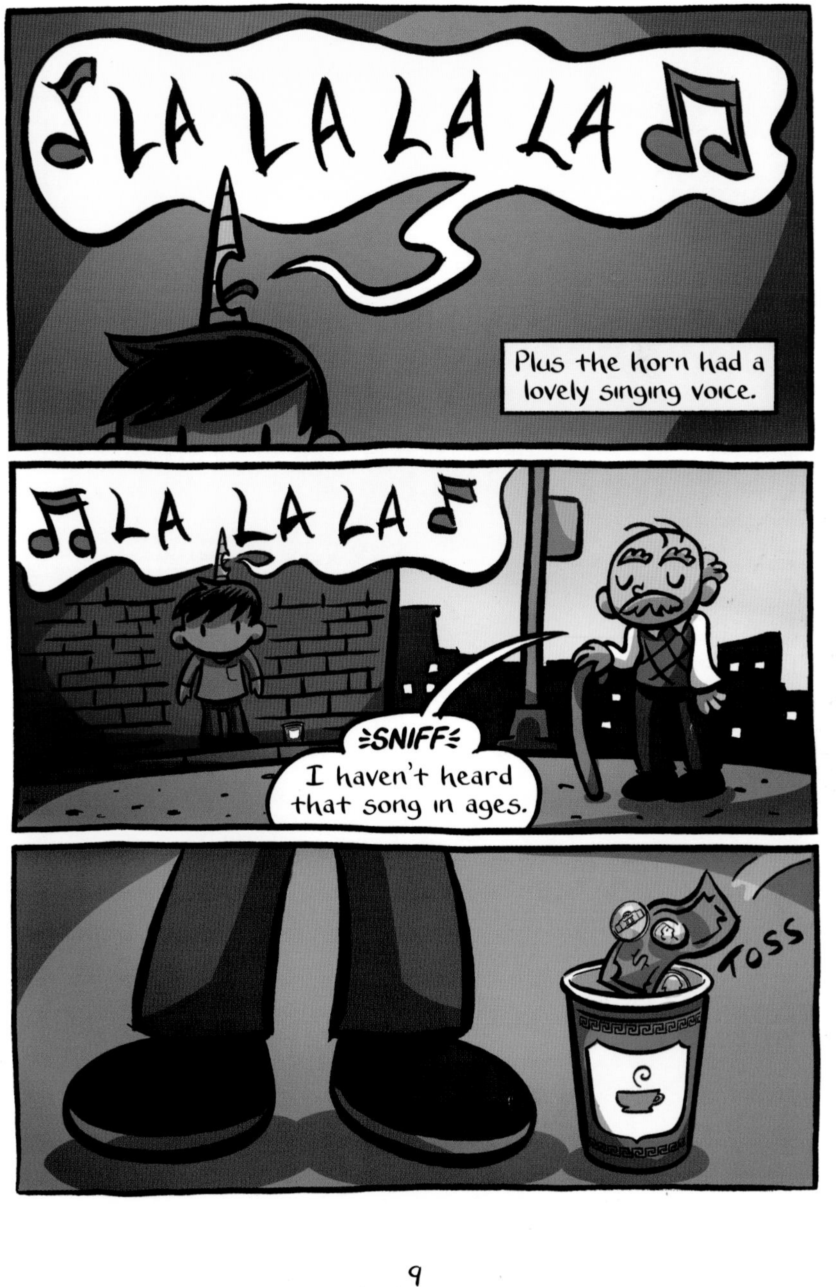
LA LA LA LA
Plus the horn had a lovely singing voice.
LA LA LA
SNIFF
I haven't heard that song in ages.
TOSS

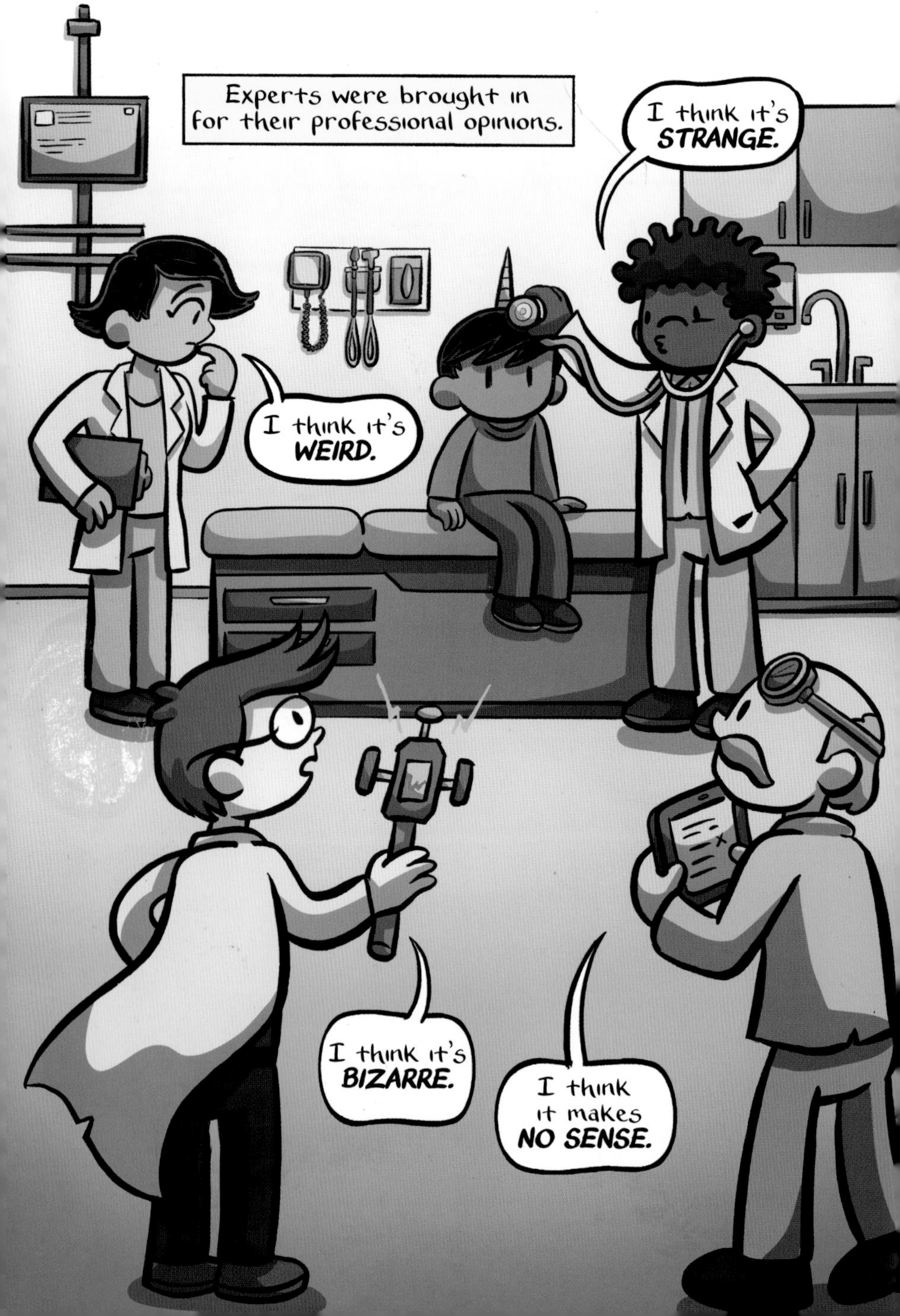
Experts were brought in for their professional opinions.
I think it's STRANGE.
I think it's WEIRD.
I think it's BIZARRE.
I think it makes NO SENSE.

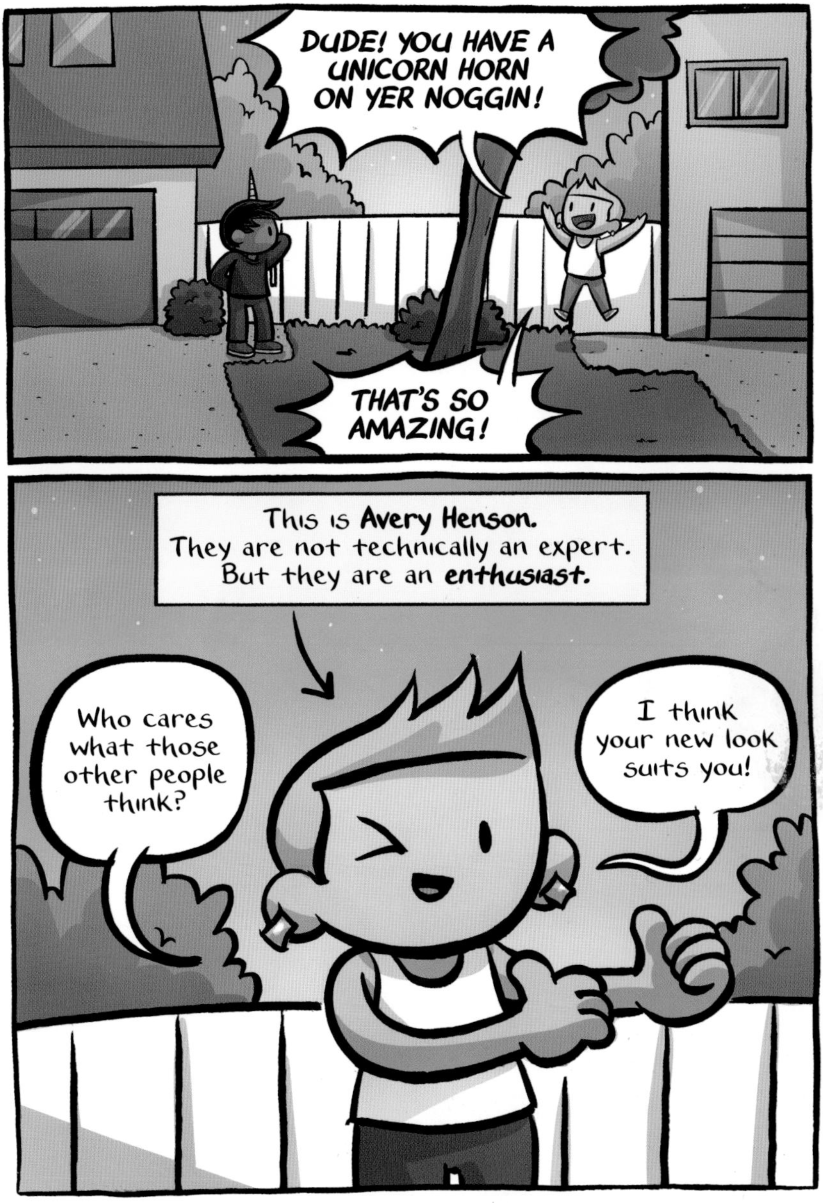
DUDE! YOU HAVE A UNICORN HORN ON YER NOGGIN!
THAT'S SO AMAZING!
This is **Avery Henson.** They are not technically an expert. But they are an **enthusiast.**
Who cares what those other people think?
I think your new look suits you!

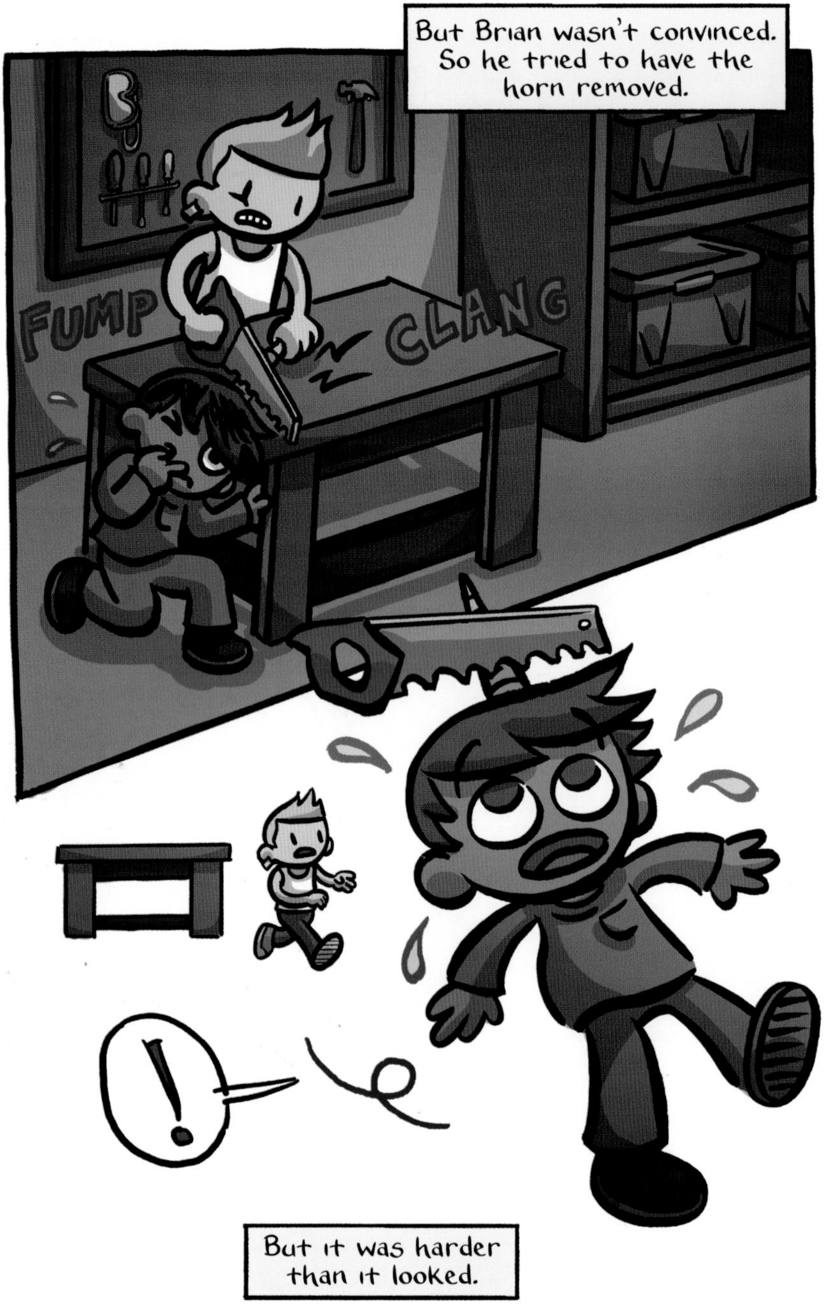
But Brian wasn't convinced. So he tried to have the horn removed.
FUMP
CLANG
!
But it was harder than it looked.

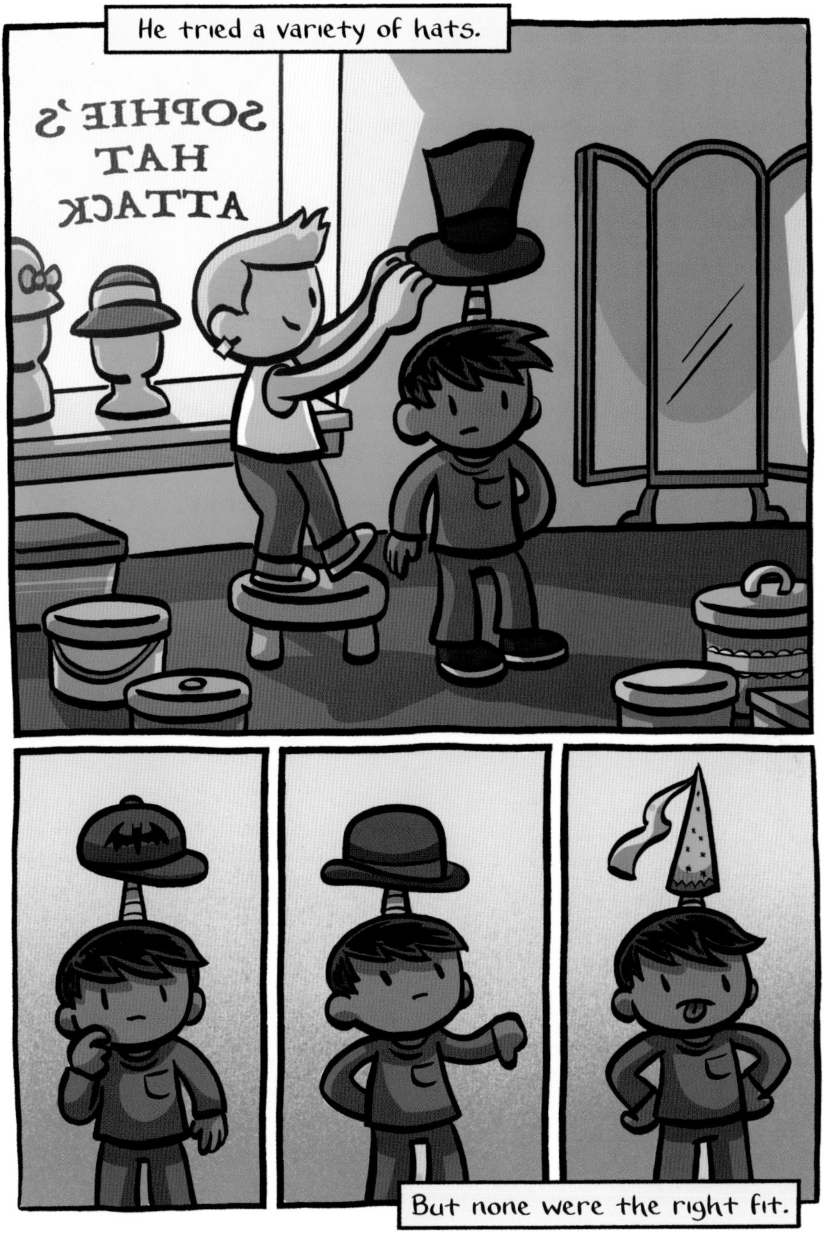
He tried a variety of hats.
SOPHIE'S HAT ATTACK
But none were the right fit.

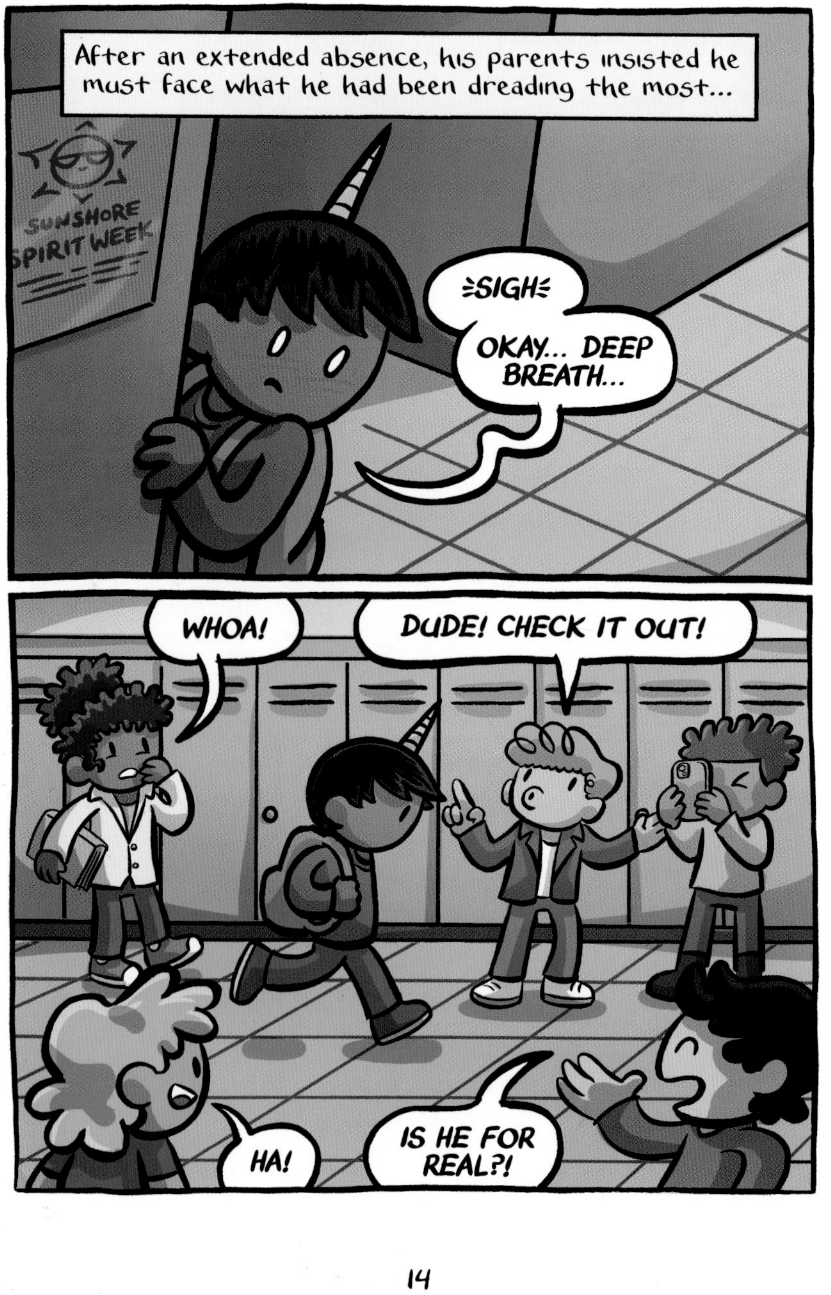
After an extended absence, his parents insisted he must face what he had been dreading the most...
SUNSHORE SPIRIT WEEK
SIGH
OKAY... DEEP BREATH...
WHOA!
DUDE! CHECK IT OUT!
HA!
IS HE FOR REAL?!

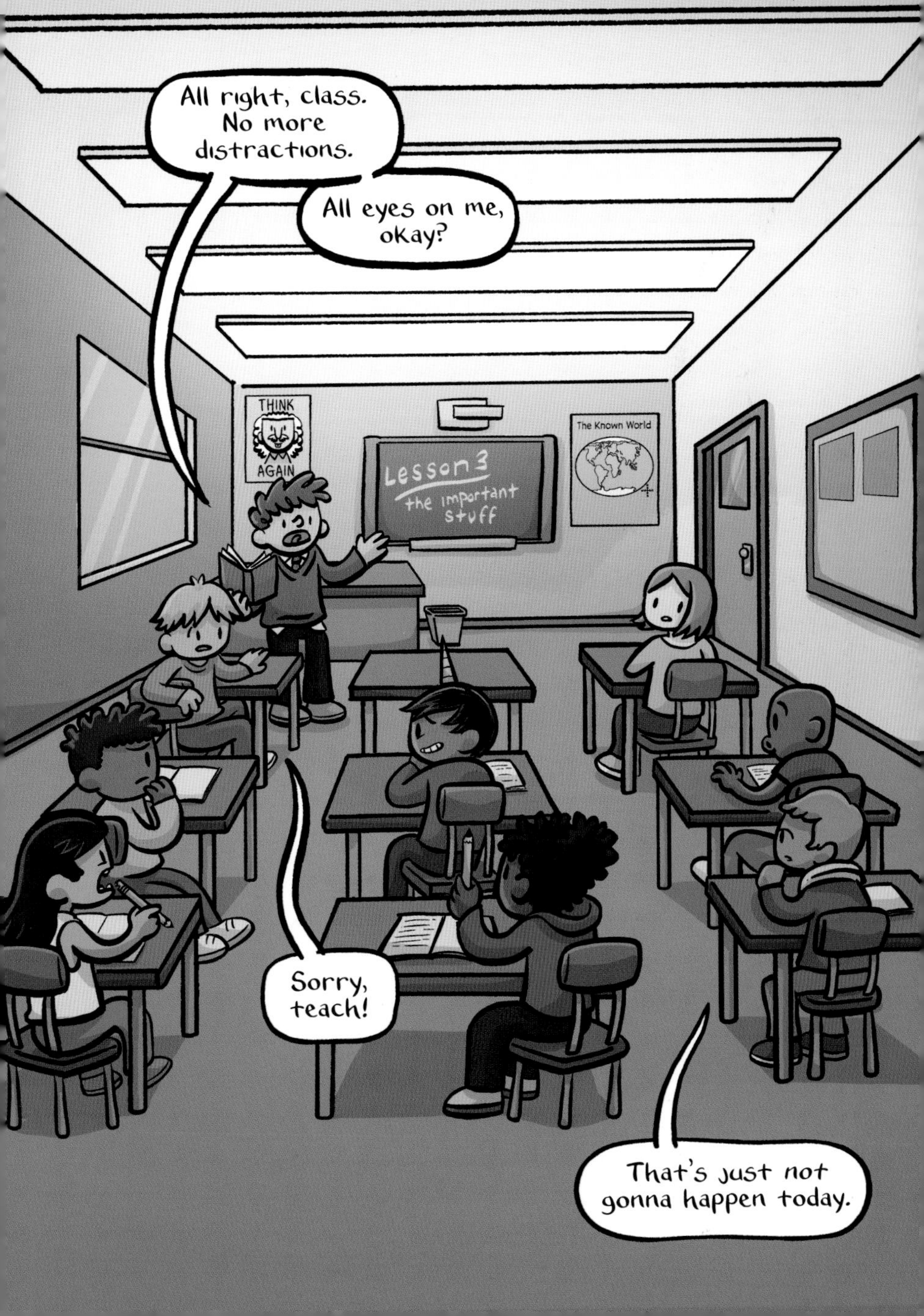
All right, class. No more distractions.
All eyes on me, okay?
THINK AGAIN
Lesson 3 the important stuff
The Known World
Sorry, teach!
That's just not gonna happen today.

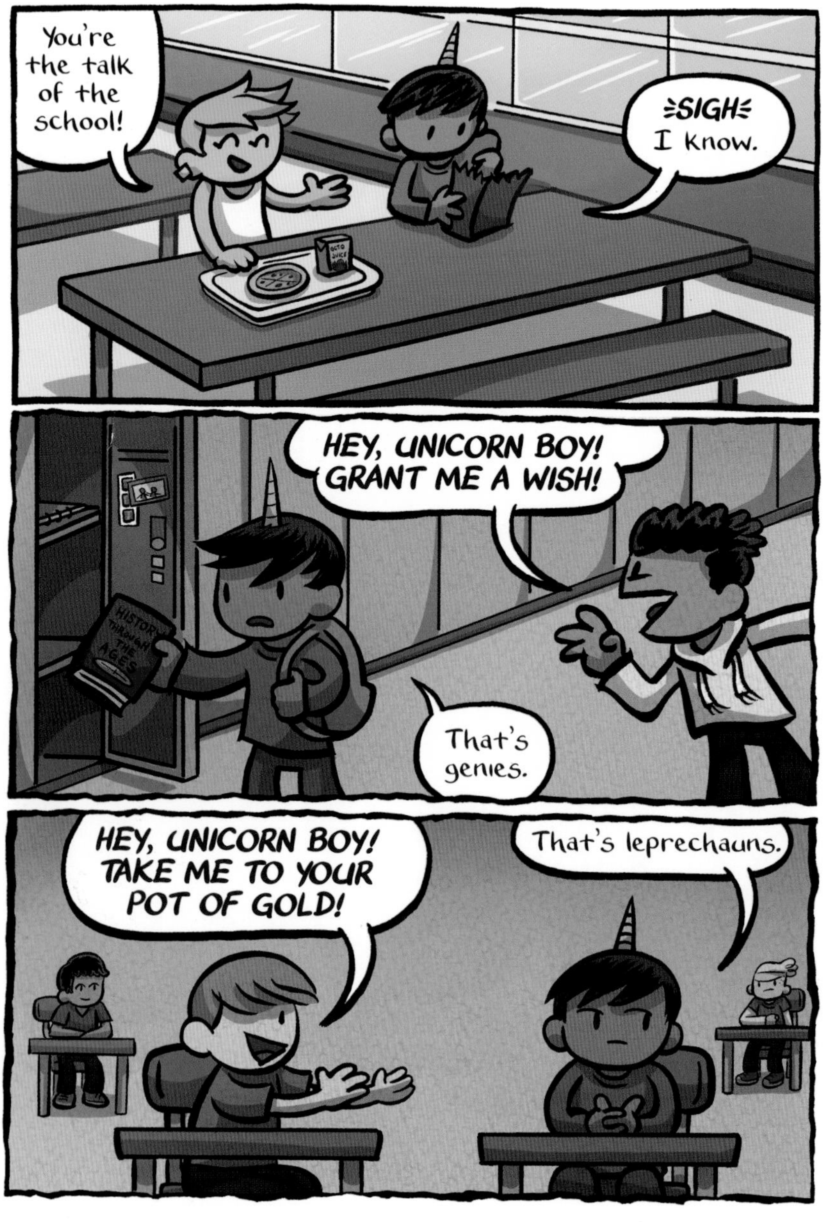
You're the talk of the school!
≶SIGH≶ I know.
HEY, UNICORN BOY! GRANT ME A WISH!
That's genies.
HISTORY THROUGH THE AGES
HEY, UNICORN BOY! TAKE ME TO YOUR POT OF GOLD!
That's leprechauns.

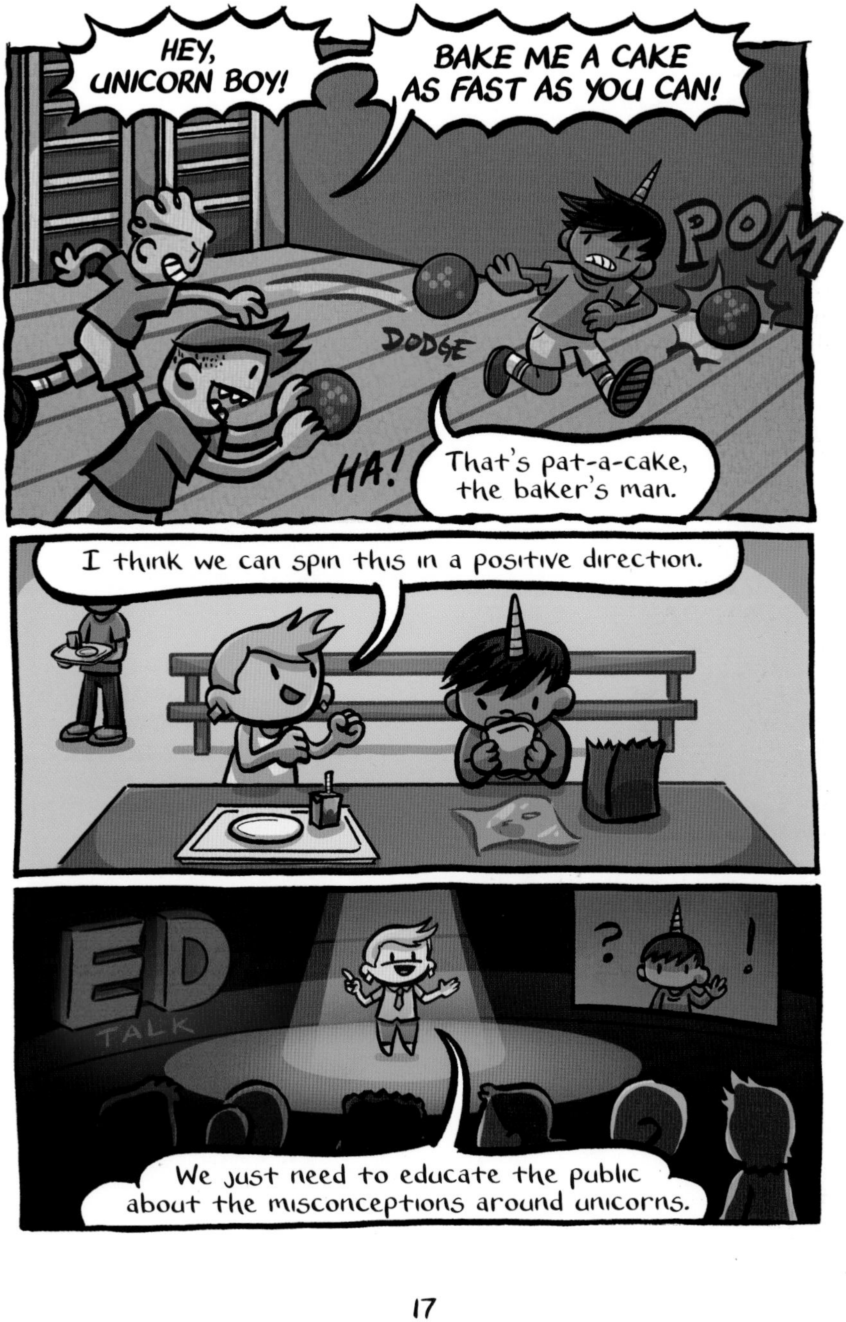

HEY, UNICORN BOY!
BAKE ME A CAKE AS FAST AS YOU CAN!
POM
DODGE
HA!
That's pat-a-cake, the baker's man.
I think we can spin this in a positive direction.
ED
TALK
? !
We just need to educate the public about the misconceptions around unicorns.

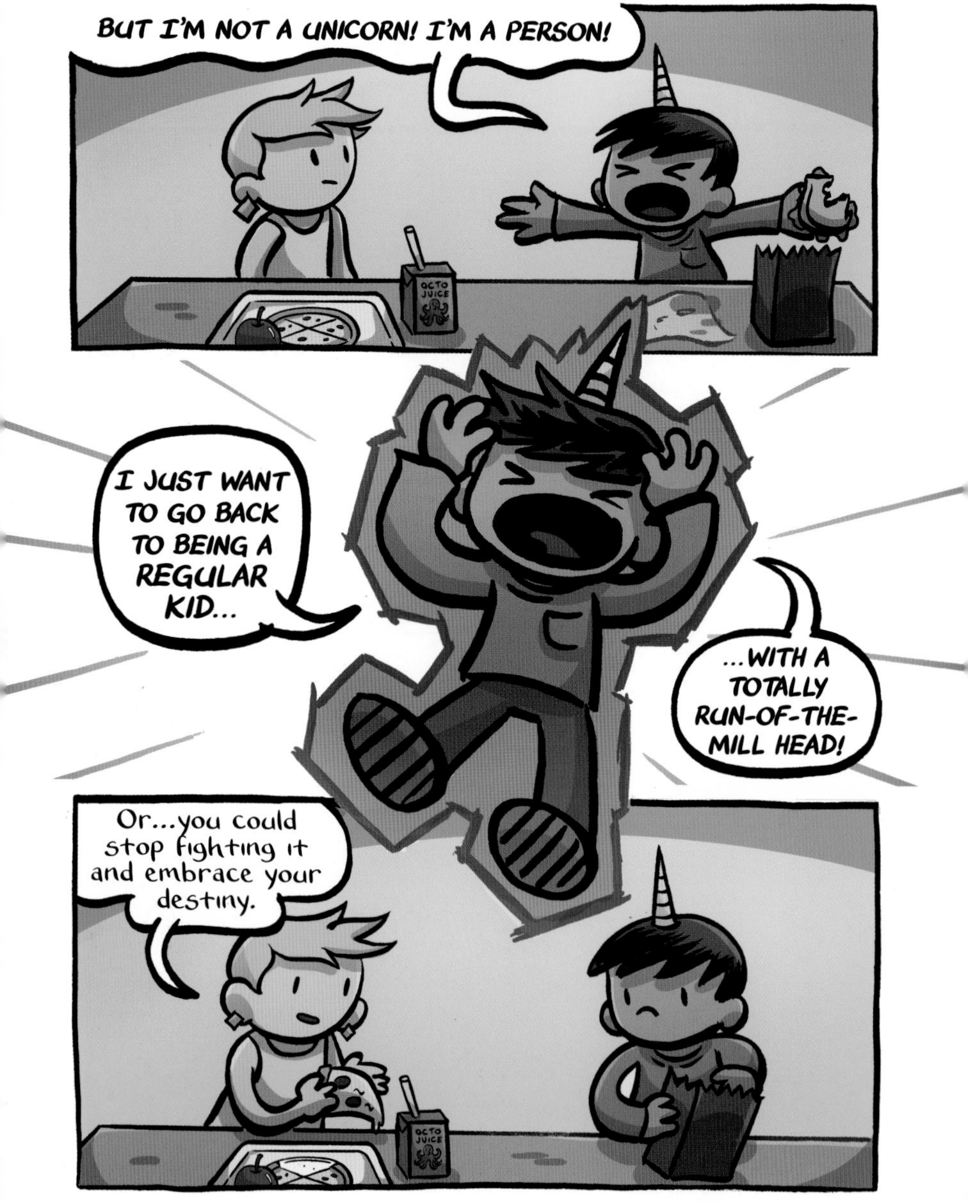
BUT I'M NOT A UNICORN! I'M A PERSON!
OCTO JUICE
I JUST WANT TO GO BACK TO BEING A REGULAR KID...
...WITH A TOTALLY RUN-OF-THE-MILL HEAD!
Or...you could stop fighting it and embrace your destiny.
OCTO JUICE

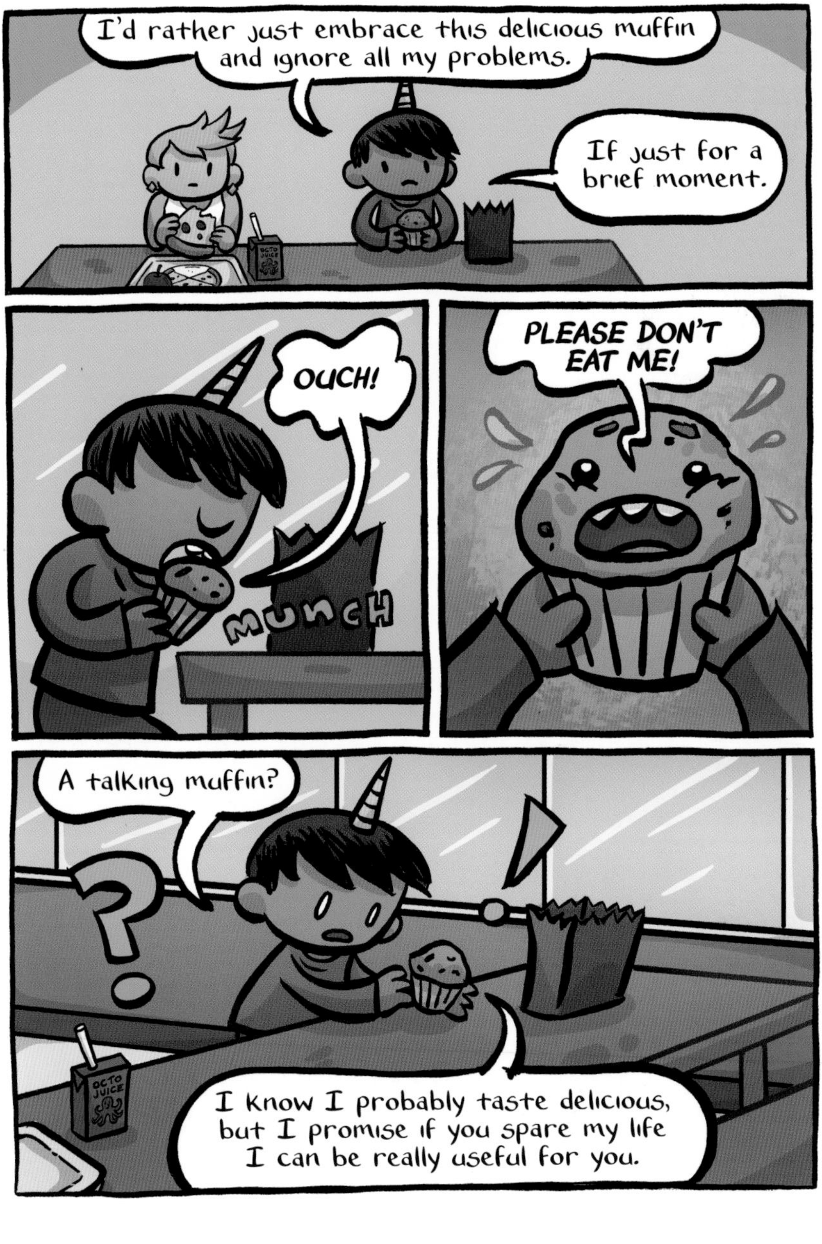
I'd rather just embrace this delicious muffin and ignore all my problems.
If just for a brief moment.
OUCH!
MUNCH
PLEASE DON'T EAT ME!
A talking muffin?
I know I probably taste delicious, but I promise if you spare my life I can be really useful for you.

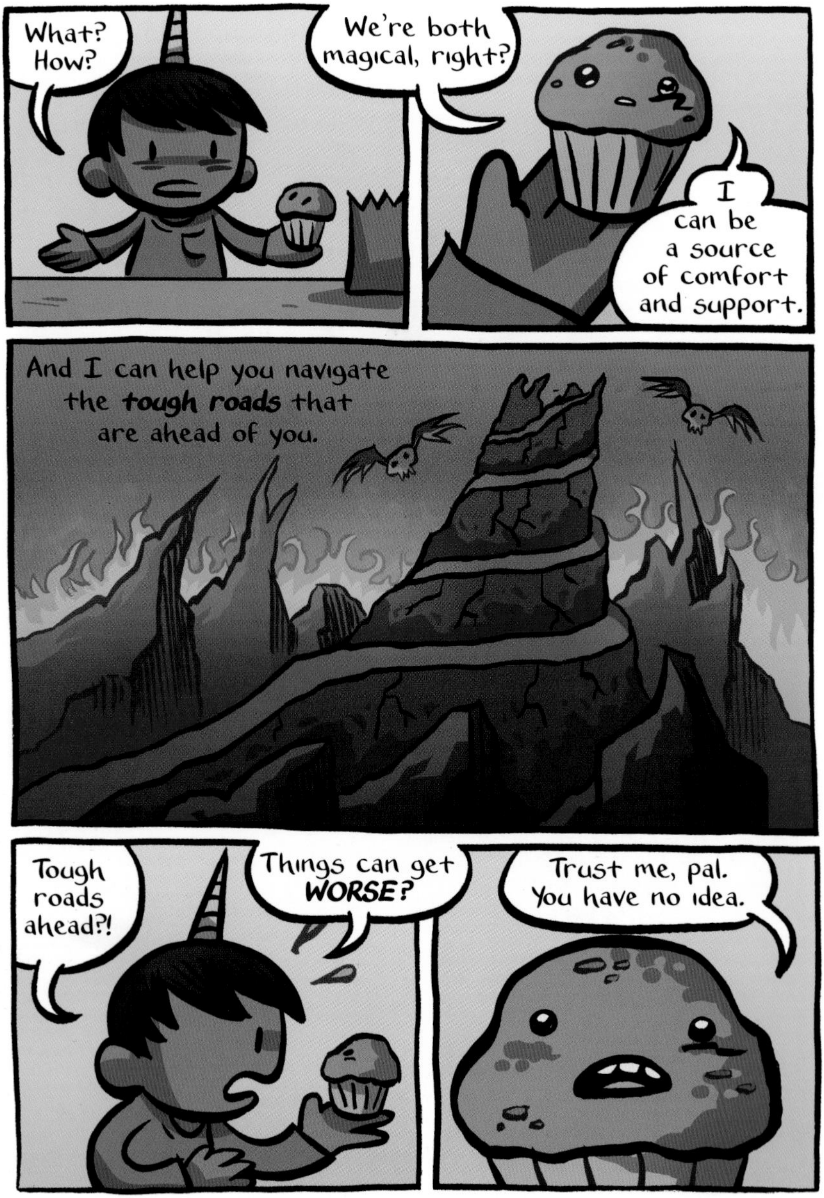
What? How?
We're both magical, right?
I can be a source of comfort and support.
And I can help you navigate the **tough roads** that are ahead of you.
Tough roads ahead?!
Things can get **WORSE?**
Trust me, pal. You have no idea.

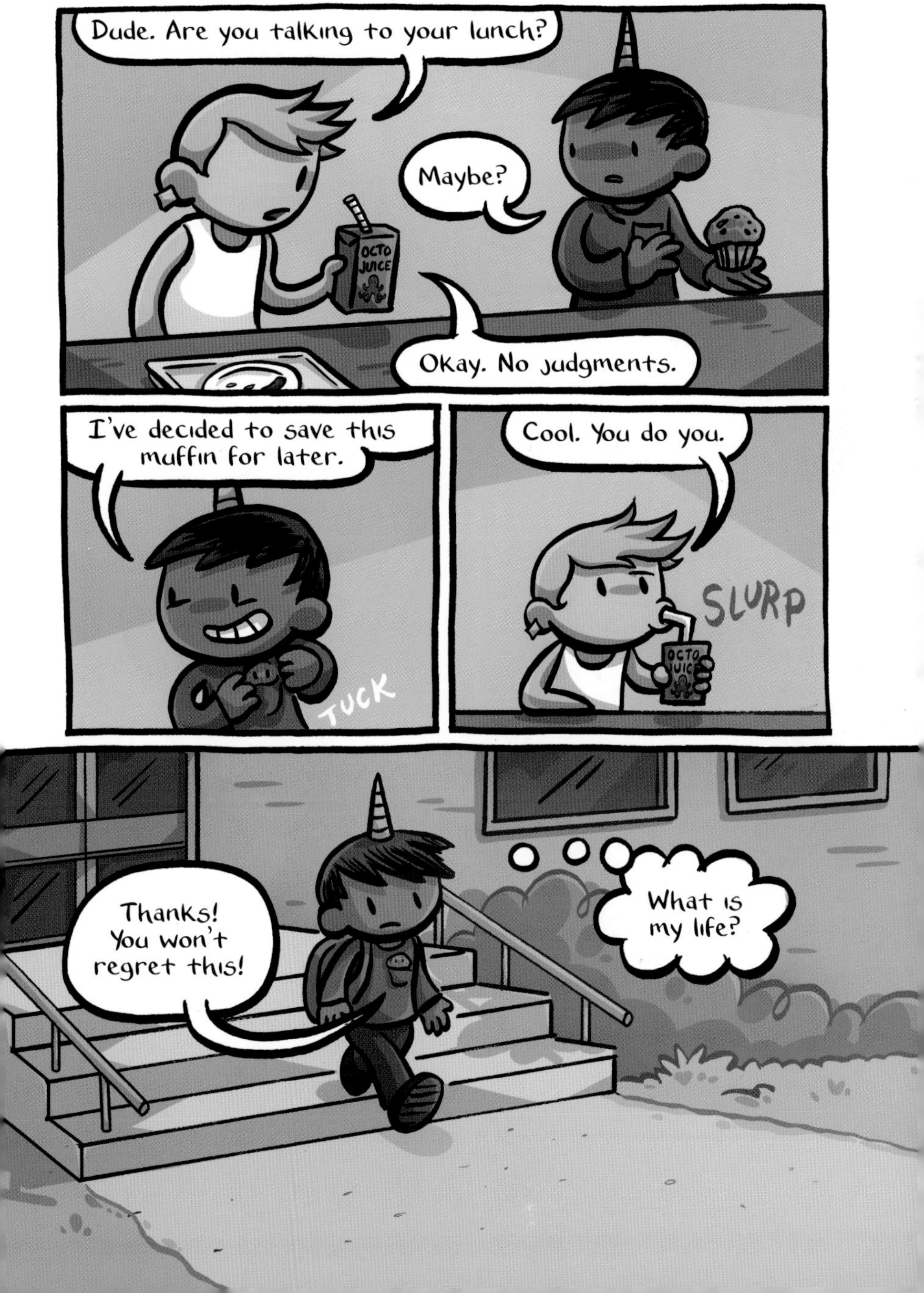
Dude. Are you talking to your lunch?
Maybe?
OCTO JUICE
Okay. No judgments.
I've decided to save this muffin for later.
TUCK
Cool. You do you.
SLURP
Thanks! You won't regret this!
What is my life?

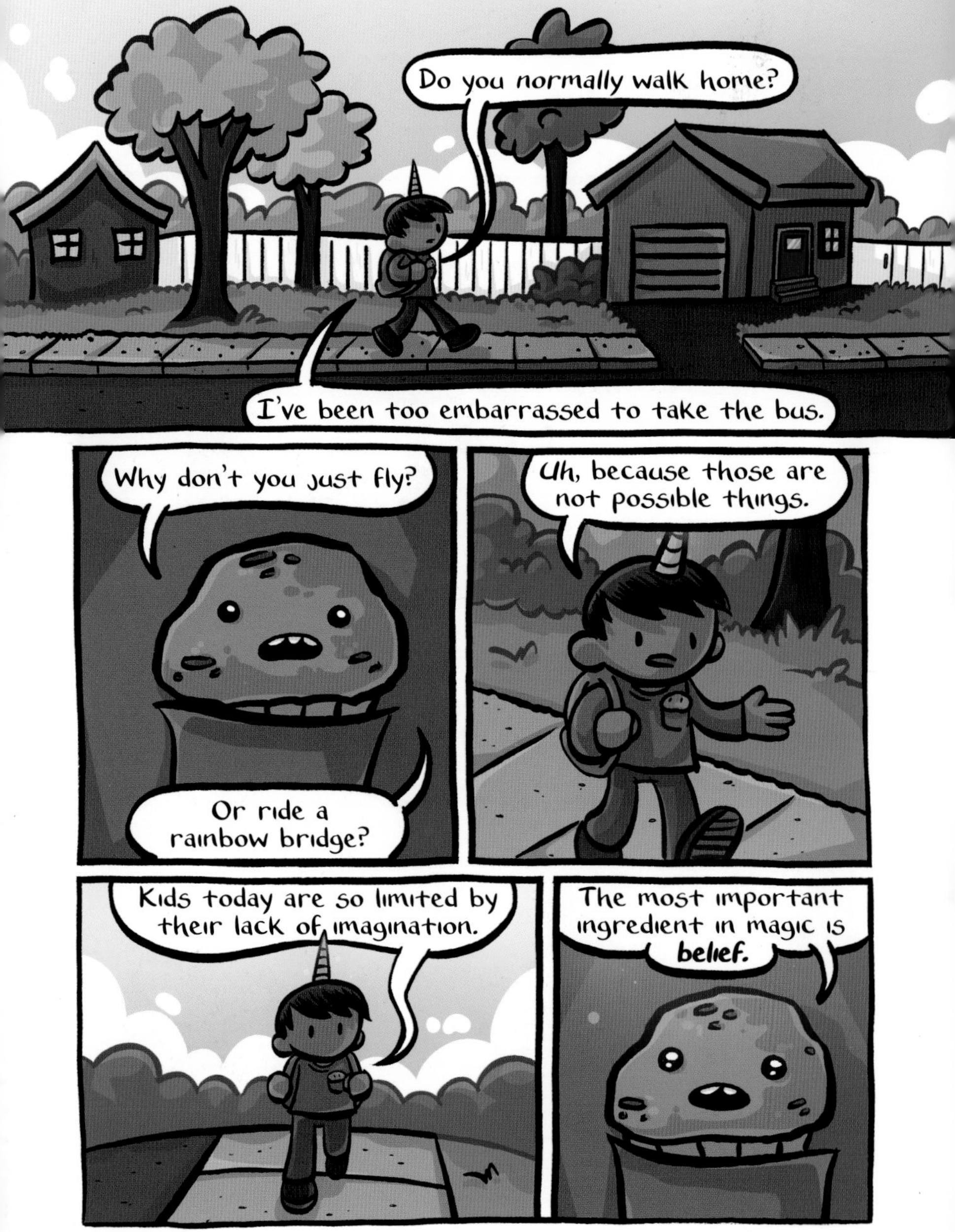
Do you normally walk home?
I've been too embarrassed to take the bus.
Why don't you just fly?
Or ride a rainbow bridge?
Uh, because those are not possible things.
Kids today are so limited by their lack of imagination.
The most important ingredient in magic is **belief.**

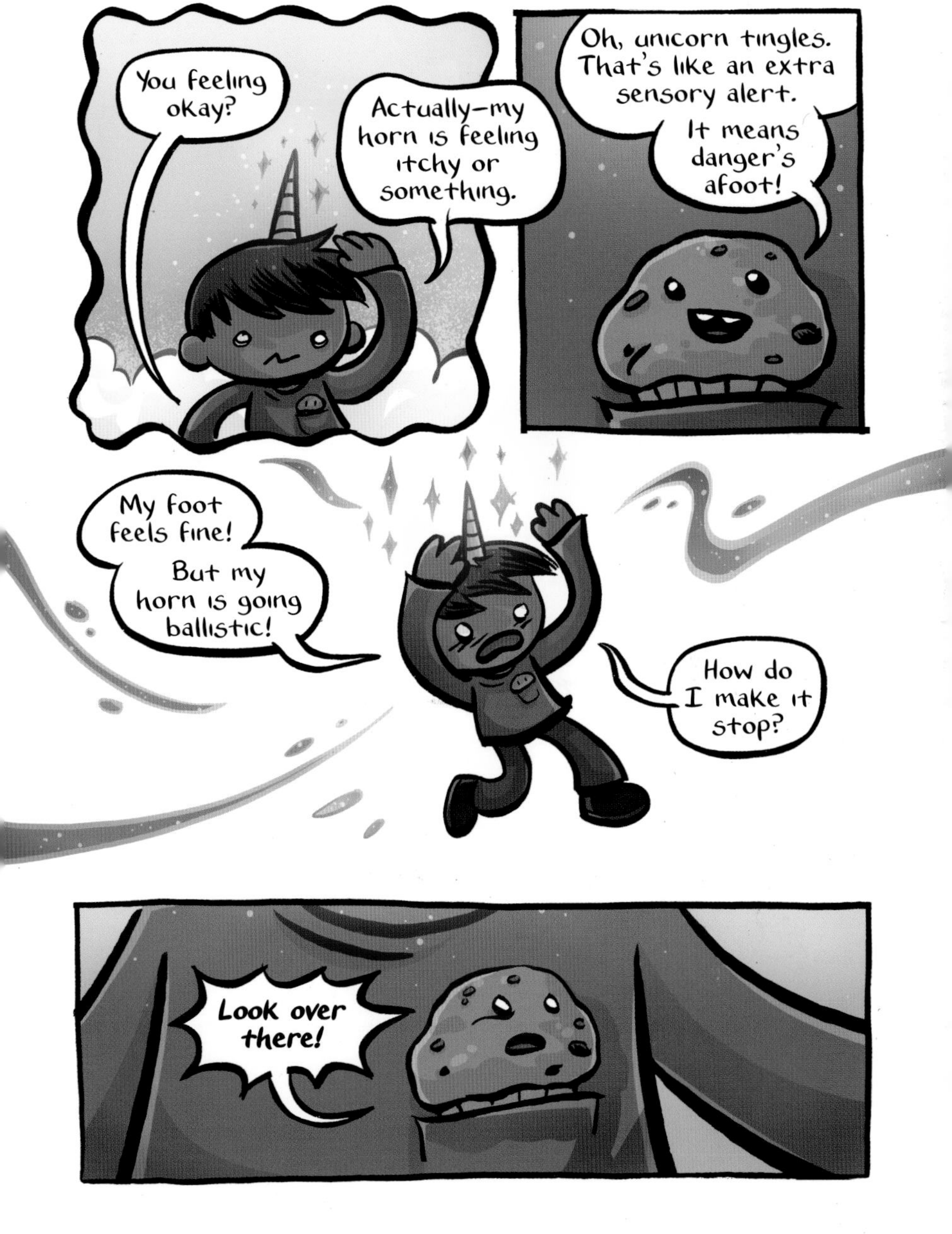
You feeling okay?
Actually—my horn is feeling itchy or something.
Oh, unicorn tingles. That's like an extra sensory alert.
It means danger's afoot!
My foot feels fine!
But my horn is going ballistic!
How do I make it stop?
Look over there!

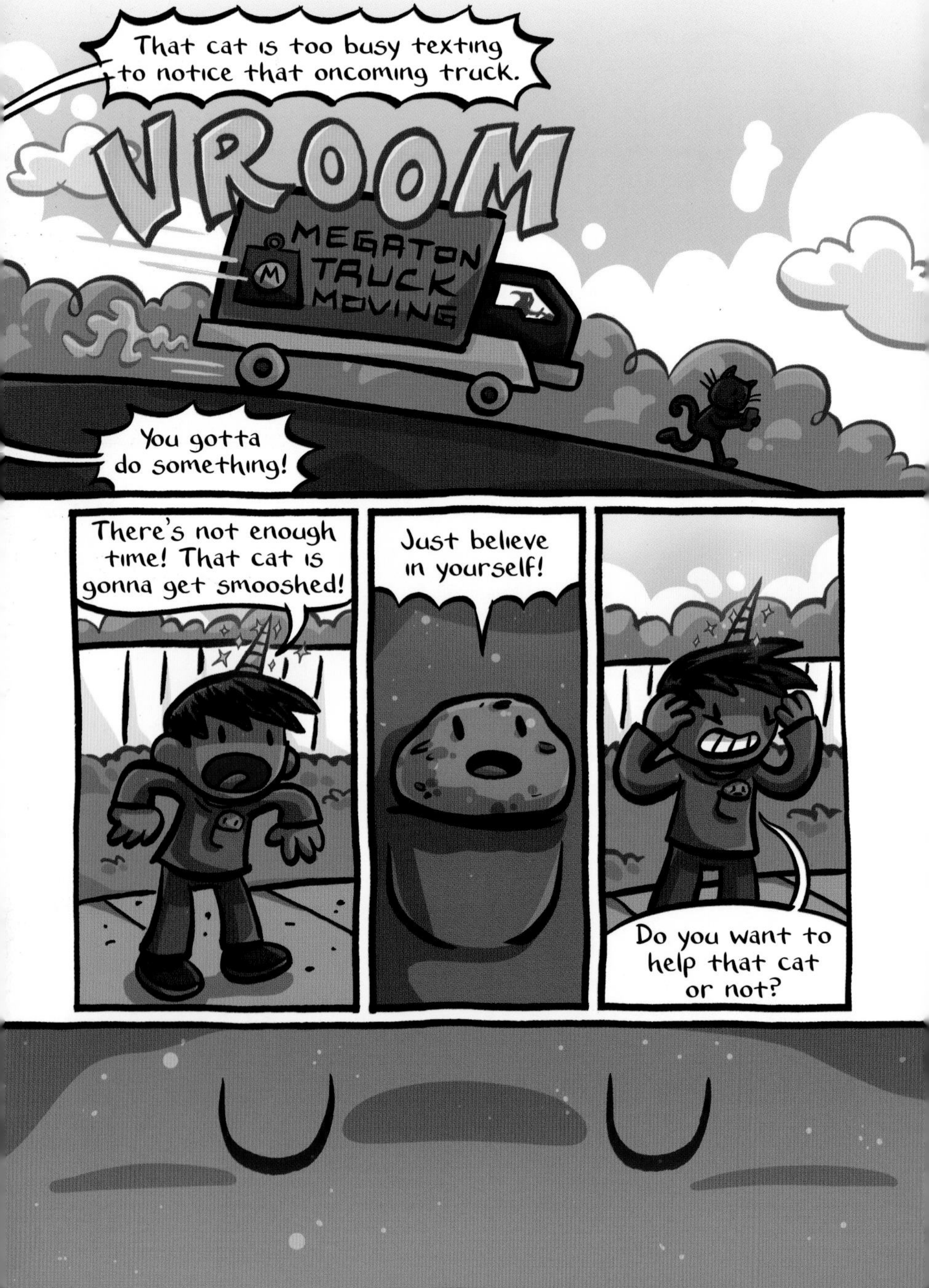
That cat is too busy texting to notice that oncoming truck.
VROOM
MEGATON TRUCK MOVING
You gotta do something!
There's not enough time! That cat is gonna get smooshed!
Just believe in yourself!
Do you want to help that cat or not?

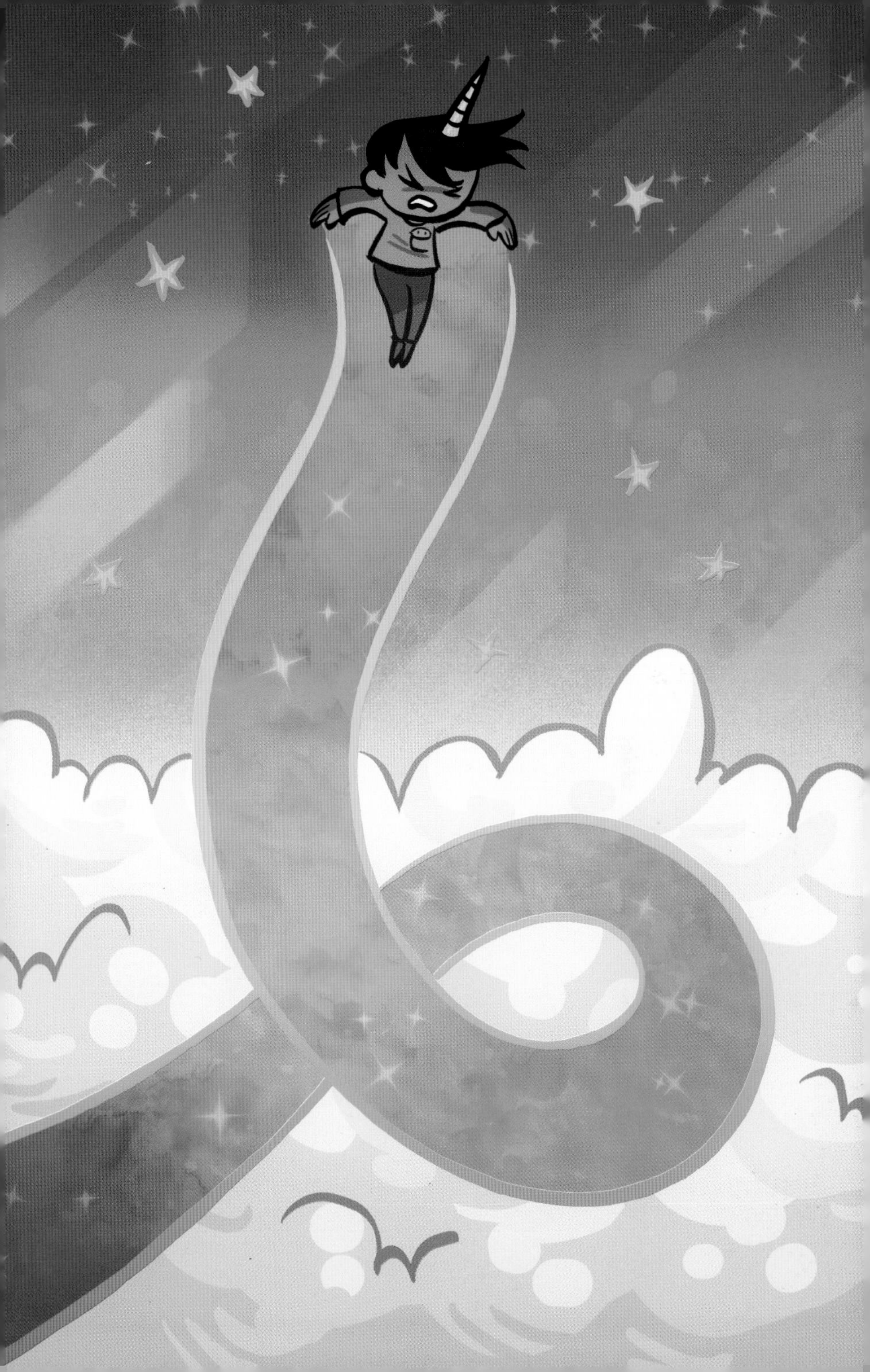

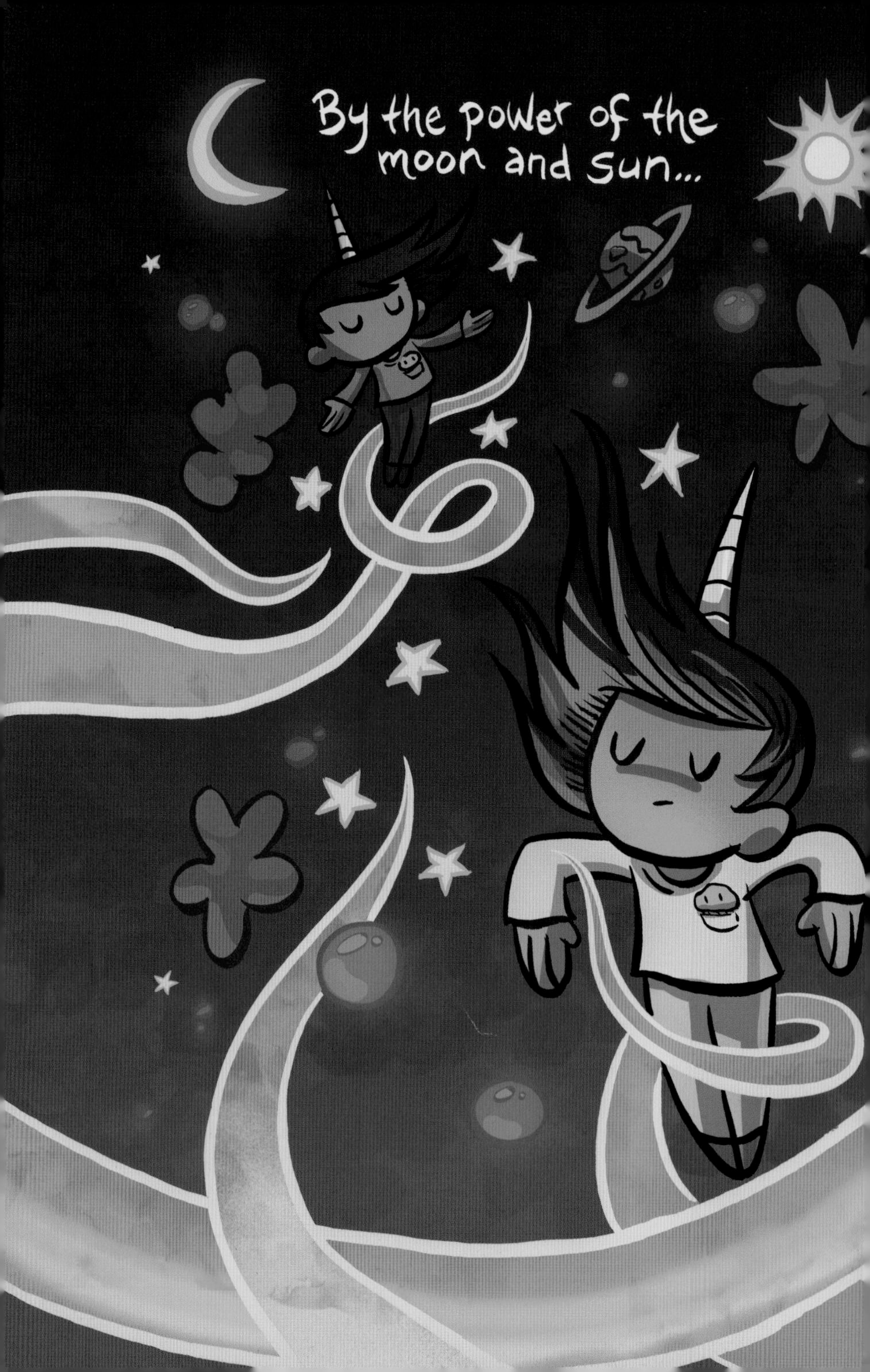
By the power of the moon and sun...

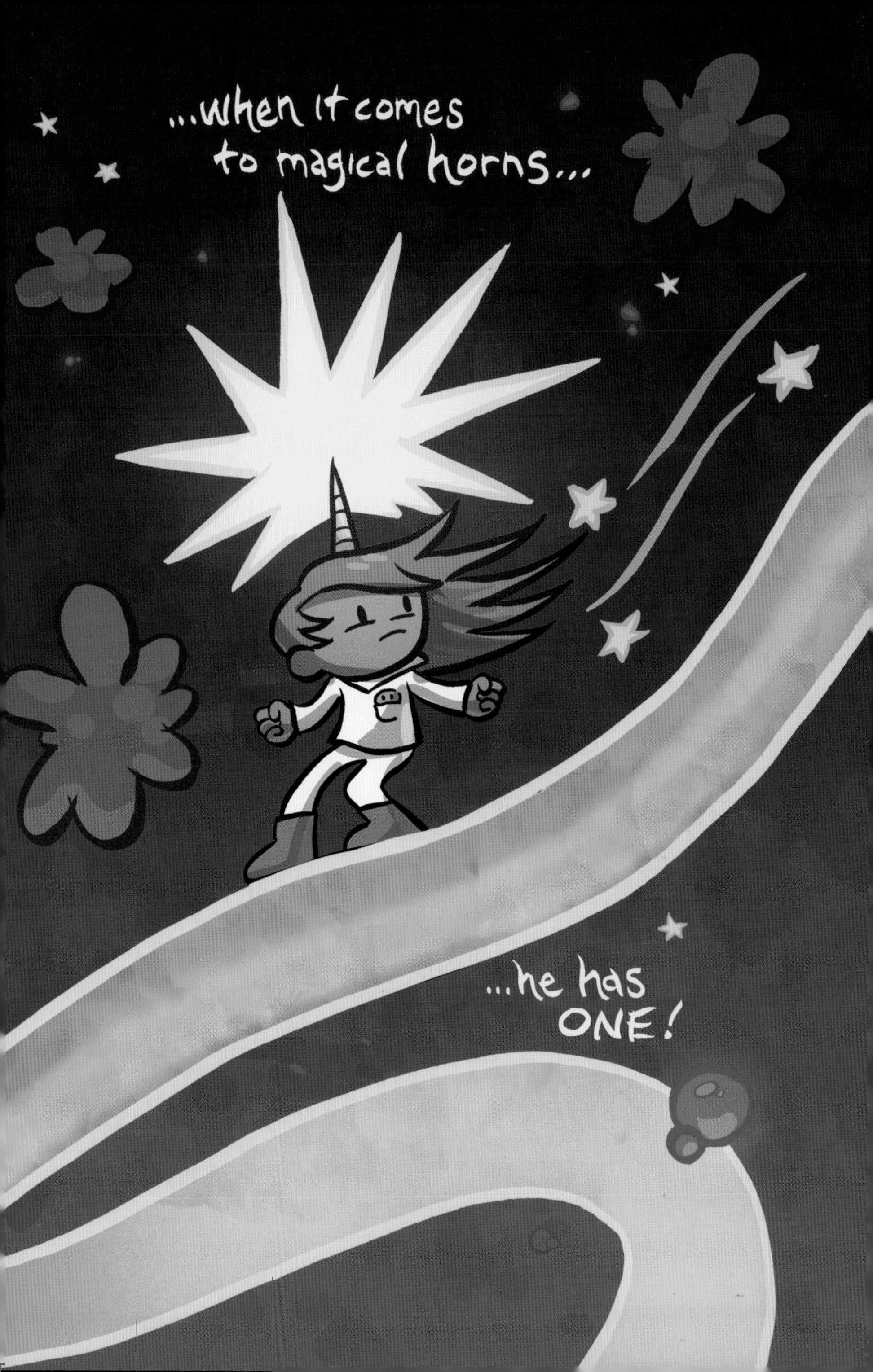
...when it comes to magical horns...
...he has ONE!

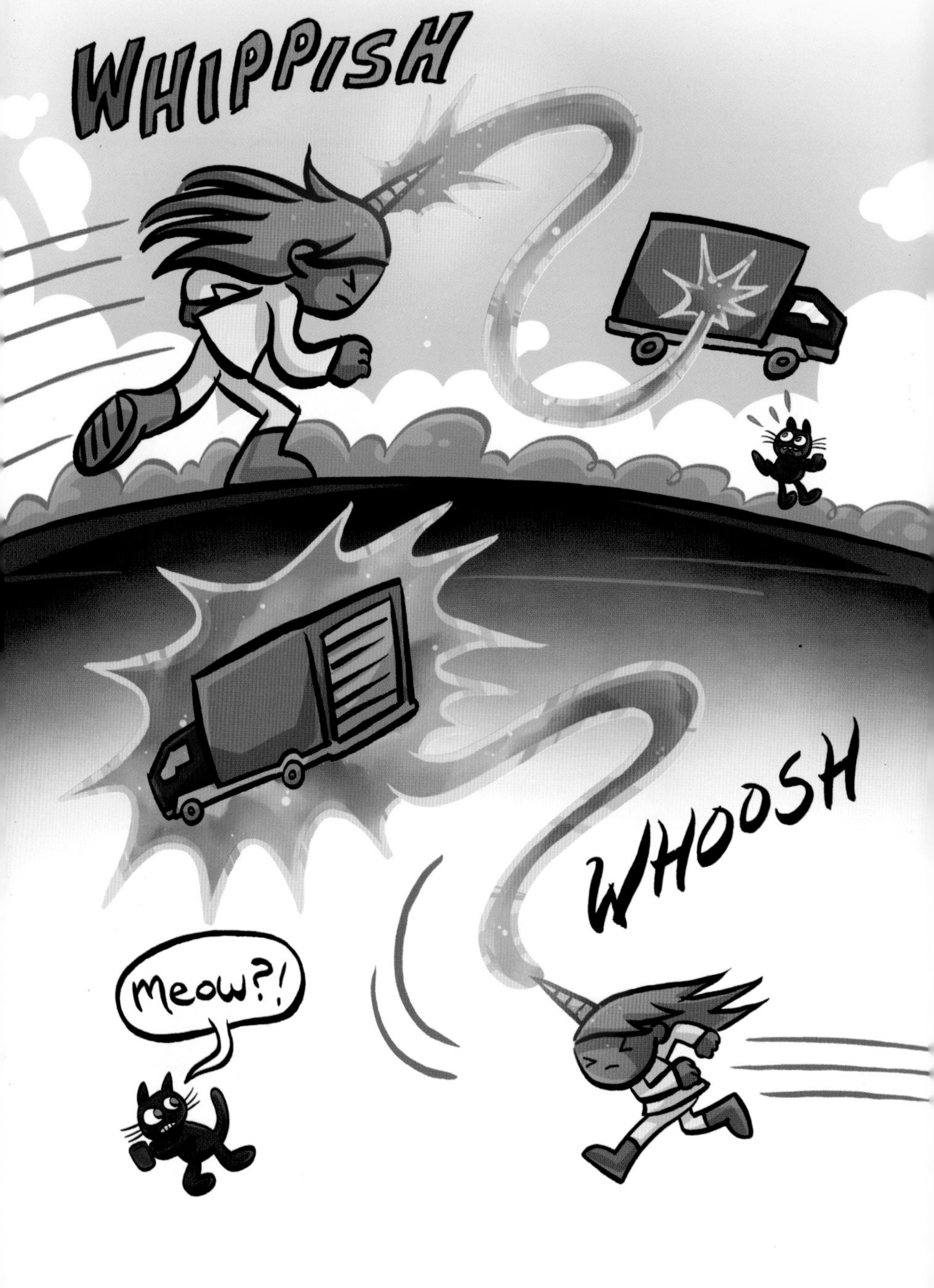
WHIPPISH
WHOOSH
meow?!

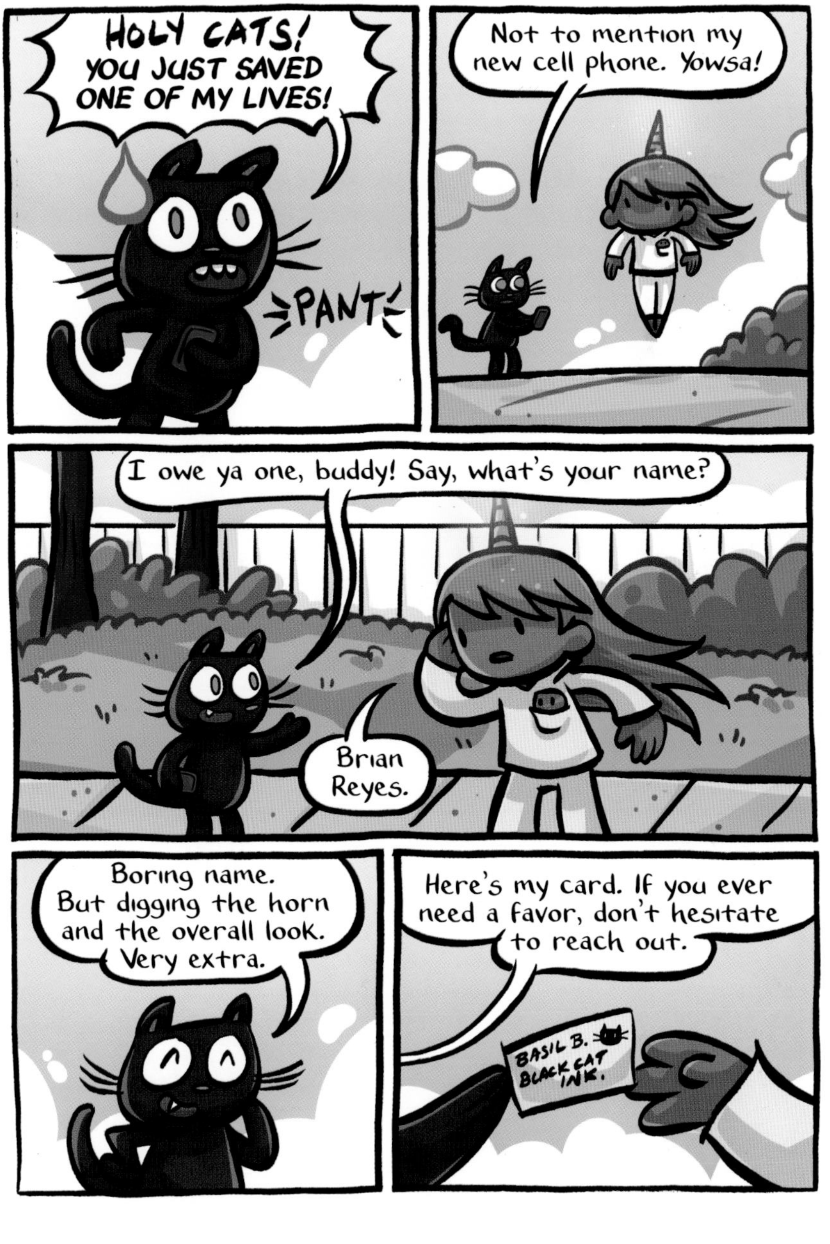
HOLY CATS! YOU JUST SAVED ONE OF MY LIVES!
PANT
Not to mention my new cell phone. Yowsa!
I owe ya one, buddy! Say, what's your name?
Brian Reyes.
Boring name. But digging the horn and the overall look. Very extra.
Here's my card. If you ever need a favor, don't hesitate to reach out.
BASIL B. BLACK CAT INK.

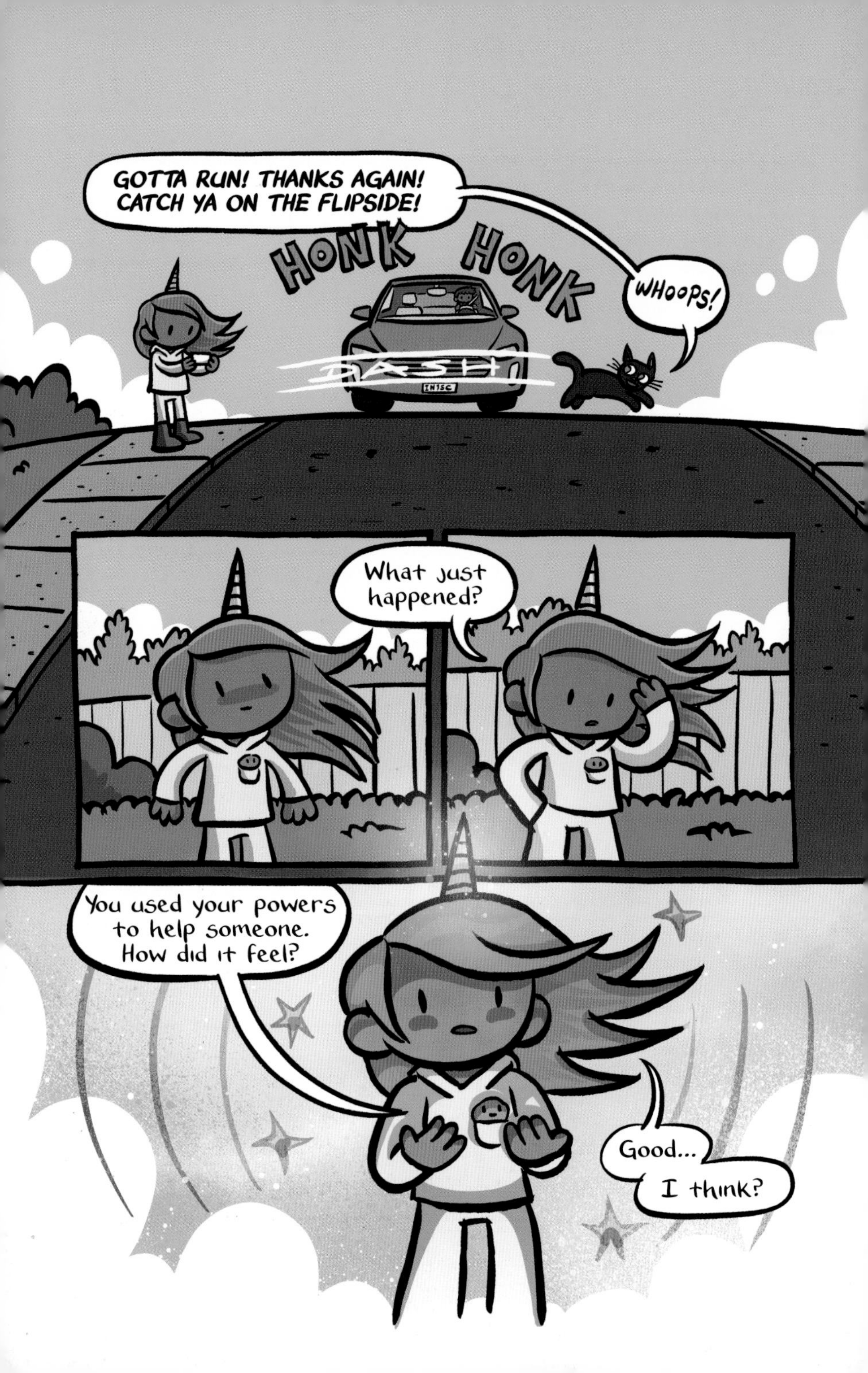
GOTTA RUN! THANKS AGAIN! CATCH YA ON THE FLIPSIDE!
HONK HONK
WHOOPS!
DASH
IN1SC
What just happened?
You used your powers to help someone. How did it feel?
Good...
I think?

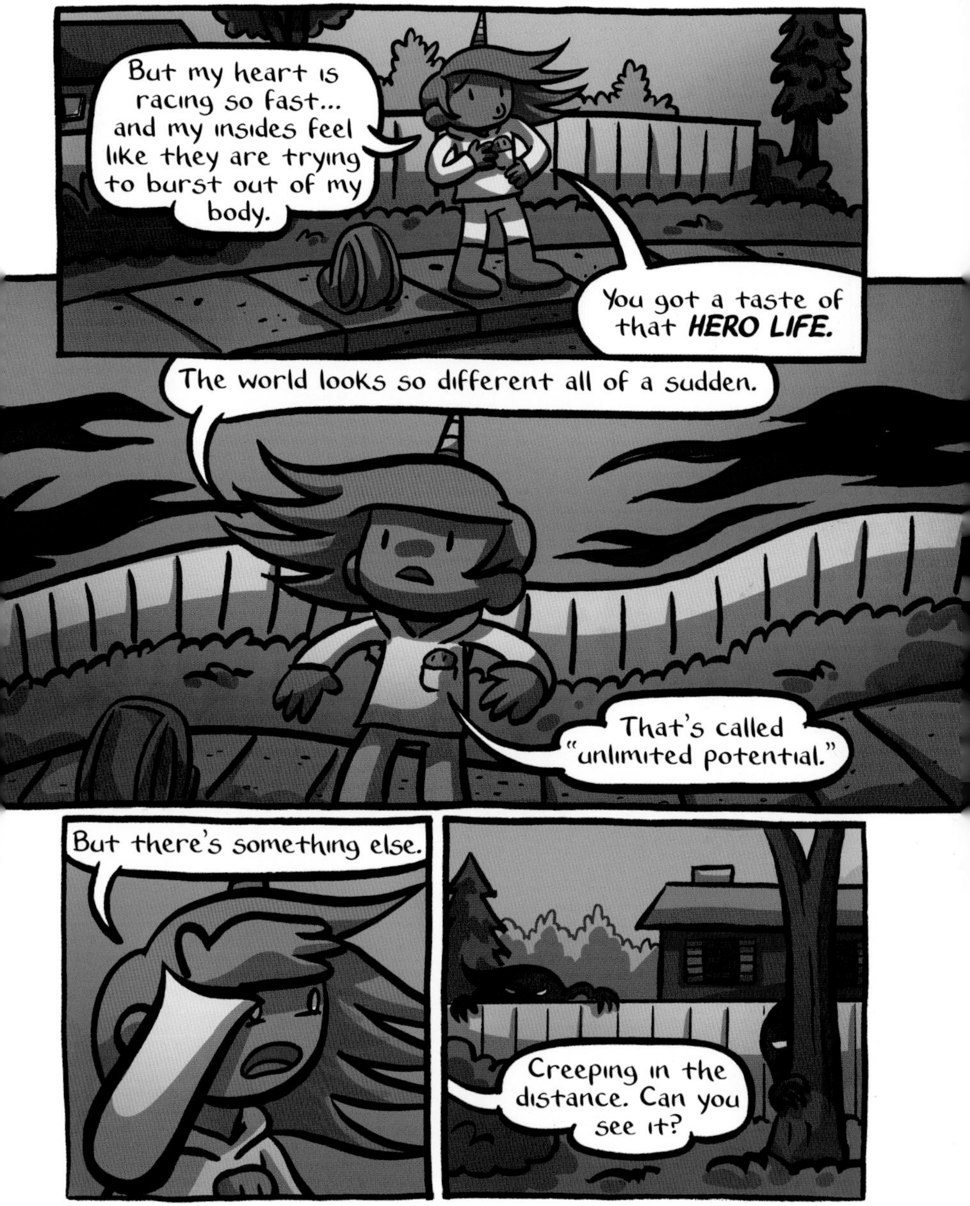

But my heart is racing so fast... and my insides feel like they are trying to burst out of my body.
You got a taste of that **HERO LIFE.**
The world looks so different all of a sudden.
That's called "unlimited potential."
But there's something else.
Creeping in the distance. Can you see it?

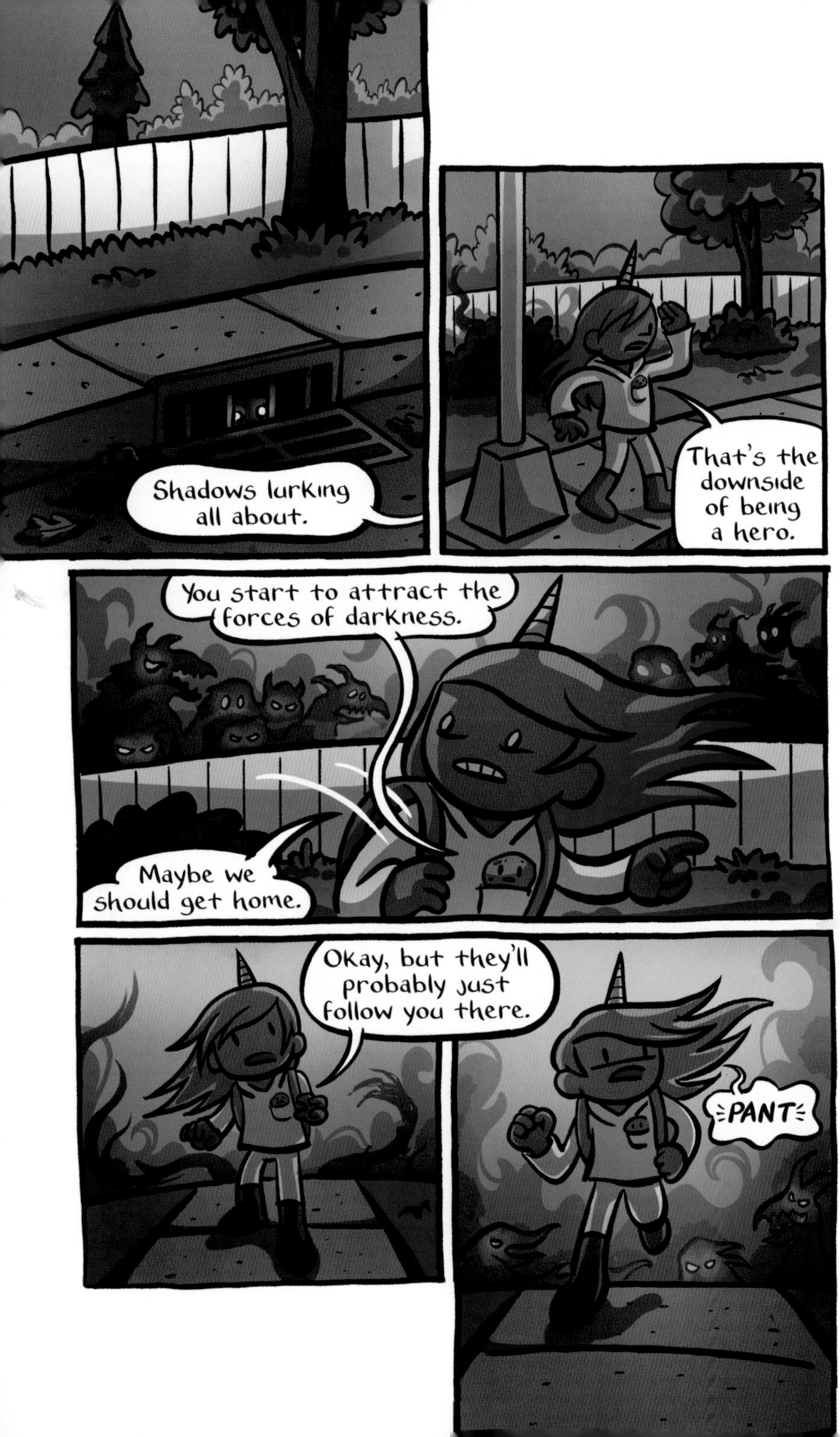
Shadows lurking all about.
That's the downside of being a hero.
You start to attract the forces of darkness.
Maybe we should get home.
Okay, but they'll probably just follow you there.
PANT

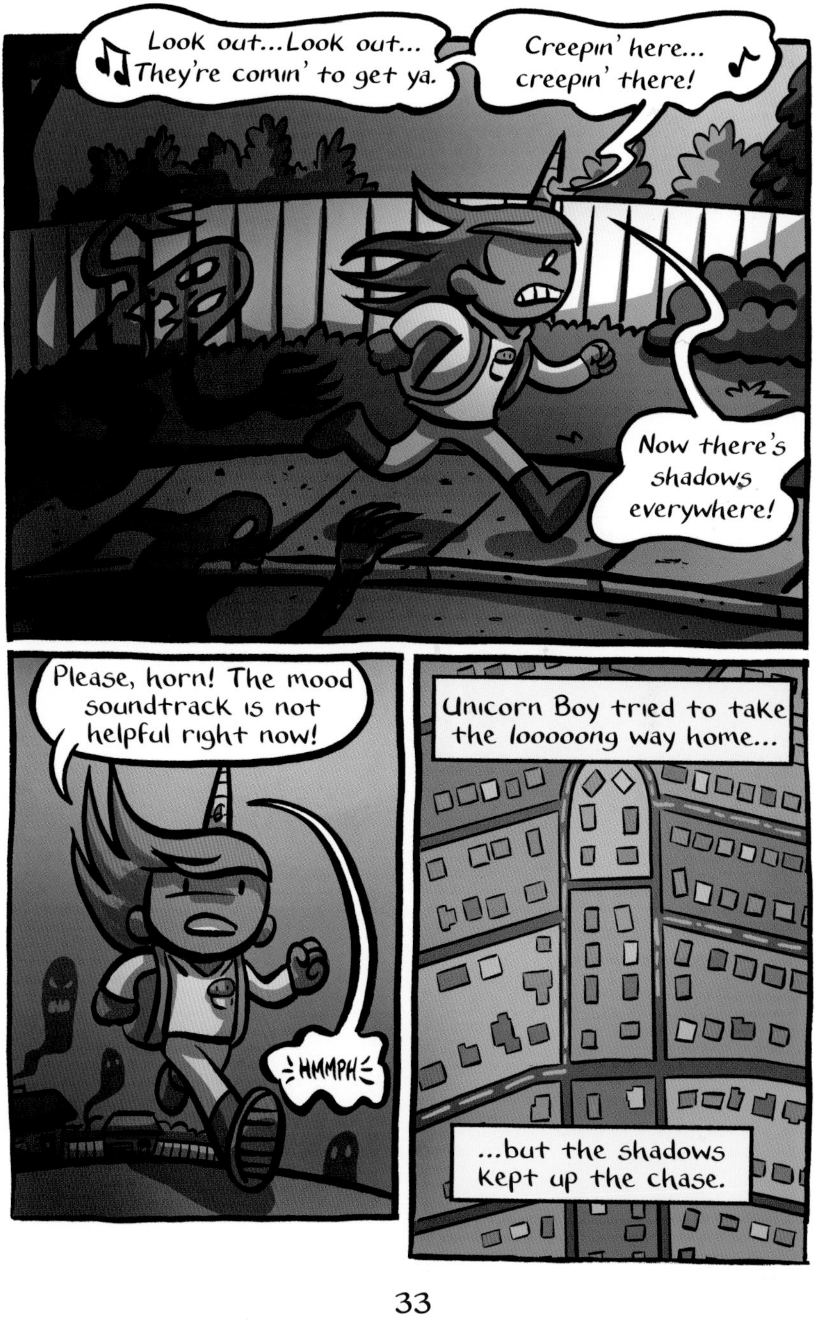
Look out...Look out... They're comin' to get ya.
Creepin' here... creepin' there!
Now there's shadows everywhere!
Please, horn! The mood soundtrack is not helpful right now!
HMMPH
Unicorn Boy tried to take the looooong way home...
...but the shadows kept up the chase.

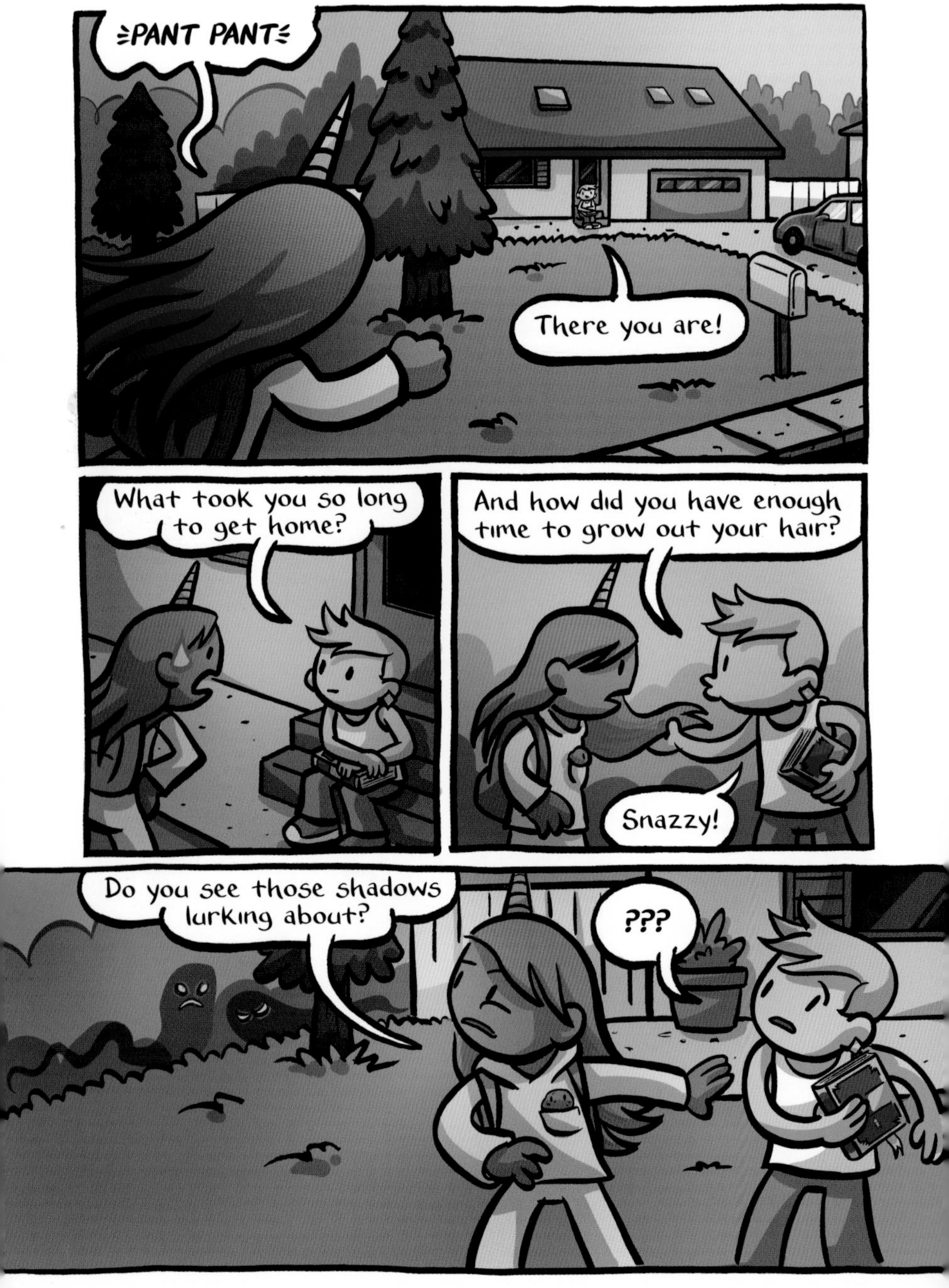
PANT PANT
There you are!
What took you so long to get home?
And how did you have enough time to grow out your hair?
Snazzy!
Do you see those shadows lurking about?
???

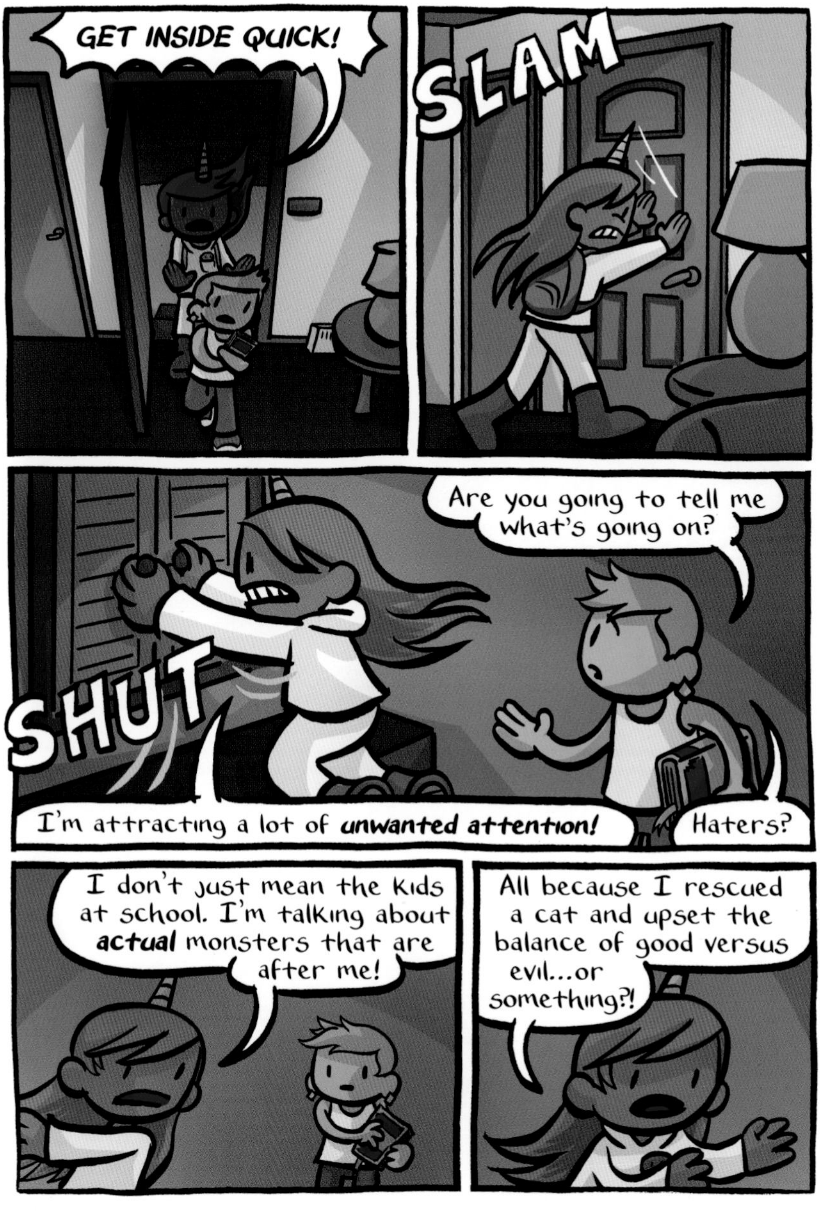
GET INSIDE QUICK!
SLAM
Are you going to tell me what's going on?
SHUT
I'm attracting a lot of **unwanted attention!**
Haters?
I don't just mean the kids at school. I'm talking about **actual** monsters that are after me!
All because I rescued a cat and upset the balance of good versus evil...or something?!

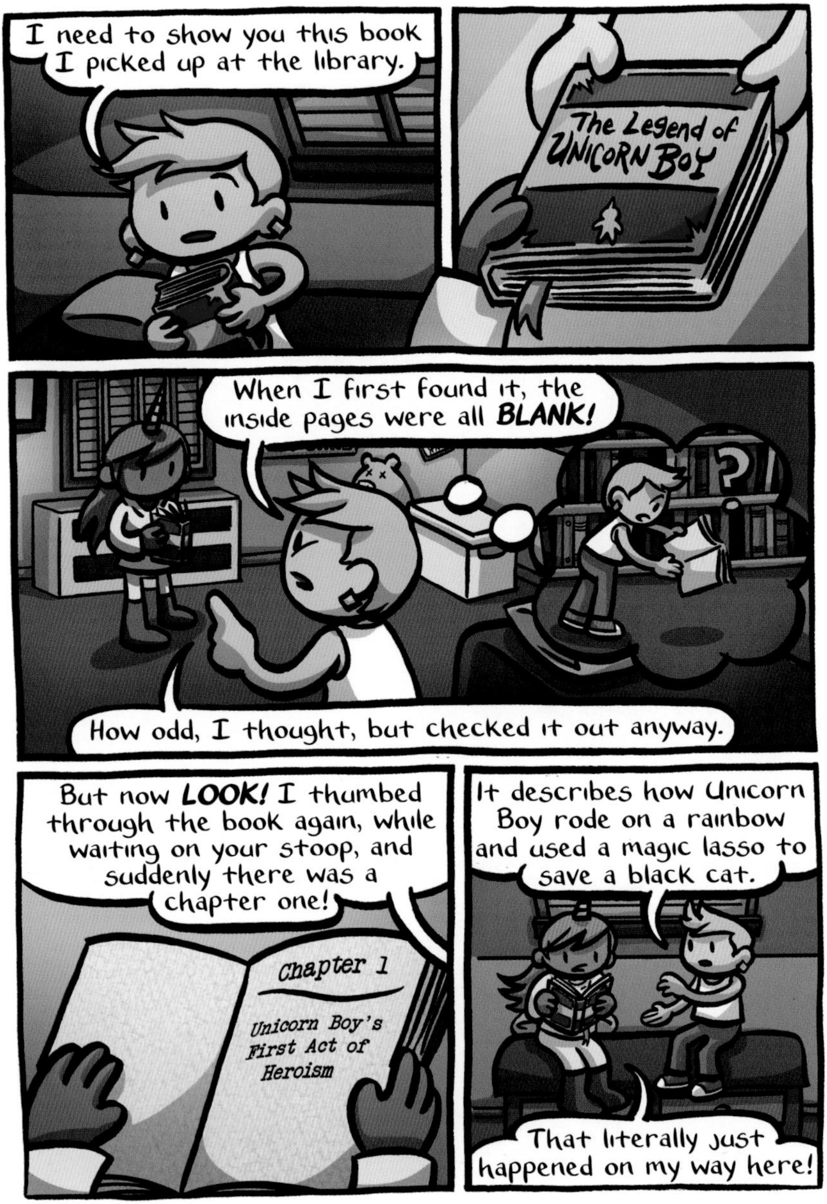

I need to show you this book I picked up at the library.
The Legend of UNICORN BOY
When I first found it, the inside pages were all **BLANK!**
How odd, I thought, but checked it out anyway.
But now **LOOK!** I thumbed through the book again, while waiting on your stoop, and suddenly there was a chapter one!
Chapter 1
Unicorn Boy's First Act of Heroism
It describes how Unicorn Boy rode on a rainbow and used a magic lasso to save a black cat.
That literally just happened on my way here!

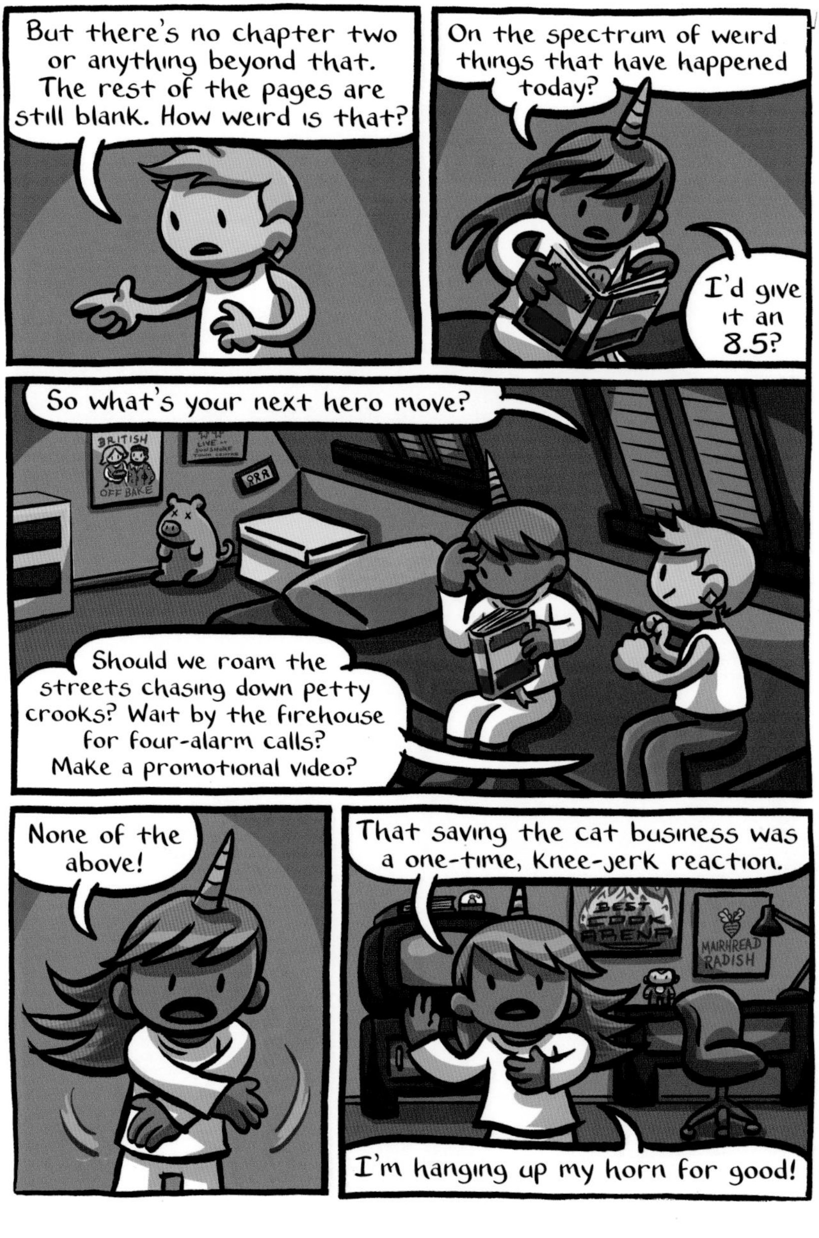
But there's no chapter two or anything beyond that. The rest of the pages are still blank. How weird is that?
On the spectrum of weird things that have happened today?
I'd give it an 8.5?
So what's your next hero move?
BRITISH OFF BAKE
Should we roam the streets chasing down petty crooks? Wait by the firehouse for four-alarm calls? Make a promotional video?
None of the above!
That saving the cat business was a one-time, knee-jerk reaction.
BEST COOK ARENA
MAIRHREAD RADISH
I'm hanging up my horn for good!

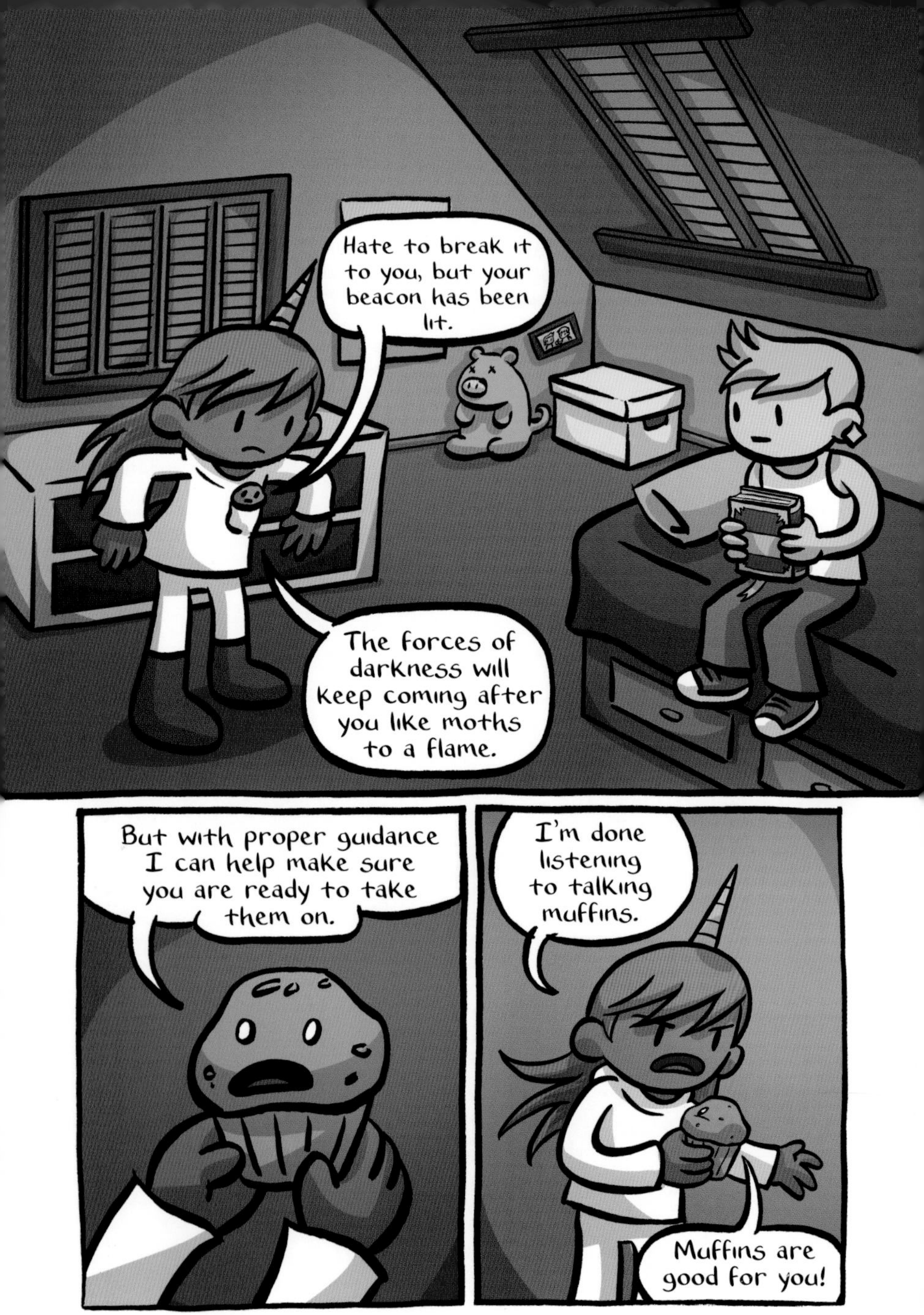
Hate to break it to you, but your beacon has been lit.
The forces of darkness will keep coming after you like moths to a flame.
But with proper guidance I can help make sure you are ready to take them on.
I'm done listening to talking muffins.
Muffins are good for you!

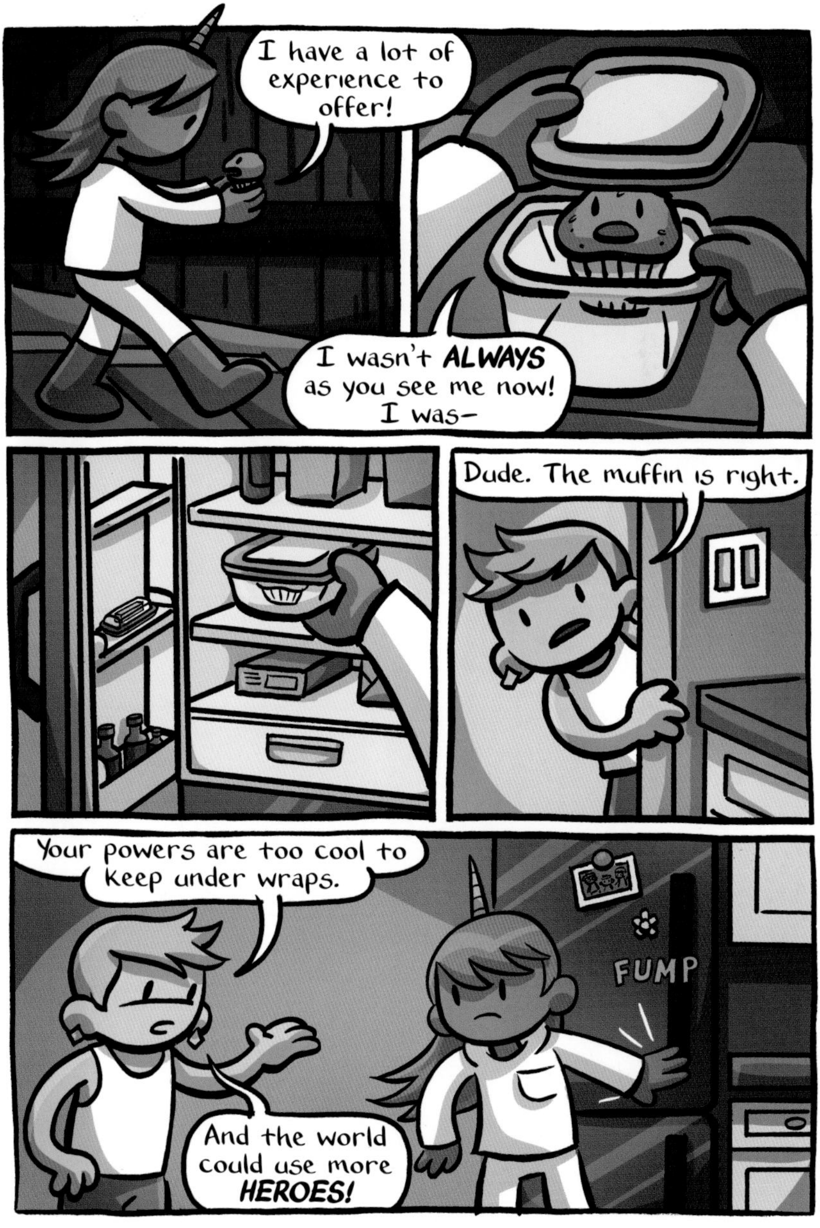
I have a lot of experience to offer!
I wasn't **ALWAYS** as you see me now! I was-
Dude. The muffin is right.
Your powers are too cool to keep under wraps.
And the world could use more ***HEROES!***
FUMP

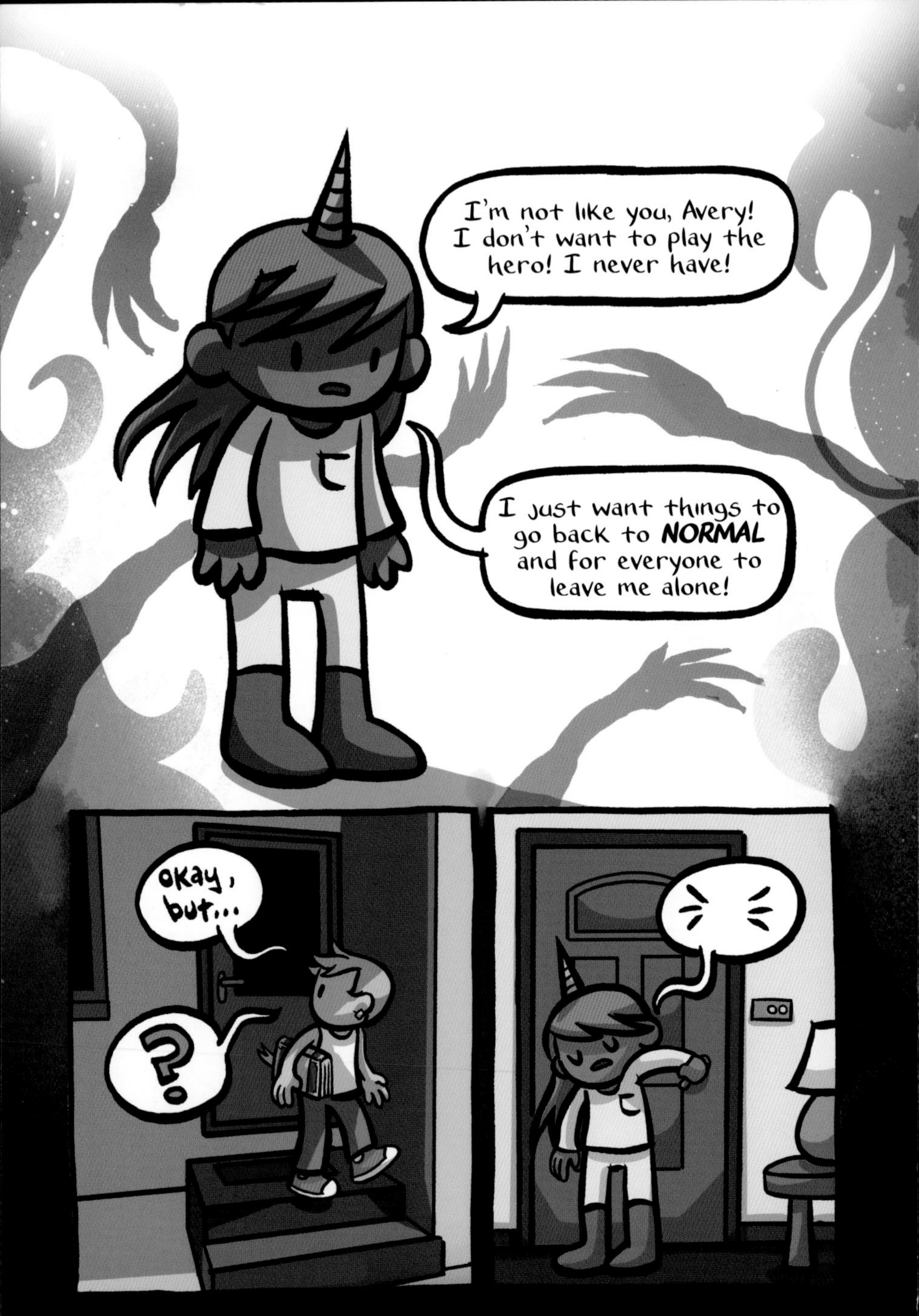
I'm not like you, Avery! I don't want to play the hero! I never have!
I just want things to go back to **NORMAL** and for everyone to leave me alone!
okay, but...
?

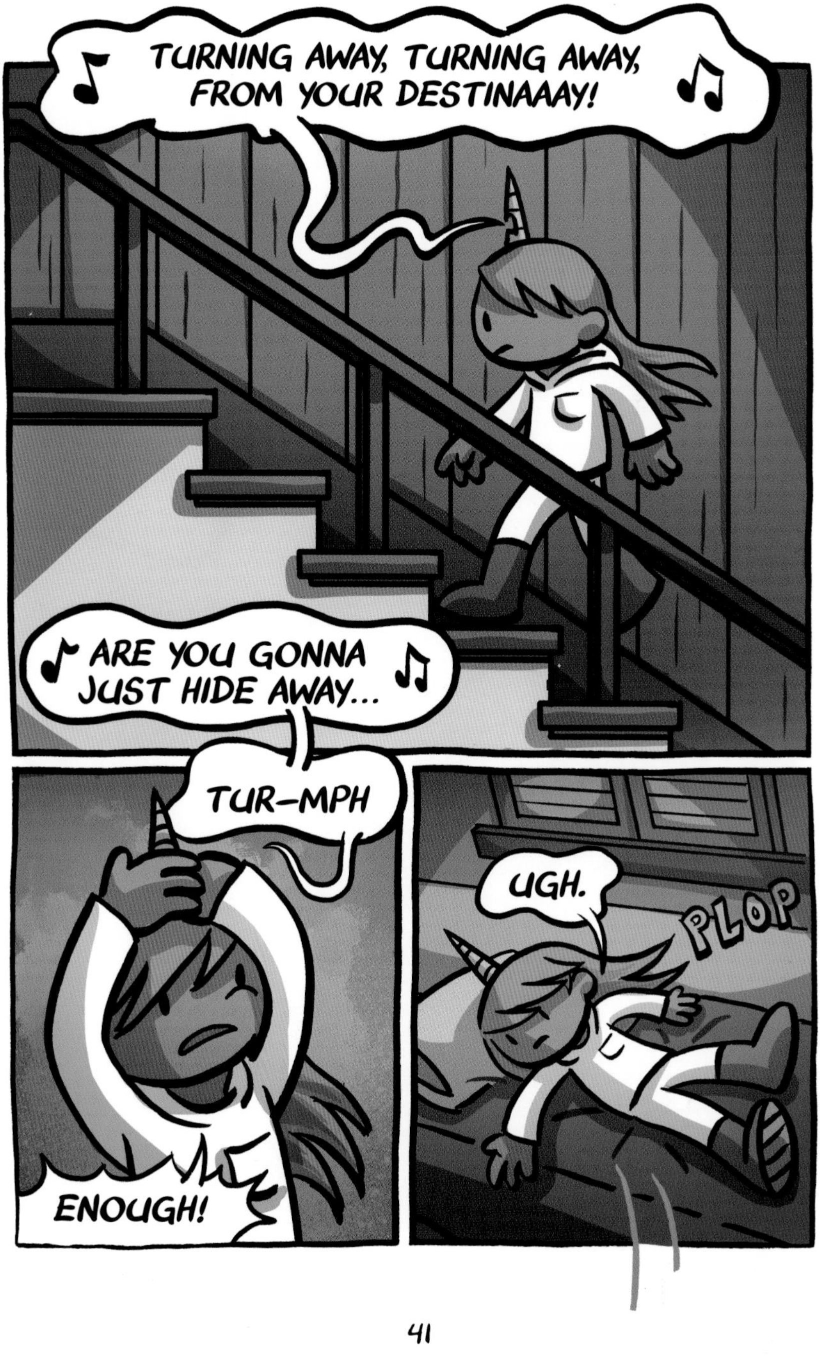
TURNING AWAY, TURNING AWAY, FROM YOUR DESTINAAAY!
ARE YOU GONNA JUST HIDE AWAY...
TUR-MPH
ENOUGH!
UGH.
PLOP

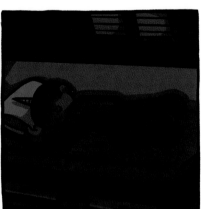

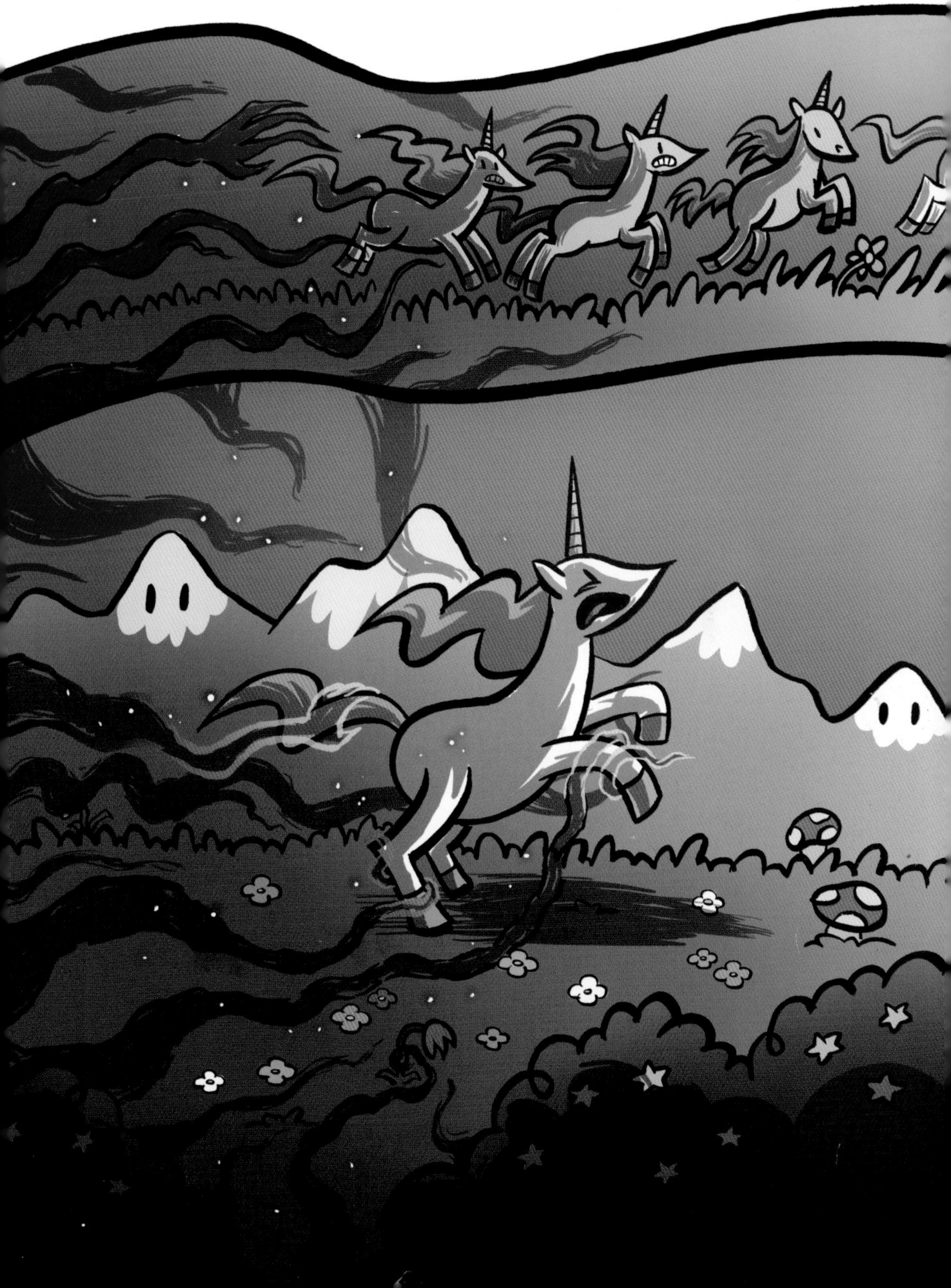

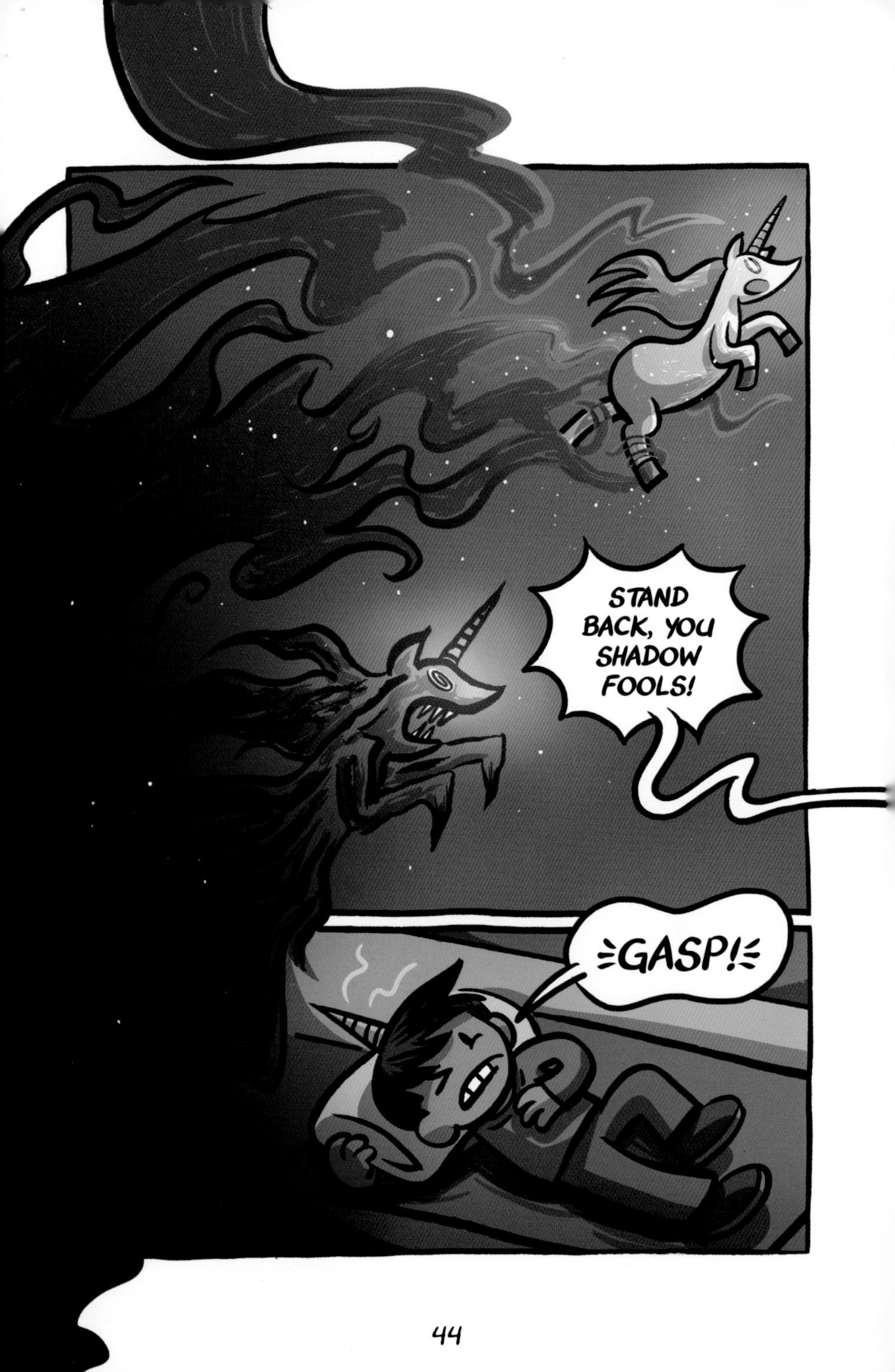
STAND BACK, YOU SHADOW FOOLS!
GASP!

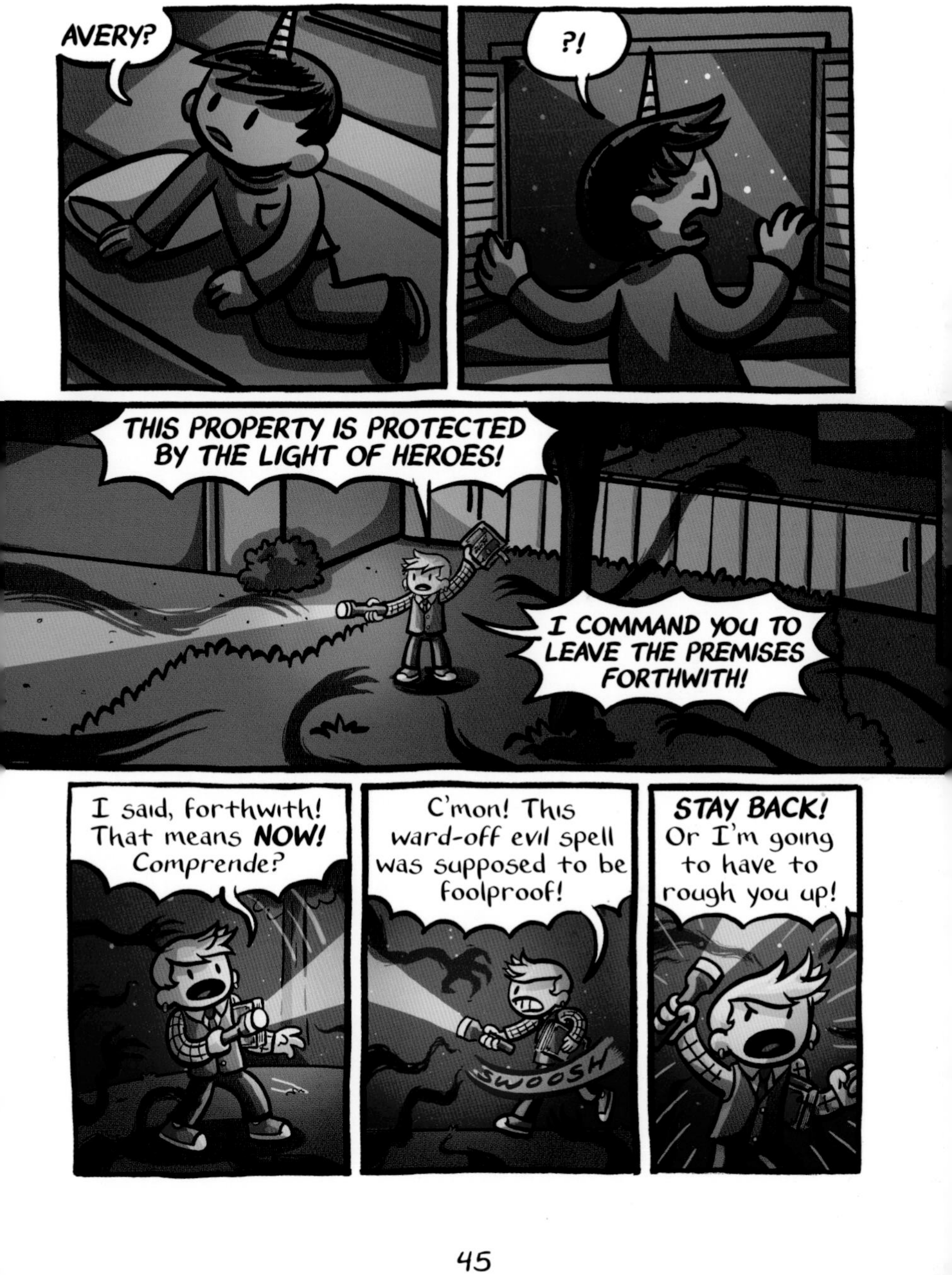
AVERY?
?!
THIS PROPERTY IS PROTECTED BY THE LIGHT OF HEROES!
I COMMAND YOU TO LEAVE THE PREMISES FORTHWITH!
I said, forthwith! That means **NOW!** Comprende?
C'mon! This ward-off evil spell was supposed to be foolproof!
SWOOSH
STAY BACK! Or I'm going to have to rough you up!

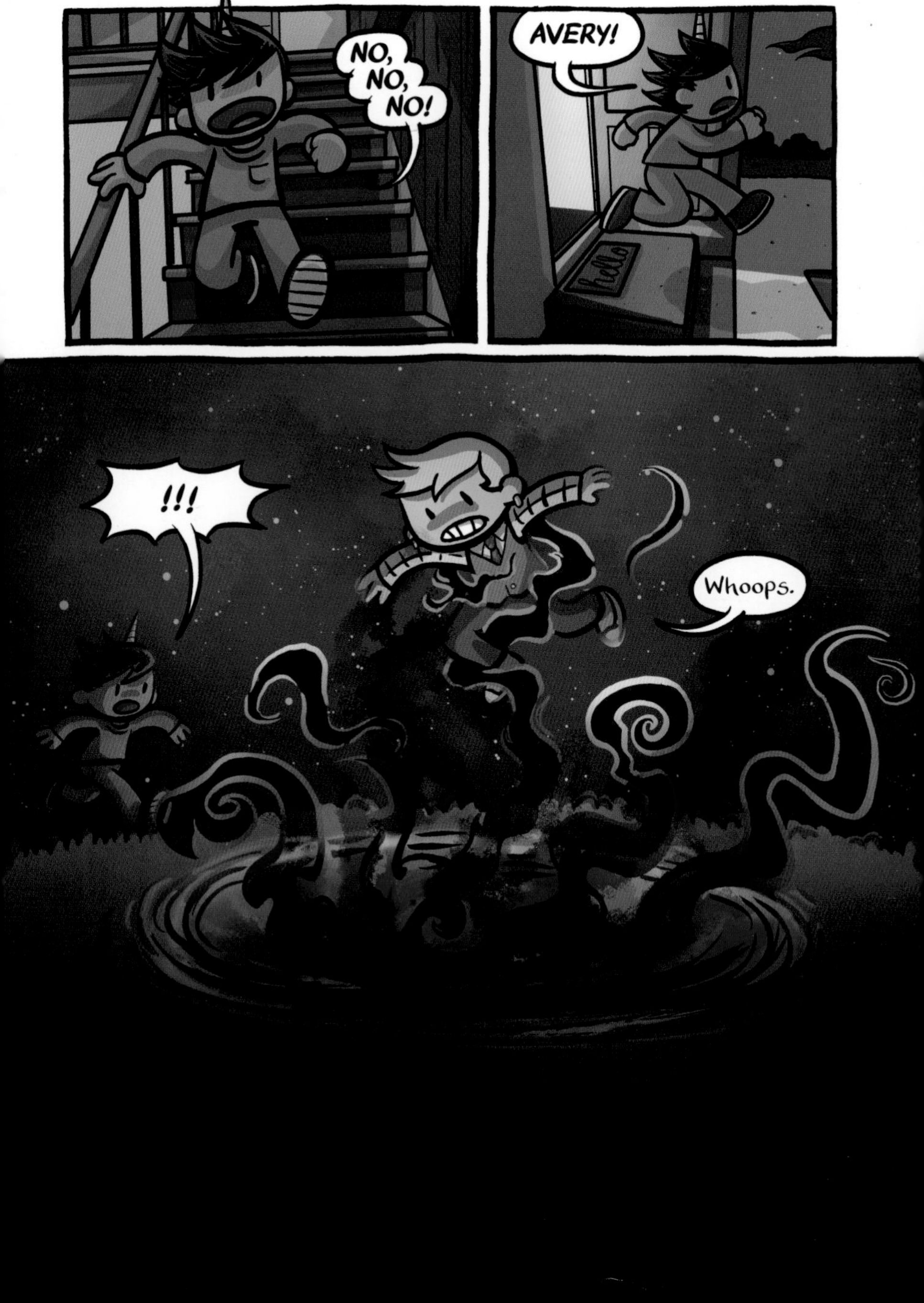
NO, NO, NO!
AVERY!
hello
!!!
Whoops.

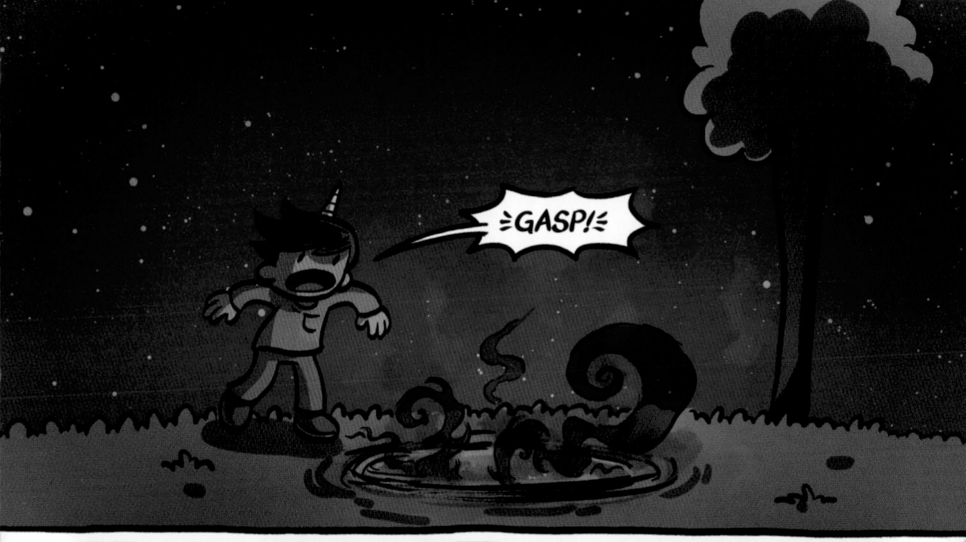
GASP!

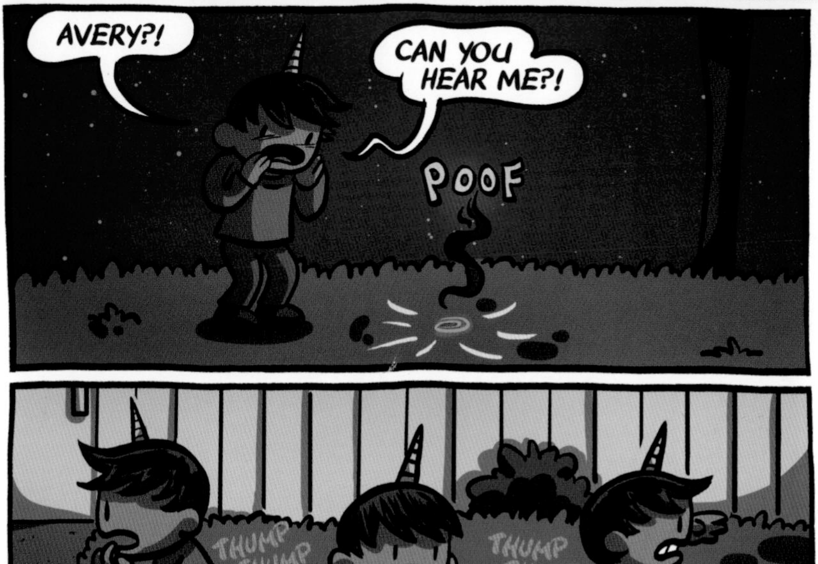
AVERY?!
CAN YOU HEAR ME?!
POOF

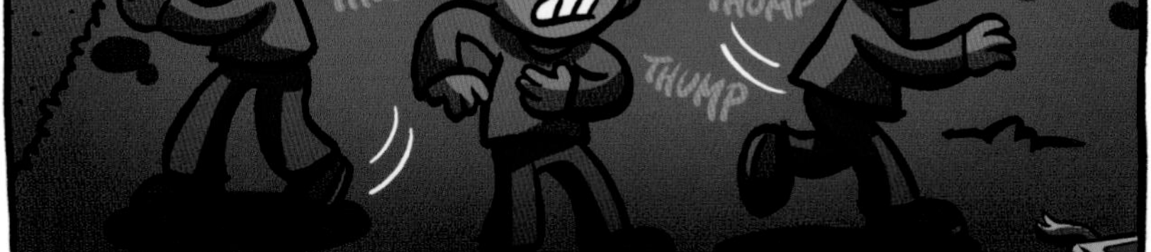
THUMP THUMP
THUMP THUMP
THUMP

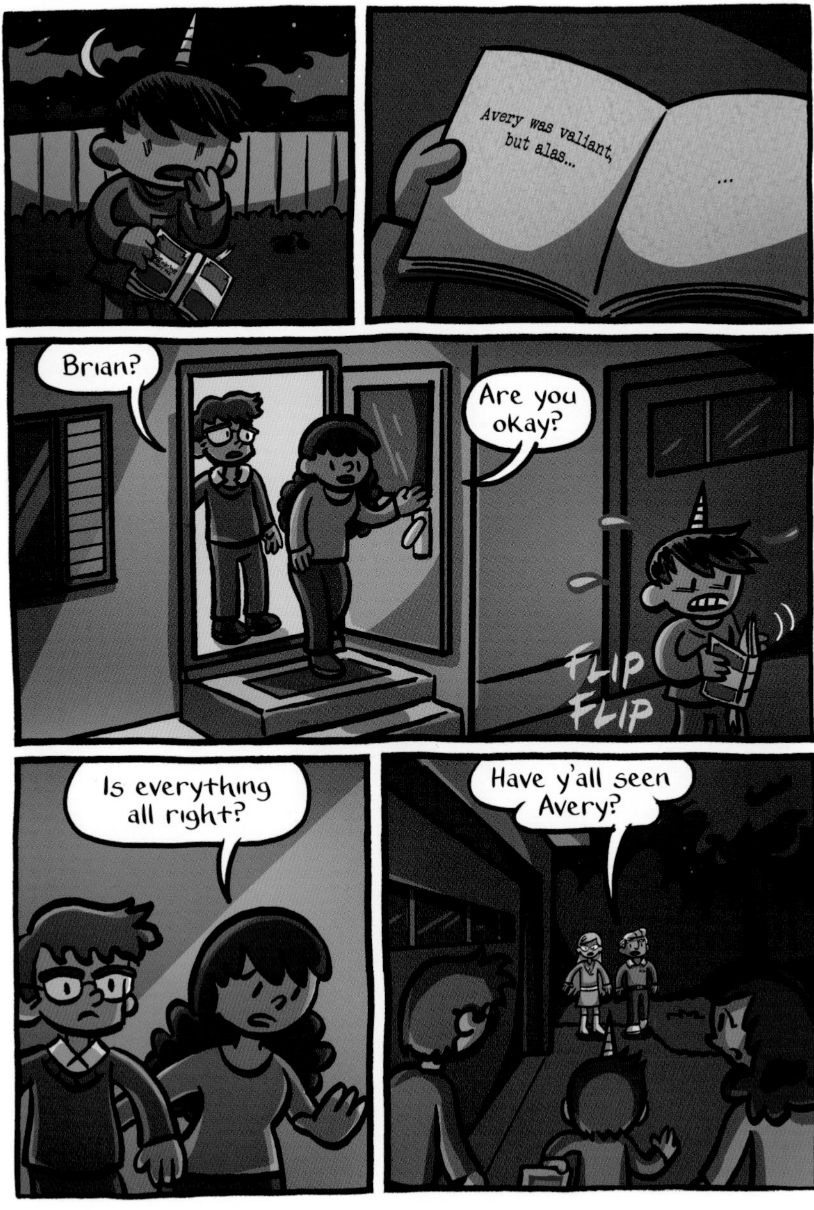
Avery was valiant, but alas...
...
Brian?
Are you okay?
FLIP FLIP
Is everything all right?
Have y'all seen Avery?

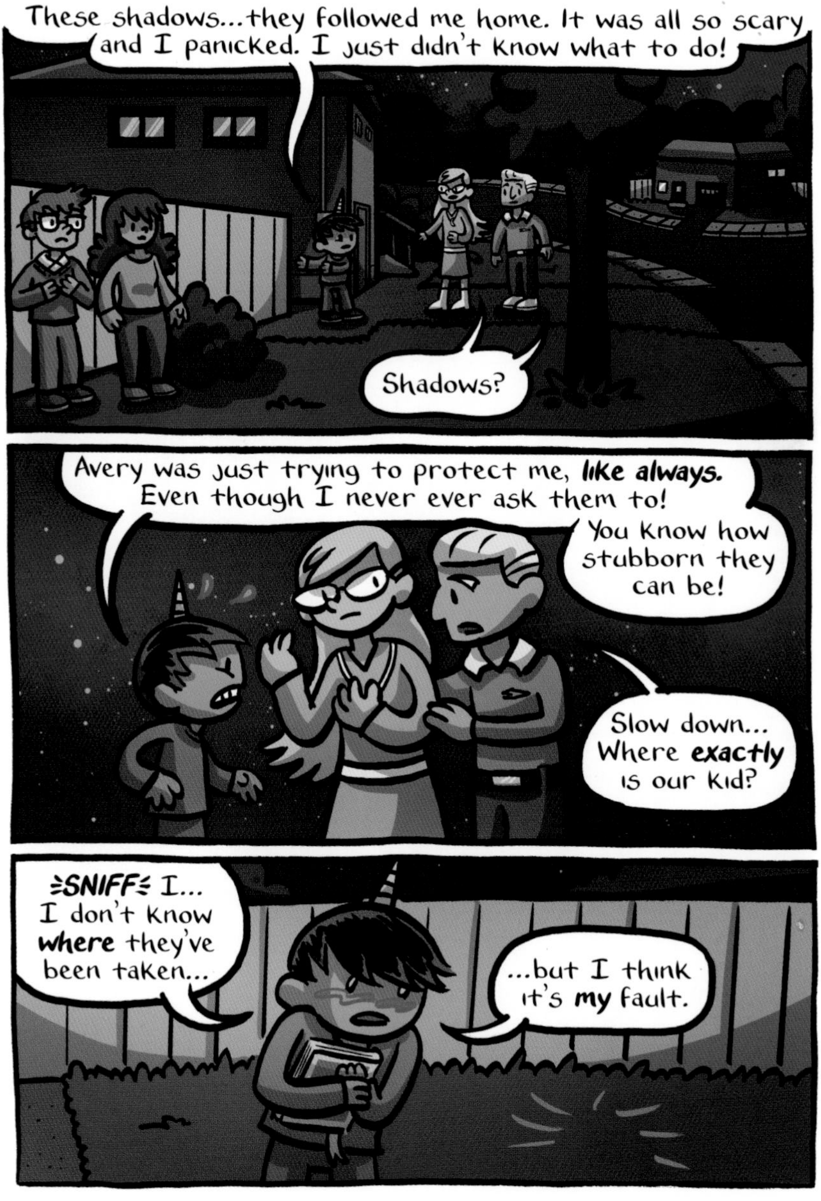
These shadows...they followed me home. It was all so scary and I panicked. I just didn't know what to do!
Shadows?
Avery was just trying to protect me, **like always.** Even though I never ever ask them to!
You know how stubborn they can be!
Slow down... Where **exactly** is our kid?
SNIFF I... I don't know **where** they've been taken...
...but I think it's **my** fault.

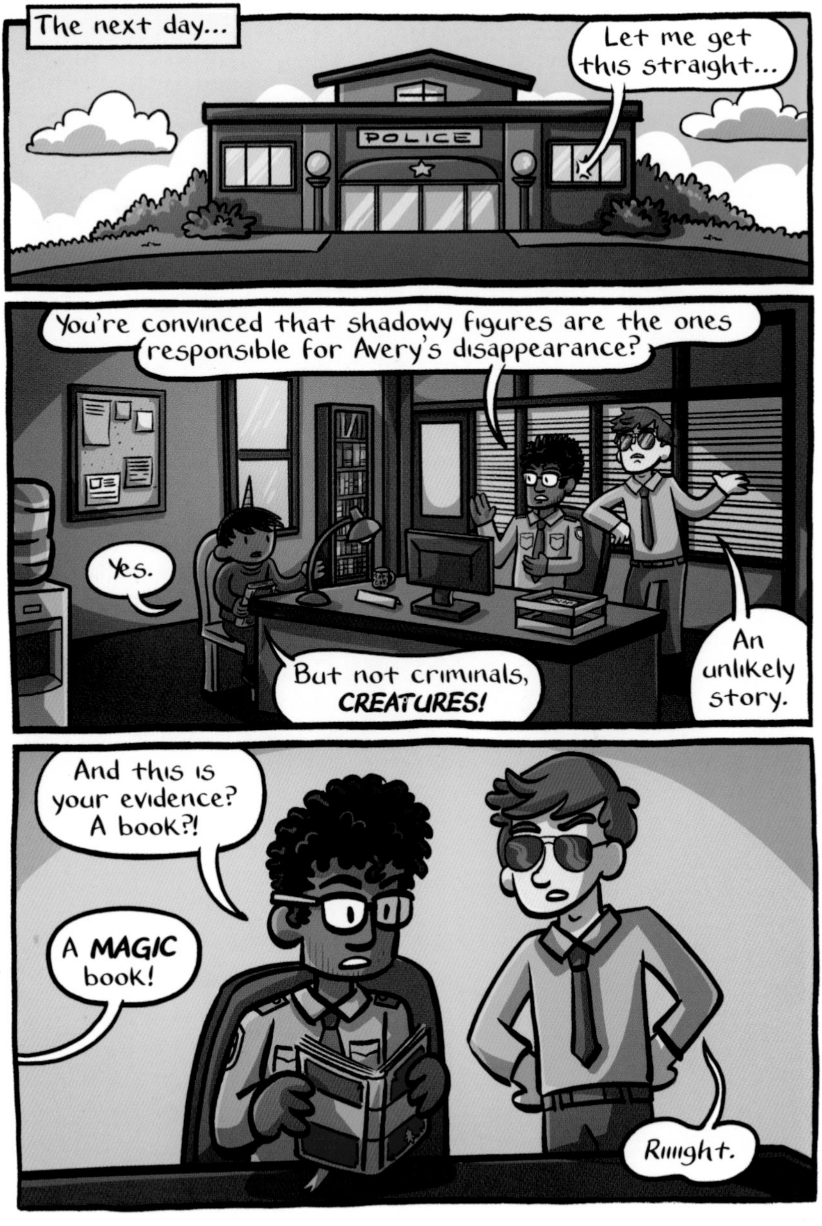
The next day...
Let me get this straight...
You're convinced that shadowy figures are the ones responsible for Avery's disappearance?
Yes.
But not criminals, **CREATURES!**
An unlikely story.
POLICE
And this is your evidence? A book?!
A **MAGIC** book!
Riiight.

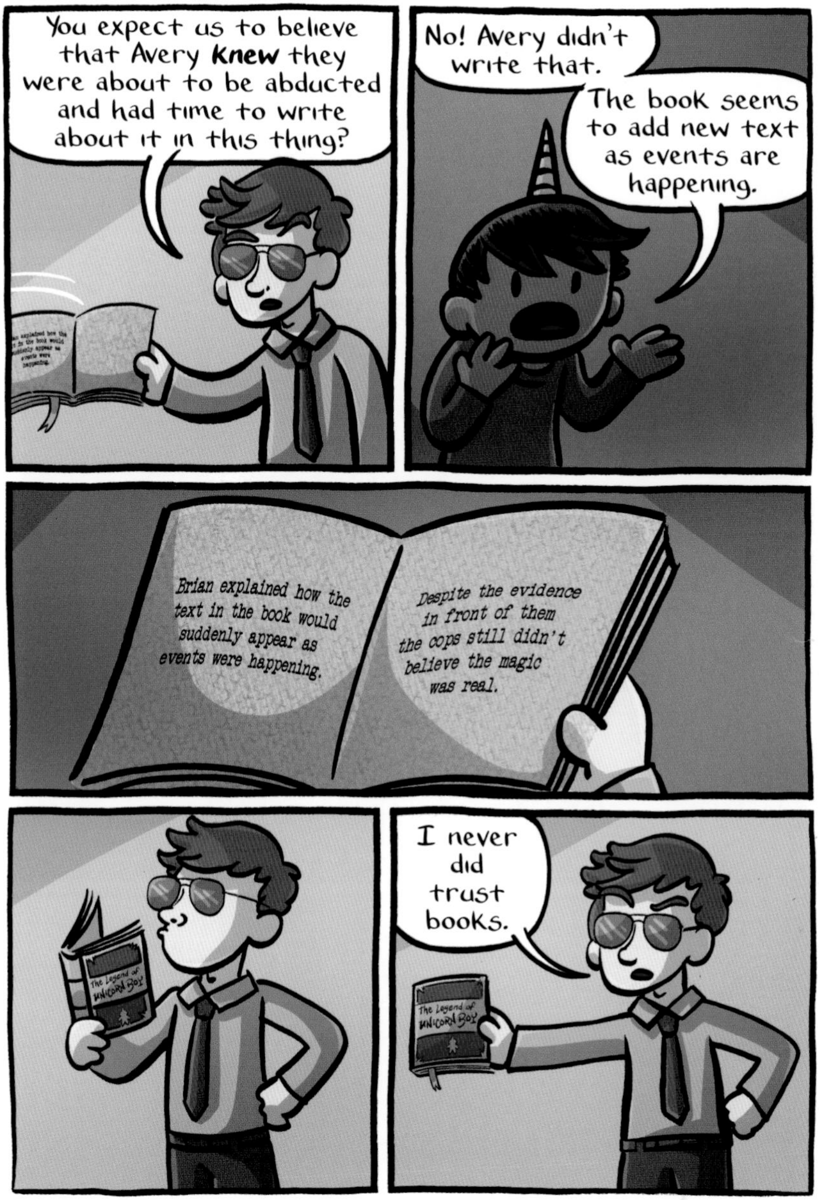
You expect us to believe that Avery **knew** they were about to be abducted and had time to write about it in this thing?
No! Avery didn't write that.
The book seems to add new text as events are happening.
Brian explained how the text in the book would suddenly appear as events were happening.
Despite the evidence in front of them the cops still didn't believe the magic was real.
The Legend of Unicorn Boy
I never did trust books.
The Legend of Unicorn Boy

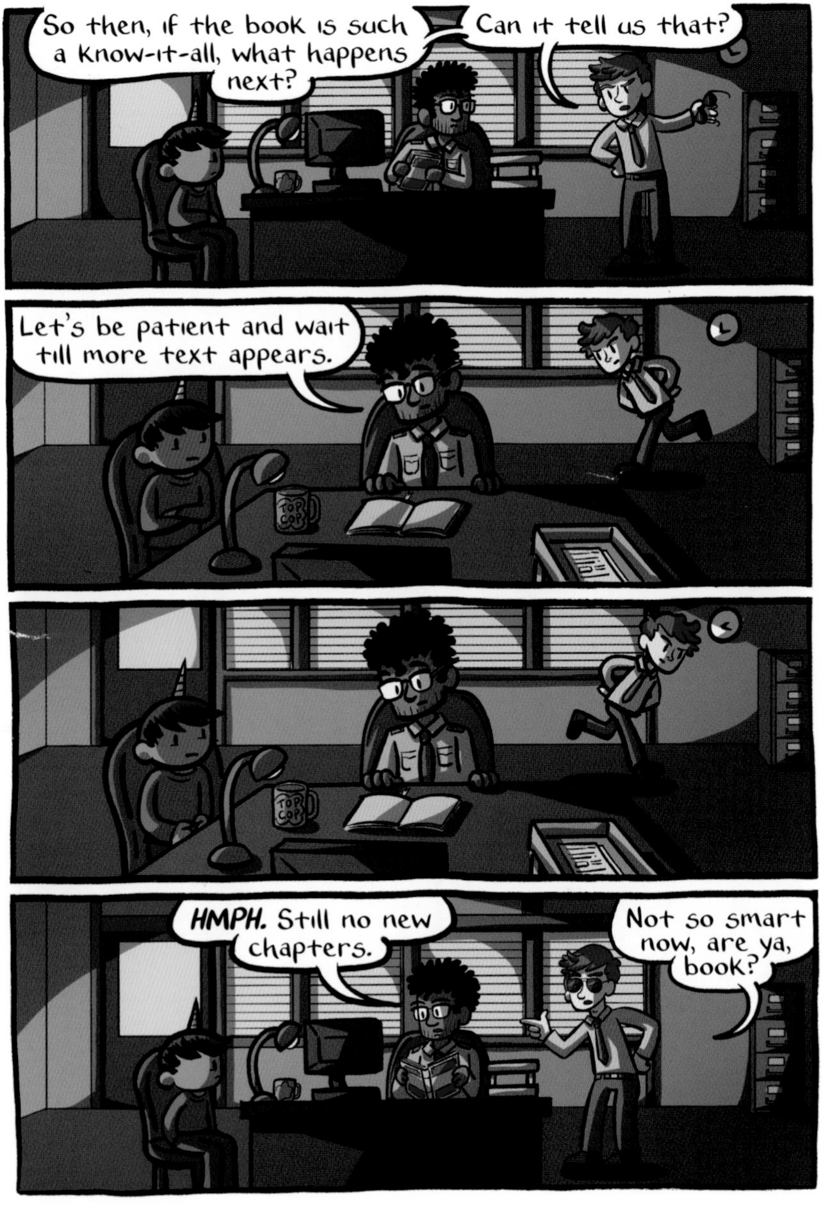
So then, if the book is such a know-it-all, what happens next?
Can it tell us that?
Let's be patient and wait till more text appears.
TOP COP
TOP COP
HMPH. Still no new chapters.
Not so smart now, are ya, book?

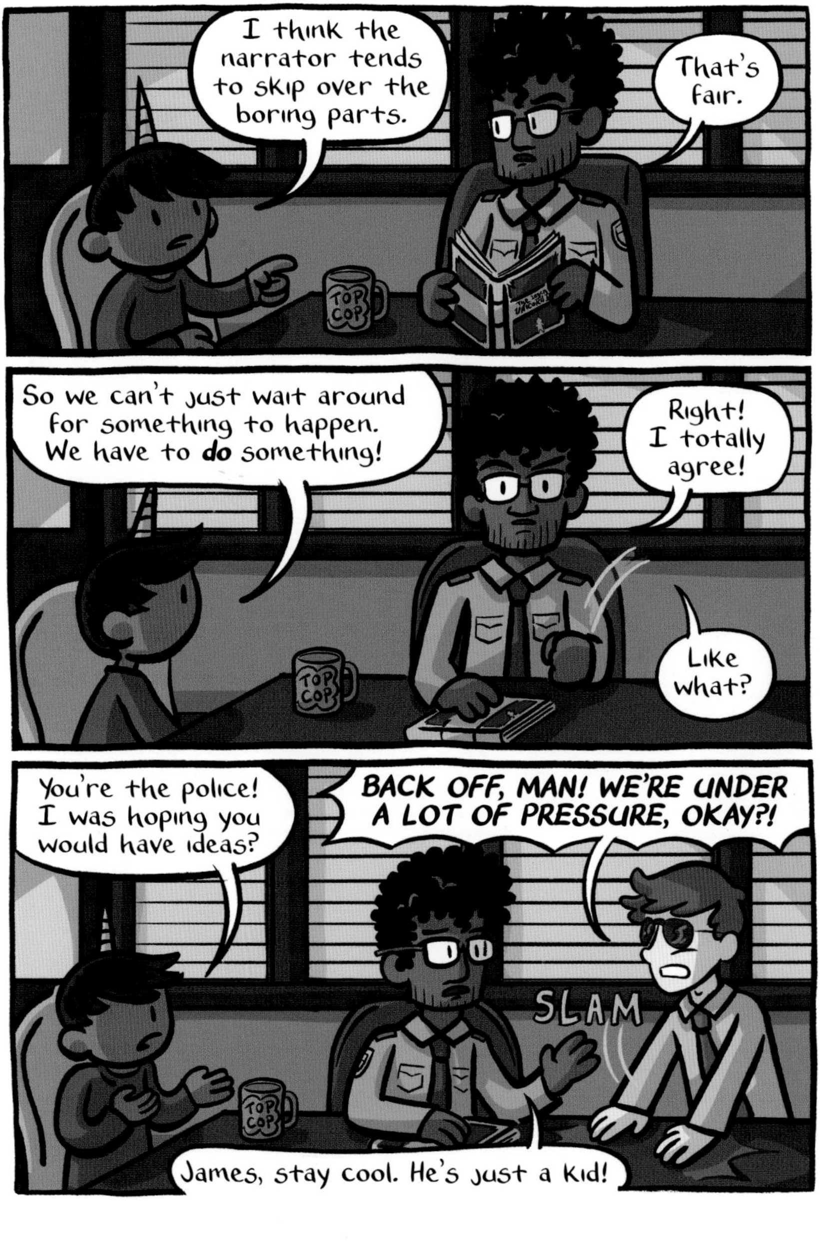
I think the narrator tends to skip over the boring parts.
That's fair.
TOP COP
So we can't just wait around for something to happen. We have to **do** something!
Right! I totally agree!
Like what?
TOP COP
You're the police! I was hoping you would have ideas?
BACK OFF, MAN! WE'RE UNDER A LOT OF PRESSURE, OKAY?!
SLAM
TOP COP
James, stay cool. He's just a kid!

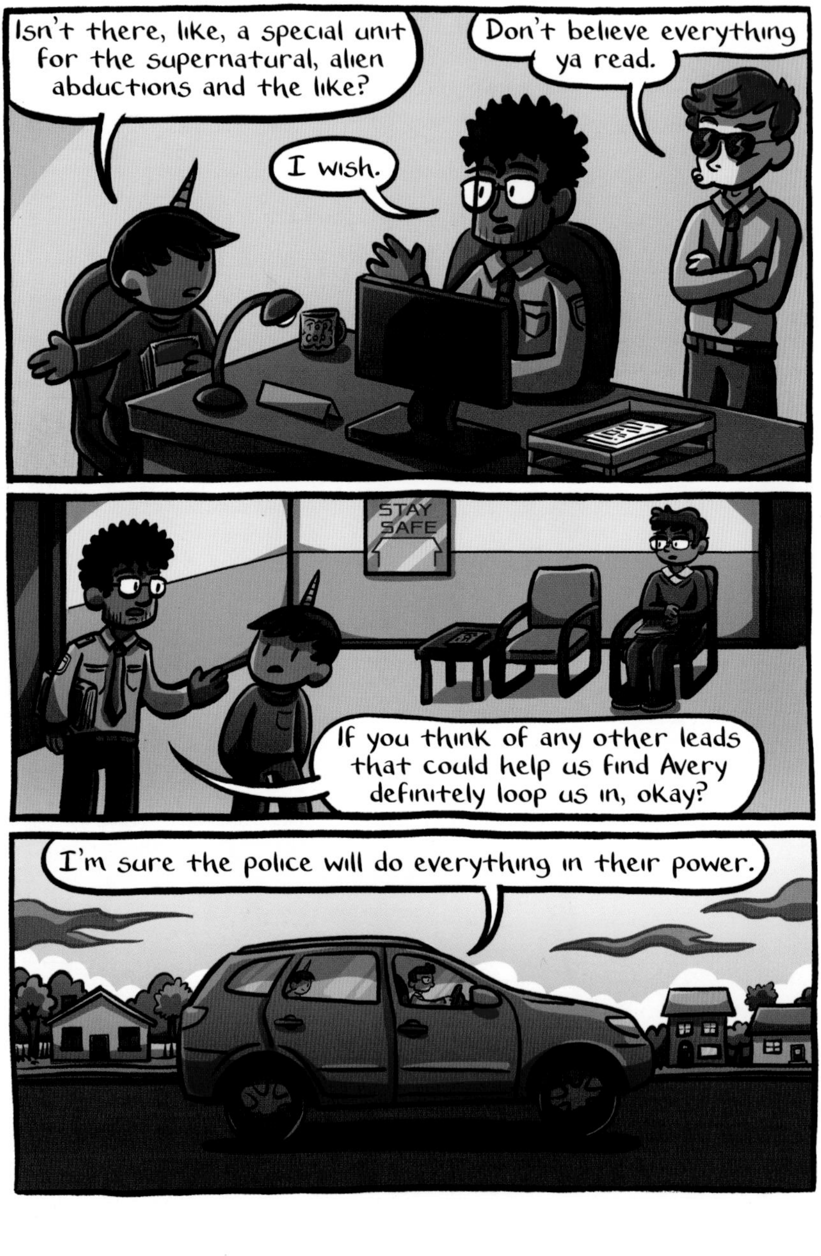
Isn't there, like, a special unit for the supernatural, alien abductions and the like?
Don't believe everything ya read.
I wish.
STAY SAFE
If you think of any other leads that could help us find Avery definitely loop us in, okay?
I'm sure the police will do everything in their power.

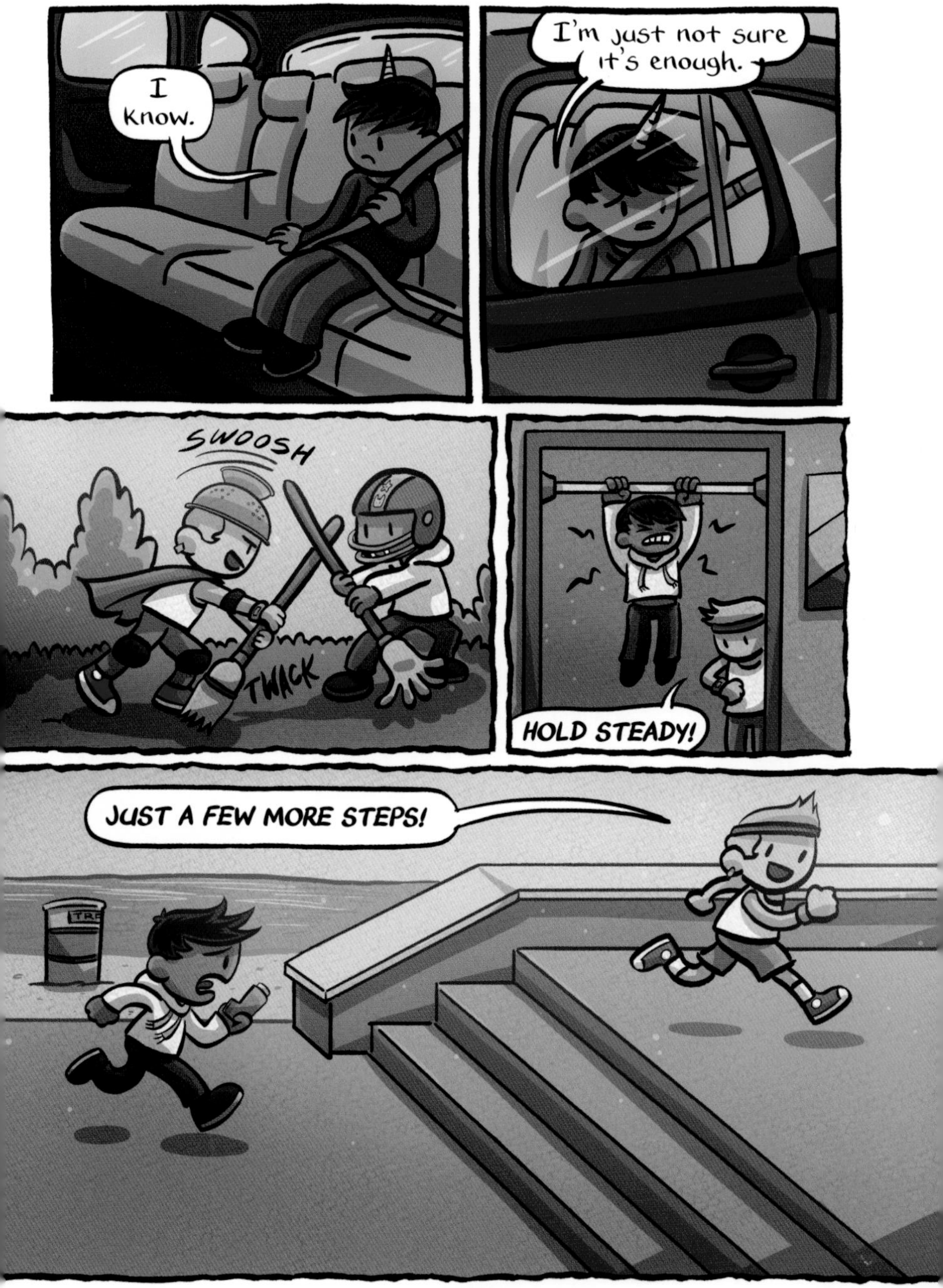
I know.
I'm just not sure it's enough.
SWOOSH
TWACK
HOLD STEADY!
JUST A FEW MORE STEPS!

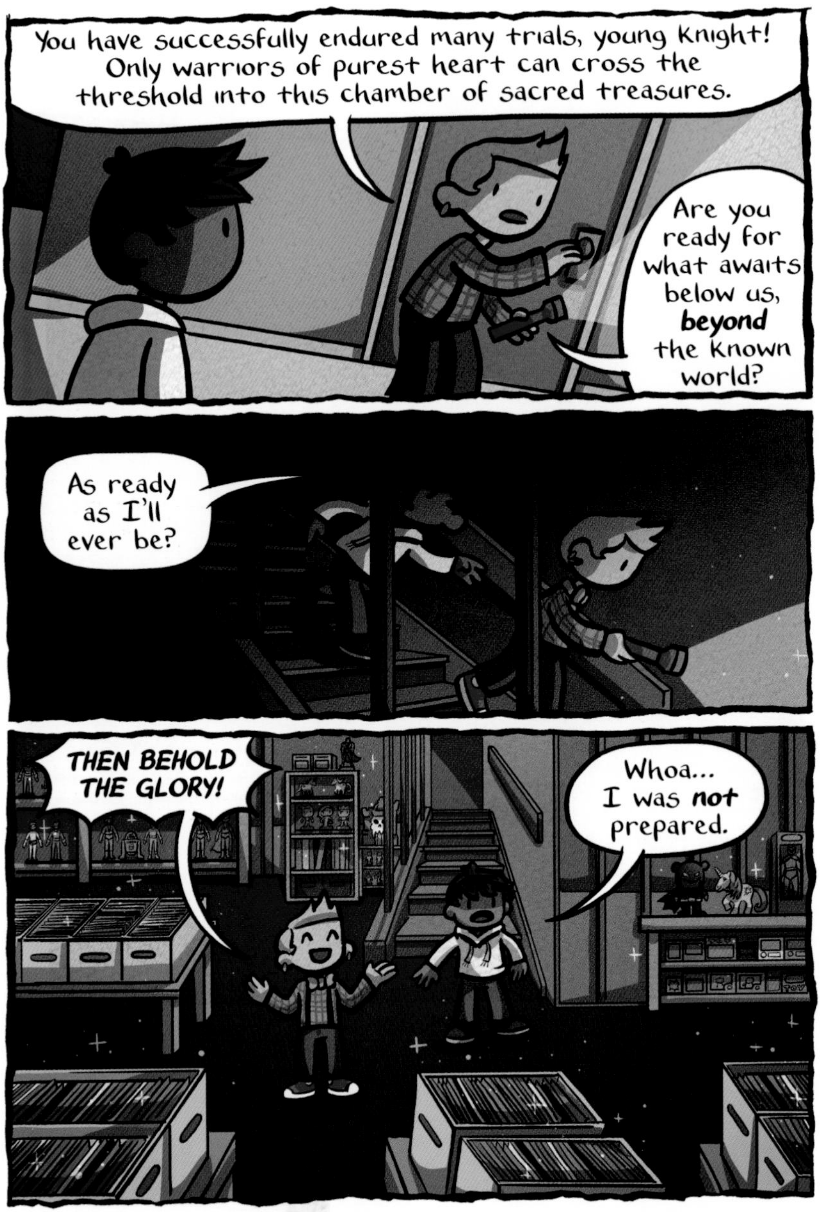
You have successfully endured many trials, young Knight! Only warriors of purest heart can cross the threshold into this chamber of sacred treasures.
Are you ready for what awaits below us, **beyond** the known world?
As ready as I'll ever be?
THEN BEHOLD THE GLORY!
Whoa... I was **not** prepared.

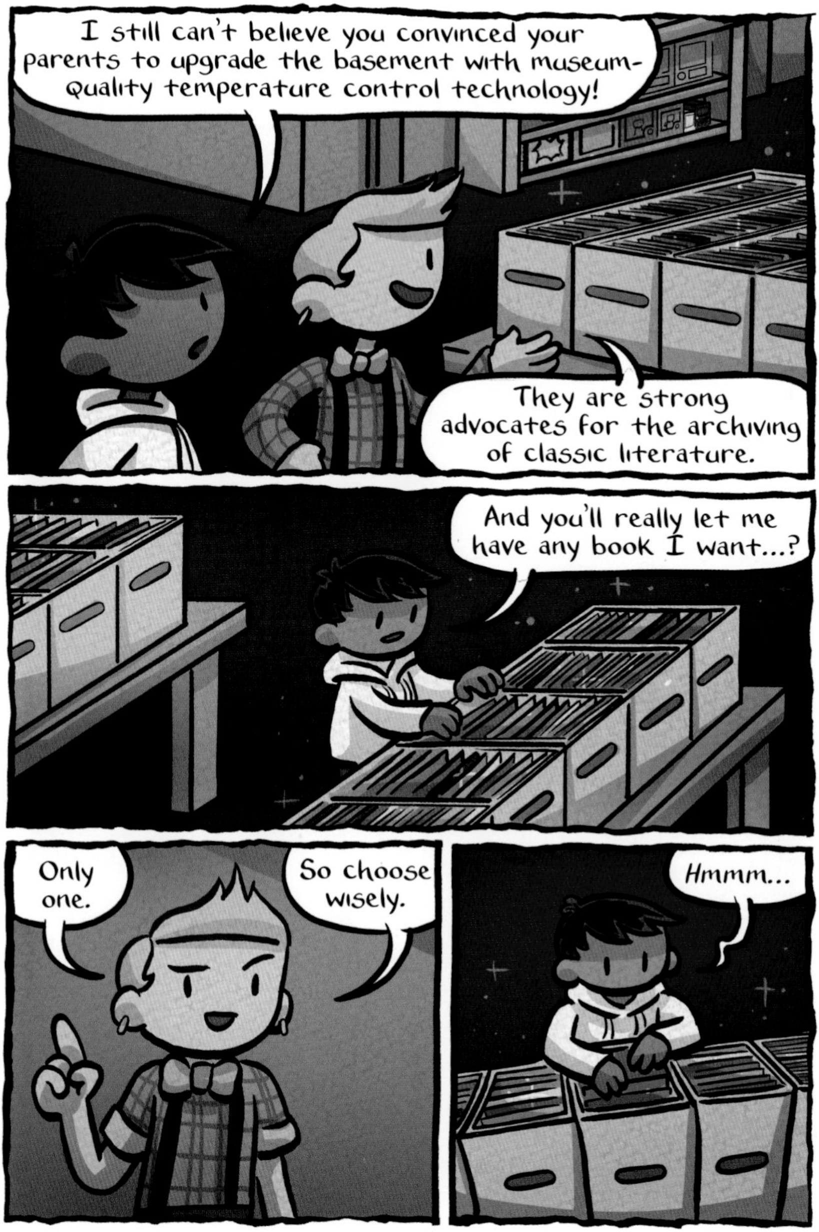
I still can't believe you convinced your parents to upgrade the basement with museum-quality temperature control technology!
They are strong advocates for the archiving of classic literature.
And you'll really let me have any book I want...?
Only one.
So choose wisely.
Hmmm...

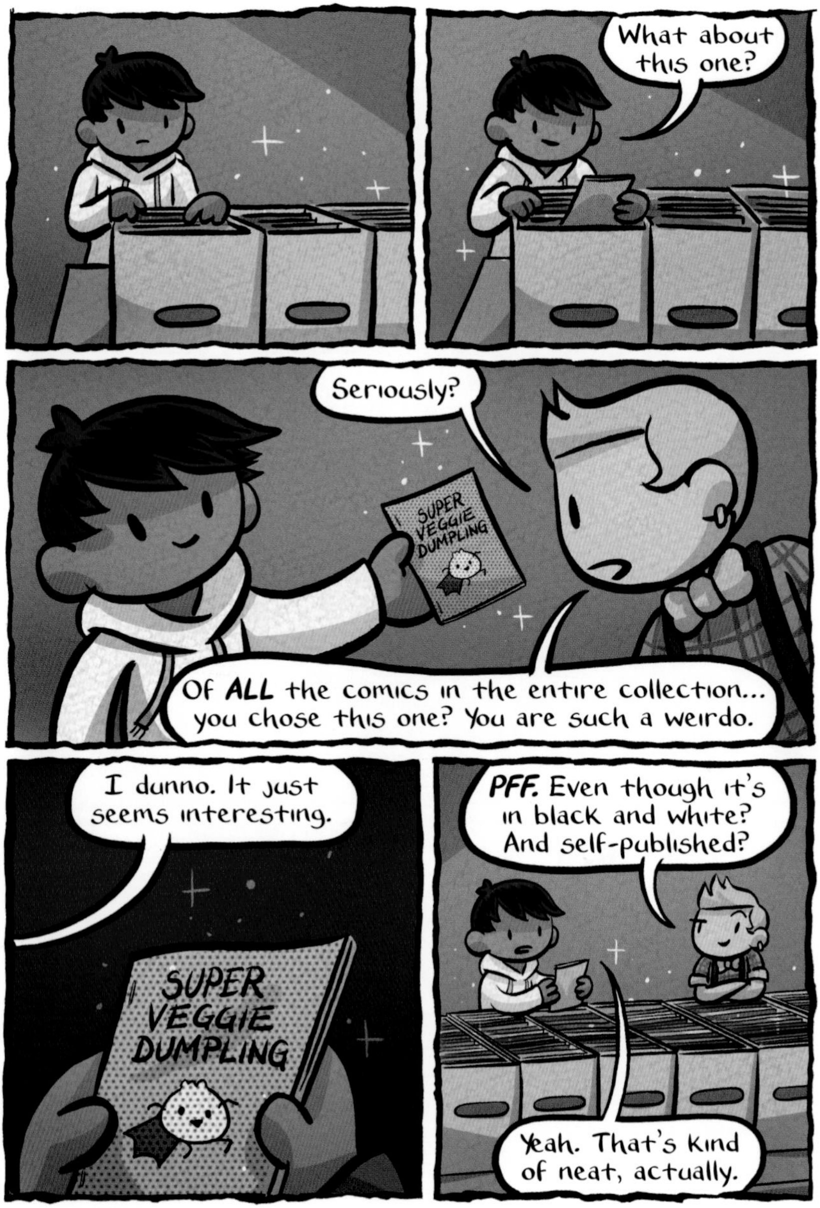
What about this one?
Seriously?
SUPER VEGGIE DUMPLING
Of ALL the comics in the entire collection... you chose this one? You are such a weirdo.
I dunno. It just seems interesting.
SUPER VEGGIE DUMPLING
PFF. Even though it's in black and white? And self-published?
Yeah. That's kind of neat, actually.

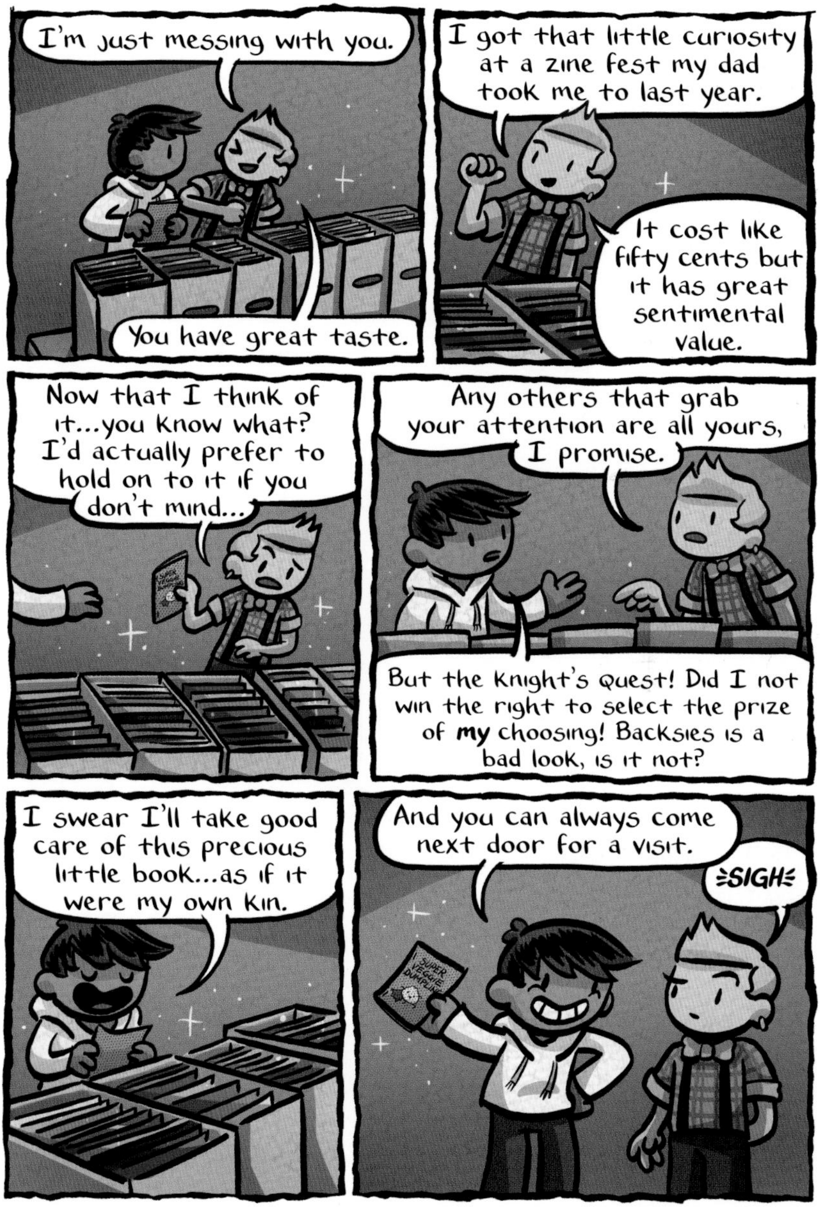
I'm just messing with you.
You have great taste.
I got that little curiosity at a zine fest my dad took me to last year.
It cost like fifty cents but it has great sentimental value.
Now that I think of it...you know what? I'd actually prefer to hold on to it if you don't mind...
SUPER VEGGIE DUMPLING
Any others that grab your attention are all yours, I promise.
But the knight's quest! Did I not win the right to select the prize of **my** choosing! Backsies is a bad look, is it not?
I swear I'll take good care of this precious little book...as if it were my own kin.
And you can always come next door for a visit.
SIGH
SUPER VEGGIE DUMPLING

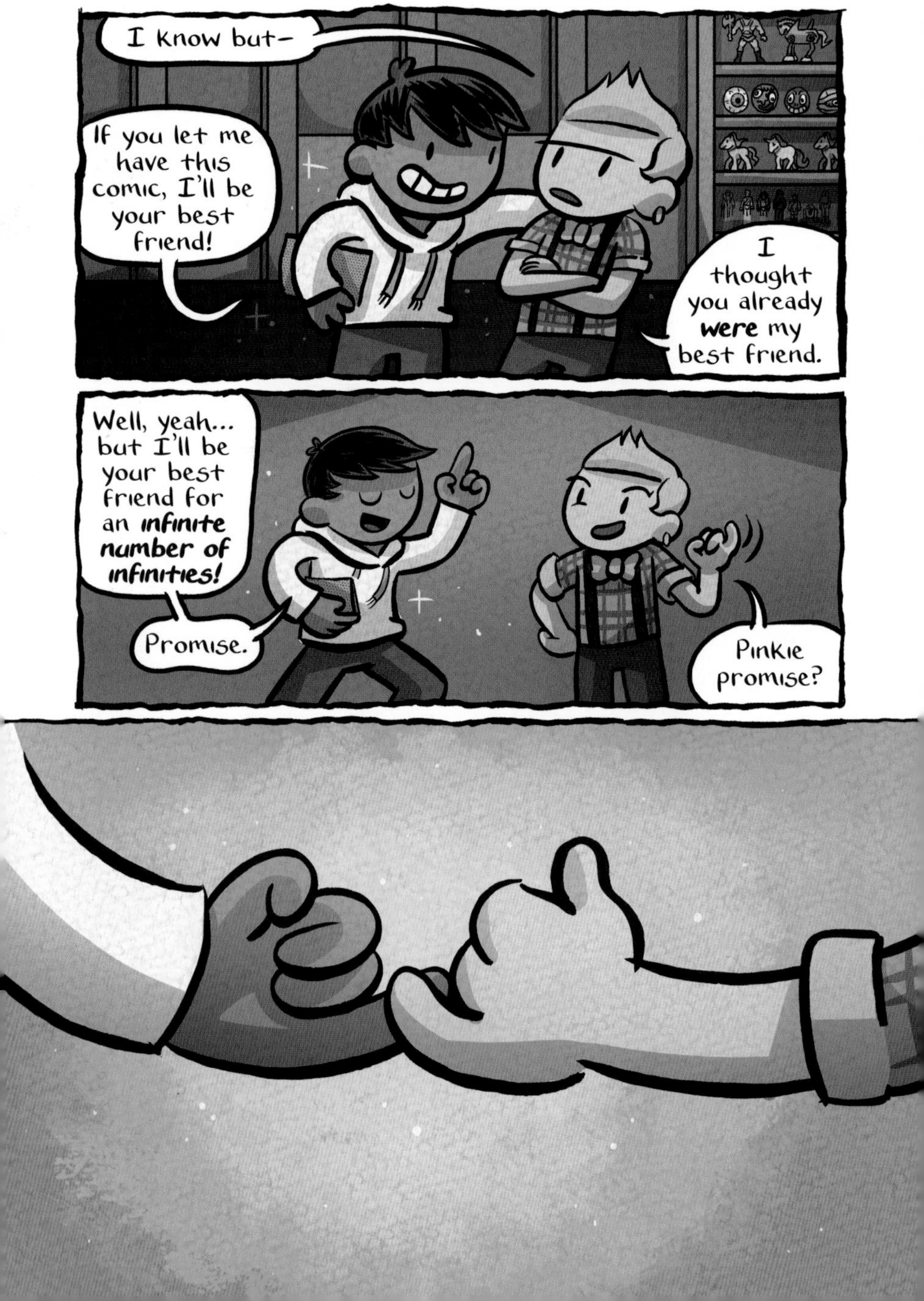
I know but–
If you let me have this comic, I'll be your best friend!
I thought you already **were** my best friend.
Well, yeah... but I'll be your best friend for an **infinite number of infinities!**
Promise.
Pinkie promise?

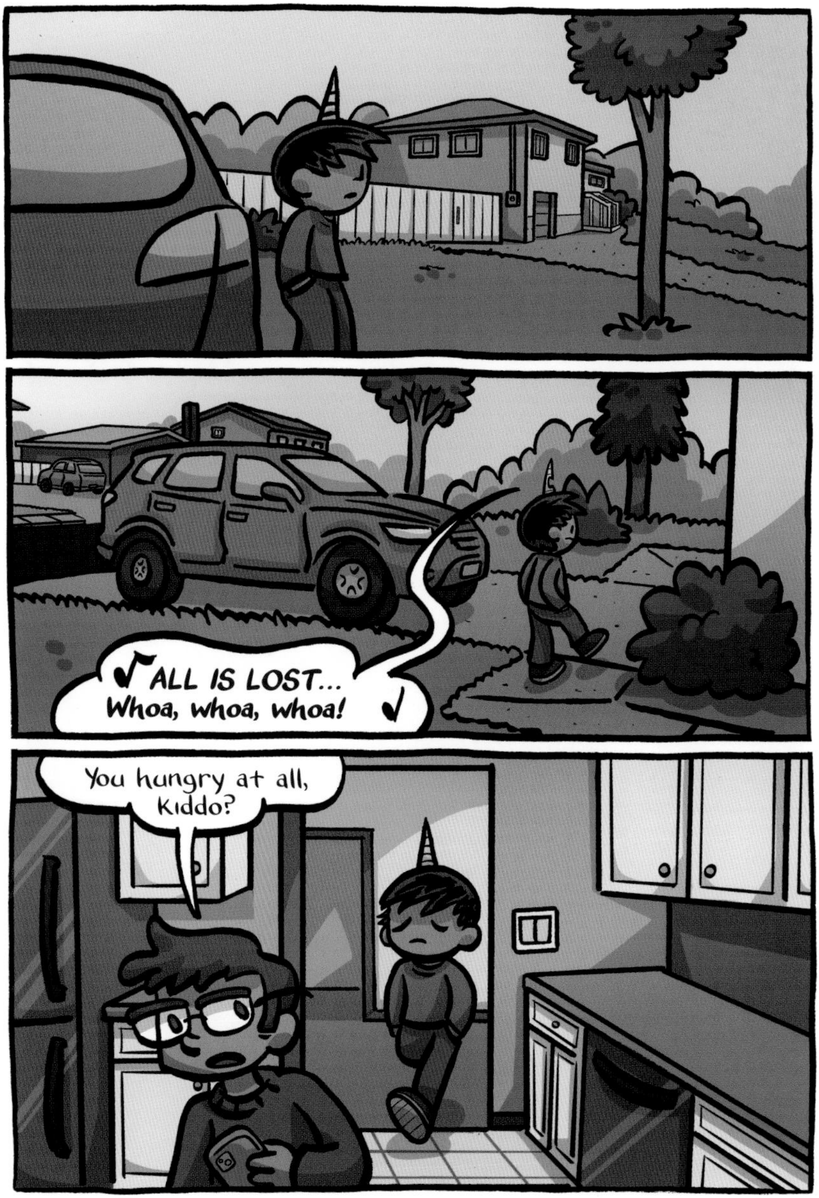
♪ALL IS LOST...
Whoa, whoa, whoa! ♪
You hungry at all, kiddo?

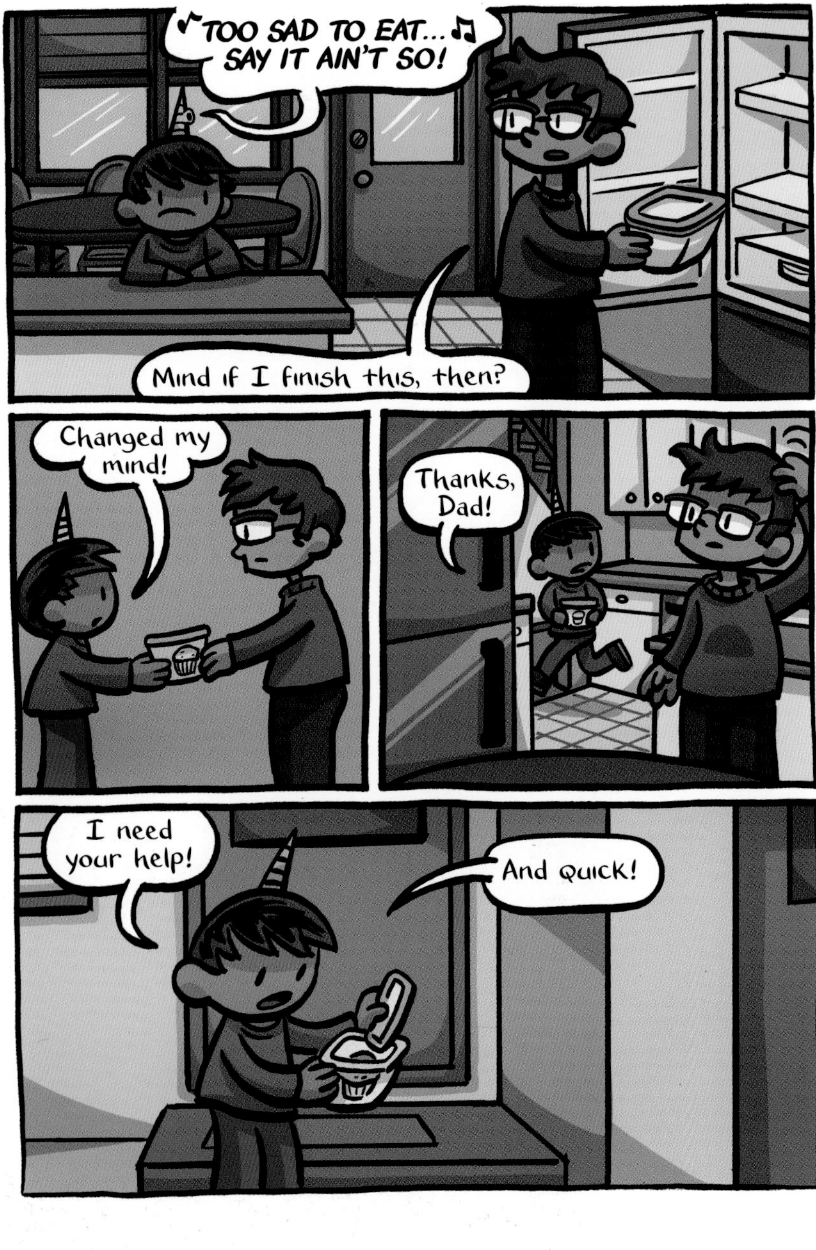
♪TOO SAD TO EAT...♫ SAY IT AIN'T SO!
Mind if I finish this, then?
Changed my mind!
Thanks, Dad!
I need your help!
And quick!

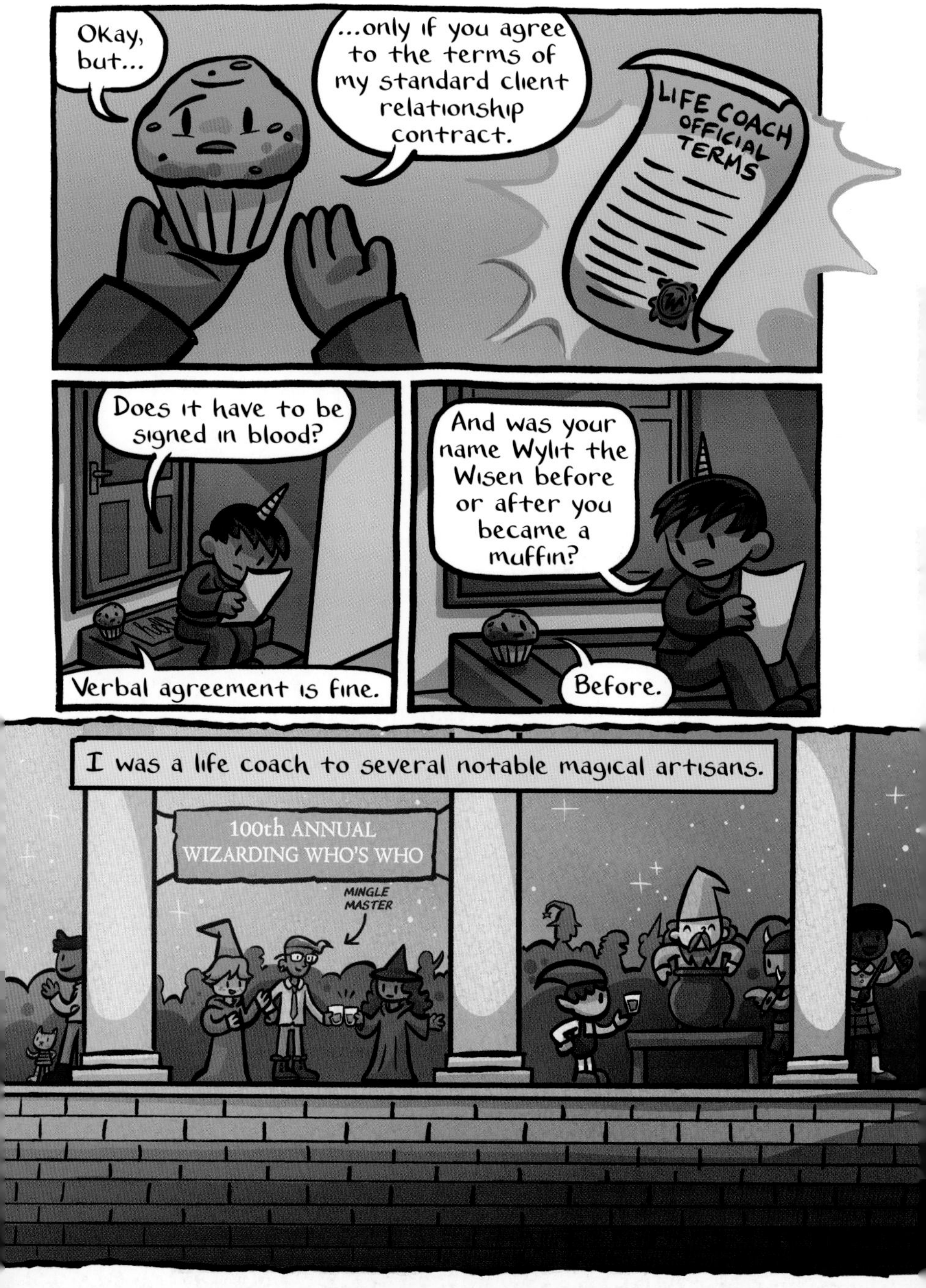
Okay, but...
...only if you agree to the terms of my standard client relationship contract.
LIFE COACH OFFICIAL TERMS
Does it have to be signed in blood?
Verbal agreement is fine.
And was your name Wylit the Wisen before or after you became a muffin?
Before.
I was a life coach to several notable magical artisans.
100th ANNUAL WIZARDING WHO'S WHO
MINGLE MASTER

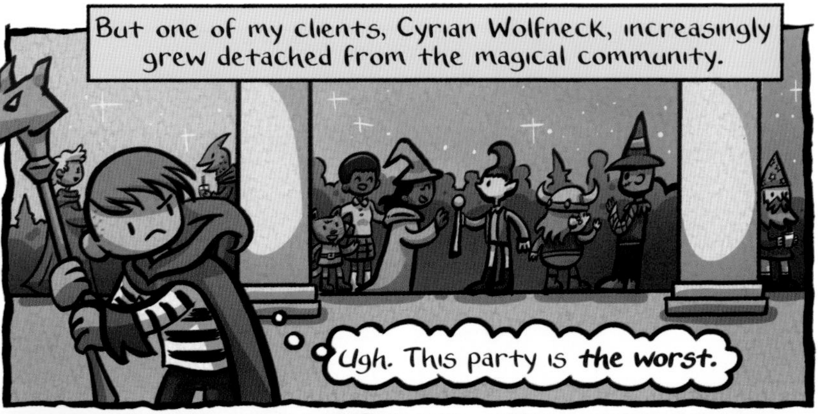
But one of my clients, Cyrian Wolfneck, increasingly grew detached from the magical community.
Ugh. This party is **the worst.**

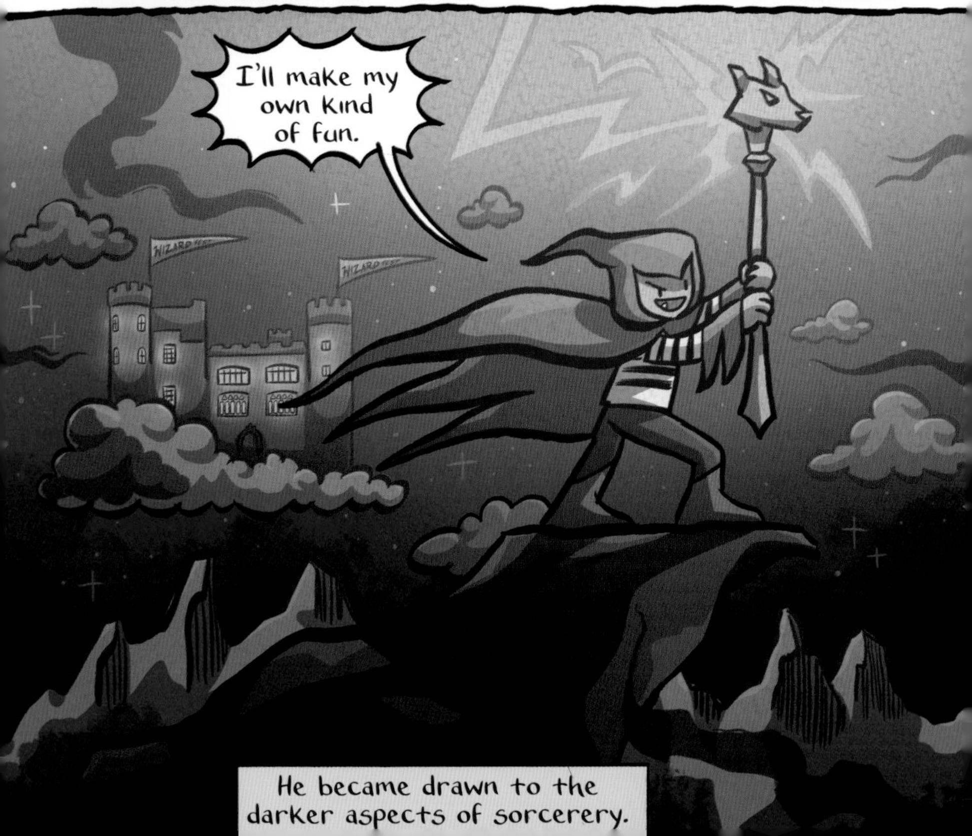
I'll make my own kind of fun.
He became drawn to the darker aspects of sorcerery.

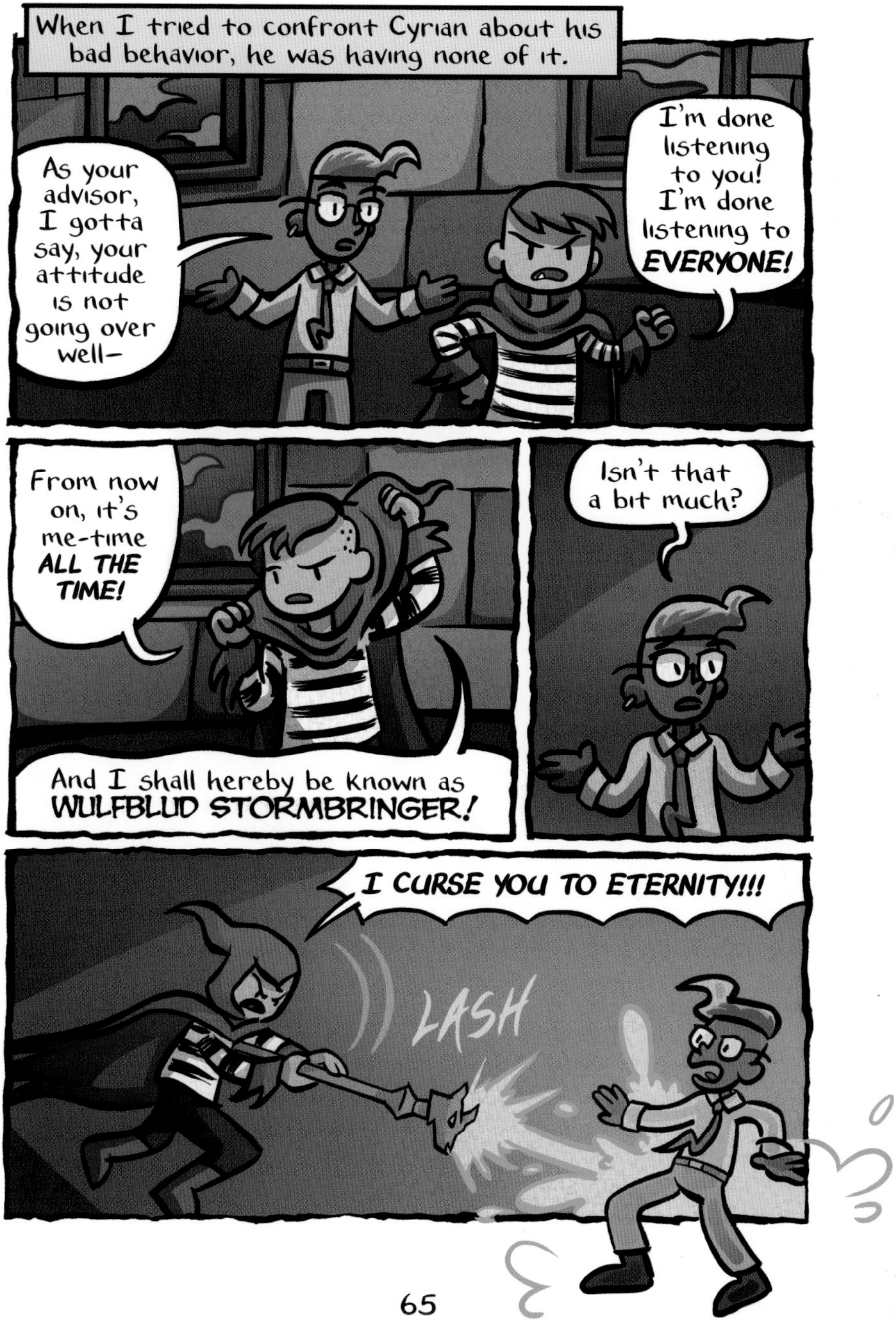
When I tried to confront Cyrian about his bad behavior, he was having none of it.
As your advisor, I gotta say, your attitude is not going over well–
I'm done listening to you! I'm done listening to EVERYONE!
From now on, it's me-time ALL THE TIME!
And I shall hereby be known as WULFBLUD STORMBRINGER!
Isn't that a bit much?
I CURSE YOU TO ETERNITY!!!
LASH

Thus, I have been trapped in this delicious form ever since.

SNIFF SNIFF

Do you mind moving me away from these ants?

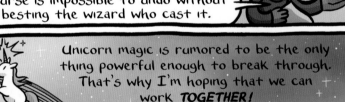

And none of those other wizards were able to help change you back?

A curse is impossible to undo without besting the wizard who cast it.

Unicorn magic is rumored to be the only thing powerful enough to break through. That's why I'm hoping that we can work *TOGETHER!*

But we can worry about my troubles later. Finding your friend might be a tad more urgent.

Okay, then.

Where do we start looking?

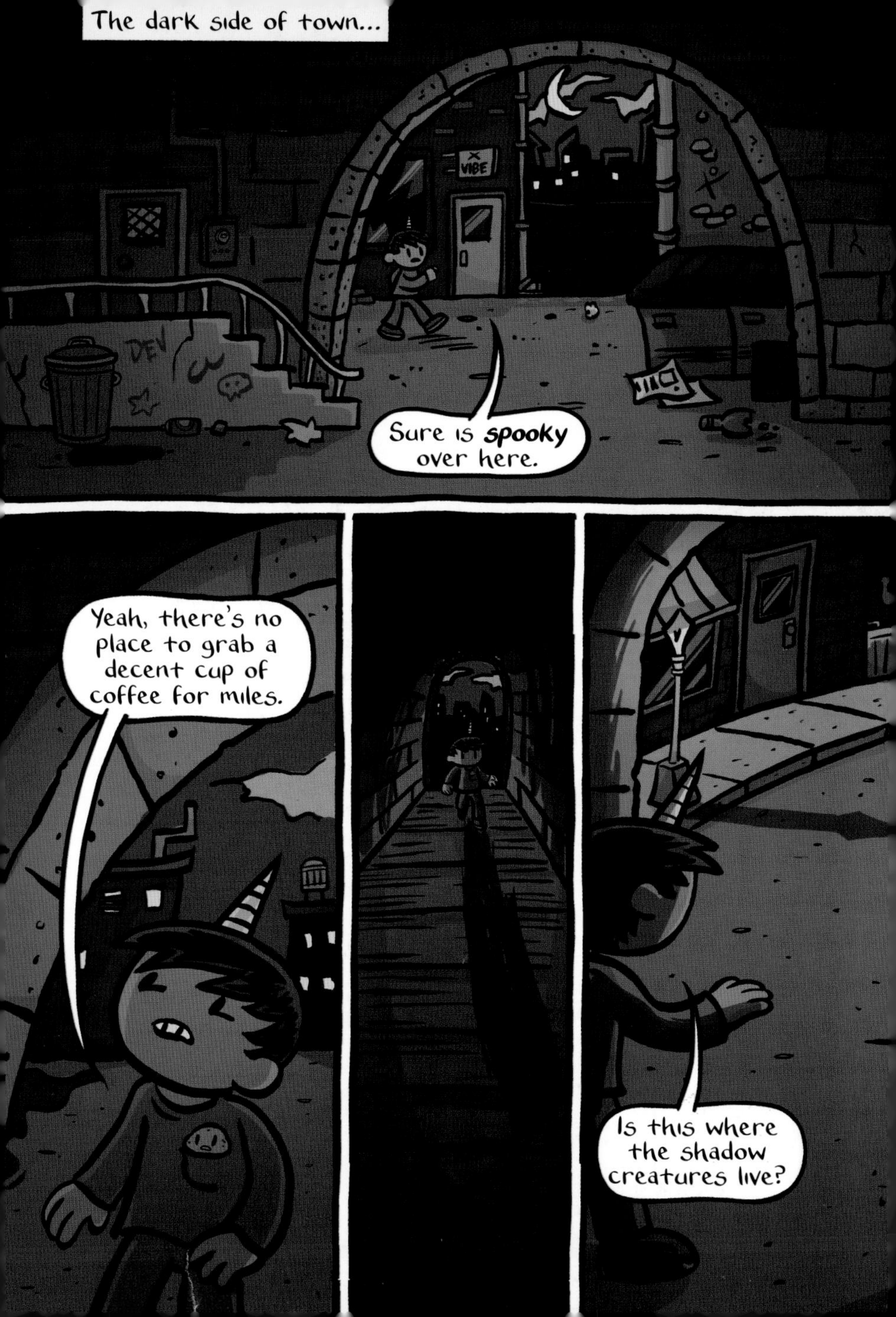
The dark side of town...
VIBE
DEV
Sure is **spooky** over here.
Yeah, there's no place to grab a decent cup of coffee for miles.
Is this where the shadow creatures live?

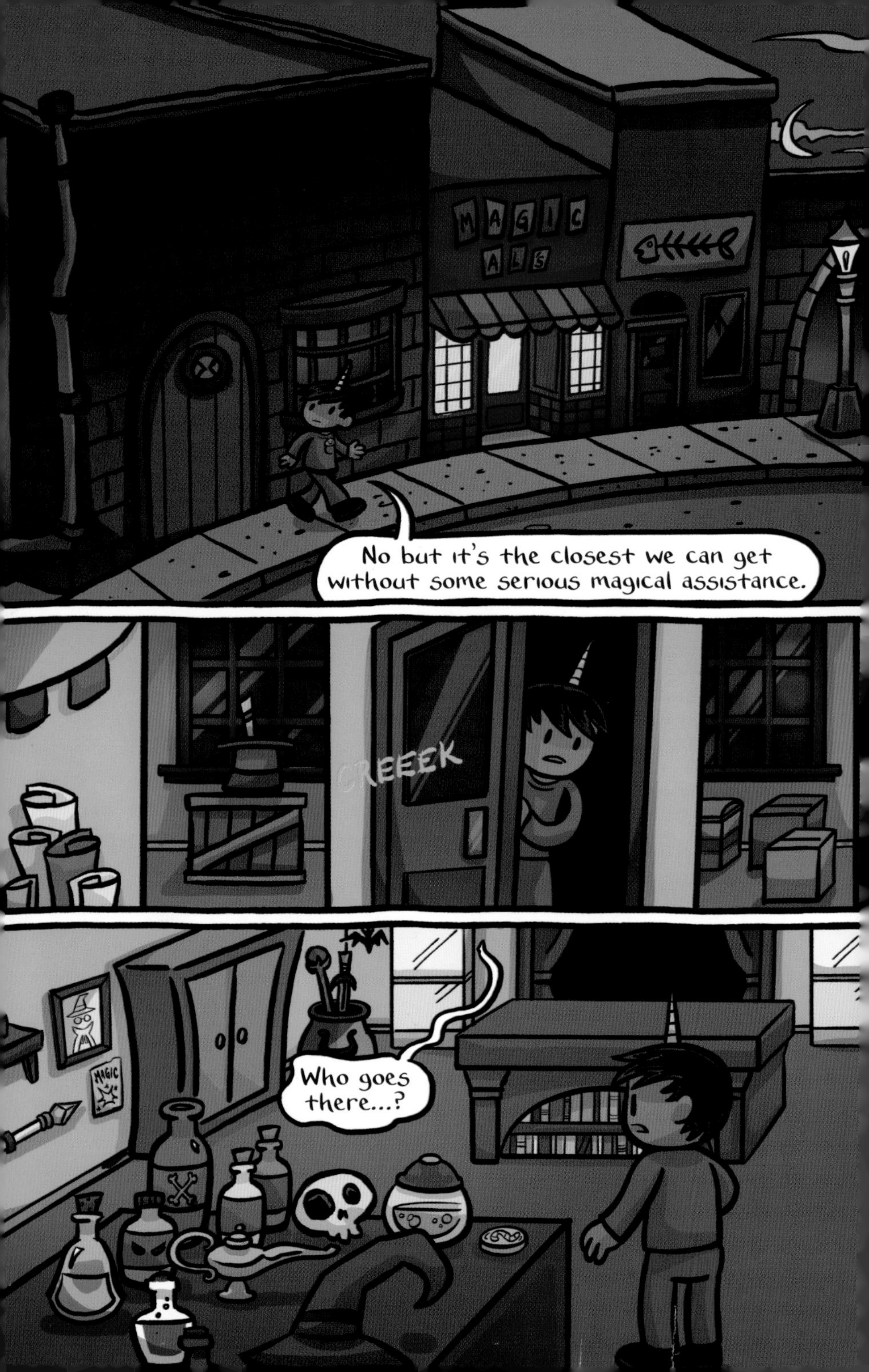
MAGIC AL'S
No but it's the closest we can get without some serious magical assistance.
CREEEK
MAGIC
Who goes there...?

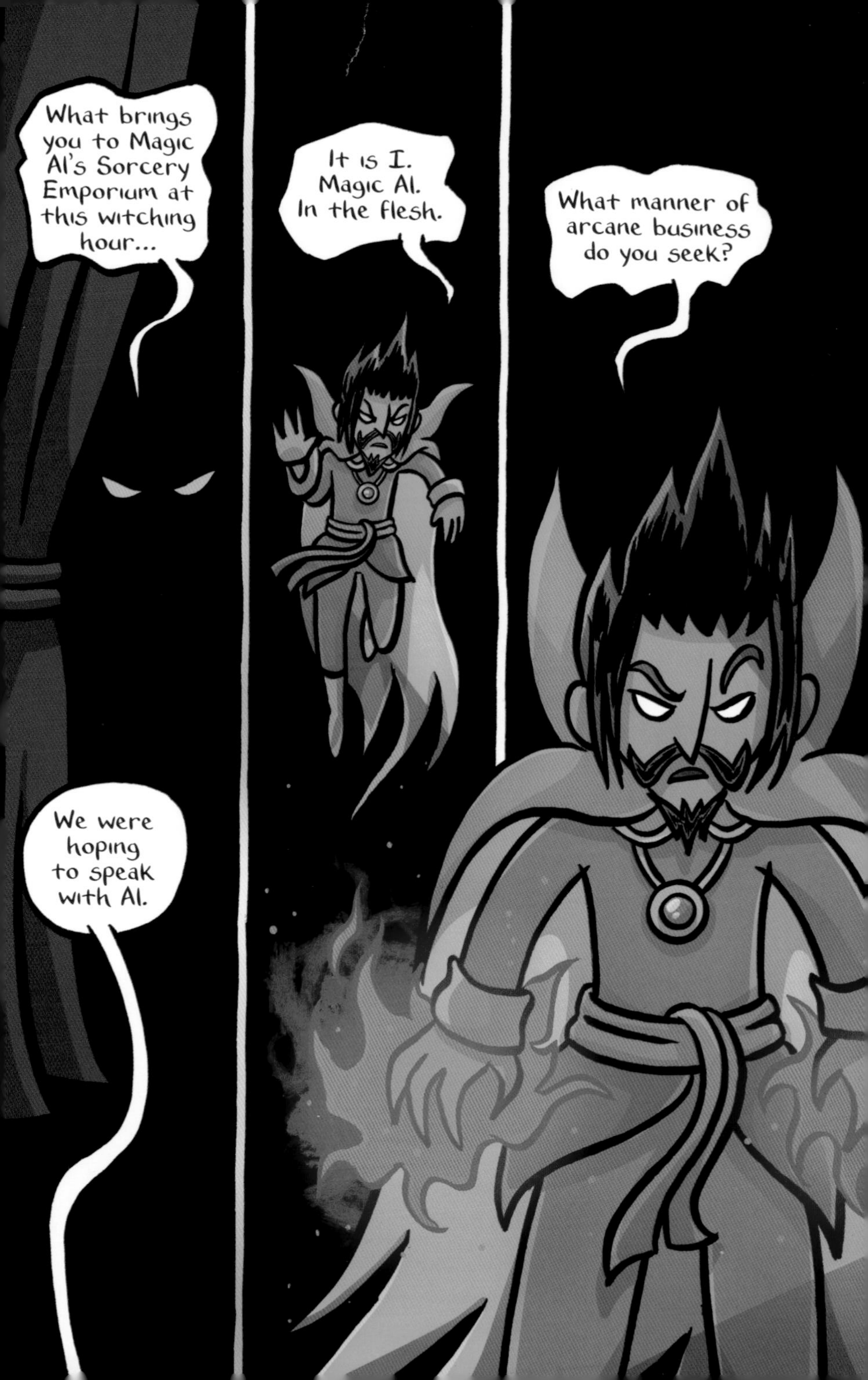
What brings you to Magic Al's Sorcery Emporium at this witching hour...
It is I. Magic Al. In the flesh.
What manner of arcane business do you seek?
We were hoping to speak with Al.

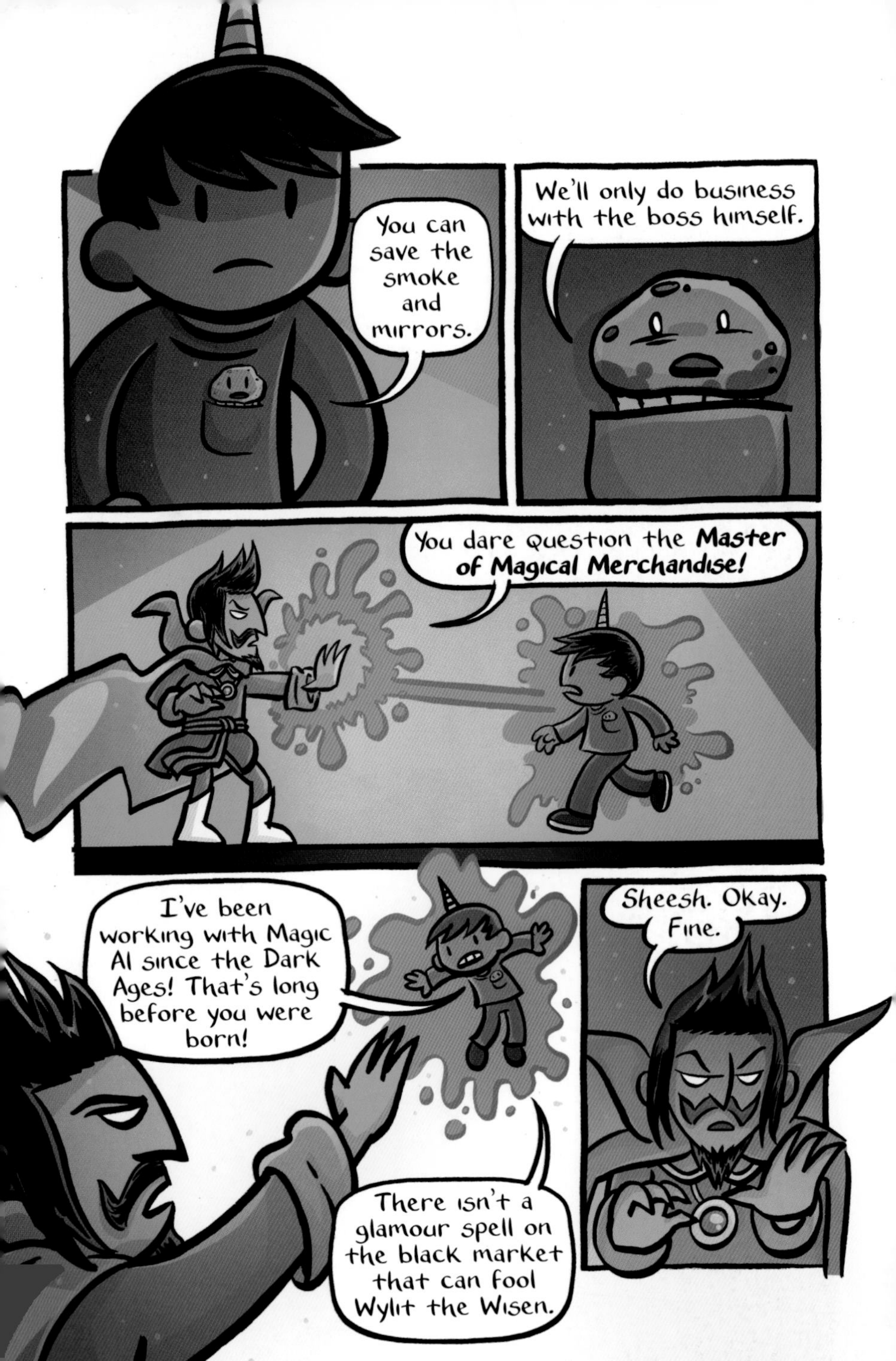
You can save the smoke and mirrors.
We'll only do business with the boss himself.
You dare question the **Master of Magical Merchandise!**
I've been working with Magic Al since the Dark Ages! That's long before you were born!
There isn't a glamour spell on the black market that can fool Wylit the Wisen.
Sheesh. Okay. Fine.

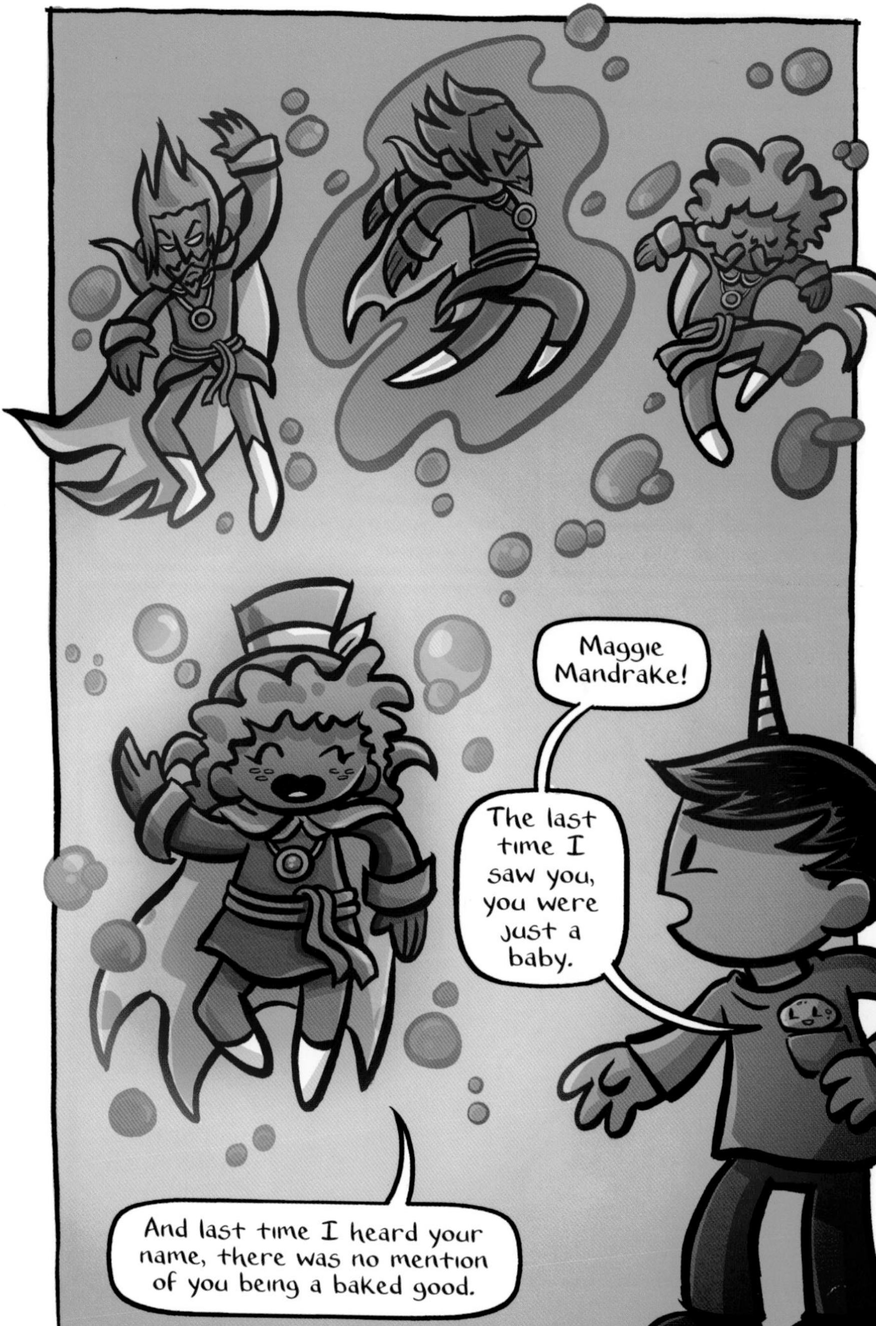
Maggie Mandrake!
The last time I saw you, you were just a baby.
And last time I heard your name, there was no mention of you being a baked good.

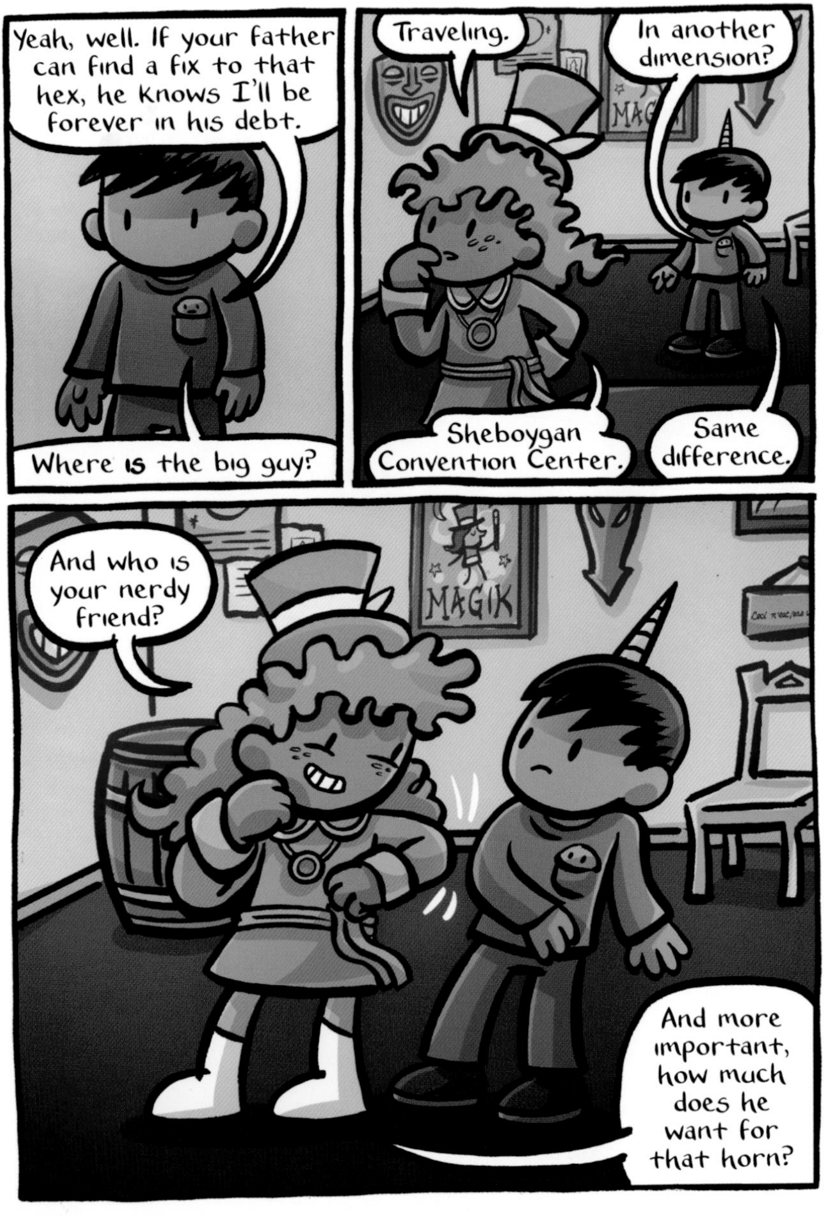

Yeah, well. If your father can find a fix to that hex, he knows I'll be forever in his debt.
Where IS the big guy?
Traveling.
In another dimension?
Sheboygan Convention Center.
Same difference.
MAGIK
And who is your nerdy friend?
And more important, how much does he want for that horn?

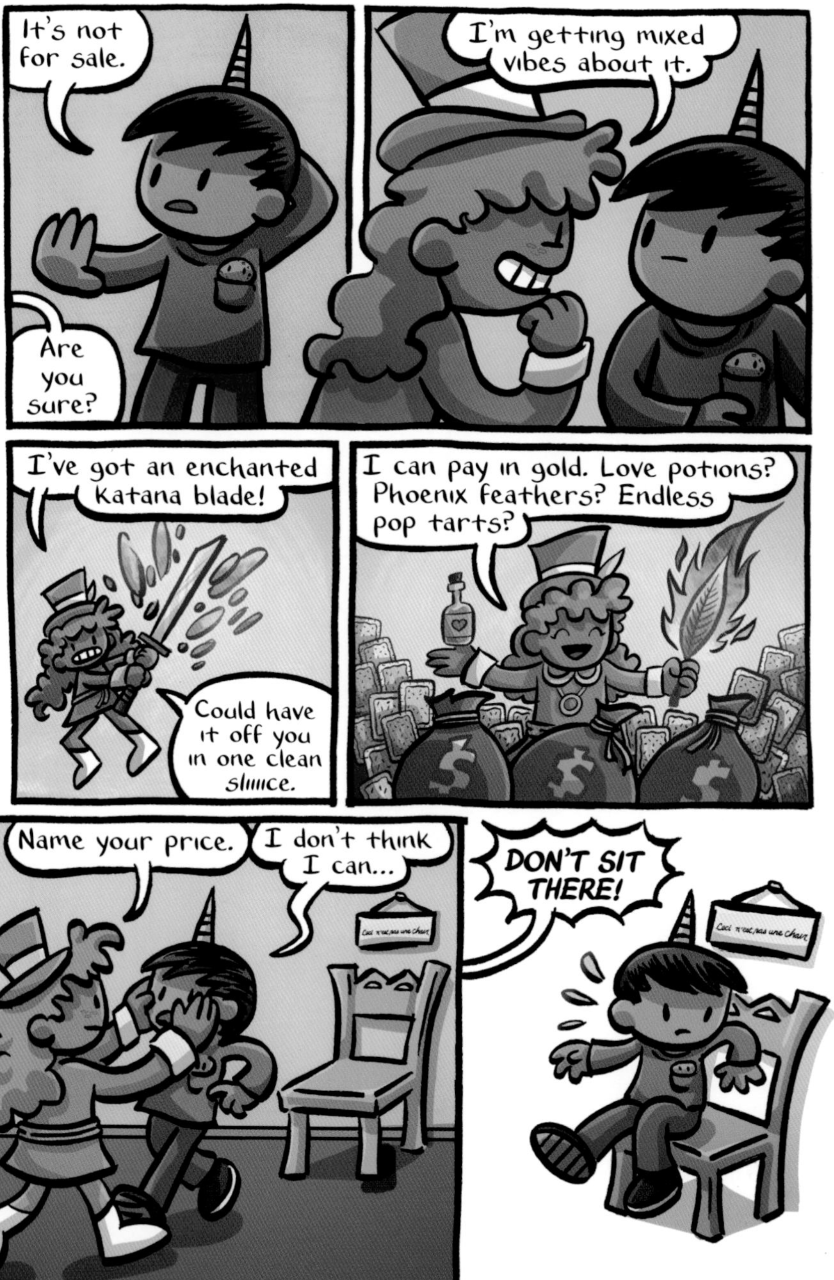
It's not for sale.
Are you sure?
I'm getting mixed vibes about it.
I've got an enchanted katana blade!
Could have it off you in one clean sliiiice.
I can pay in gold. Love potions? Phoenix feathers? Endless pop tarts?
Name your price.
I don't think I can...
DON'T SIT THERE!

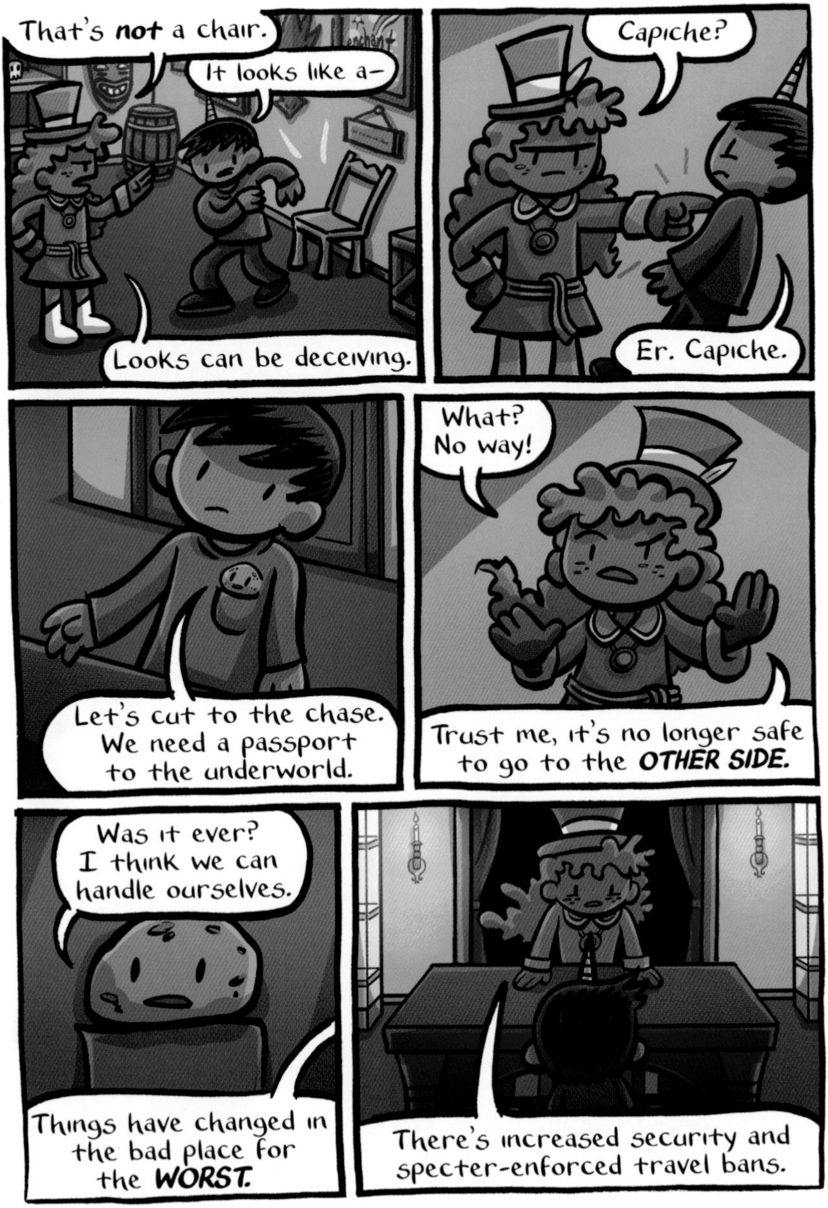
That's **not** a chair.
It looks like a—
Looks can be deceiving.
Capiche?
Er. Capiche.
Let's cut to the chase. We need a passport to the underworld.
What? No way!
Trust me, it's no longer safe to go to the **OTHER SIDE.**
Was it ever? I think we can handle ourselves.
Things have changed in the bad place for the **WORST.**
There's increased security and specter-enforced travel bans.

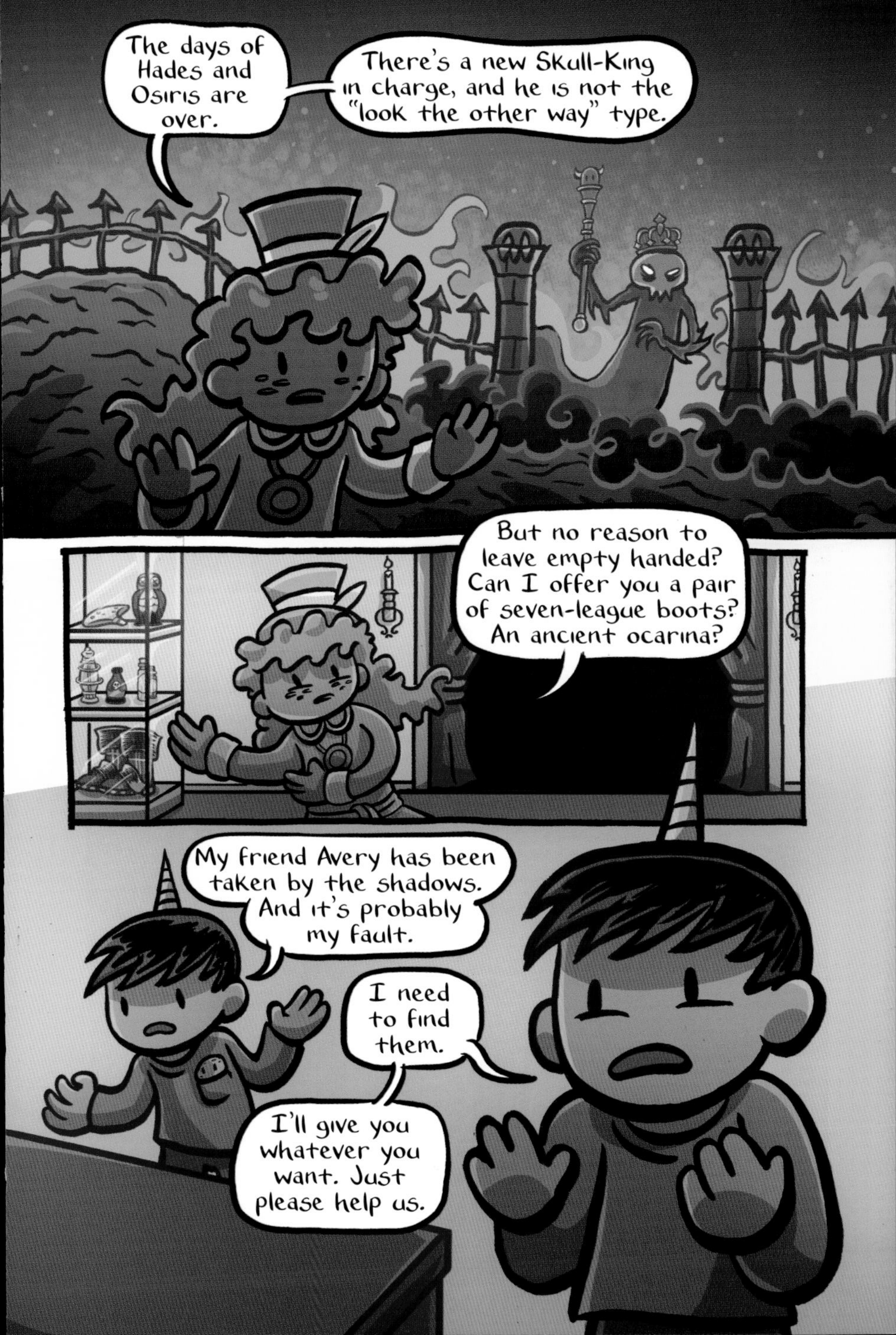
The days of Hades and Osiris are over.
There's a new Skull-King in charge, and he is not the "look the other way" type.
But no reason to leave empty handed? Can I offer you a pair of seven-league boots? An ancient ocarina?
My friend Avery has been taken by the shadows. And it's probably my fault.
I need to find them.
I'll give you whatever you want. Just please help us.

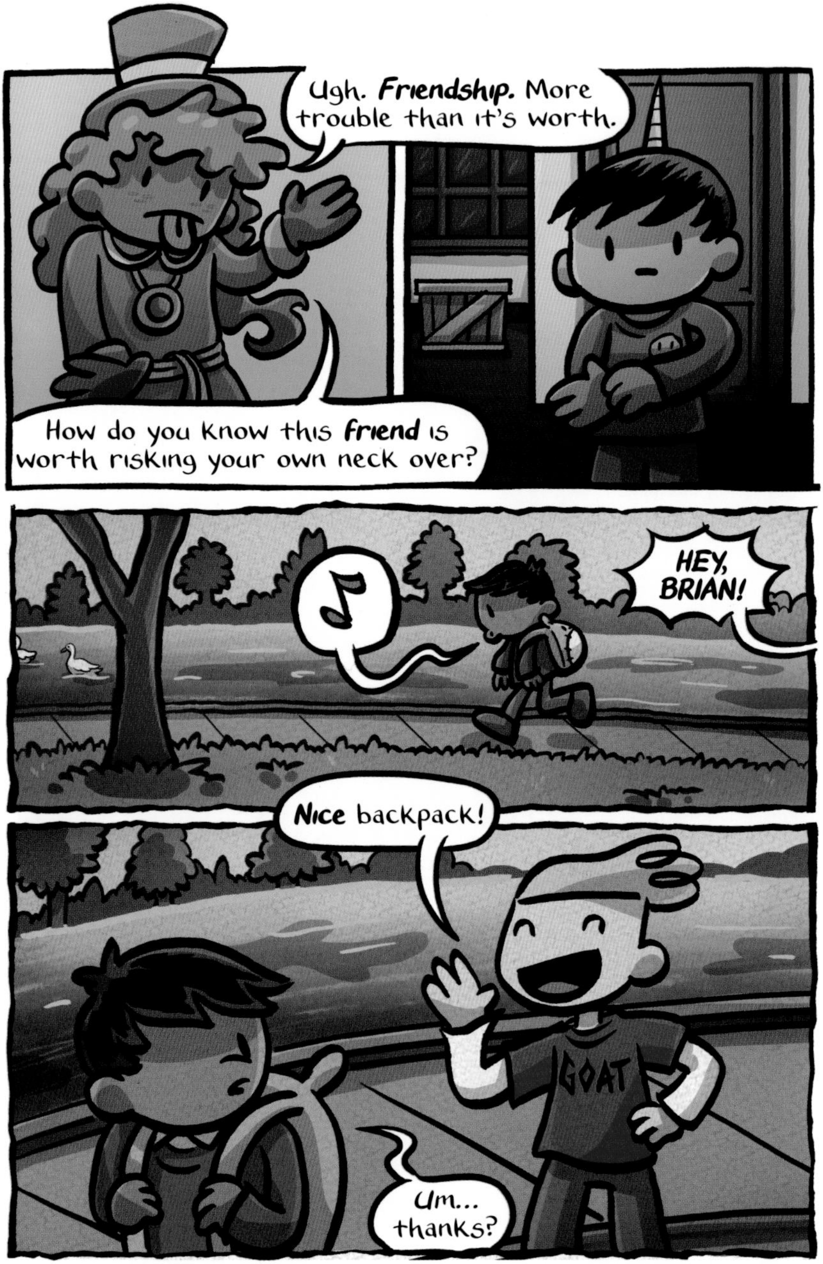
Ugh. **Friendship.** More trouble than it's worth.
How do you know this **friend** is worth risking your own neck over?
HEY, BRIAN!
Nice backpack!
GOAT
Um... thanks?

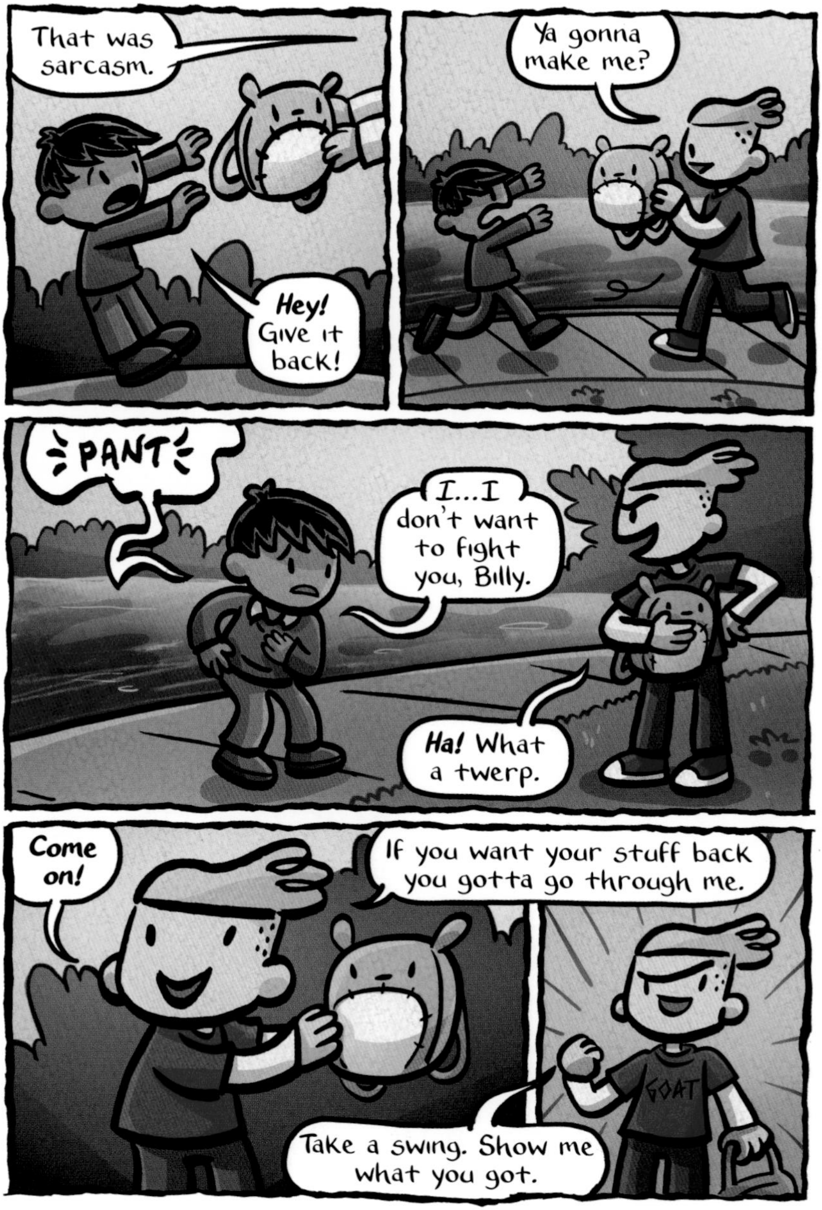
That was sarcasm.
Hey! Give it back!
Ya gonna make me?
PANT
I...I don't want to fight you, Billy.
Ha! What a twerp.
Come on!
If you want your stuff back you gotta go through me.
GOAT
Take a swing. Show me what you got.

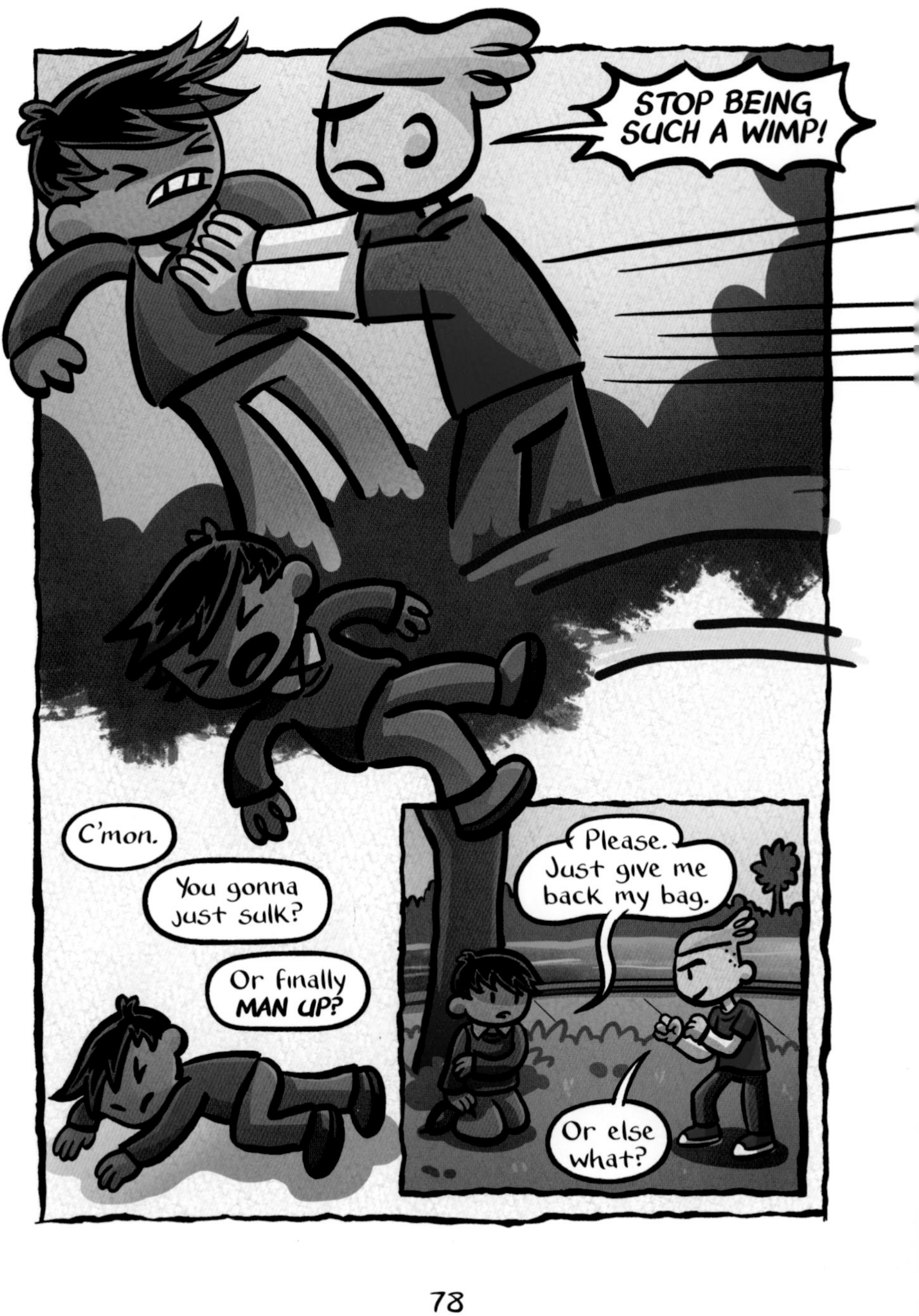
STOP BEING SUCH A WIMP!
C'mon.
You gonna just sulk?
Or finally MAN UP?
Please. Just give me back my bag.
Or else what?

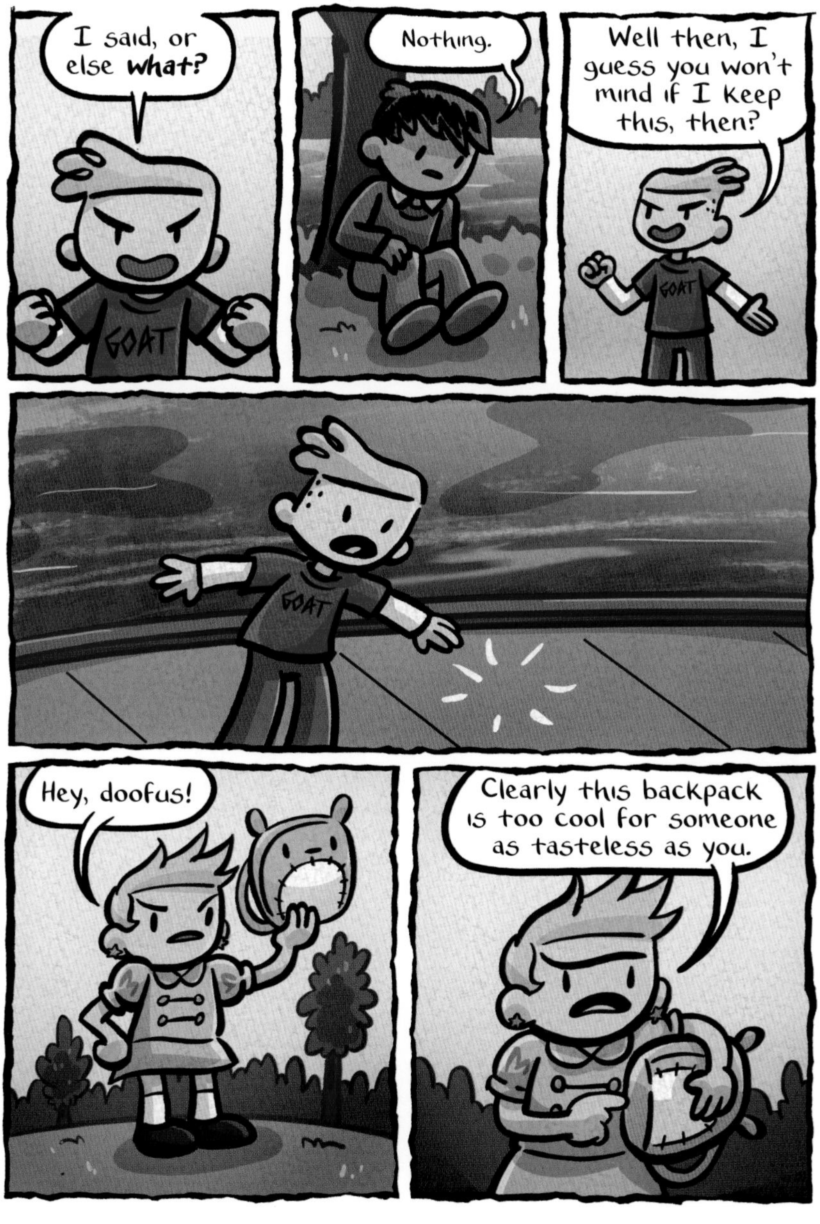

I said, or else what?
Nothing.
Well then, I guess you won't mind if I keep this, then?
GOAT
Hey, doofus!
Clearly this backpack is too cool for someone as tasteless as you.

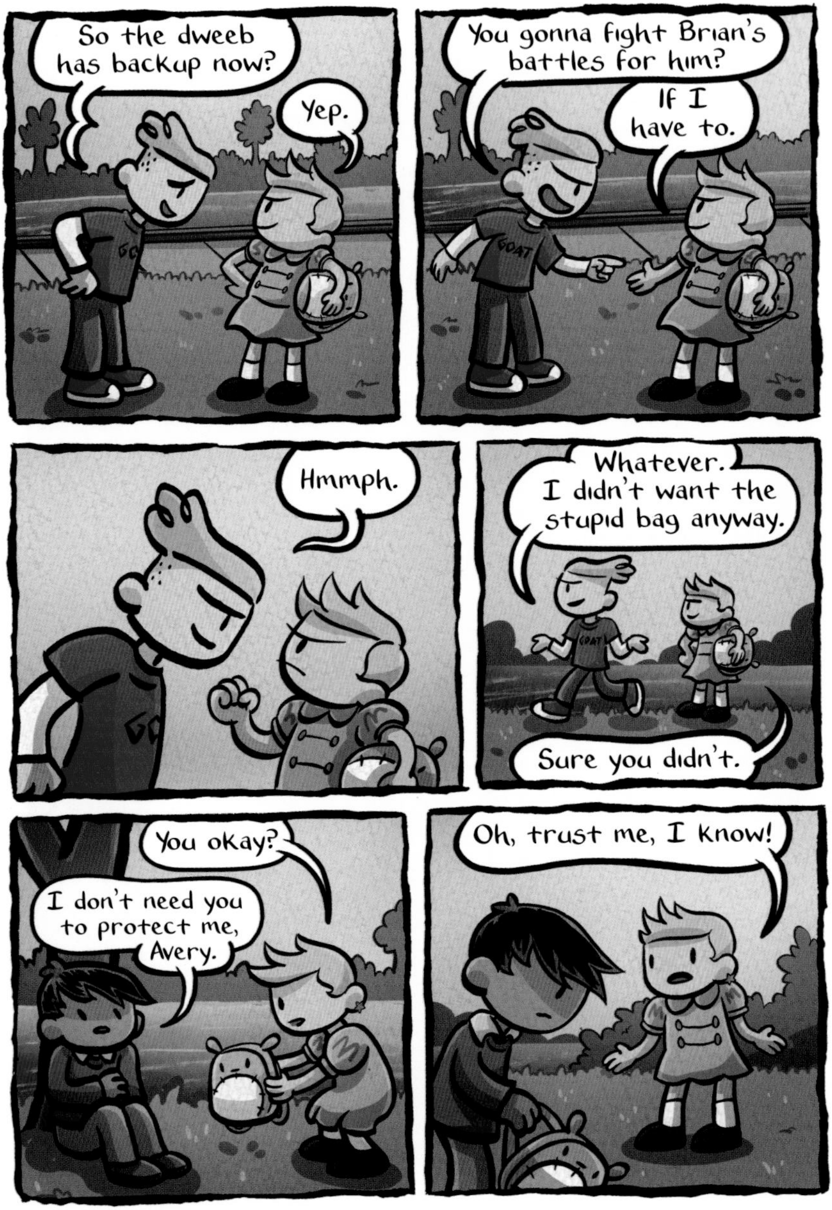
So the dweeb has backup now?
Yep.
You gonna fight Brian's battles for him?
If I have to.
Hmmph.
Whatever. I didn't want the stupid bag anyway.
Sure you didn't.
You okay?
I don't need you to protect me, Avery.
Oh, trust me, I know!

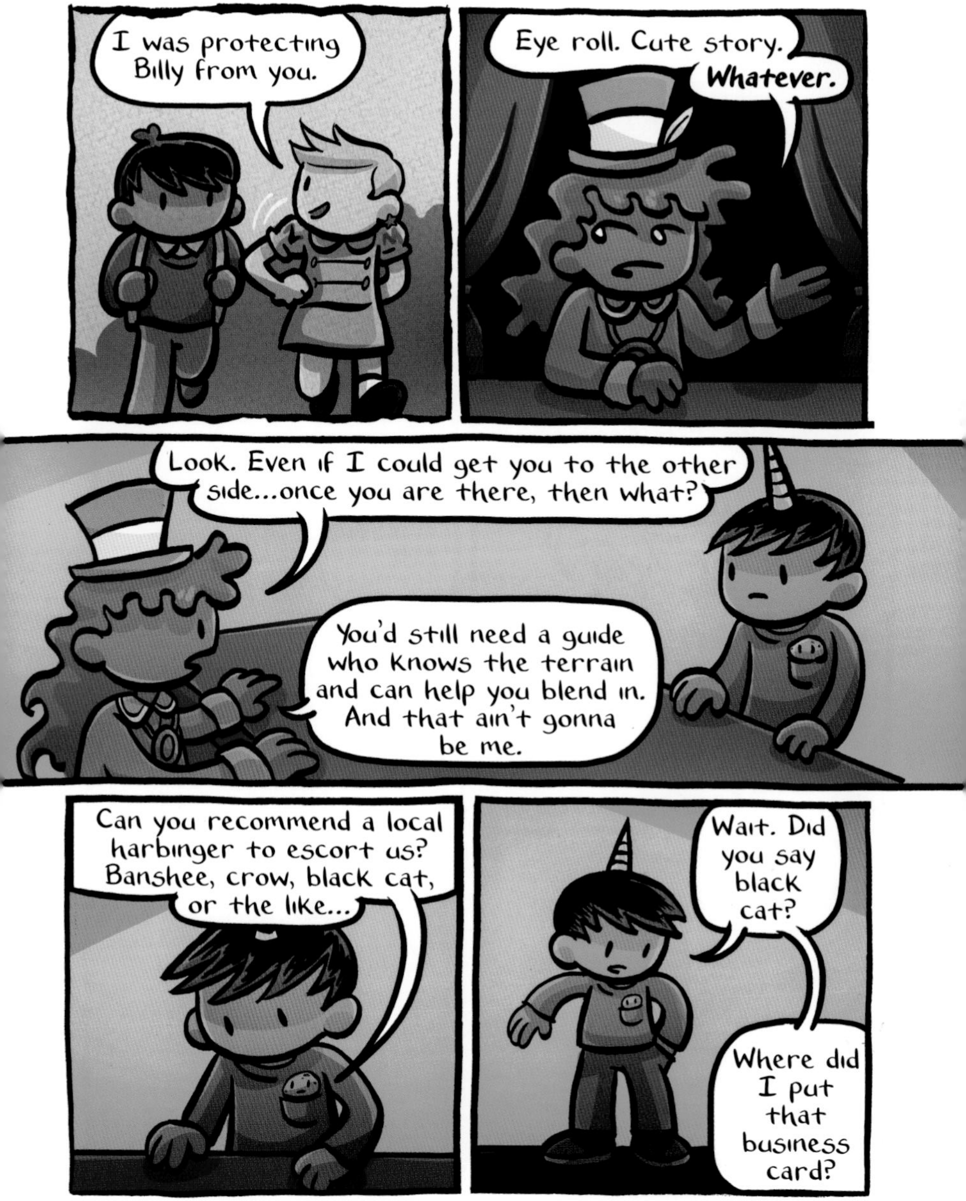
I was protecting Billy from you.
Eye roll. Cute story.
Whatever.
Look. Even if I could get you to the other side...once you are there, then what?
You'd still need a guide who knows the terrain and can help you blend in. And that ain't gonna be me.
Can you recommend a local harbinger to escort us? Banshee, crow, black cat, or the like...
Wait. Did you say black cat?
Where did I put that business card?

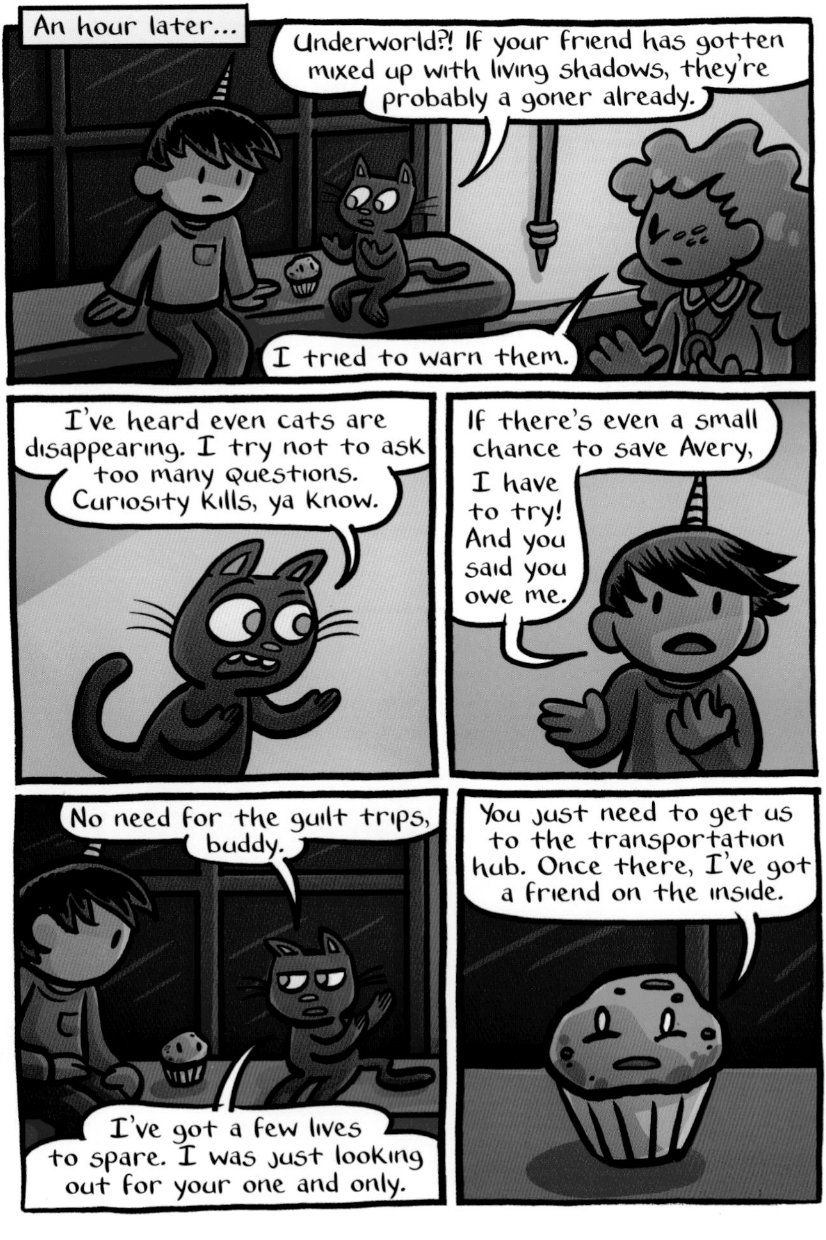
An hour later...
Underworld?! If your friend has gotten mixed up with living shadows, they're probably a goner already.
I tried to warn them.
I've heard even cats are disappearing. I try not to ask too many questions. Curiosity kills, ya know.
If there's even a small chance to save Avery,
I have to try! And you said you owe me.
No need for the guilt trips, buddy.
I've got a few lives to spare. I was just looking out for your one and only.
You just need to get us to the transportation hub. Once there, I've got a friend on the inside.

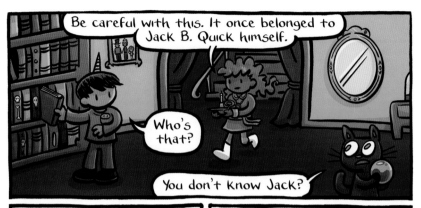

Be careful with this. It once belonged to Jack B. Quick himself.

Who's that?

You don't know Jack?

I thought everyone knew Jack. Dude was a legend at jumping over candlesticks.

Y'all ready? Once I light this thing you'll only have about a wick's eve to cross over and back again.

Once the wax melts, you'll be stuck on one side or the other.

And considering I still ain't been paid, I'd prefer my horn makes it back here in one piece.

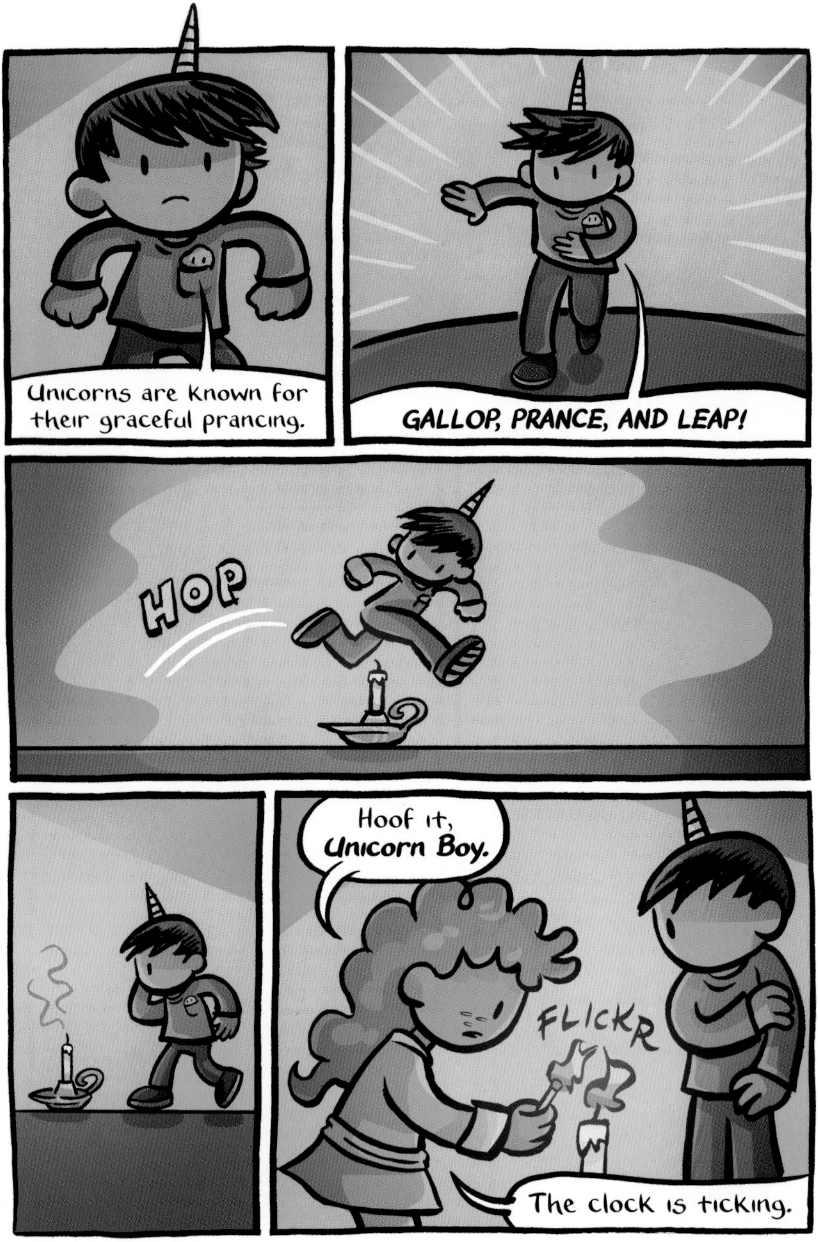
Unicorns are known for their graceful prancing.
GALLOP, PRANCE, AND LEAP!
HOP
Hoof it, Unicorn Boy.
FLICKR
The clock is ticking.

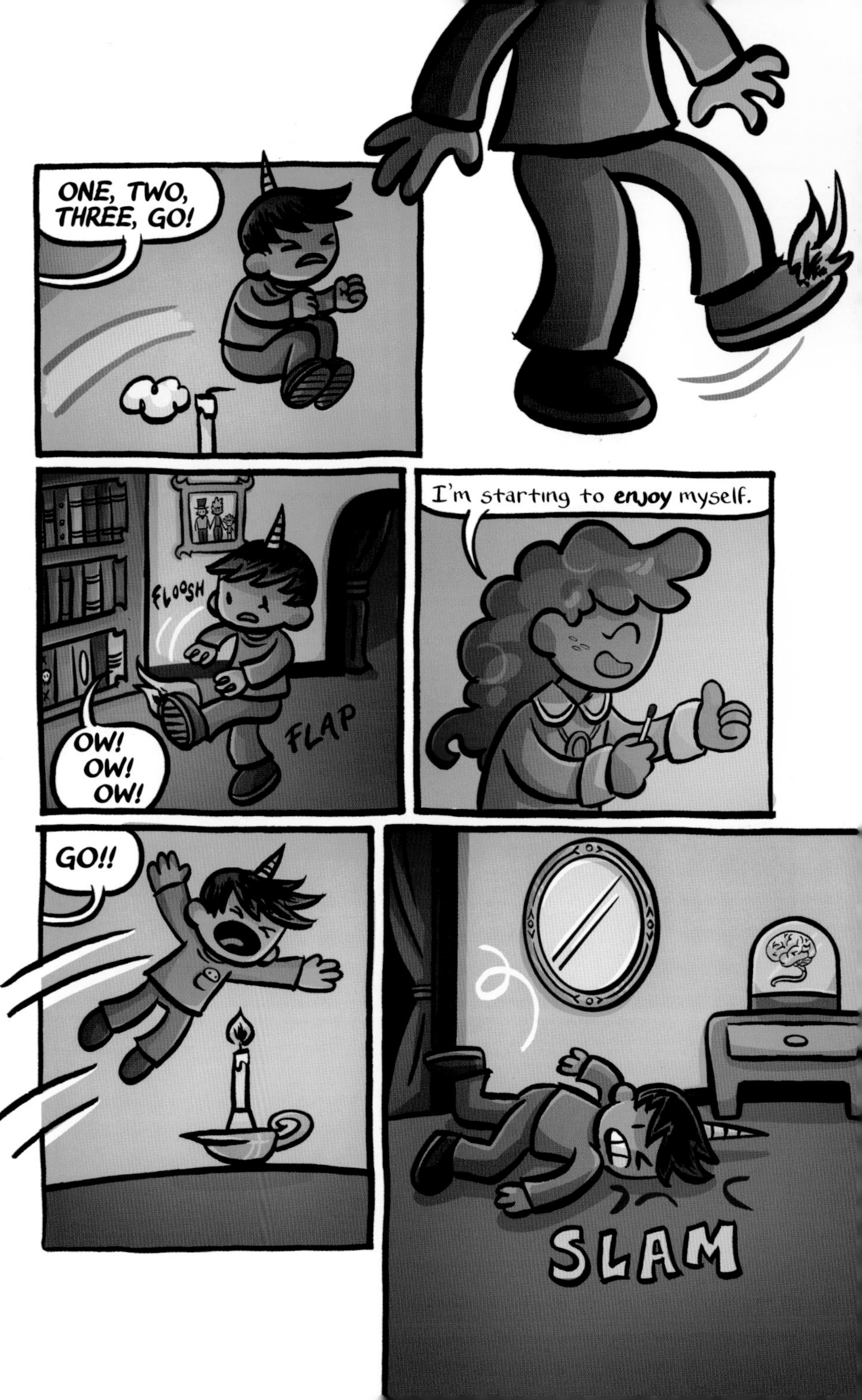
ONE, TWO, THREE, GO!
FLOOSH
OW! OW! OW!
FLAP
I'm starting to **enjoy** myself.
GO!!
SLAM

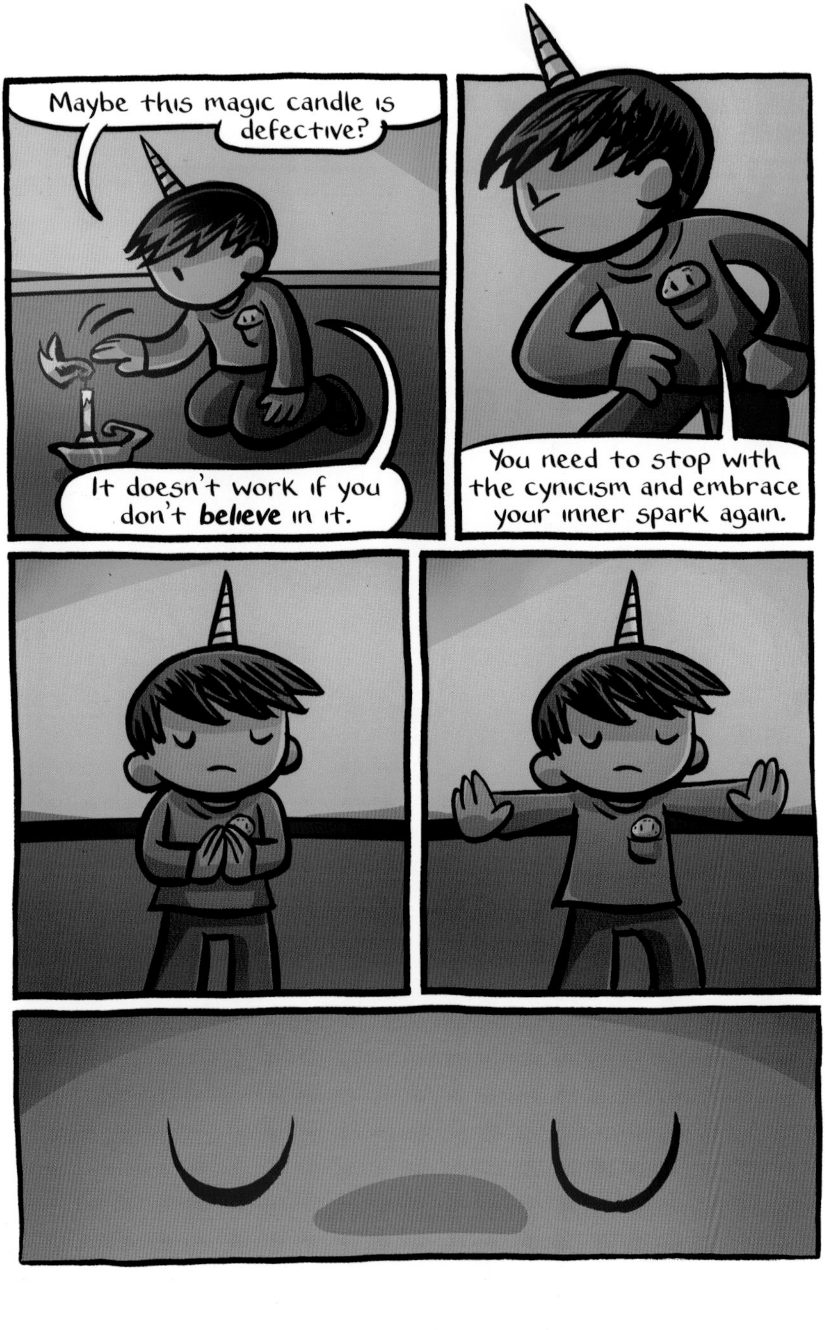

Maybe this magic candle is defective?
It doesn't work if you don't **believe** in it.
You need to stop with the cynicism and embrace your inner spark again.

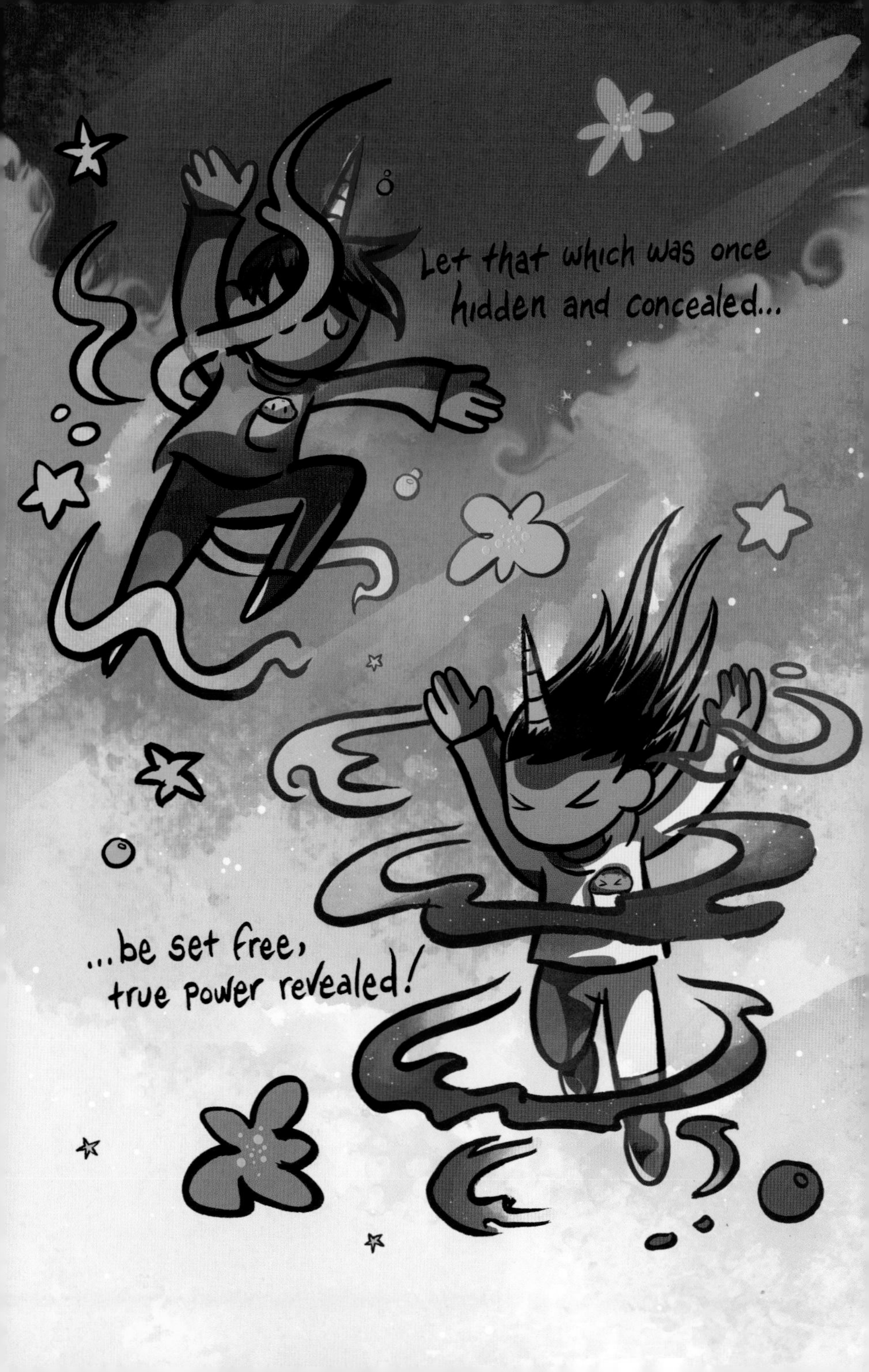
Let that which was once hidden and concealed...
...be set free, true power revealed!

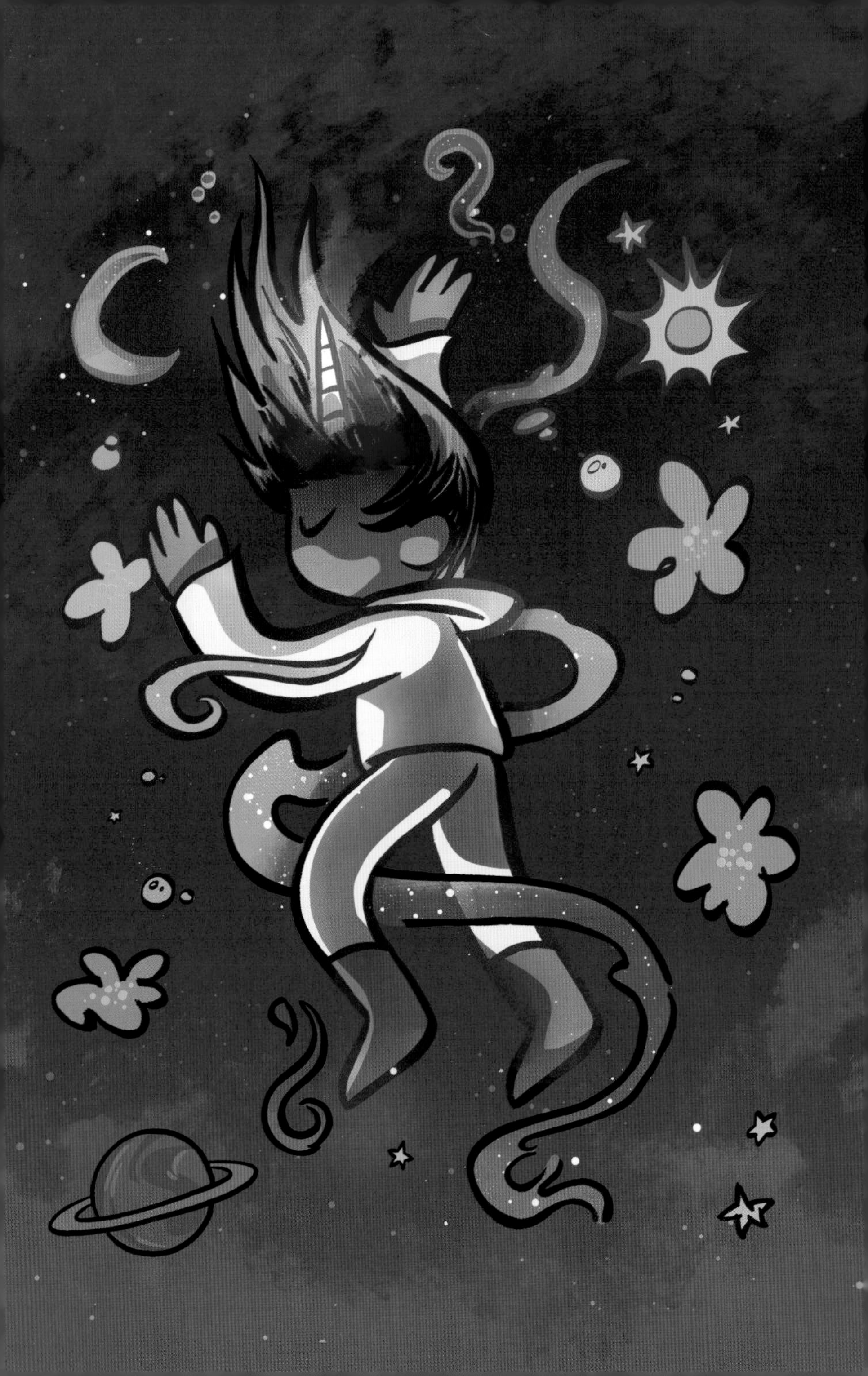

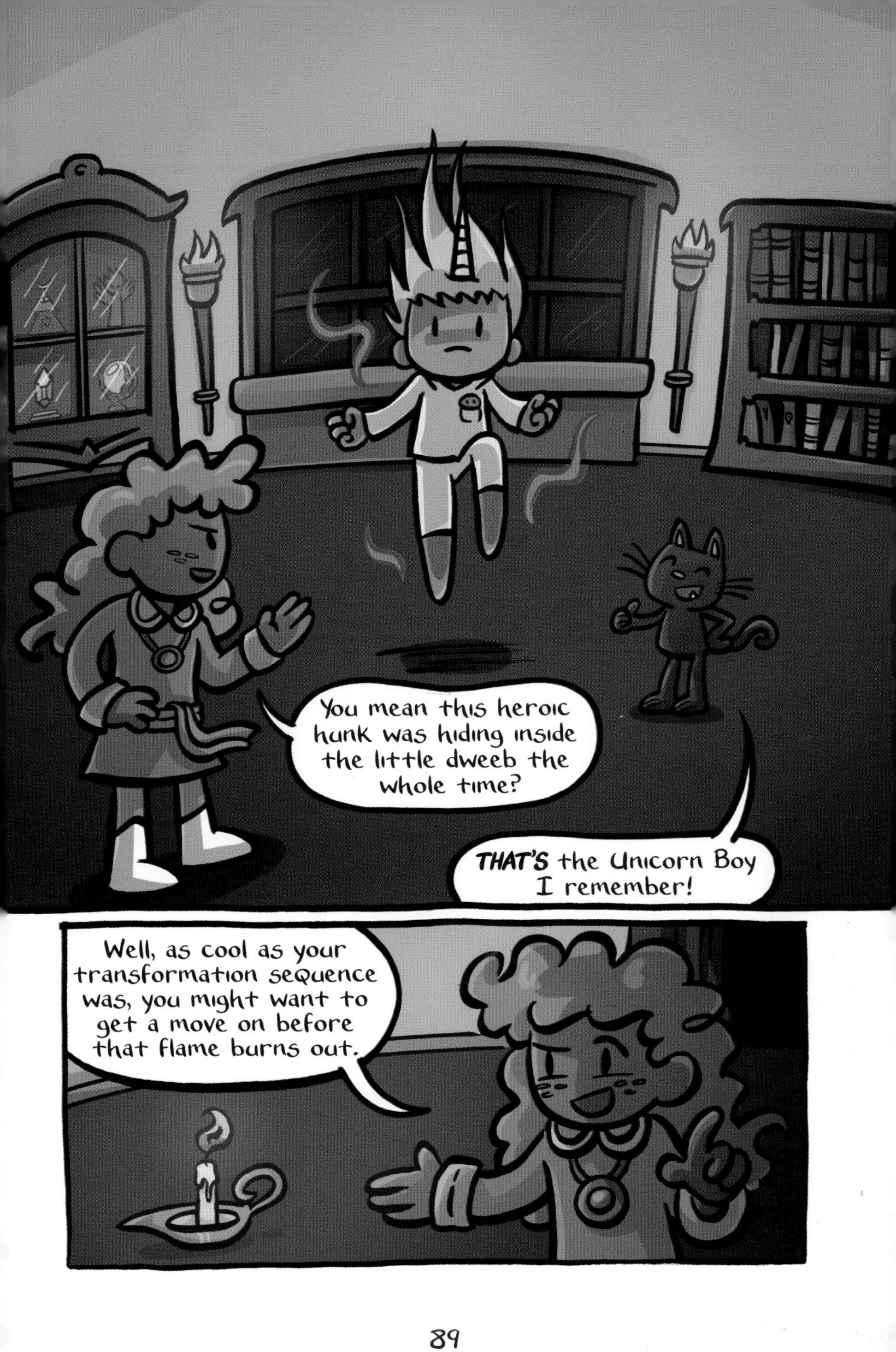
You mean this heroic hunk was hiding inside the little dweeb the whole time?
THAT'S the Unicorn Boy I remember!
Well, as cool as your transformation sequence was, you might want to get a move on before that flame burns out.

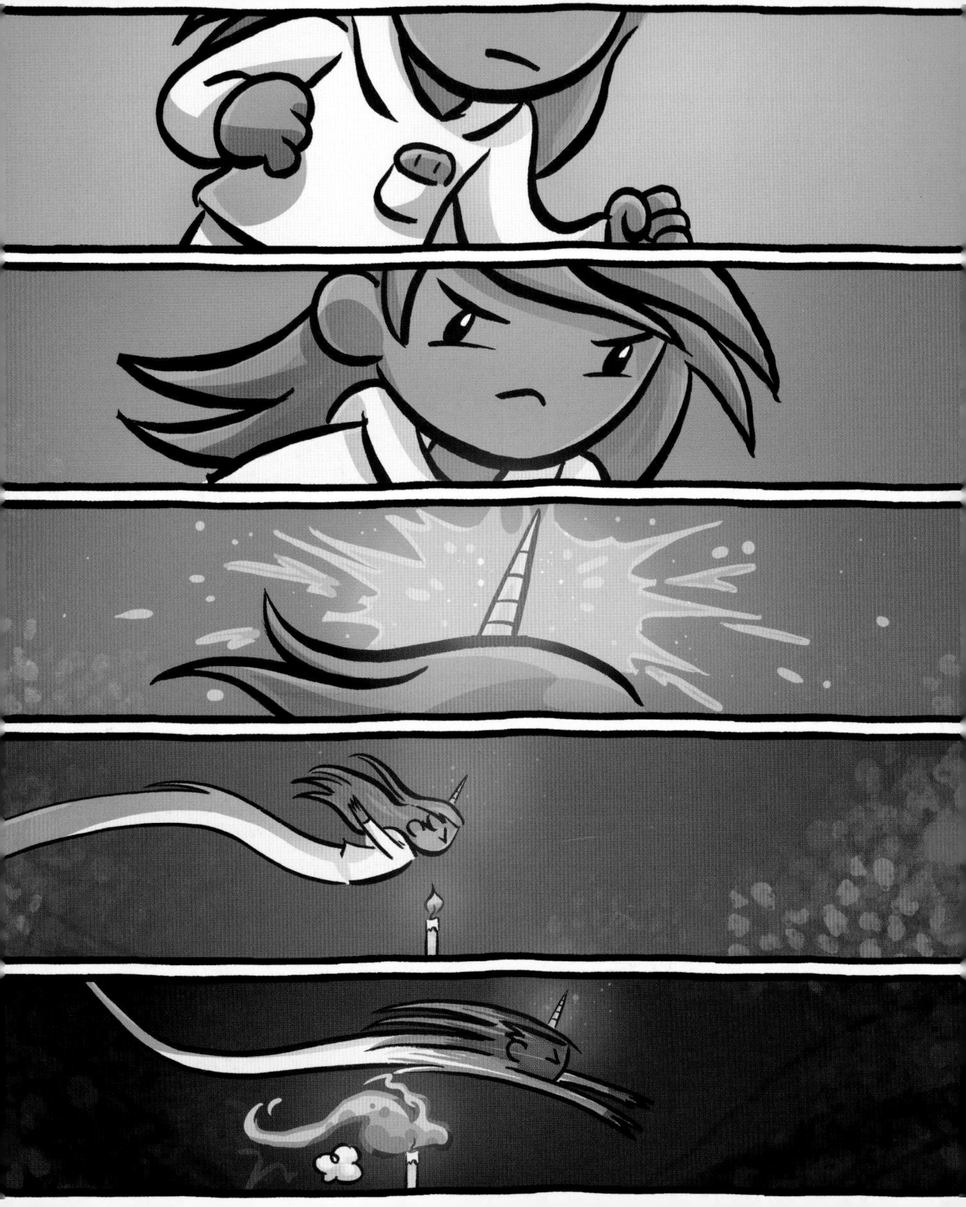

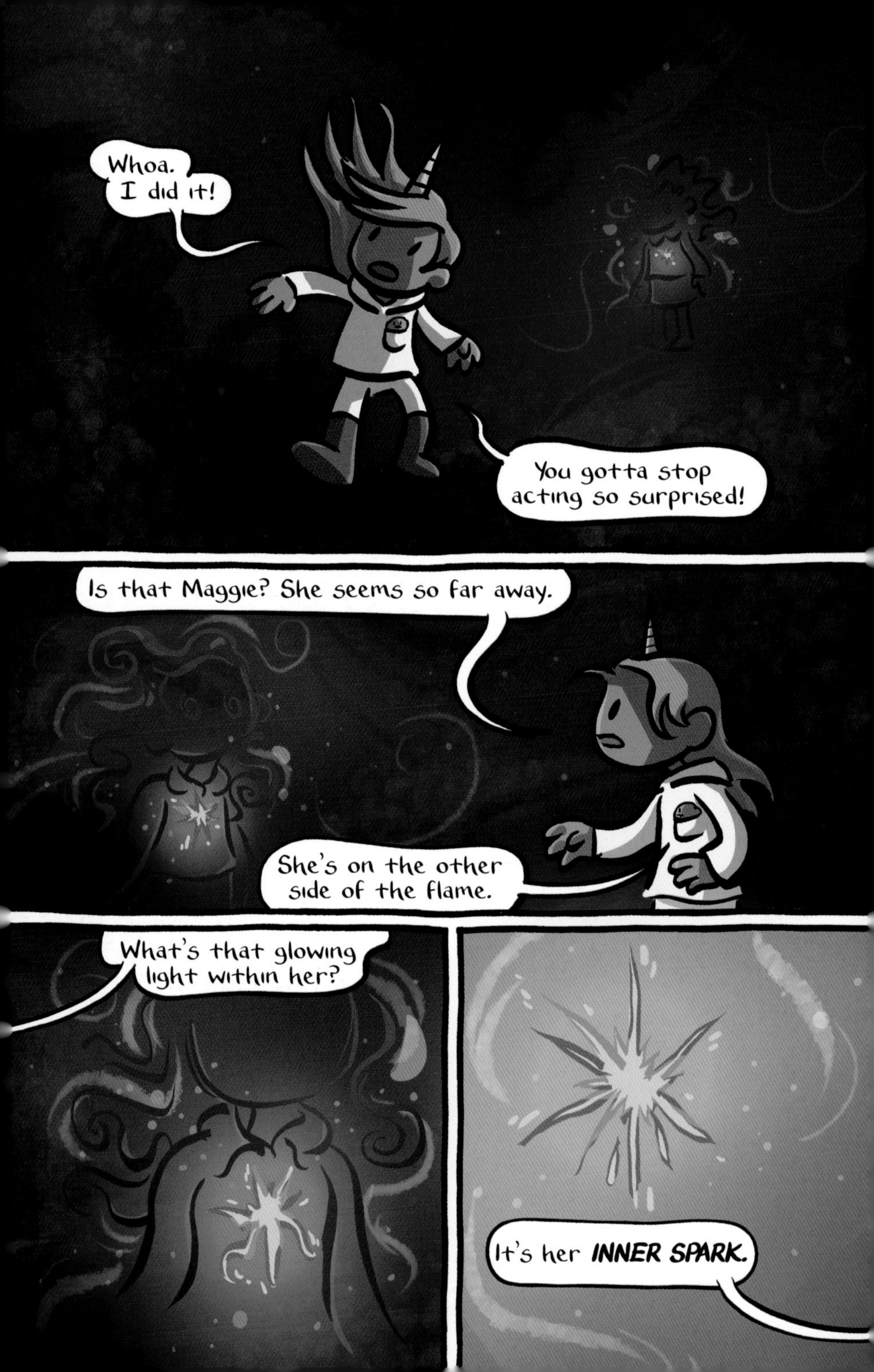
Whoa. I did it!
You gotta stop acting so surprised!
Is that Maggie? She seems so far away.
She's on the other side of the flame.
What's that glowing light within her?
It's her **INNER SPARK.**

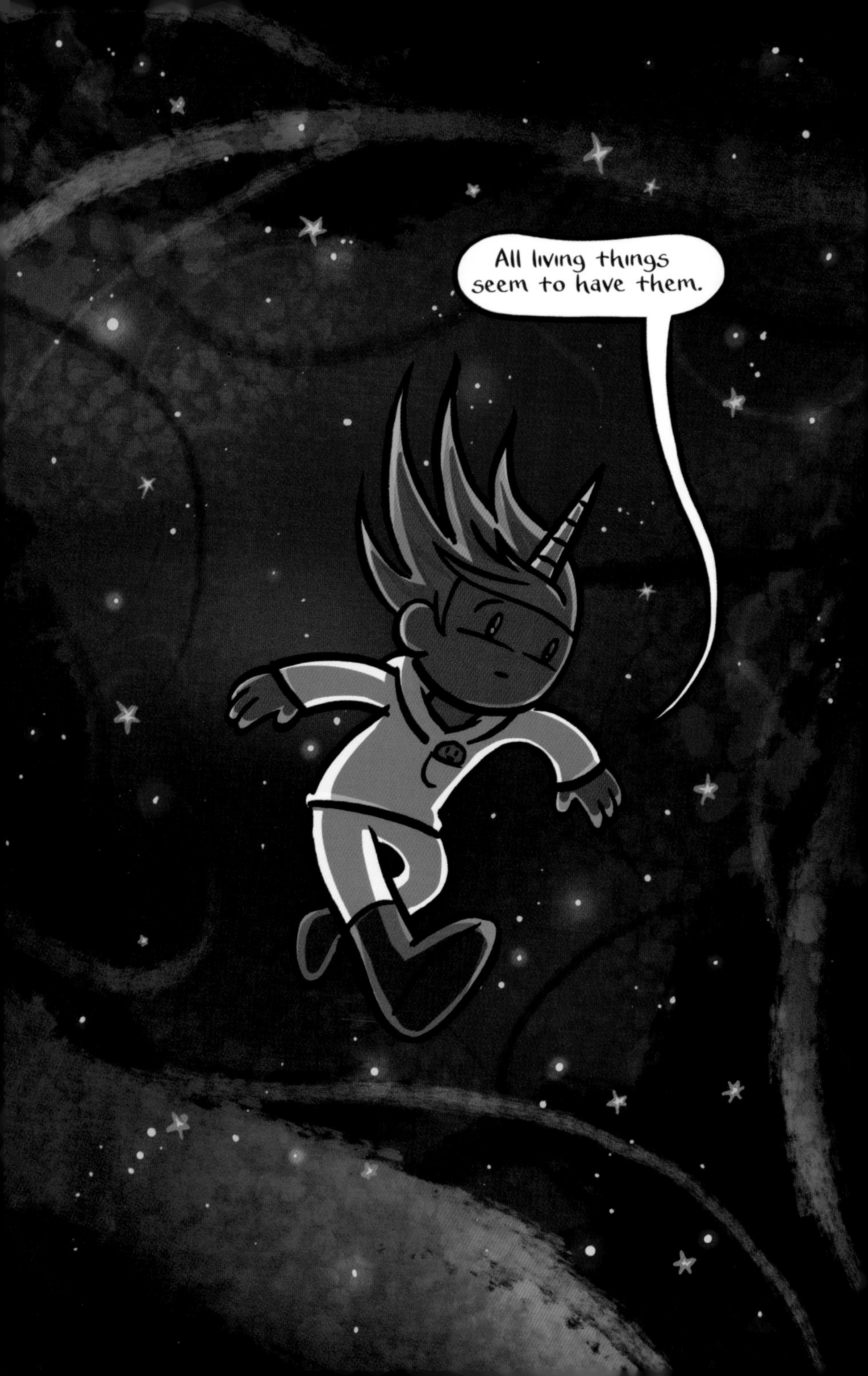
All living things seem to have them.

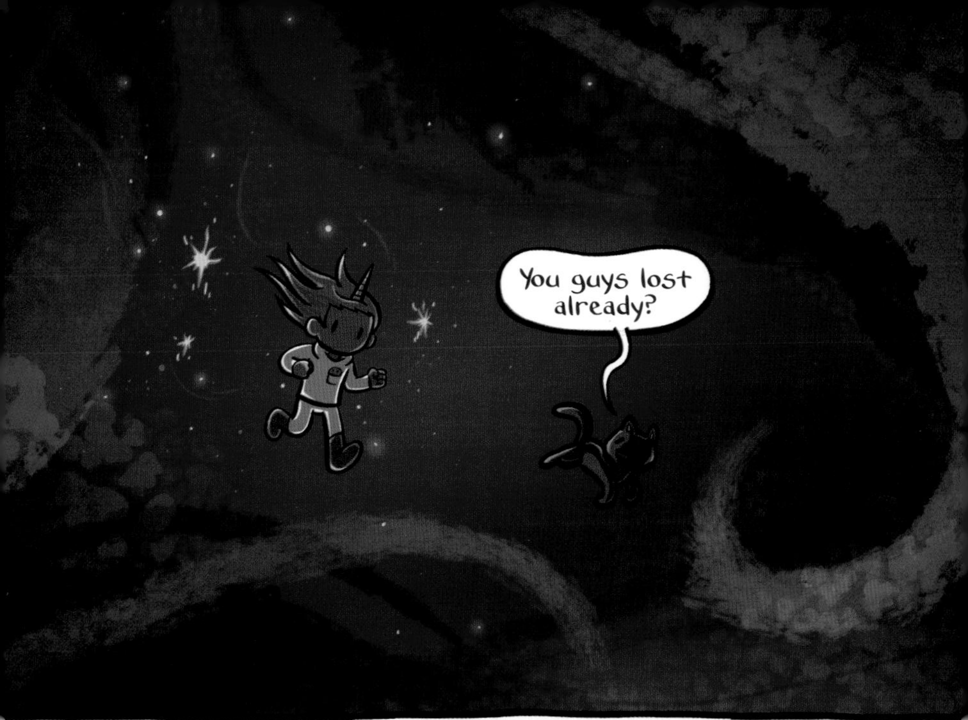
You guys lost already?
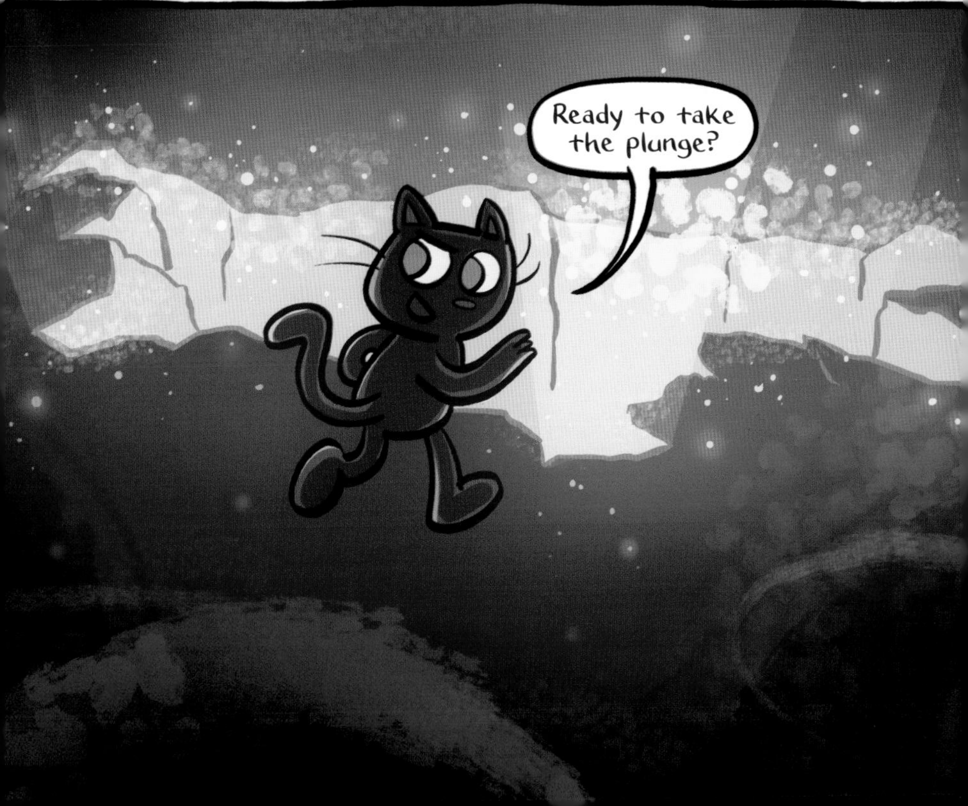
Ready to take the plunge?

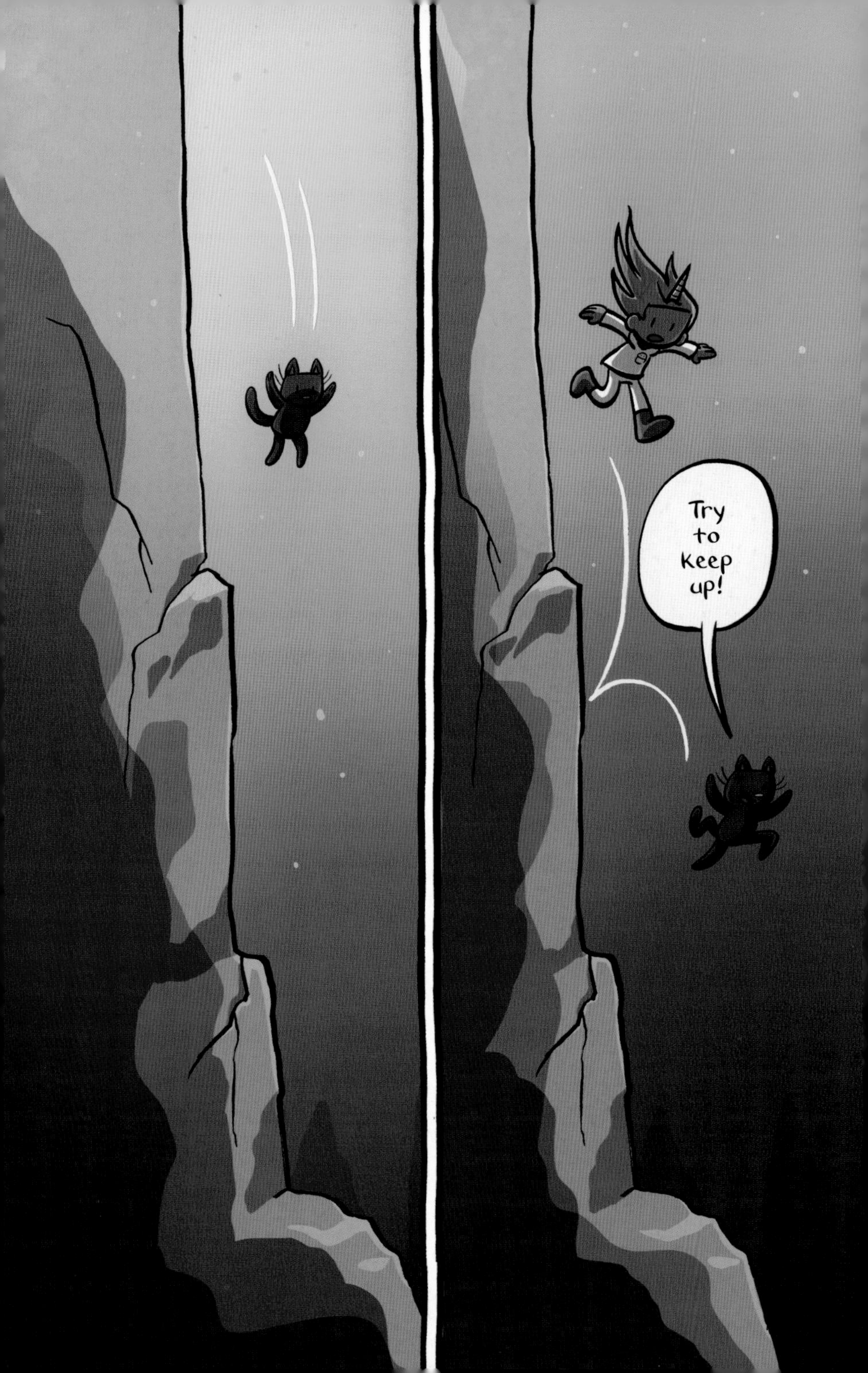
Try to keep up!

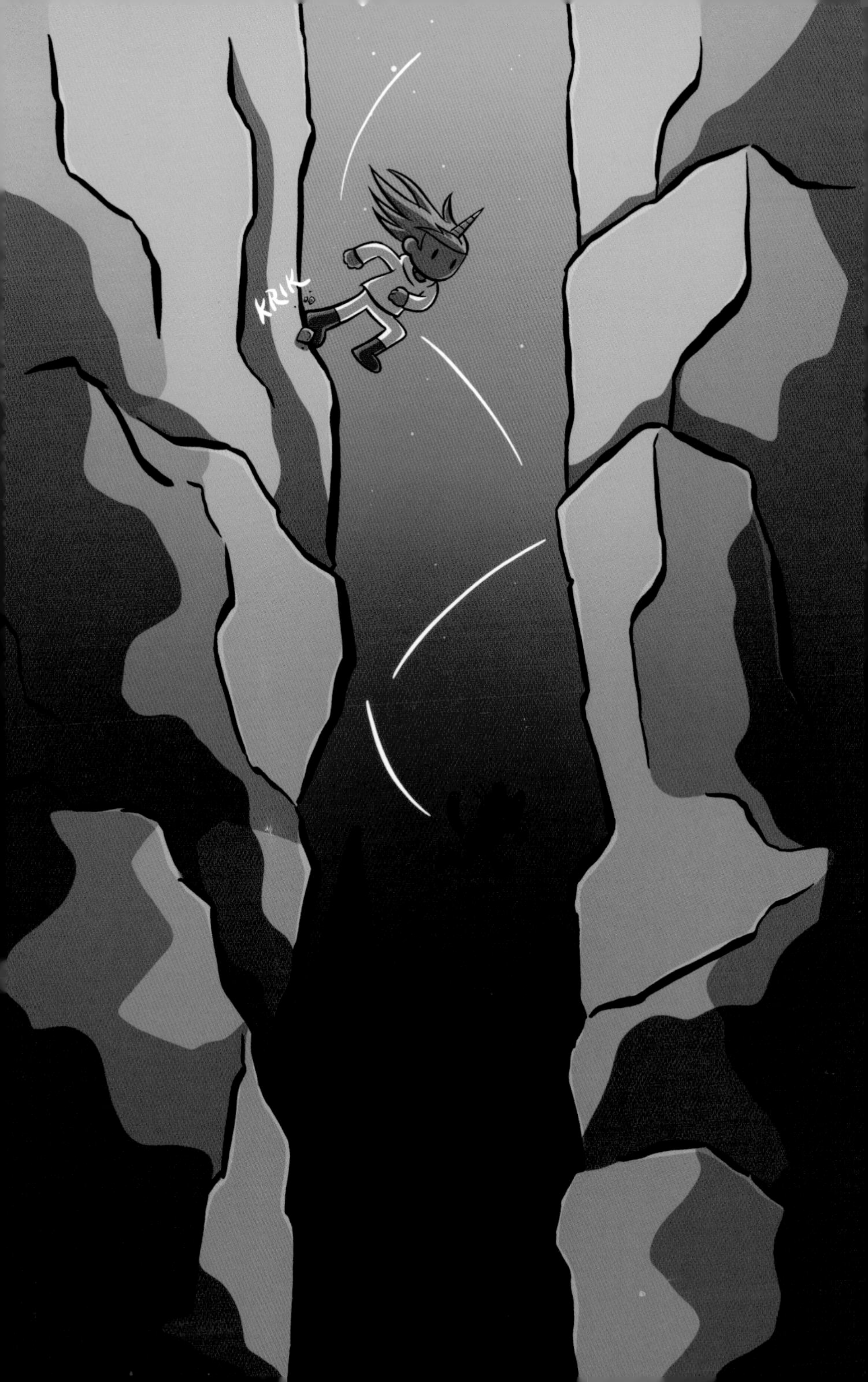
KRIK

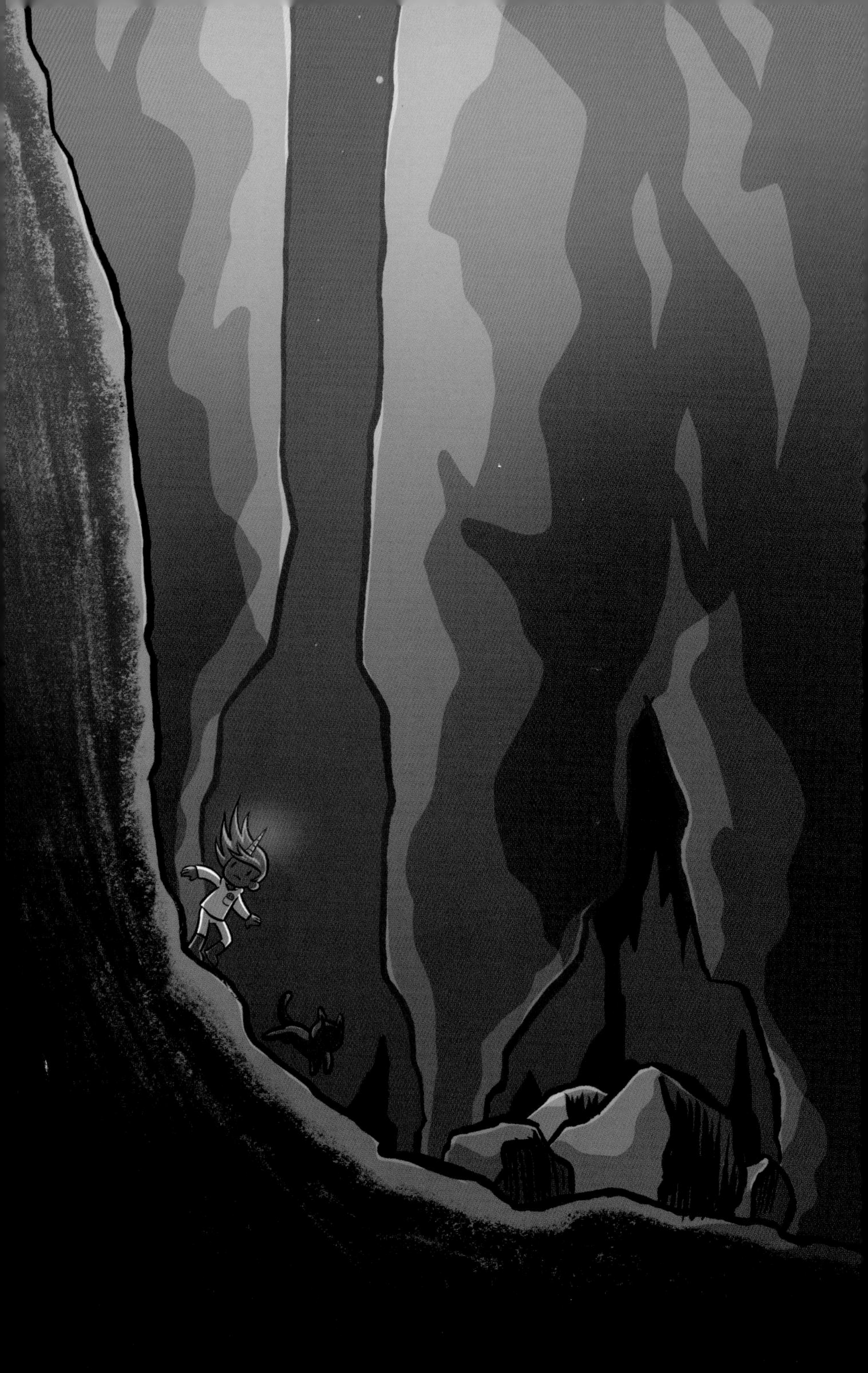

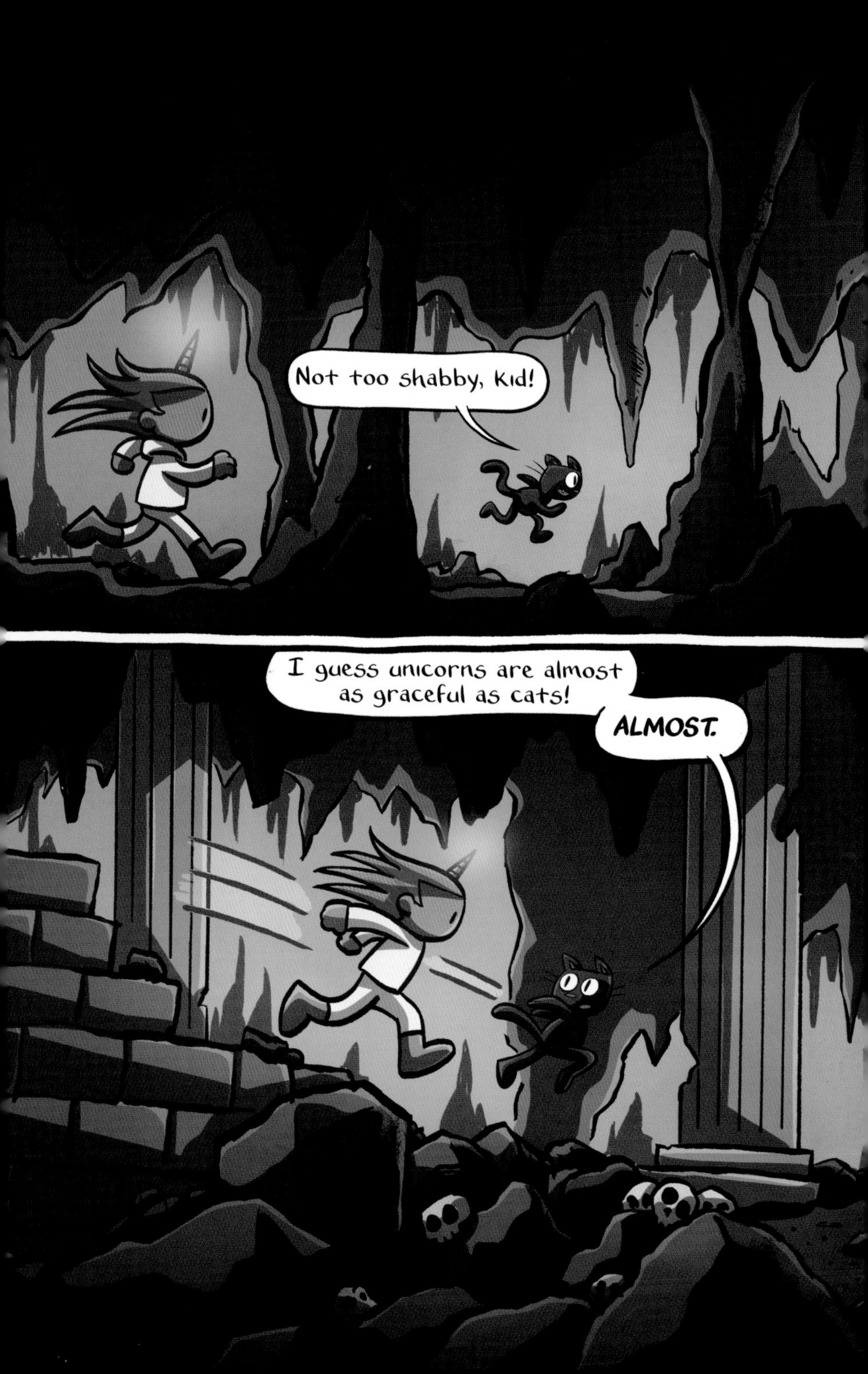
Not too shabby, kid!
I guess unicorns are almost as graceful as cats!
ALMOST.

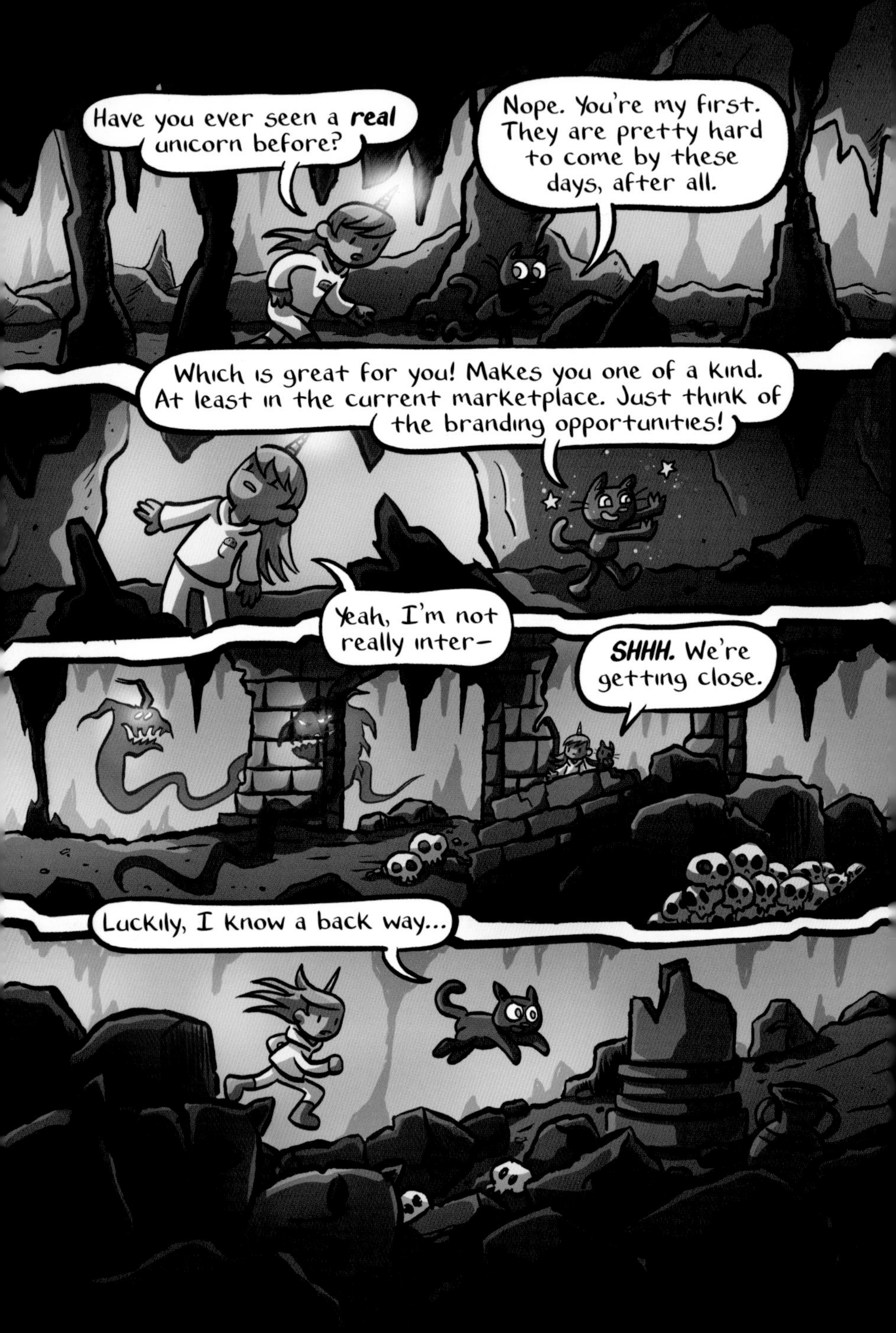
Have you ever seen a **real** unicorn before?
Nope. You're my first. They are pretty hard to come by these days, after all.
Which is great for you! Makes you one of a kind. At least in the current marketplace. Just think of the branding opportunities!
Yeah, I'm not really inter-
SHHH. We're getting close.
Luckily, I know a back way...

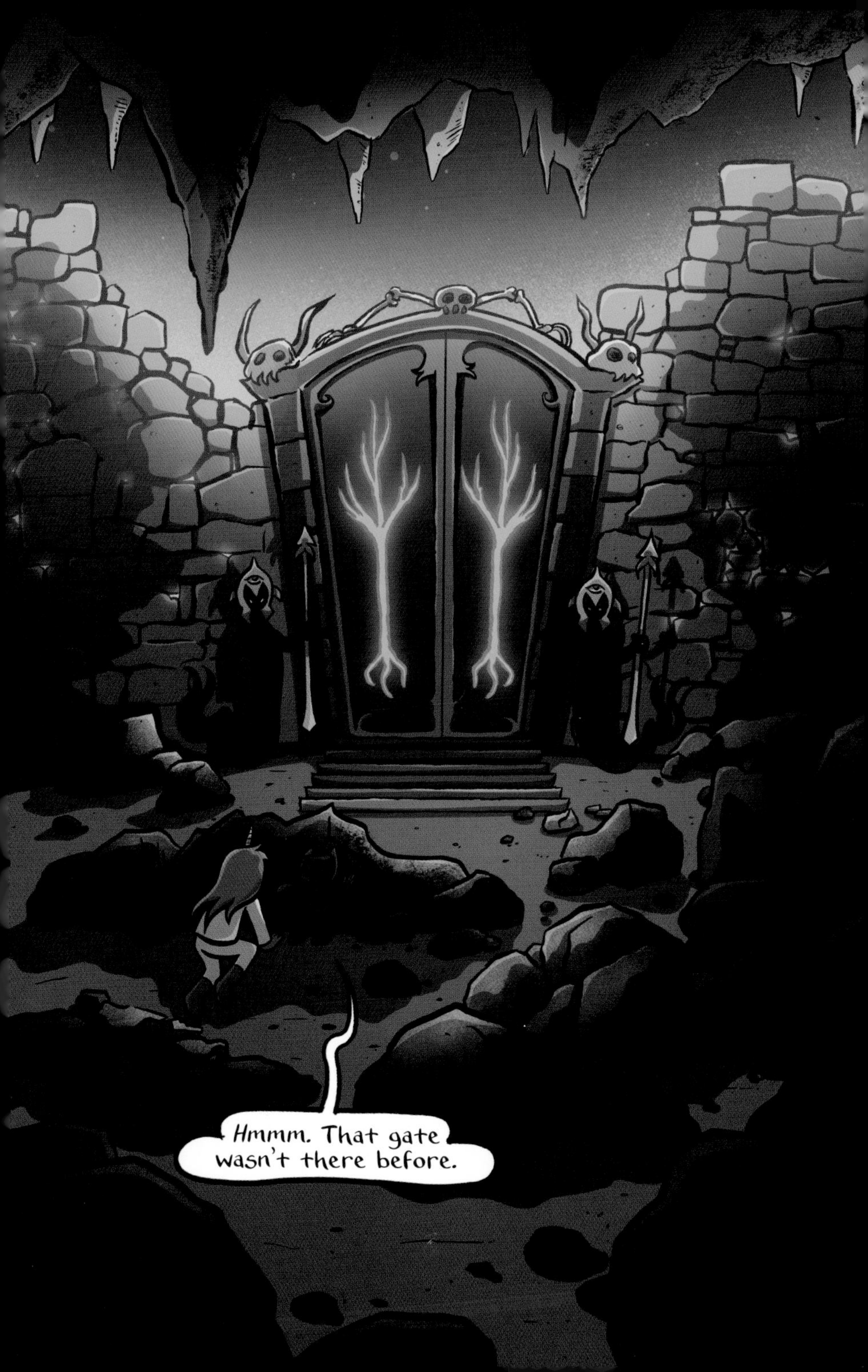
Hmmm. That gate wasn't there before.

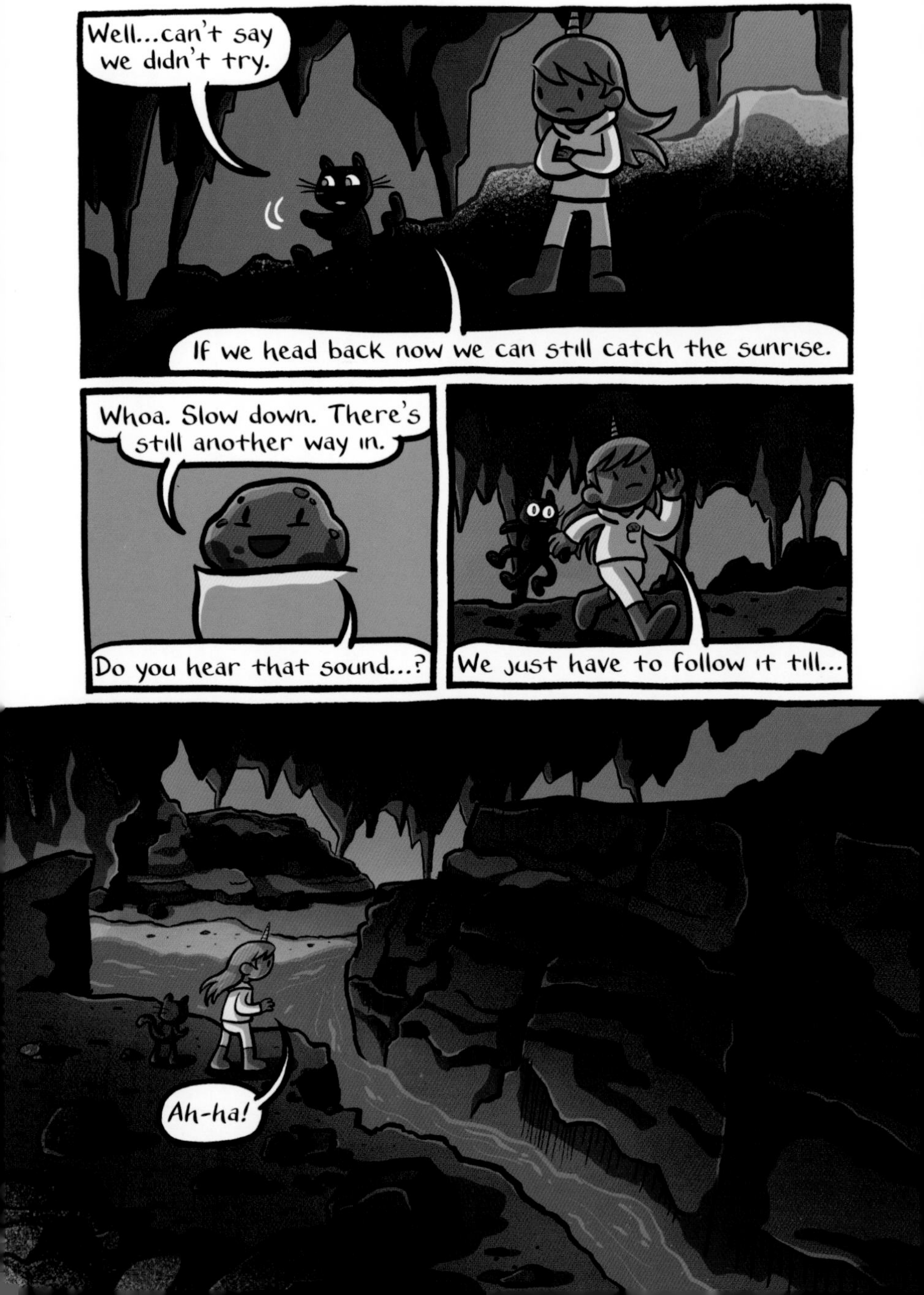
Well...can't say we didn't try.
If we head back now we can still catch the sunrise.
Whoa. Slow down. There's still another way in.
Do you hear that sound...?
We just have to follow it till...
Ah-ha!

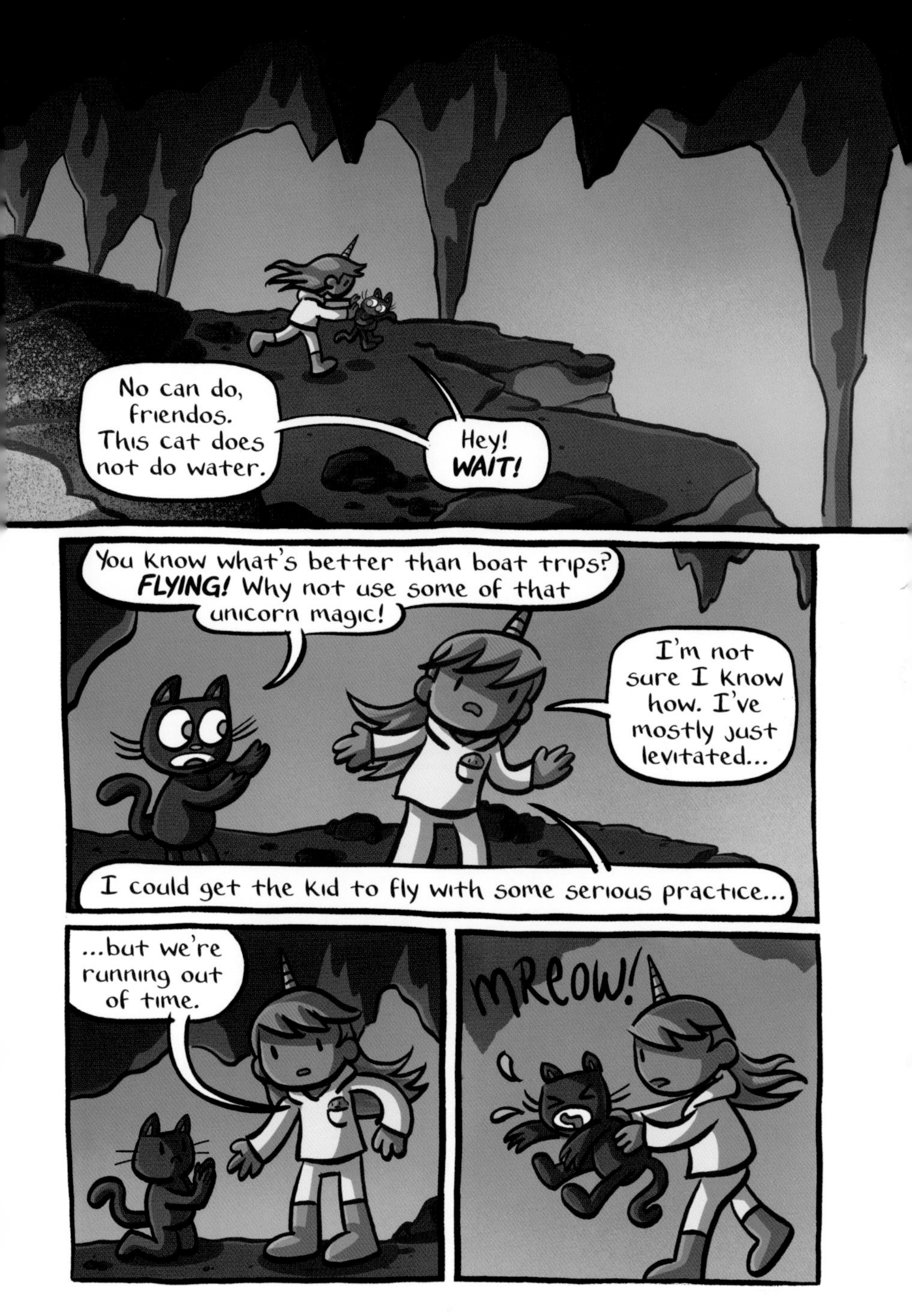
No can do, friendos. This cat does not do water.
Hey! WAIT!
You know what's better than boat trips? FLYING! Why not use some of that unicorn magic!
I'm not sure I know how. I've mostly just levitated...
I could get the kid to fly with some serious practice...
...but we're running out of time.
MREOW!

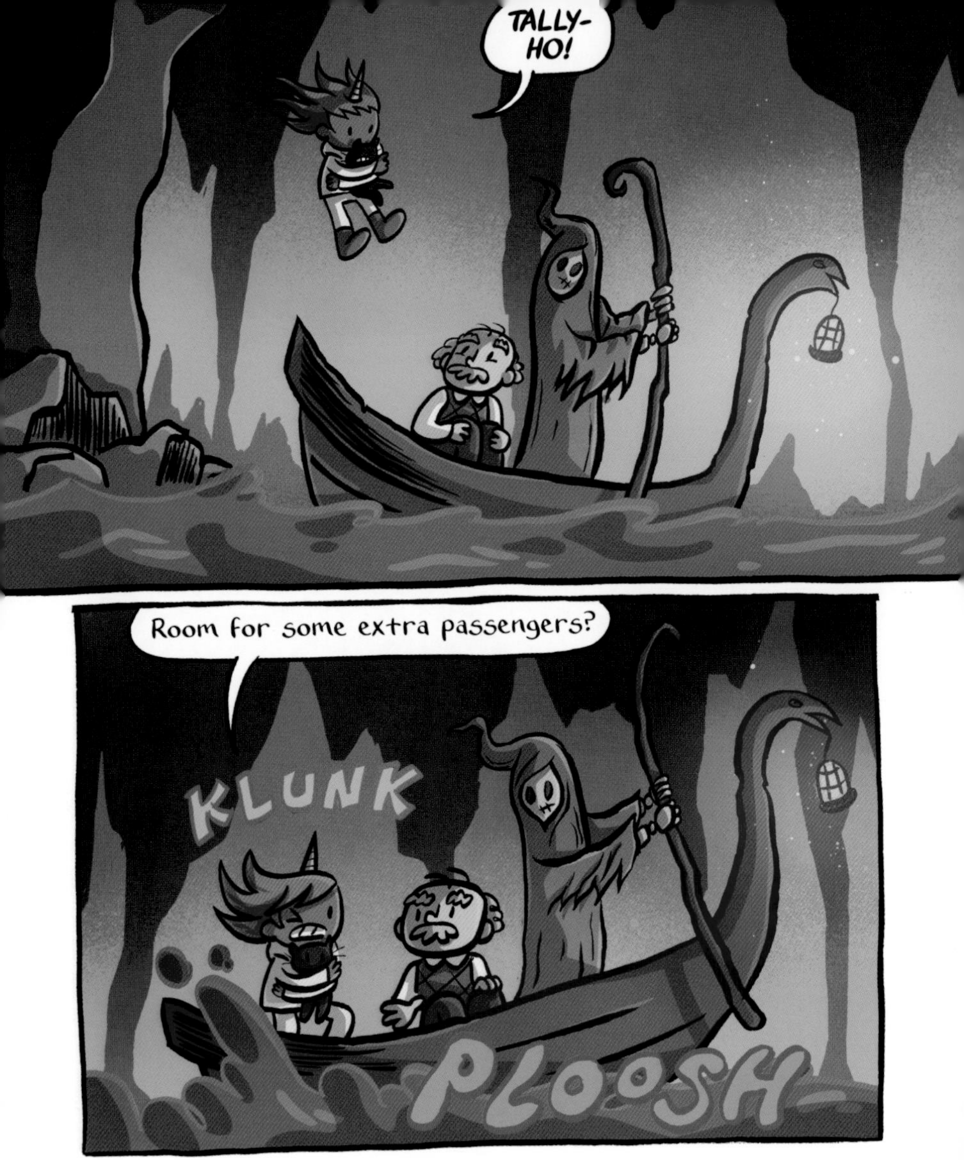
TALLY-HO!
Room for some extra passengers?
KLUNK
PLOOSH

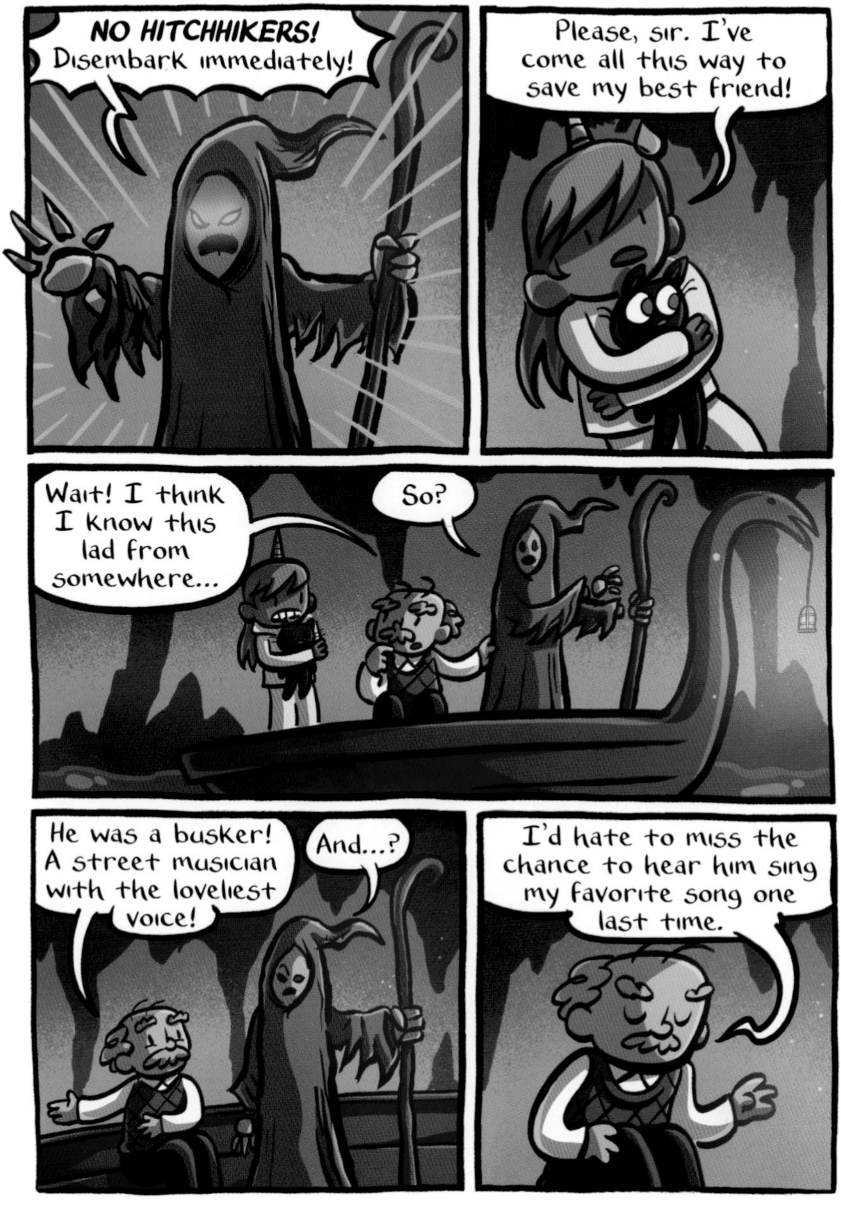
NO HITCHHIKERS! Disembark immediately!
Please, sir. I've come all this way to save my best friend!
Wait! I think I know this lad from somewhere...
So?
He was a busker! A street musician with the loveliest voice!
And...?
I'd hate to miss the chance to hear him sing my favorite song one last time.

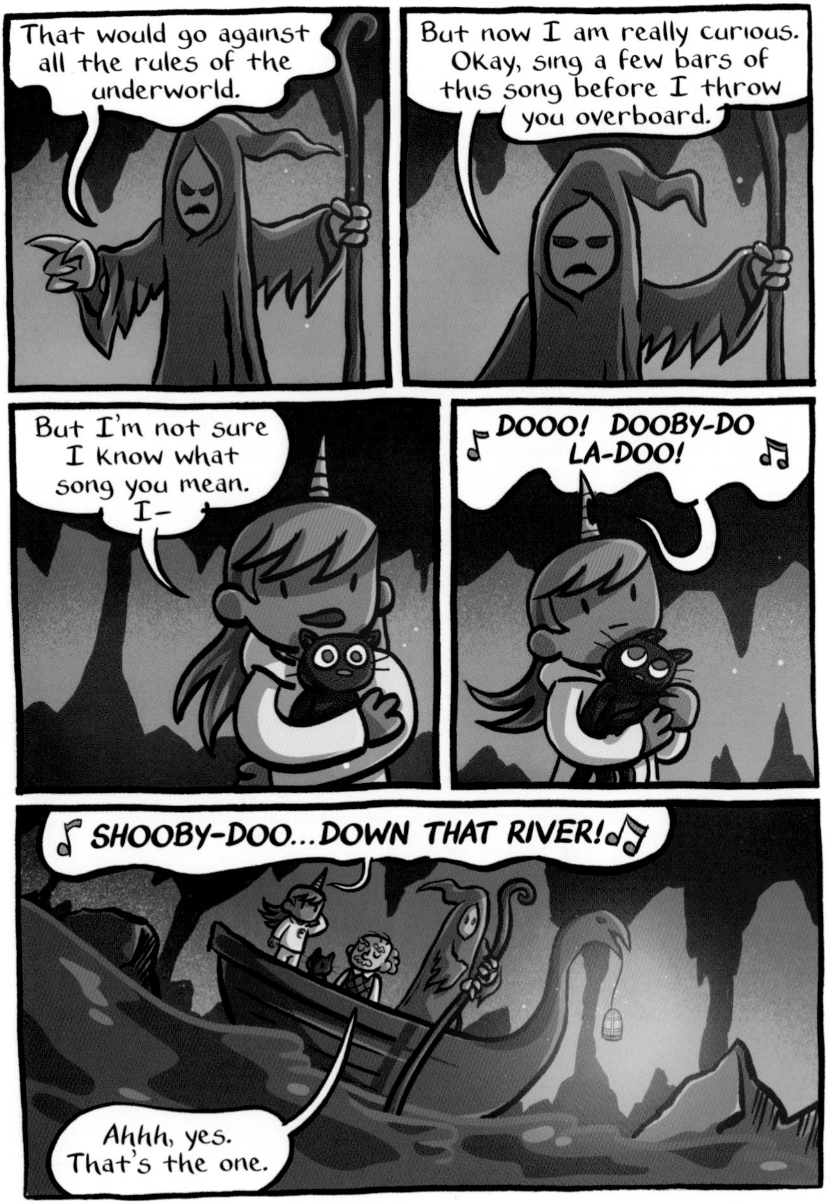
That would go against all the rules of the underworld.
But now I am really curious. Okay, sing a few bars of this song before I throw you overboard.
But I'm not sure I know what song you mean. I–
DOOO! DOOBY-DO LA-DOO!
SHOOBY-DOO...DOWN THAT RIVER!
Ahhh, yes. That's the one.

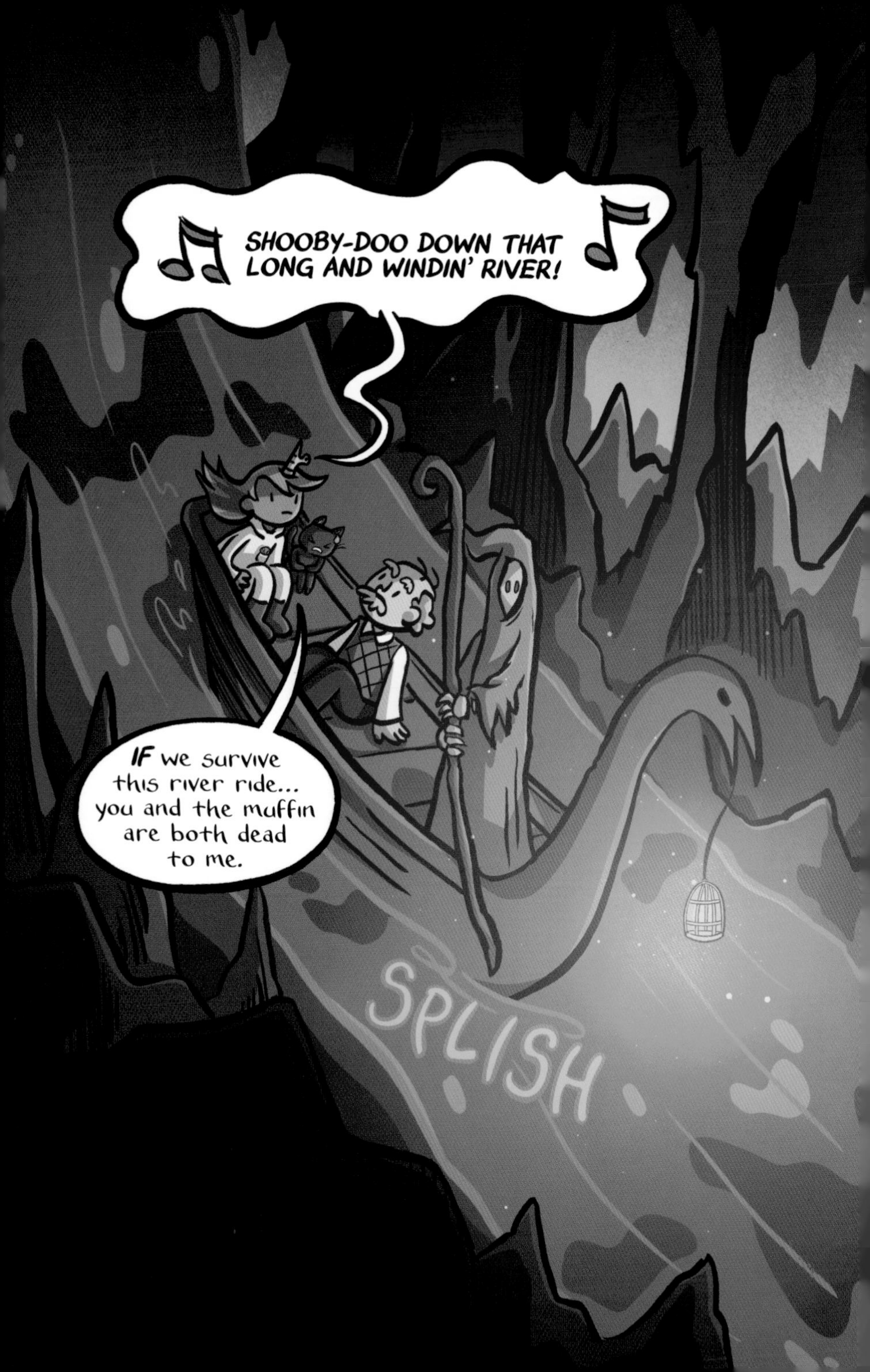
SHOOBY-DOO DOWN THAT LONG AND WINDIN' RIVER!
IF we survive this river ride... you and the muffin are both dead to me.
SPLISH

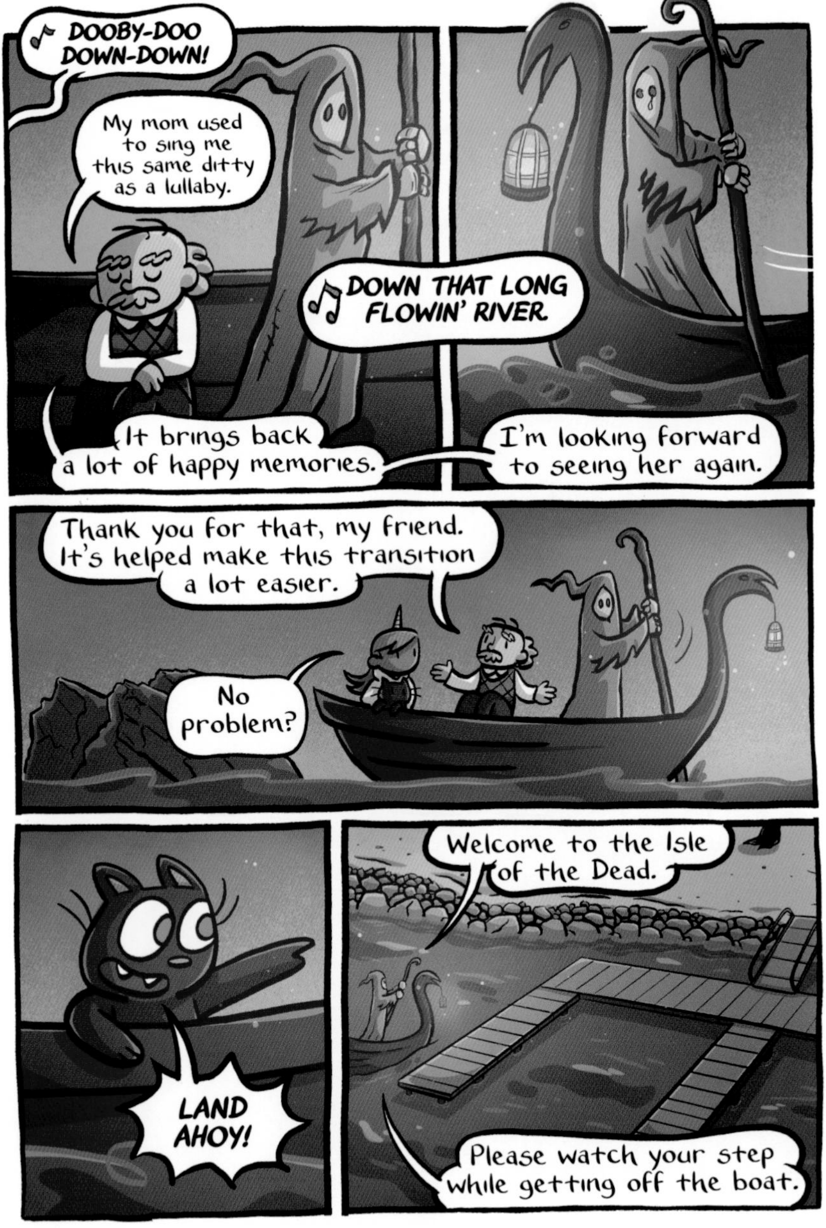
DOOBY-DOO DOWN-DOWN!
My mom used to sing me this same ditty as a lullaby.
DOWN THAT LONG FLOWIN' RIVER
It brings back a lot of happy memories.
I'm looking forward to seeing her again.
Thank you for that, my friend. It's helped make this transition a lot easier.
No problem?
LAND AHOY!
Welcome to the Isle of the Dead.
Please watch your step while getting off the boat.

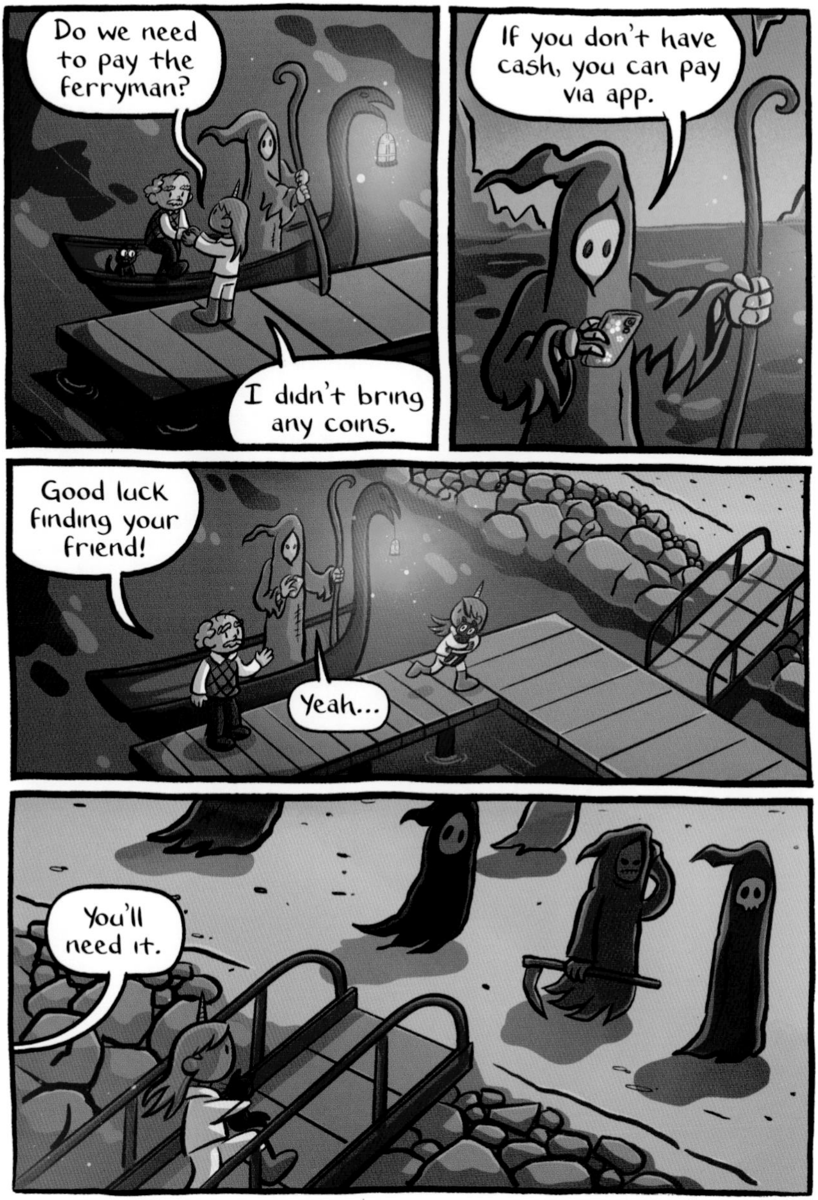
Do we need to pay the ferryman?
I didn't bring any coins.
If you don't have cash, you can pay via app.
Good luck finding your friend!
Yeah...
You'll need it.

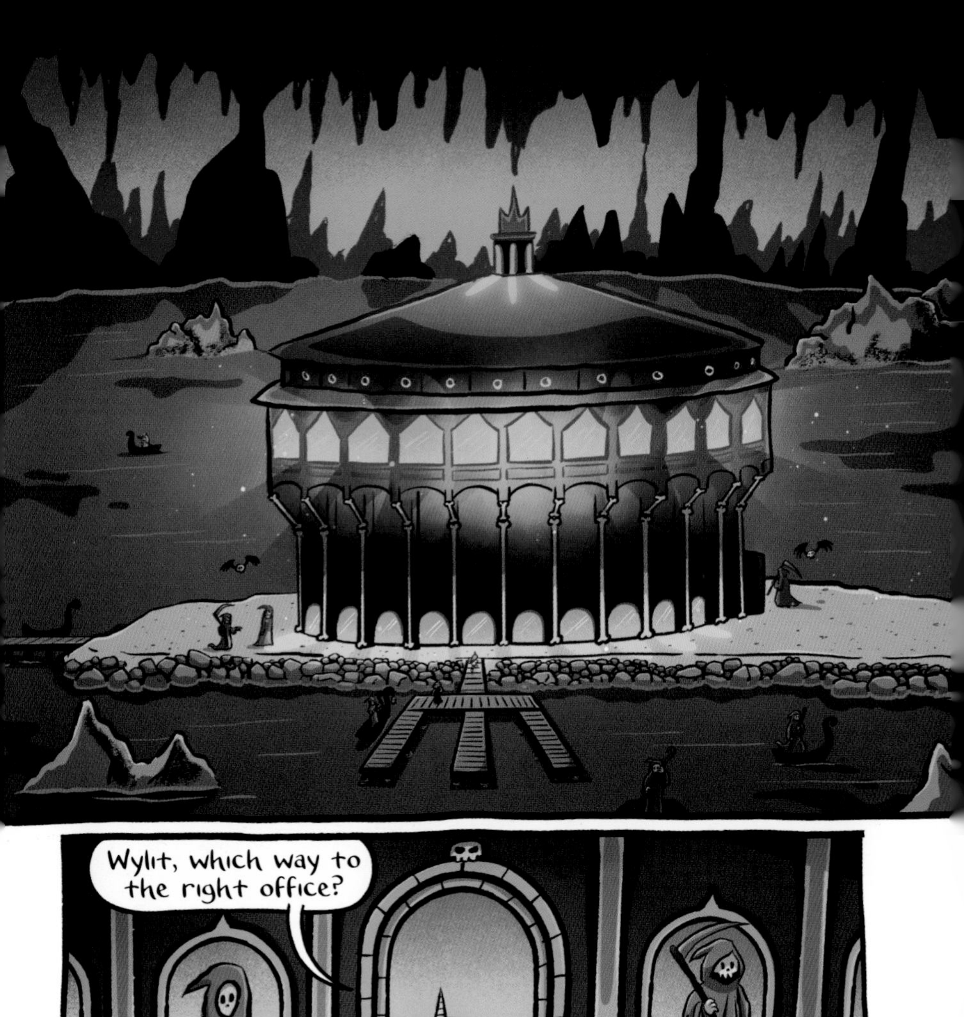

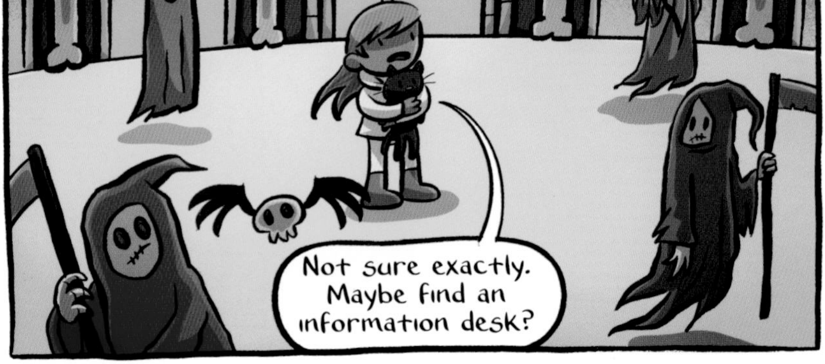
Wylit, which way to the right office?
Not sure exactly. Maybe find an information desk?

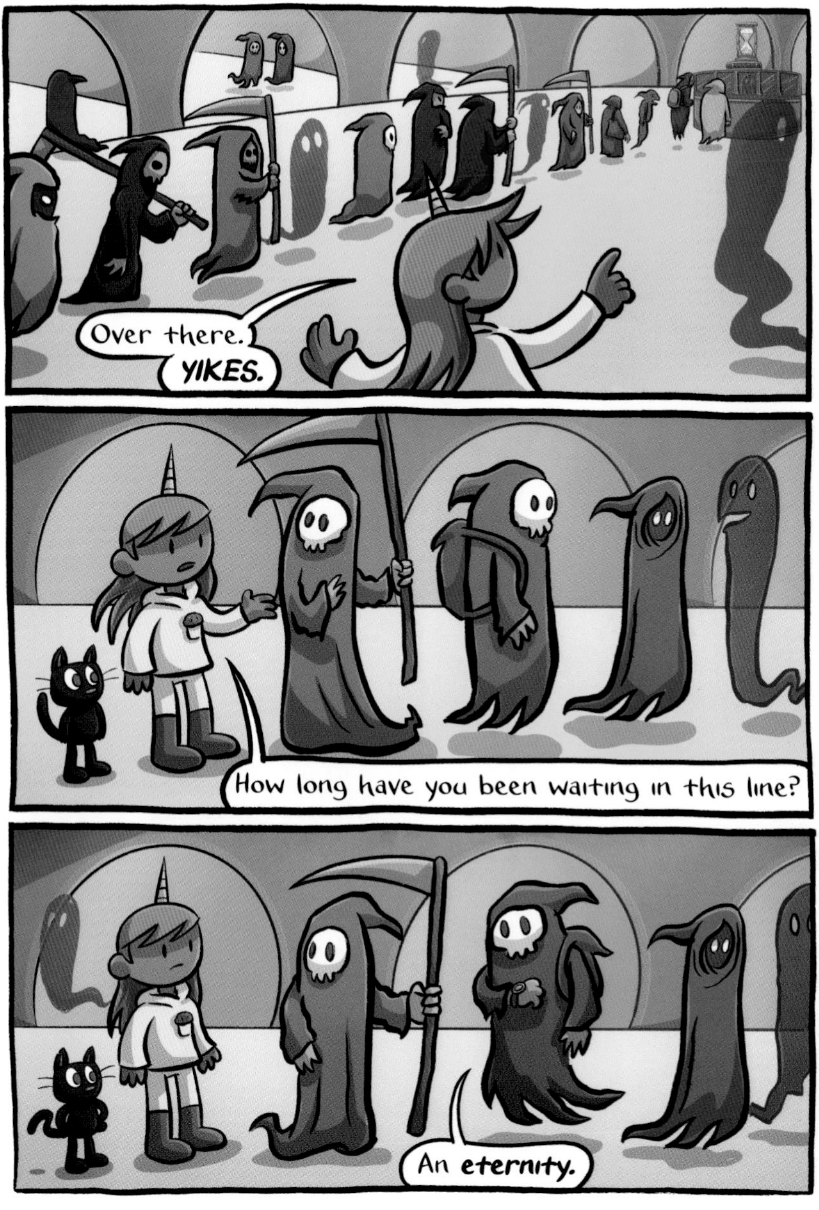
Over there.
YIKES.
How long have you been waiting in this line?
An eternity.

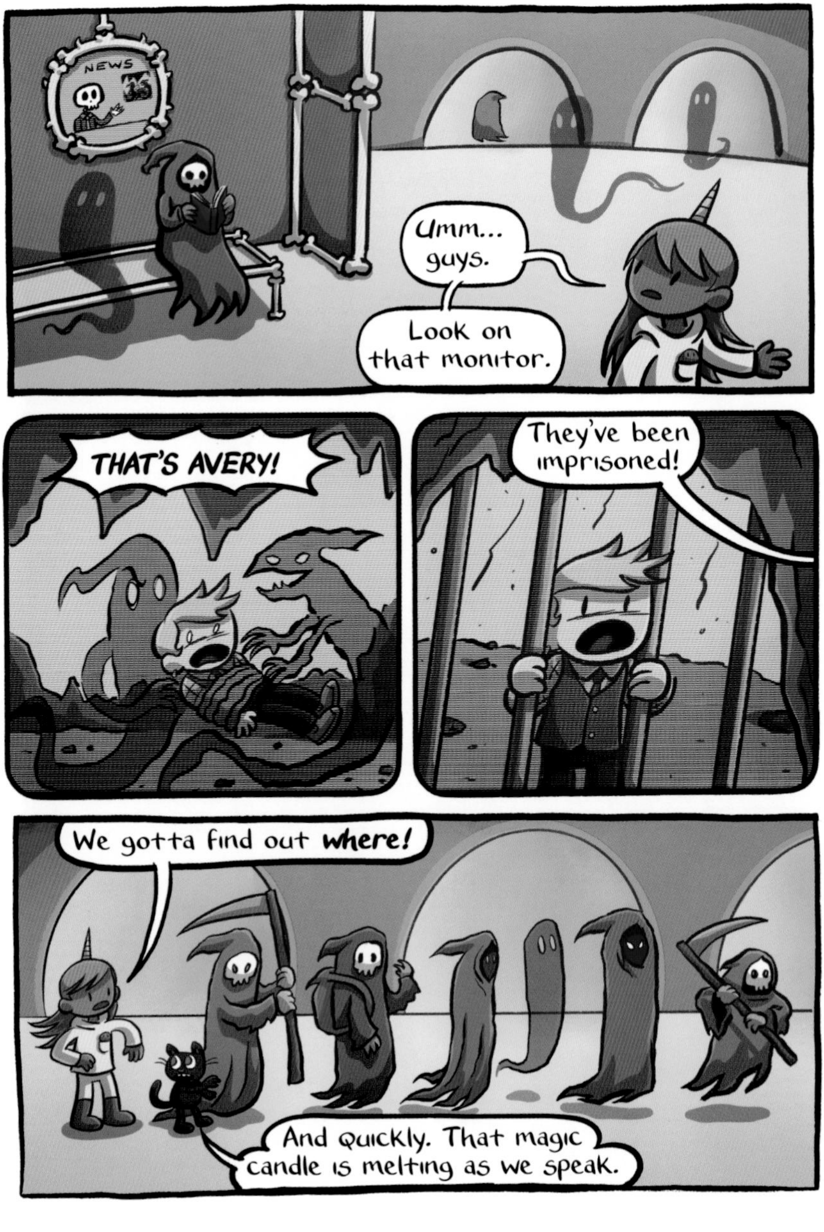
NEWS
Umm... guys.
Look on that monitor.
THAT'S AVERY!
They've been imprisoned!
We gotta find out **where!**
And quickly. That magic candle is melting as we speak.

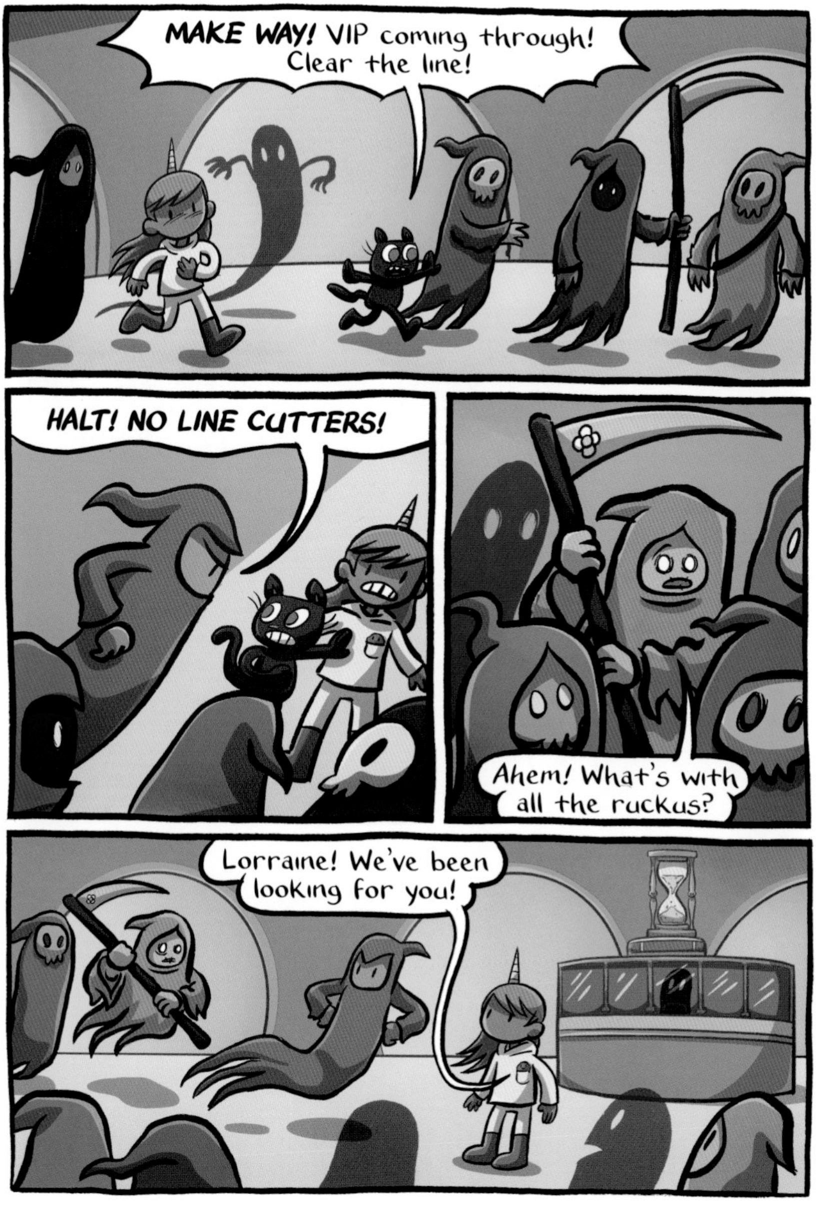
MAKE WAY! VIP coming through! Clear the line!
HALT! NO LINE CUTTERS!
Ahem! What's with all the ruckus?
Lorraine! We've been looking for you!

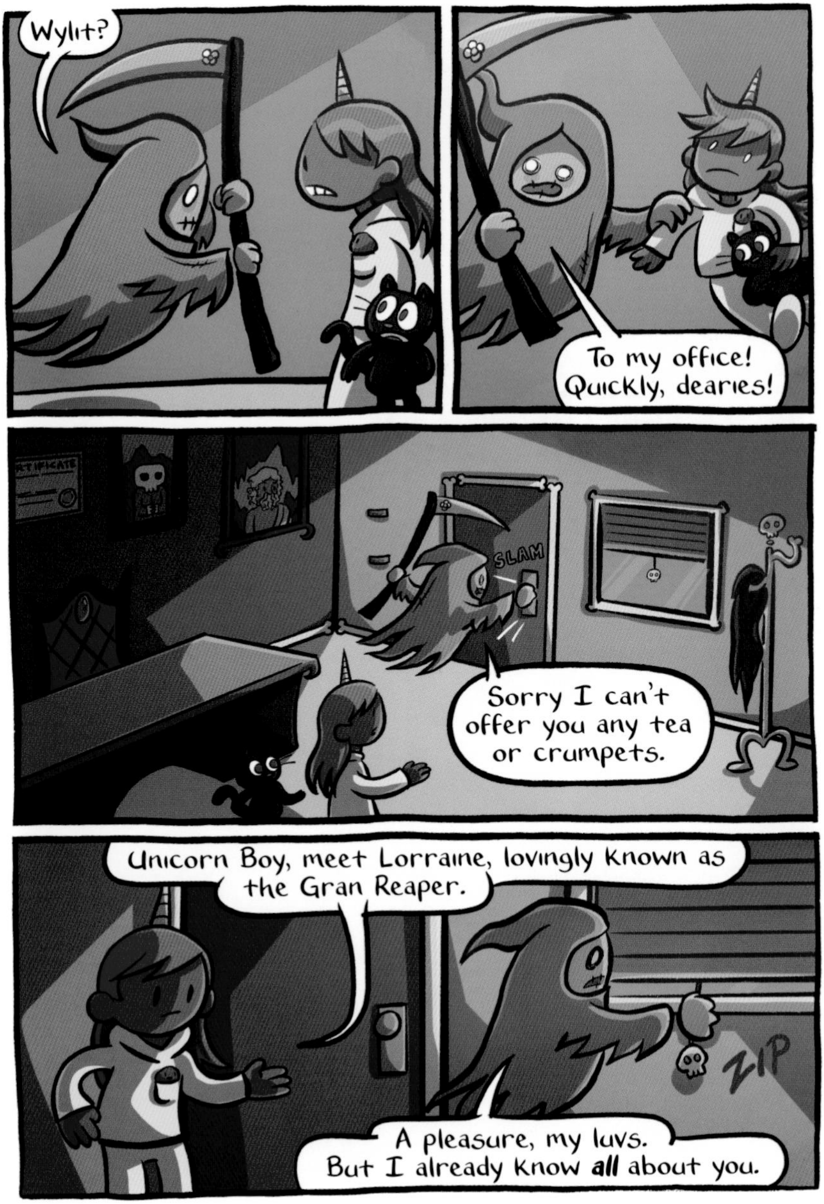
Wylit?
To my office! Quickly, dearies!
SLAM
Sorry I can't offer you any tea or crumpets.
Unicorn Boy, meet Lorraine, lovingly known as the Gran Reaper.
ZIP
A pleasure, my luvs. But I already know **all** about you.

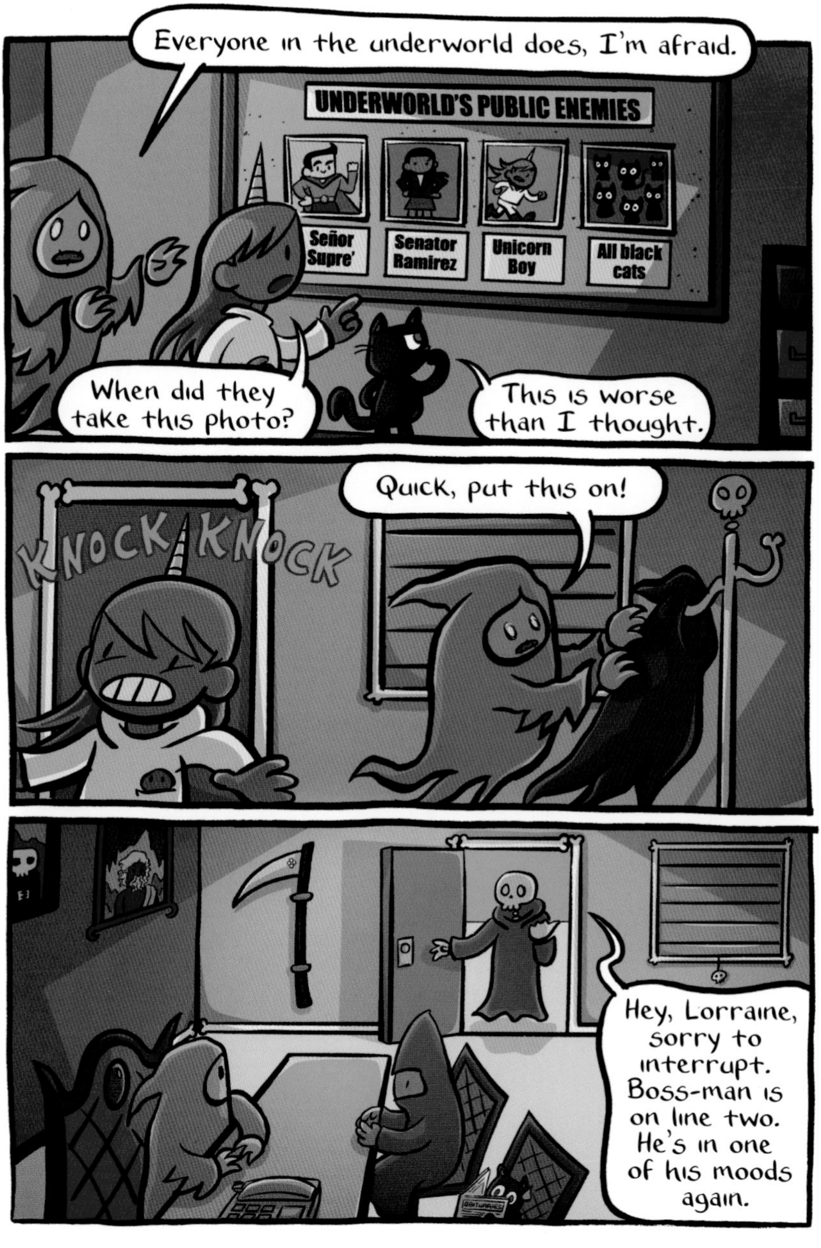
Everyone in the underworld does, I'm afraid.
UNDERWORLD'S PUBLIC ENEMIES
Señor Supre'
Senator Ramirez
Unicorn Boy
All black cats
When did they take this photo?
This is worse than I thought.
KNOCK KNOCK
Quick, put this on!
Hey, Lorraine, sorry to interrupt. Boss-man is on line two. He's in one of his moods again.

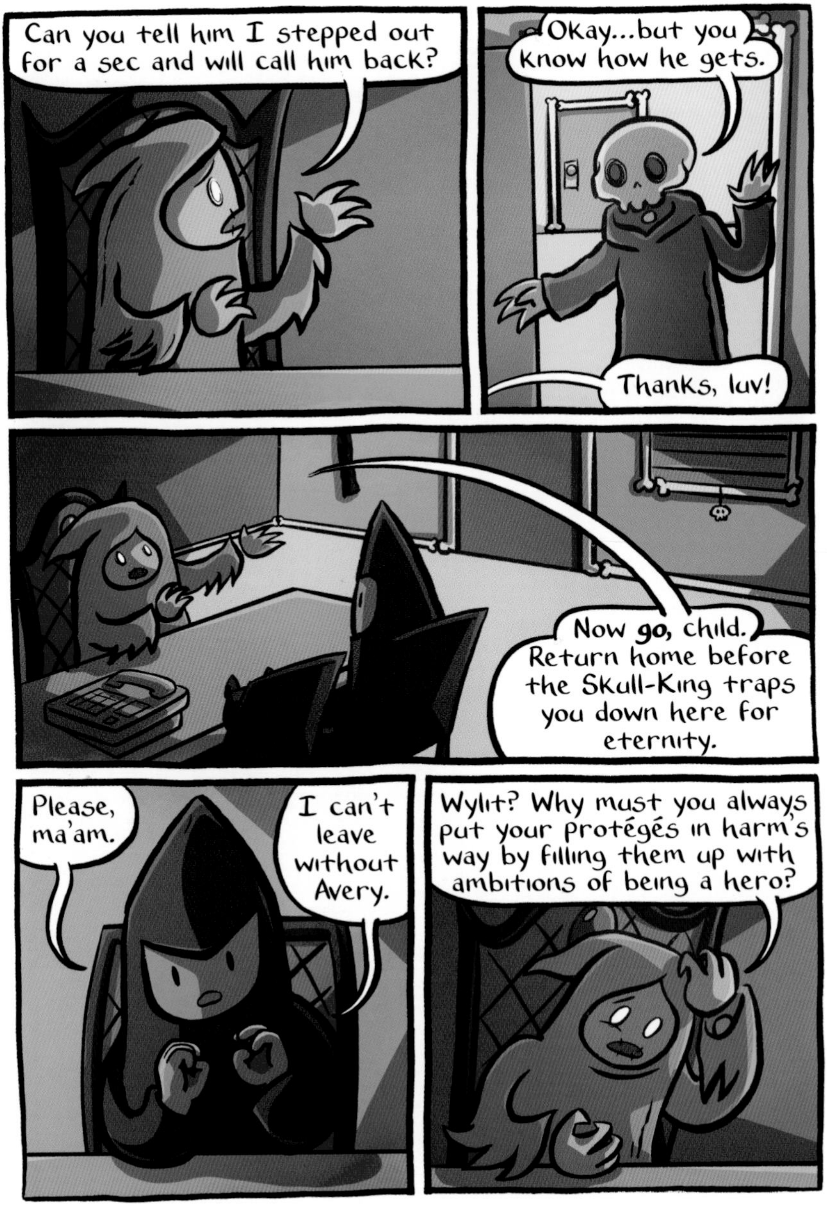
Can you tell him I stepped out for a sec and will call him back?
Okay...but you know how he gets.
Thanks, luv!
Now go, child. Return home before the Skull-King traps you down here for eternity.
Please, ma'am.
I can't leave without Avery.
Wylit? Why must you always put your protégés in harm's way by filling them up with ambitions of being a hero?

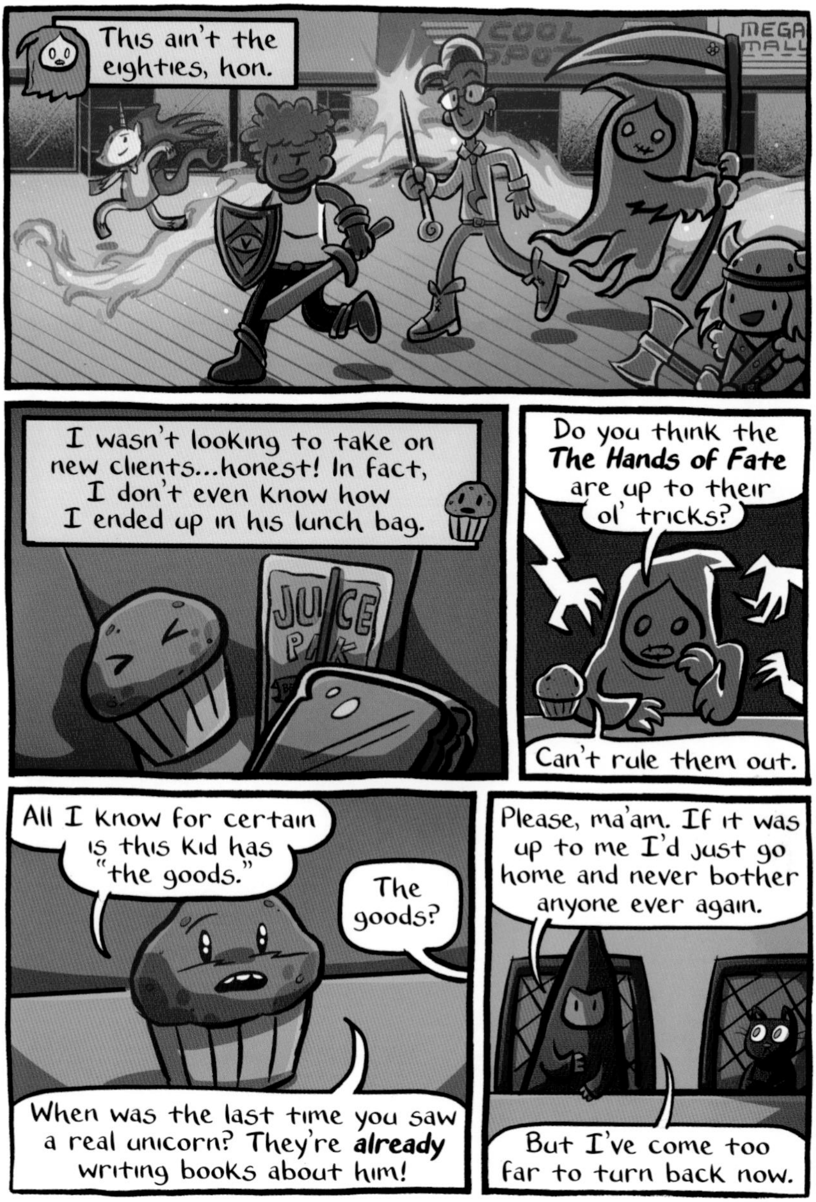

This ain't the eighties, hon.
COOL SPOT
MEGA MALL
I wasn't looking to take on new clients...honest! In fact, I don't even know how I ended up in his lunch bag.
JUICE PAK
Do you think the **The Hands of Fate** are up to their ol' tricks?
Can't rule them out.
All I know for certain is this kid has "the goods."
The goods?
When was the last time you saw a real unicorn? They're **already** writing books about him!
Please, ma'am. If it was up to me I'd just go home and never bother anyone ever again.
But I've come too far to turn back now.

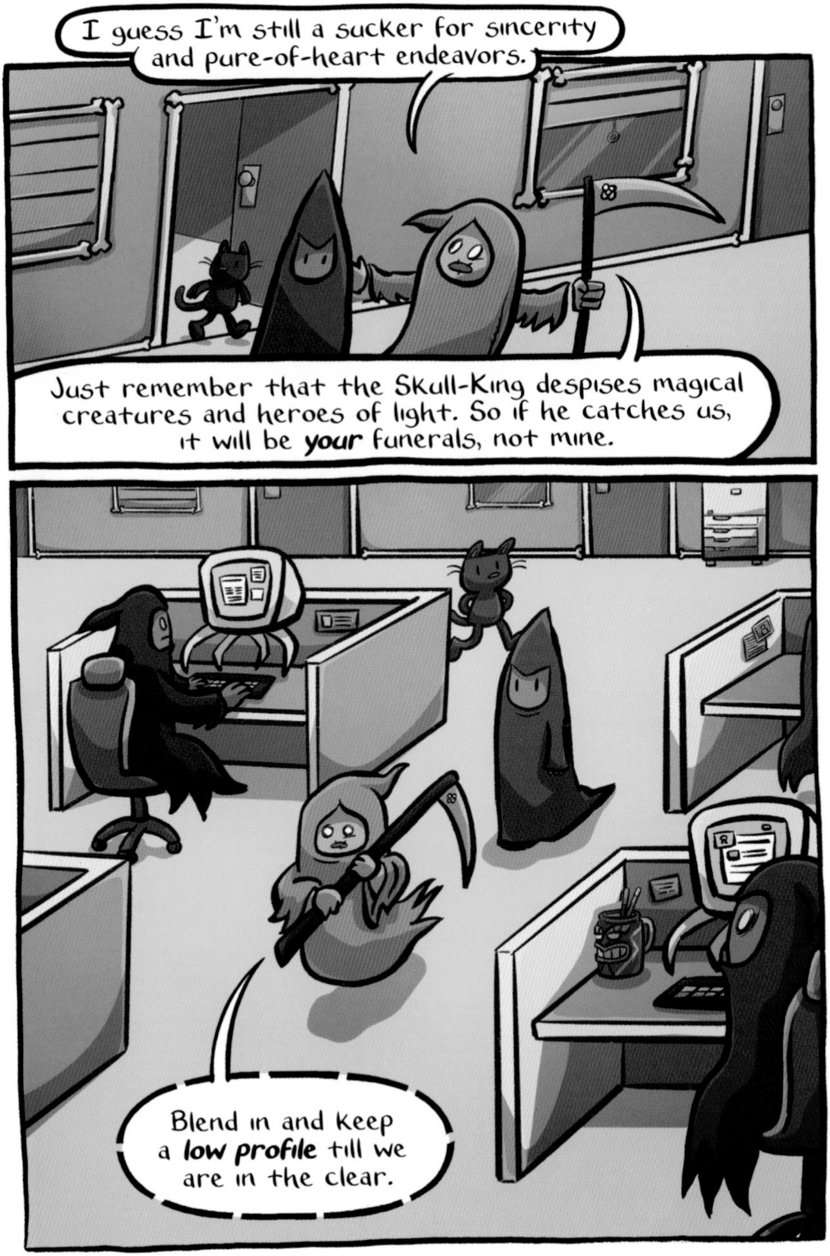
I guess I'm still a sucker for sincerity and pure-of-heart endeavors.
Just remember that the Skull-King despises magical creatures and heroes of light. So if he catches us, it will be **your** funerals, not mine.
Blend in and keep a **low profile** till we are in the clear.

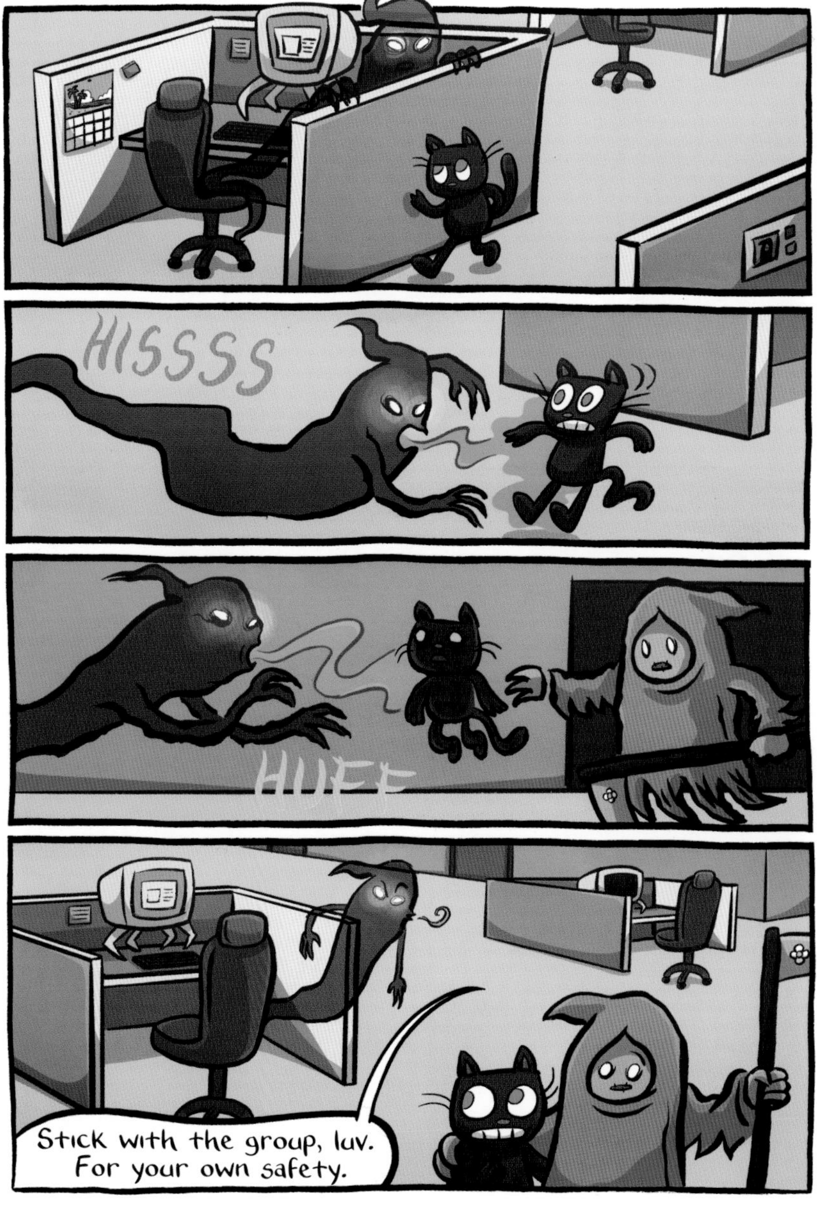
HISSSS
HUFF
Stick with the group, luv.
For your own safety.

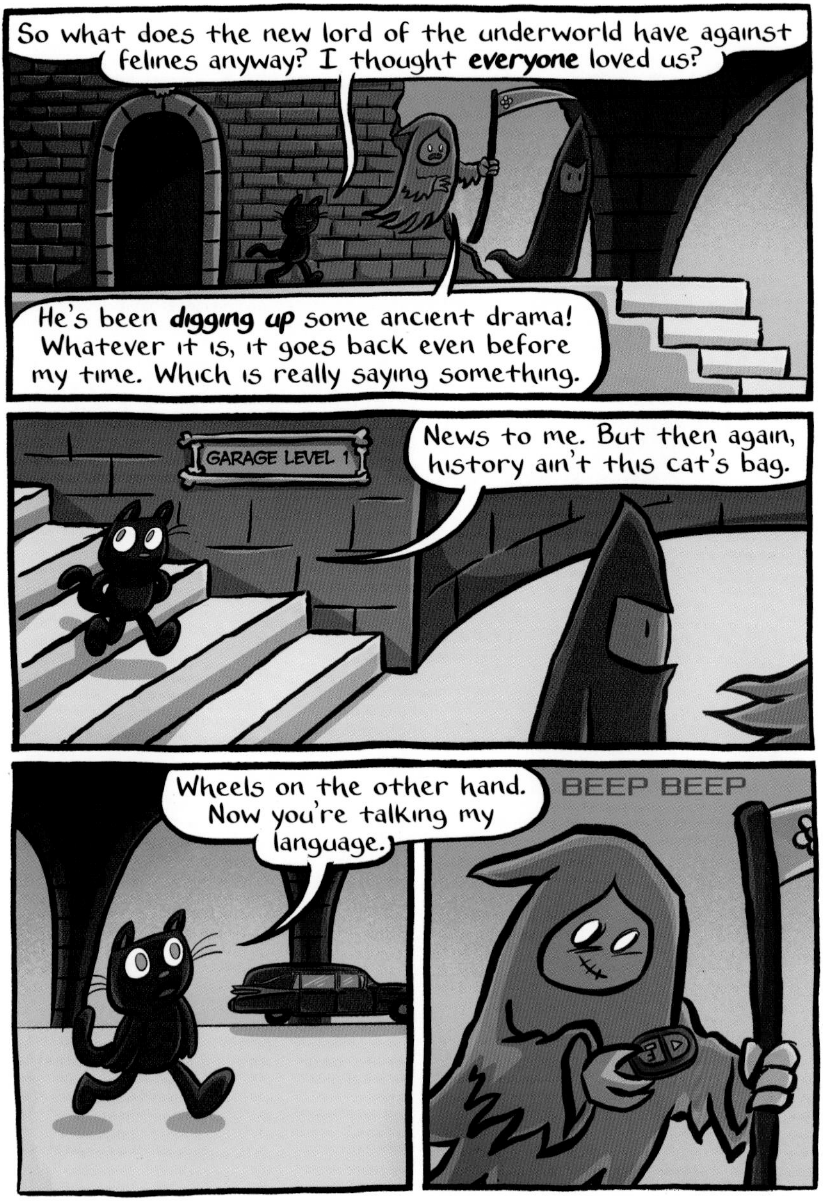

So what does the new lord of the underworld have against felines anyway? I thought **everyone** loved us?
He's been **digging up** some ancient drama! Whatever it is, it goes back even before my time. Which is really saying something.
GARAGE LEVEL 1
News to me. But then again, history ain't this cat's bag.
Wheels on the other hand. Now you're talking my language.
BEEP BEEP

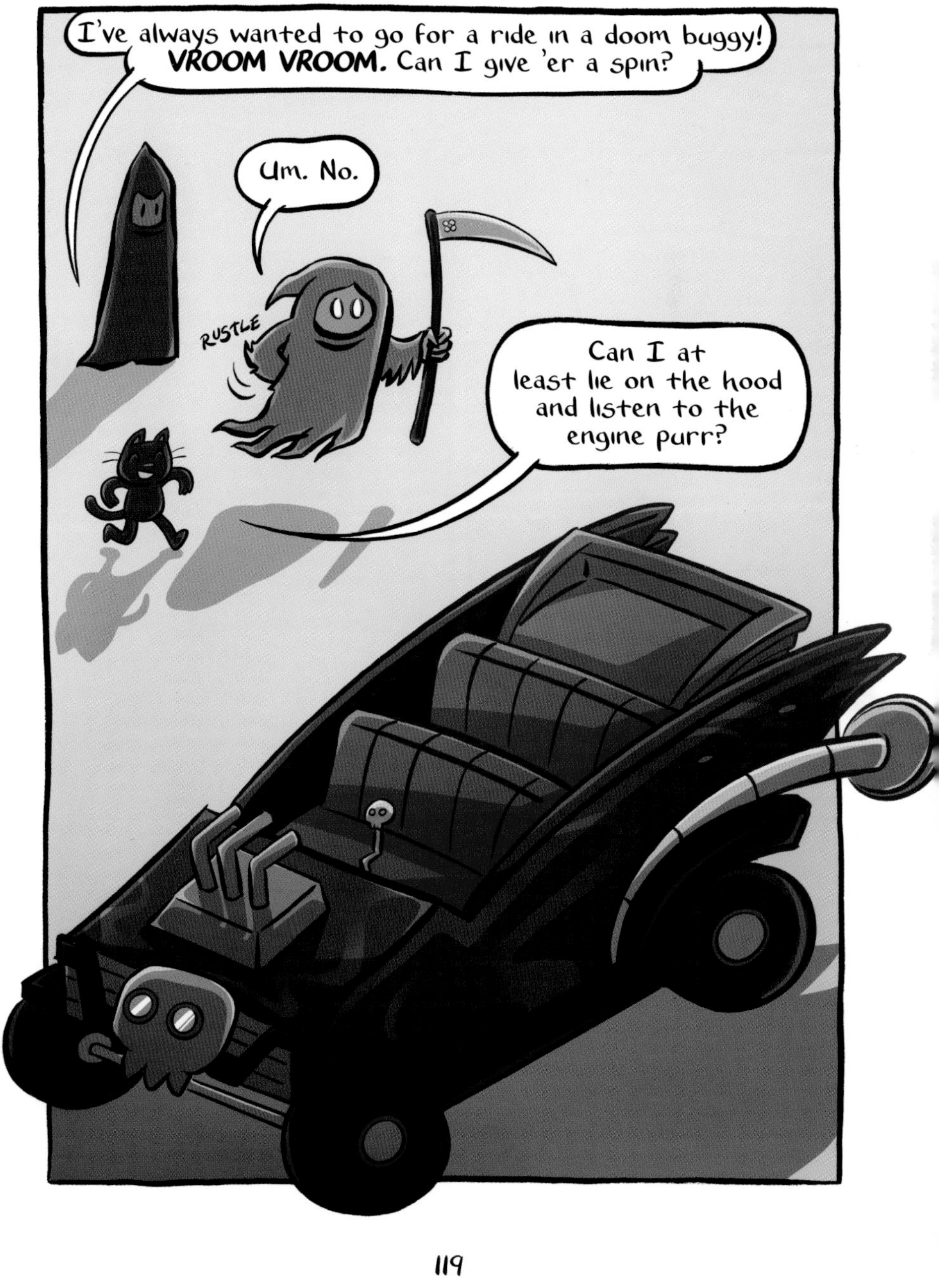
I've always wanted to go for a ride in a doom buggy! VROOM VROOM. Can I give 'er a spin?
Um. No.
RUSTLE
Can I at least lie on the hood and listen to the engine purr?

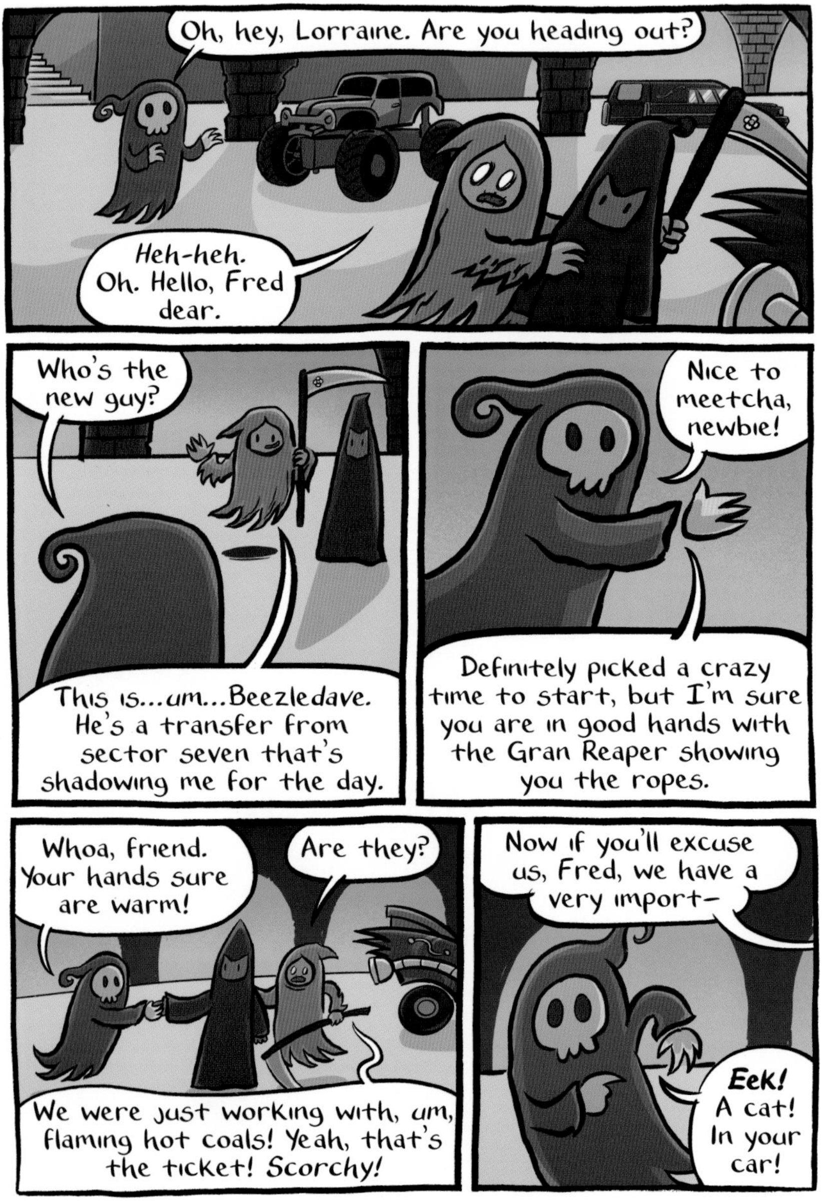
Oh, hey, Lorraine. Are you heading out?
Heh-heh. Oh. Hello, Fred dear.
Who's the new guy?
This is...um...Beezledave. He's a transfer from sector seven that's shadowing me for the day.
Nice to meetcha, newbie!
Definitely picked a crazy time to start, but I'm sure you are in good hands with the Gran Reaper showing you the ropes.
Whoa, friend. Your hands sure are warm!
Are they?
We were just working with, um, flaming hot coals! Yeah, that's the ticket! Scorchy!
Now if you'll excuse us, Fred, we have a very import–
Eek! A cat! In your car!

BAD KITTY! Scoot over!

Should I report the feline to the proper authorities?

Oh, don't trouble yourself. I'll lock up this naughty ragamuffin myself.

Ragamuffin? I'm a noble Bombay, thank you very much.

CLUTCH

VROOOM

Sector seven?

Wait a second... There is no sector seven.

Hold up, Lorraine! I think that new kid might be an *IMPOSTER!*

VRRR

Hold on tight, lads!

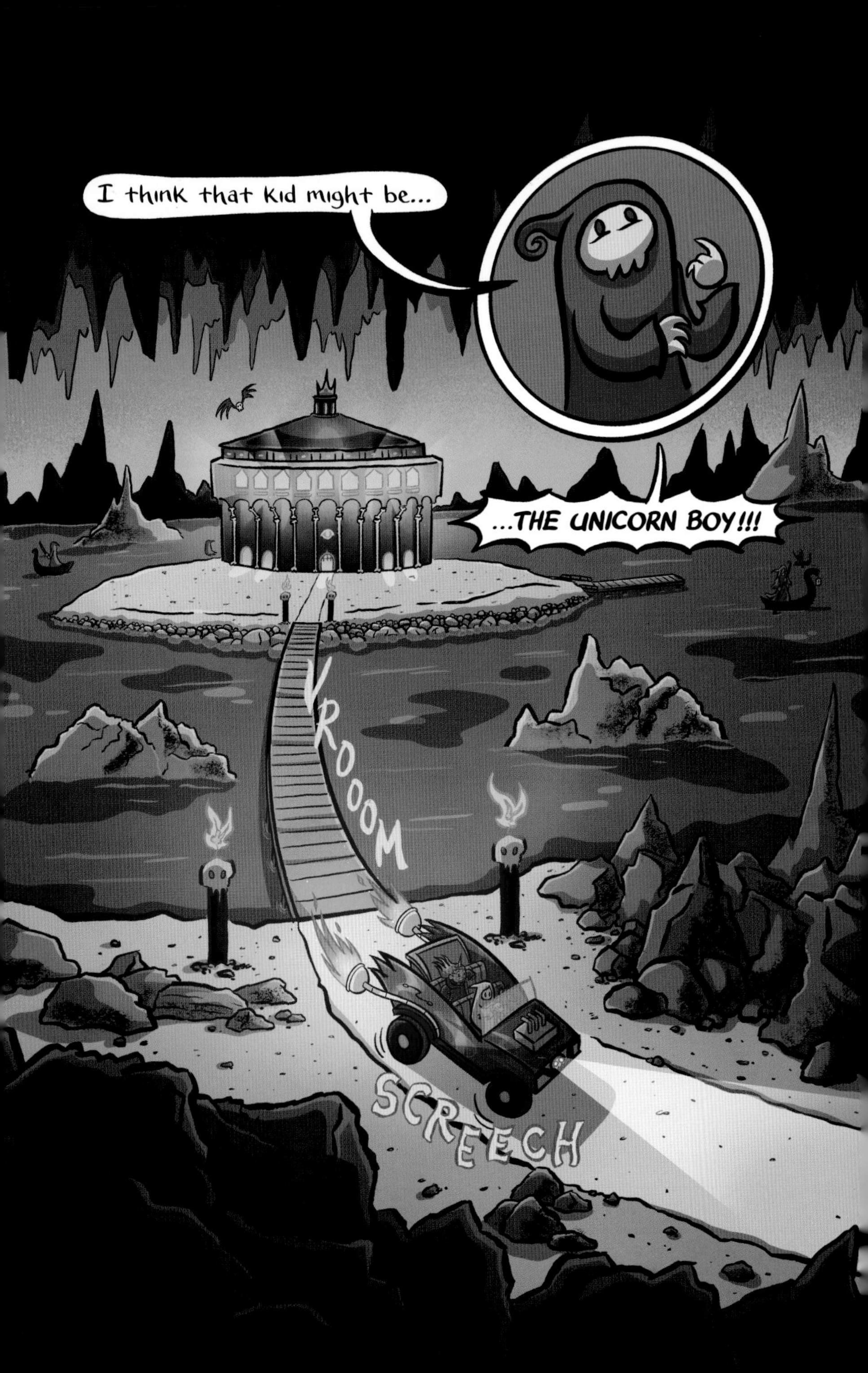
I think that kid might be...
...THE UNICORN BOY!!!
VROOOM
SCREECH

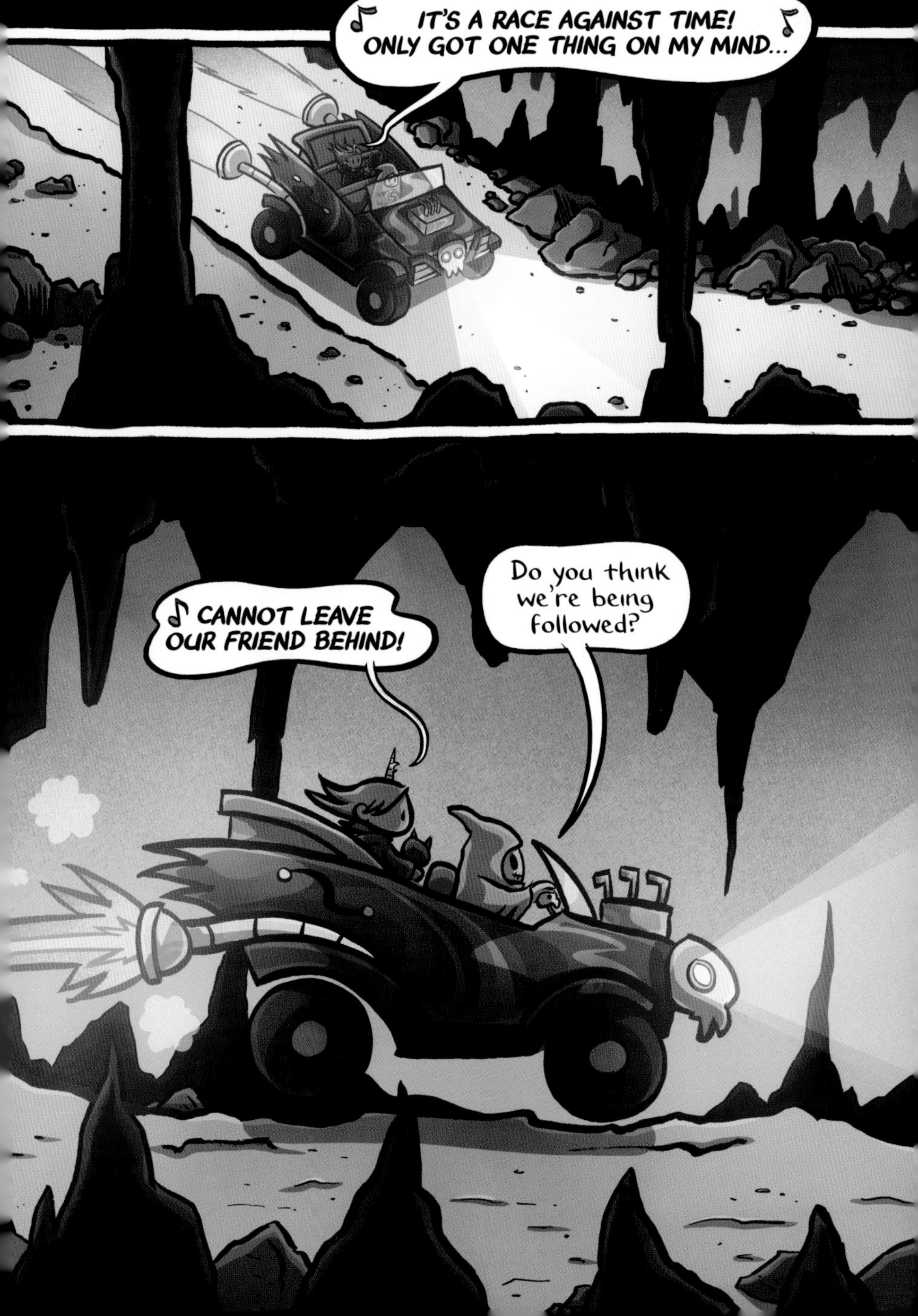
♪ IT'S A RACE AGAINST TIME! ONLY GOT ONE THING ON MY MIND... ♪
♪ CANNOT LEAVE OUR FRIEND BEHIND!
Do you think we're being followed?

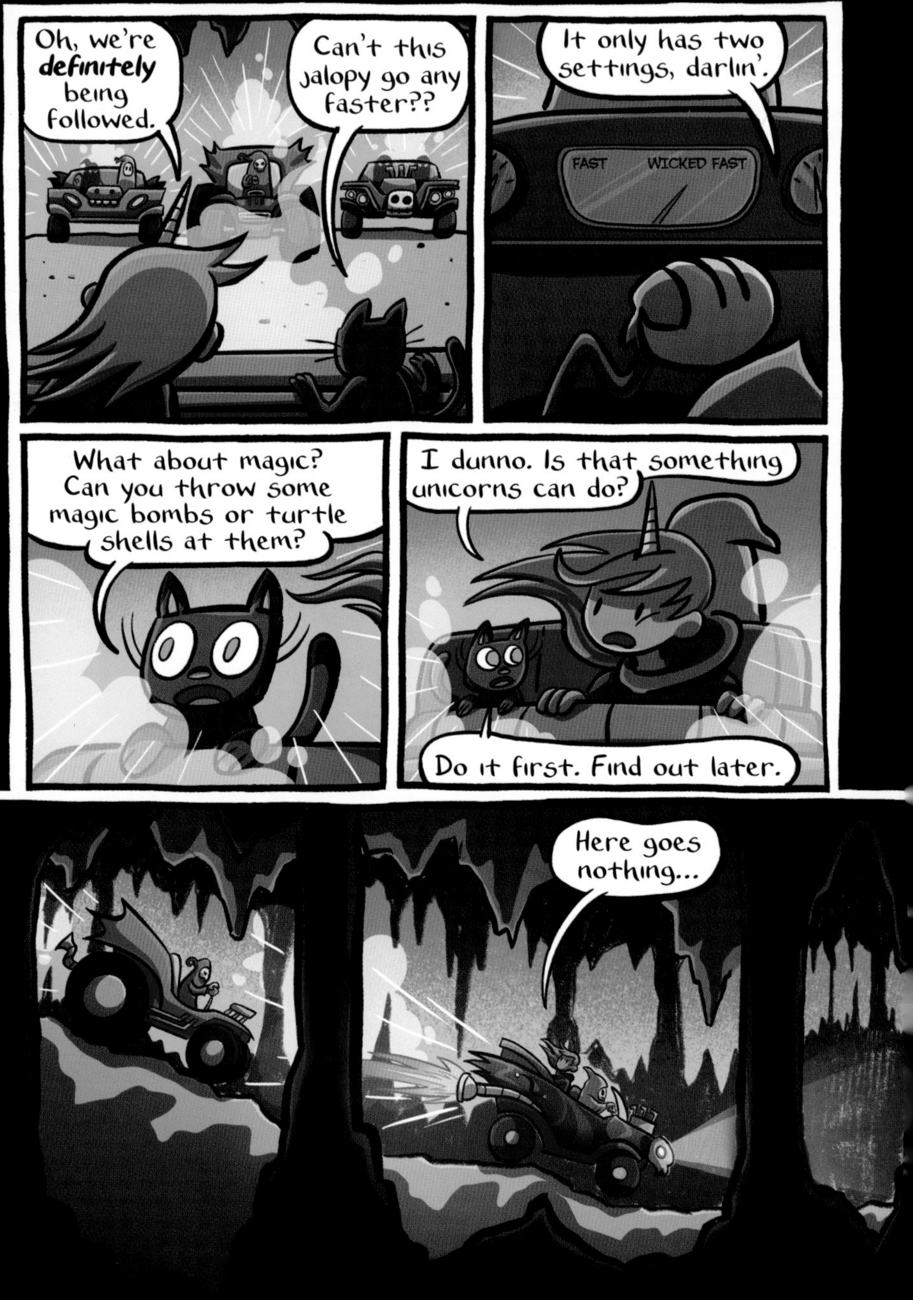
Oh, we're **definitely** being followed.
Can't this jalopy go any faster??
It only has two settings, darlin'.
FAST
WICKED FAST
What about magic? Can you throw some magic bombs or turtle shells at them?
I dunno. Is that something unicorns can do?
Do it first. Find out later.
Here goes nothing...

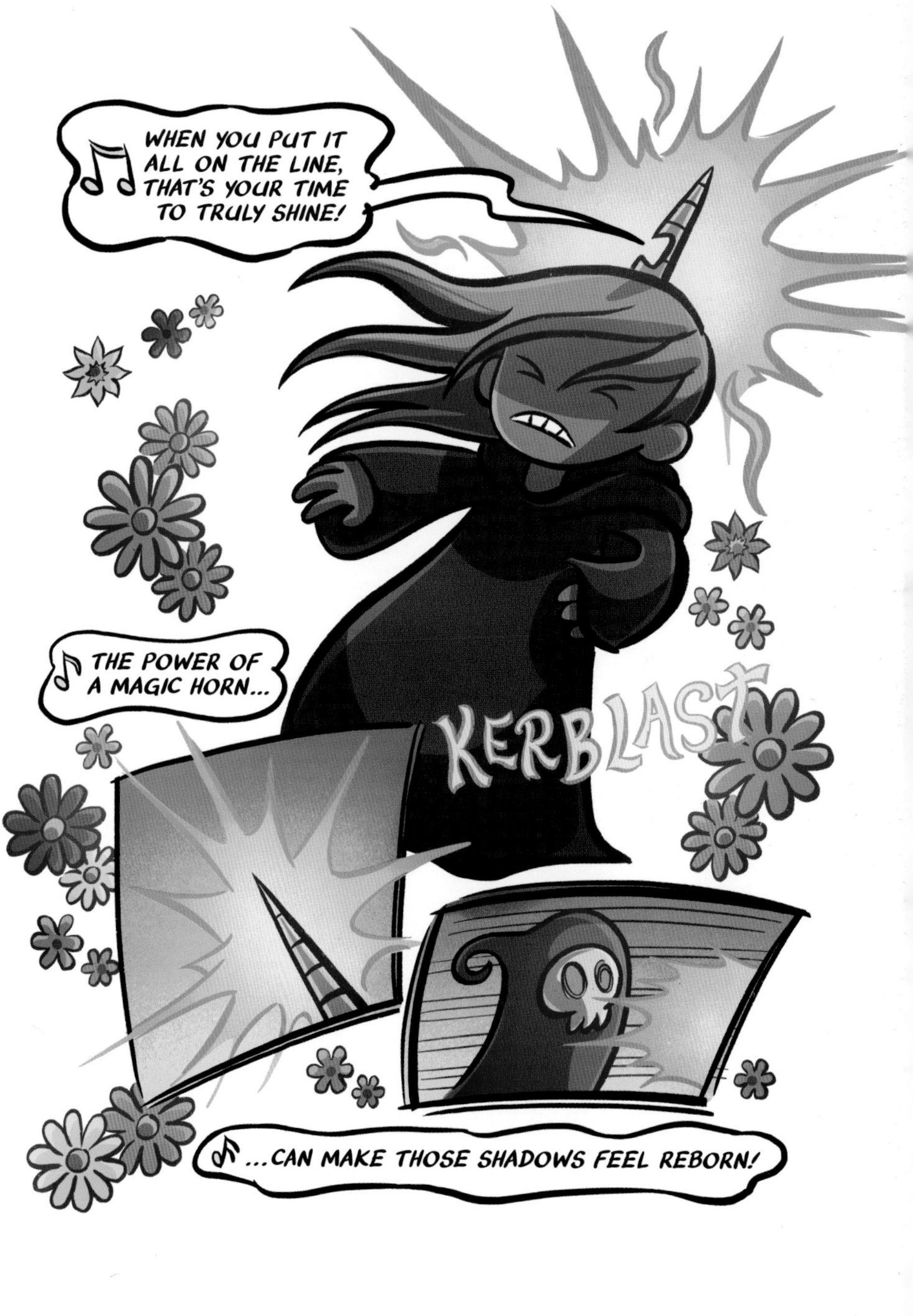
♫ WHEN YOU PUT IT ALL ON THE LINE, THAT'S YOUR TIME TO TRULY SHINE!
♪ THE POWER OF A MAGIC HORN...
KERBLAST
♪ ...CAN MAKE THOSE SHADOWS FEEL REBORN!

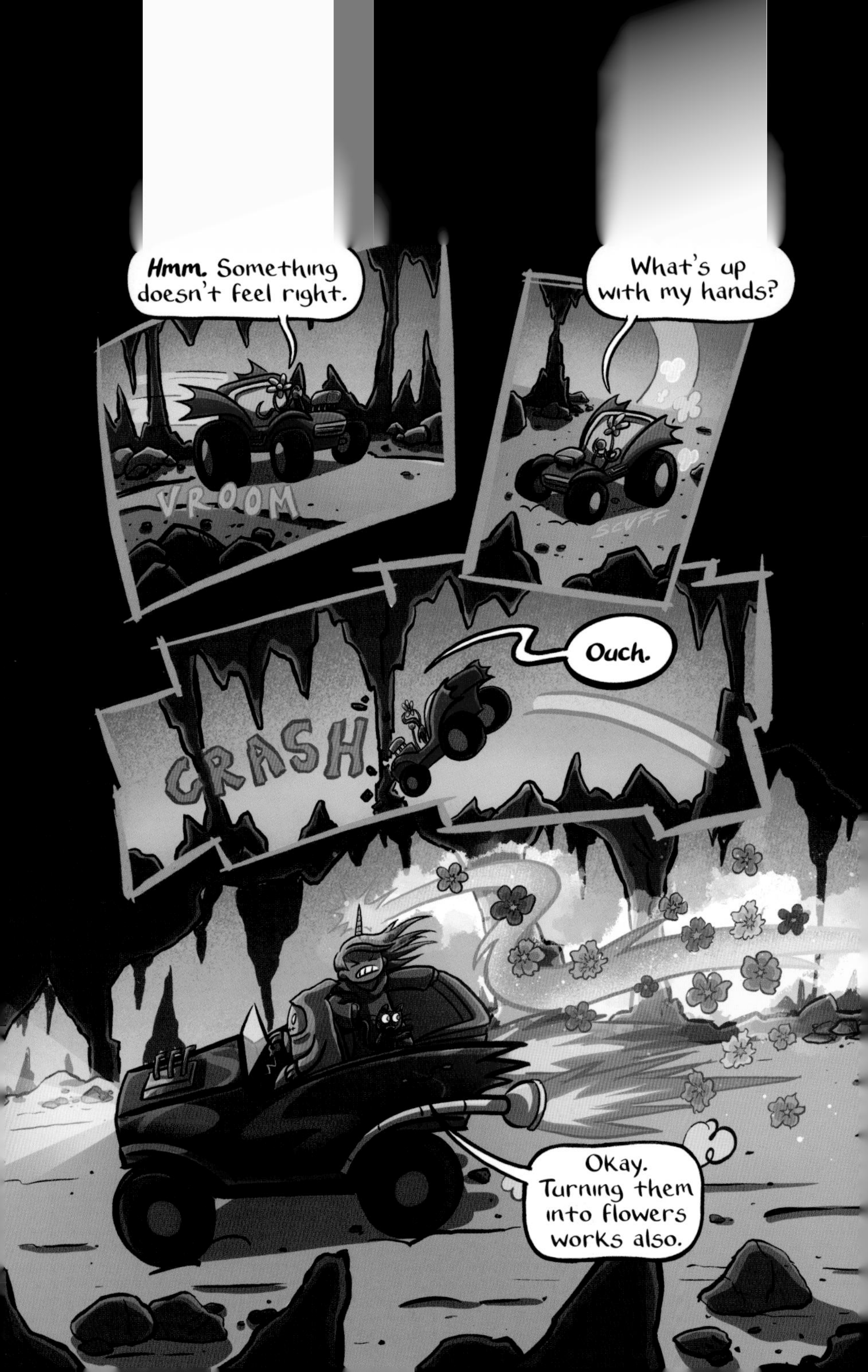

Hmm. Something doesn't feel right.
VROOM
What's up with my hands?
SCUFF
CRASH
Ouch.
Okay. Turning them into flowers works also.

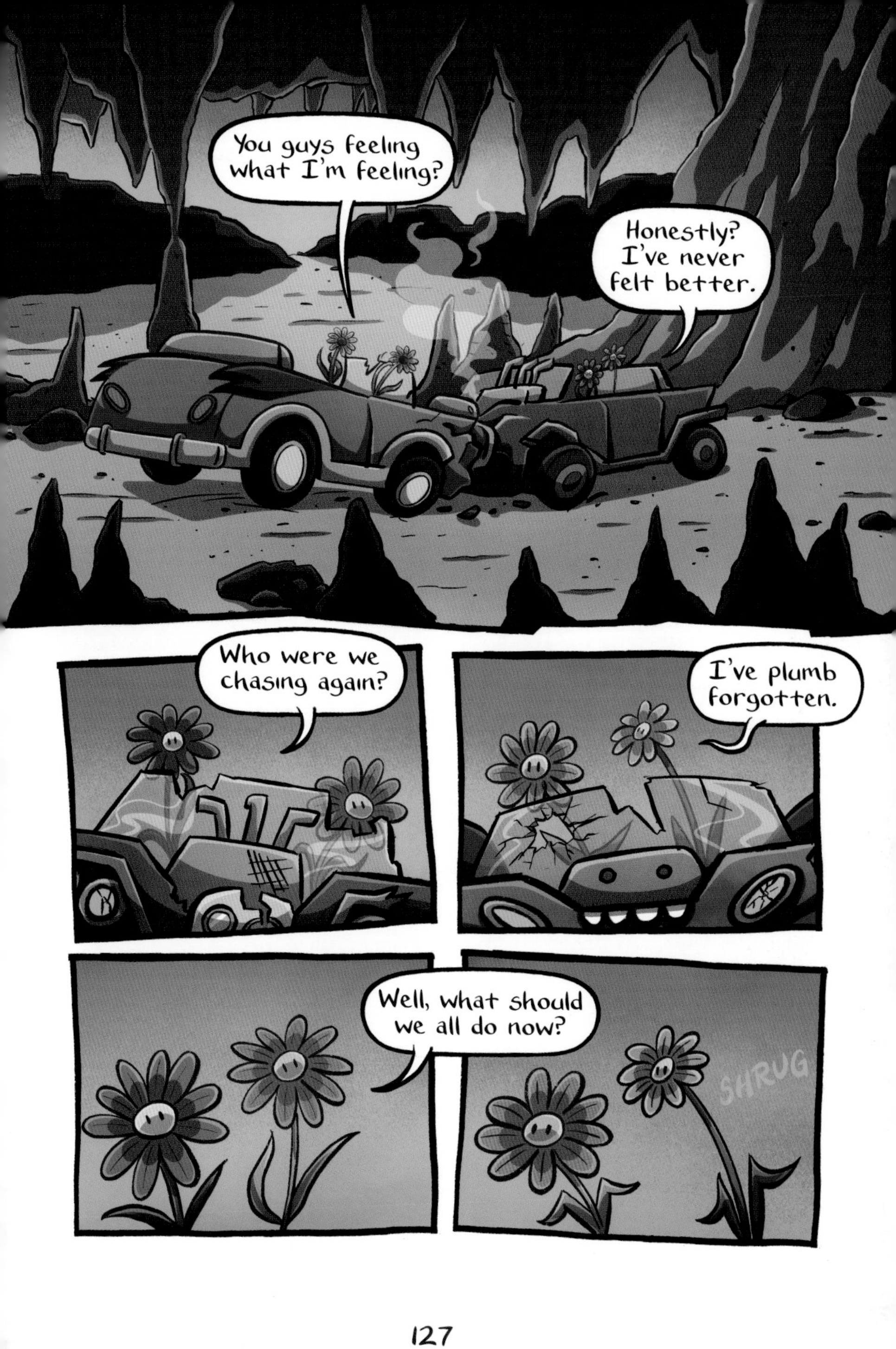
You guys feeling what I'm feeling?
Honestly? I've never felt better.
Who were we chasing again?
I've plumb forgotten.
Well, what should we all do now?
SHRUG

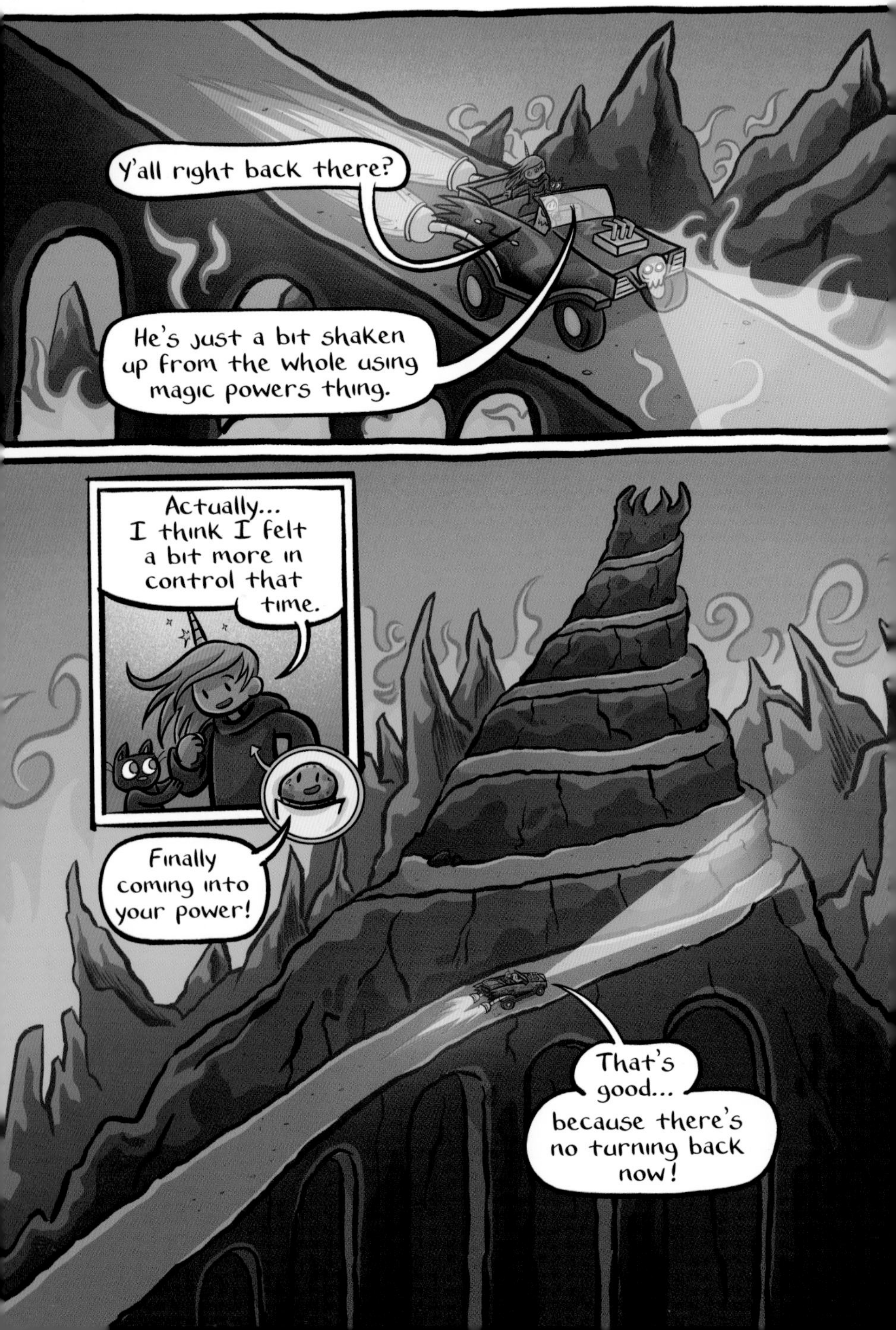
Y'all right back there?
He's just a bit shaken up from the whole using magic powers thing.
Actually... I think I felt a bit more in control that time.
Finally coming into your power!
That's good... because there's no turning back now!

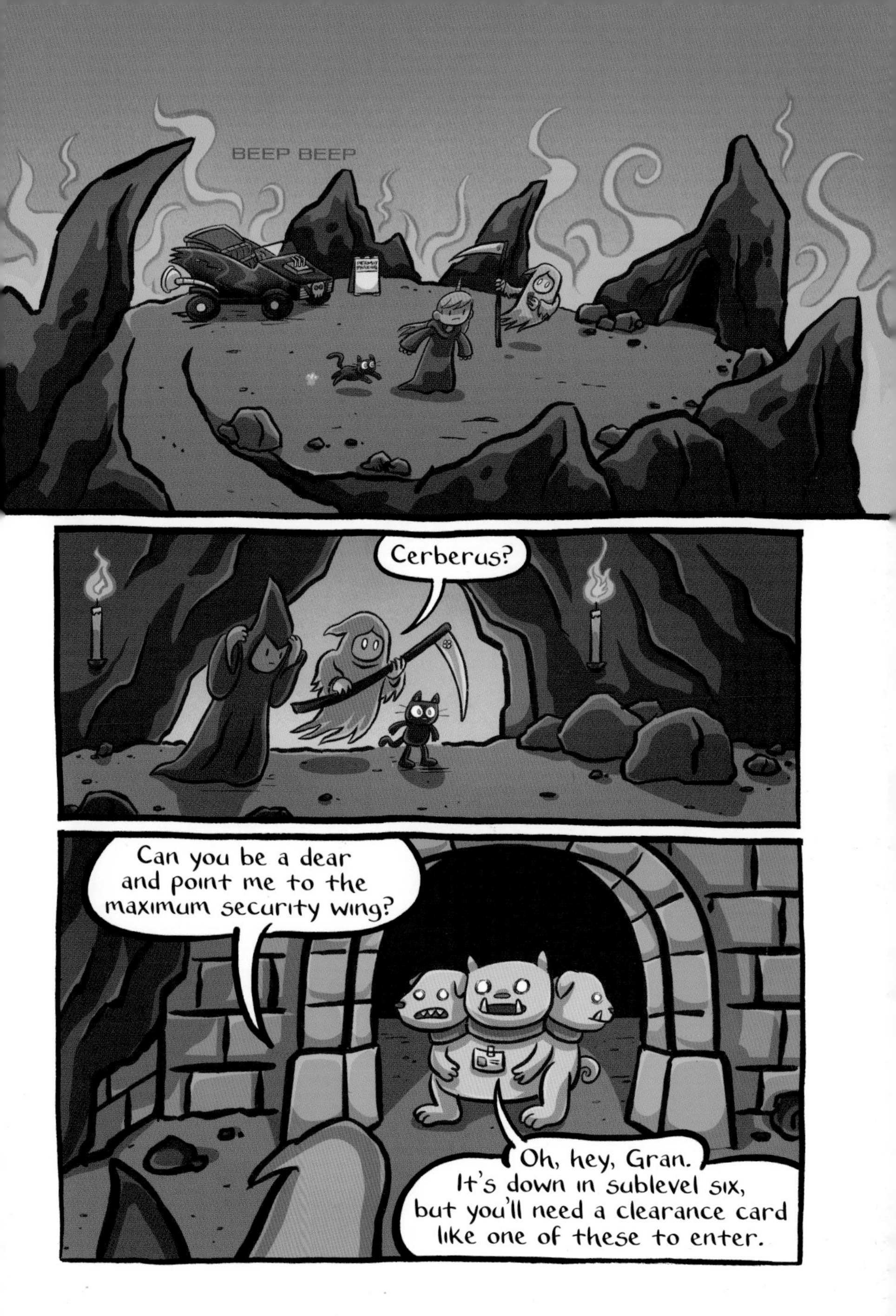
BEEP BEEP
Cerberus?
Can you be a dear and point me to the maximum security wing?
Oh, hey, Gran. It's down in sublevel six, but you'll need a clearance card like one of these to enter.

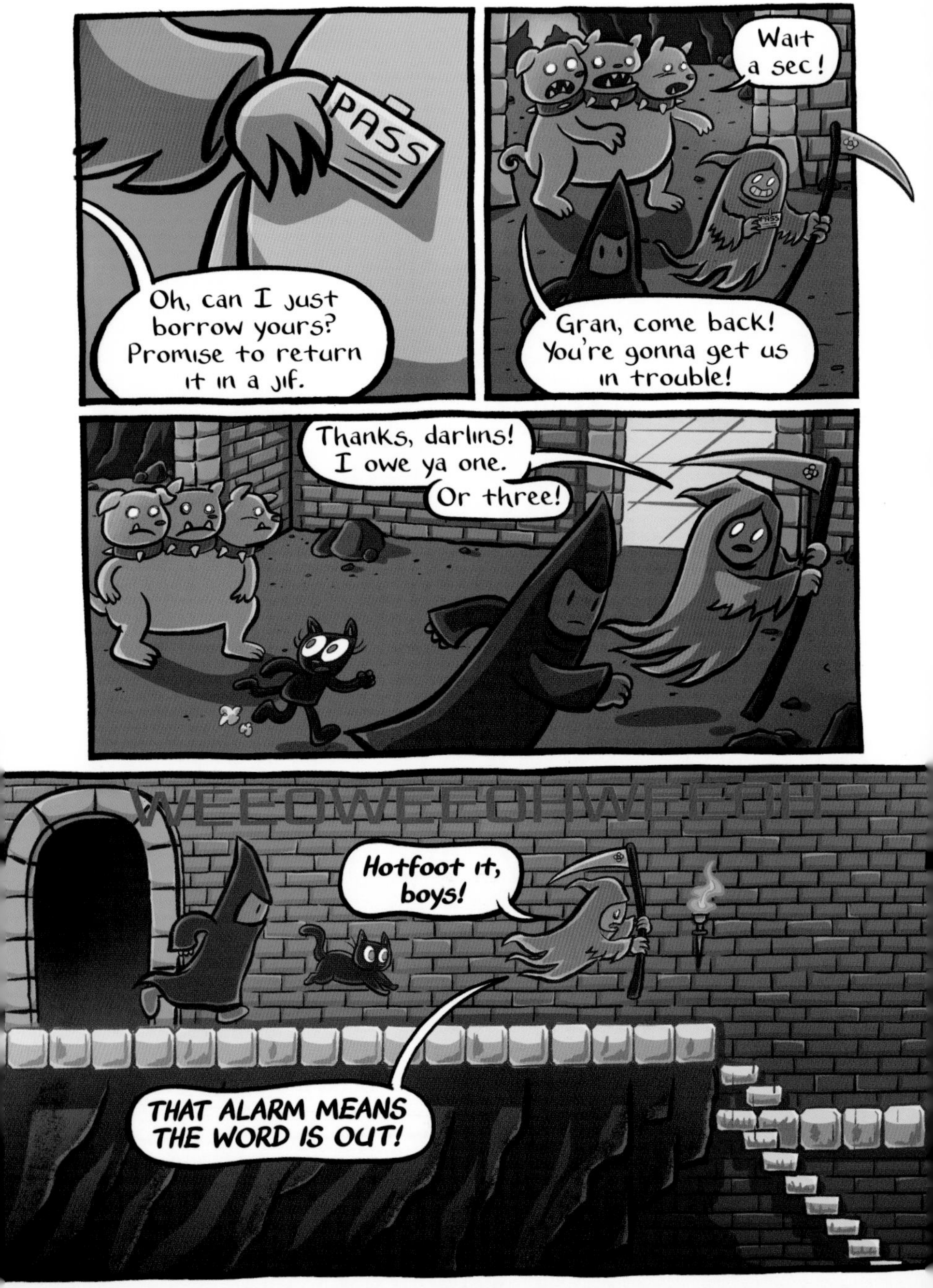
Oh, can I just borrow yours? Promise to return it in a jif.
PASS
Wait a sec!
Gran, come back! You're gonna get us in trouble!
Thanks, darlins! I owe ya one.
Or three!
WEEOWEEOHWEEOH
Hotfoot it, boys!
THAT ALARM MEANS THE WORD IS OUT!

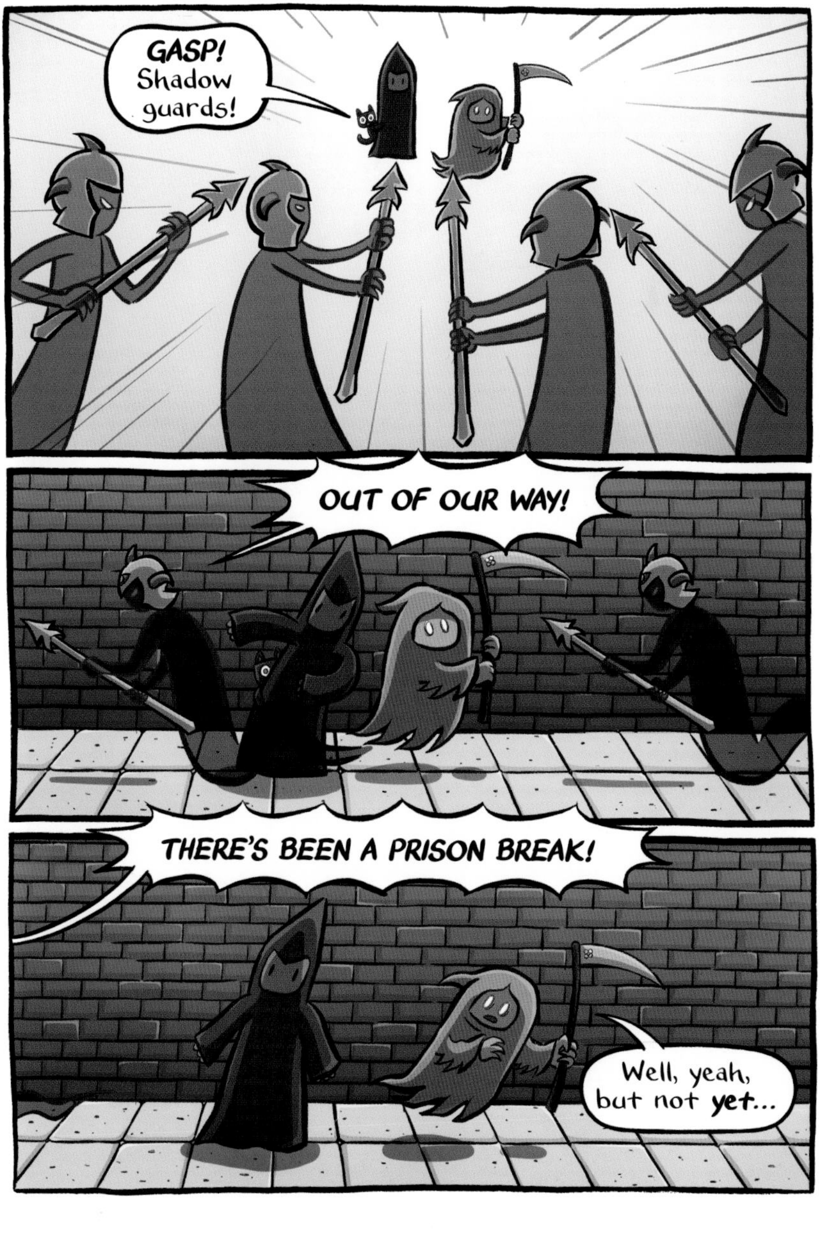
GASP! Shadow guards!
OUT OF OUR WAY!
THERE'S BEEN A PRISON BREAK!
Well, yeah, but not yet...

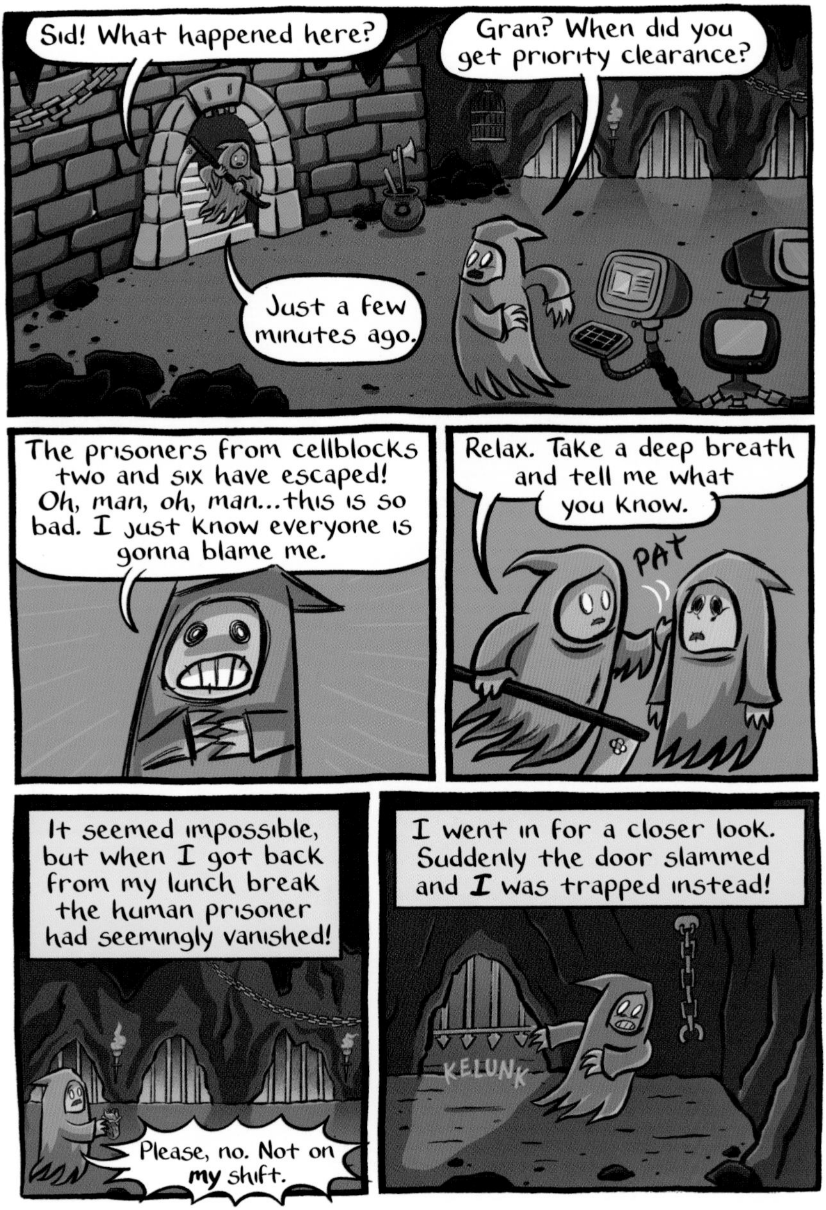
Sid! What happened here?
Gran? When did you get priority clearance?
Just a few minutes ago.
The prisoners from cellblocks two and six have escaped! Oh, man, oh, man...this is so bad. I just know everyone is gonna blame me.
Relax. Take a deep breath and tell me what you know.
PAT
It seemed impossible, but when I got back from my lunch break the human prisoner had seemingly vanished!
Please, no. Not on **my** shift.
I went in for a closer look. Suddenly the door slammed and I was trapped instead!
KELUNK

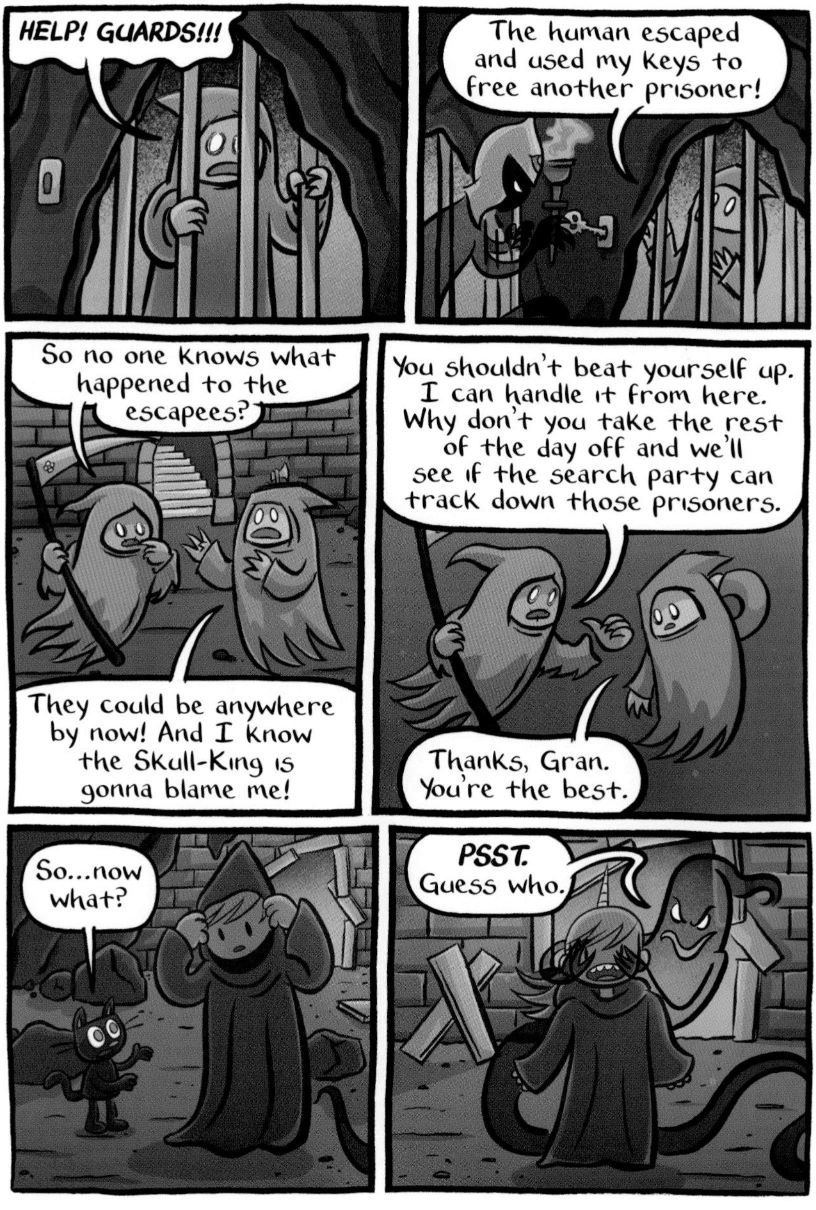
HELP! GUARDS!!!
The human escaped and used my keys to free another prisoner!
So no one knows what happened to the escapees?
They could be anywhere by now! And I know the Skull-King is gonna blame me!
You shouldn't beat yourself up. I can handle it from here. Why don't you take the rest of the day off and we'll see if the search party can track down those prisoners.
Thanks, Gran. You're the best.
So...now what?
PSST.
Guess who.

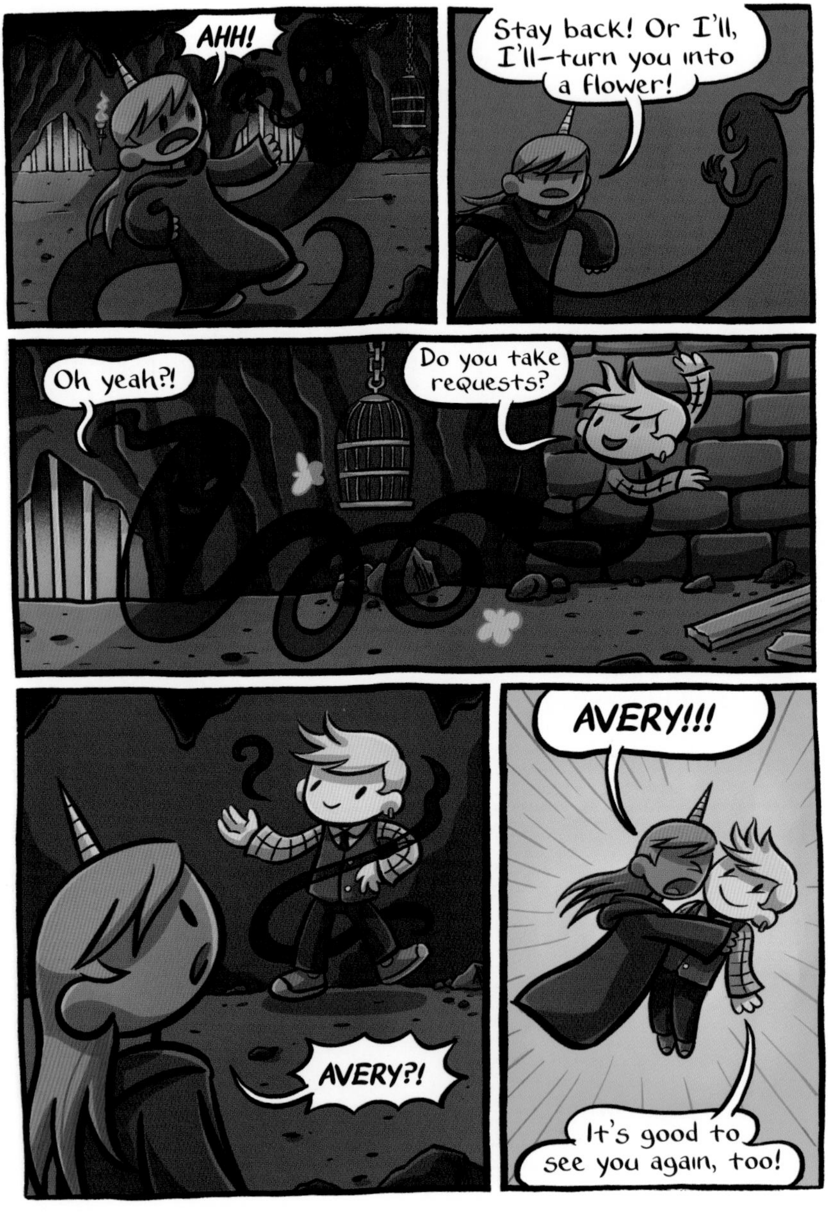
AHH!
Stay back! Or I'll, I'll—turn you into a flower!
Oh yeah?!
Do you take requests?
AVERY?!
AVERY!!!
It's good to see you again, too!

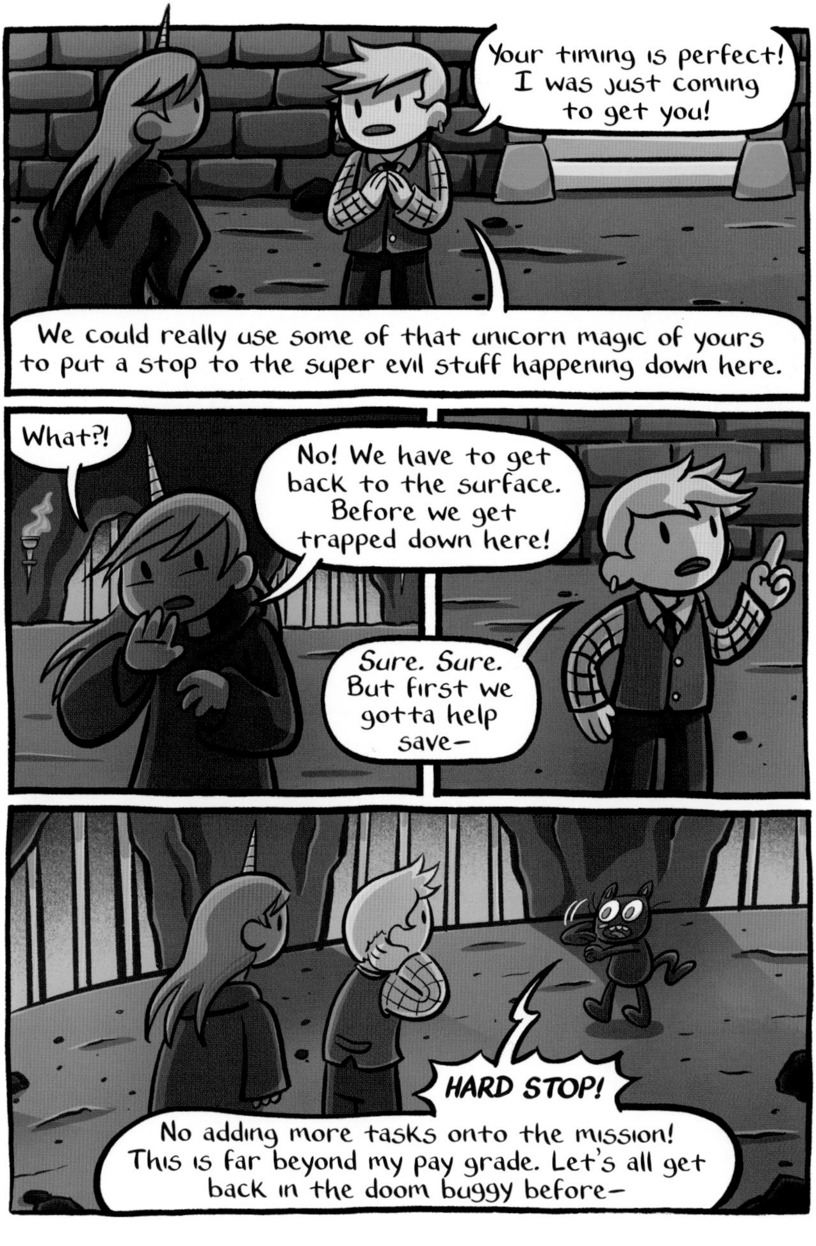
Your timing is perfect! I was just coming to get you!
We could really use some of that unicorn magic of yours to put a stop to the super evil stuff happening down here.
What?!
No! We have to get back to the surface. Before we get trapped down here!
Sure. Sure. But first we gotta help save—
HARD STOP!
No adding more tasks onto the mission! This is far beyond my pay grade. Let's all get back in the doom buggy before—

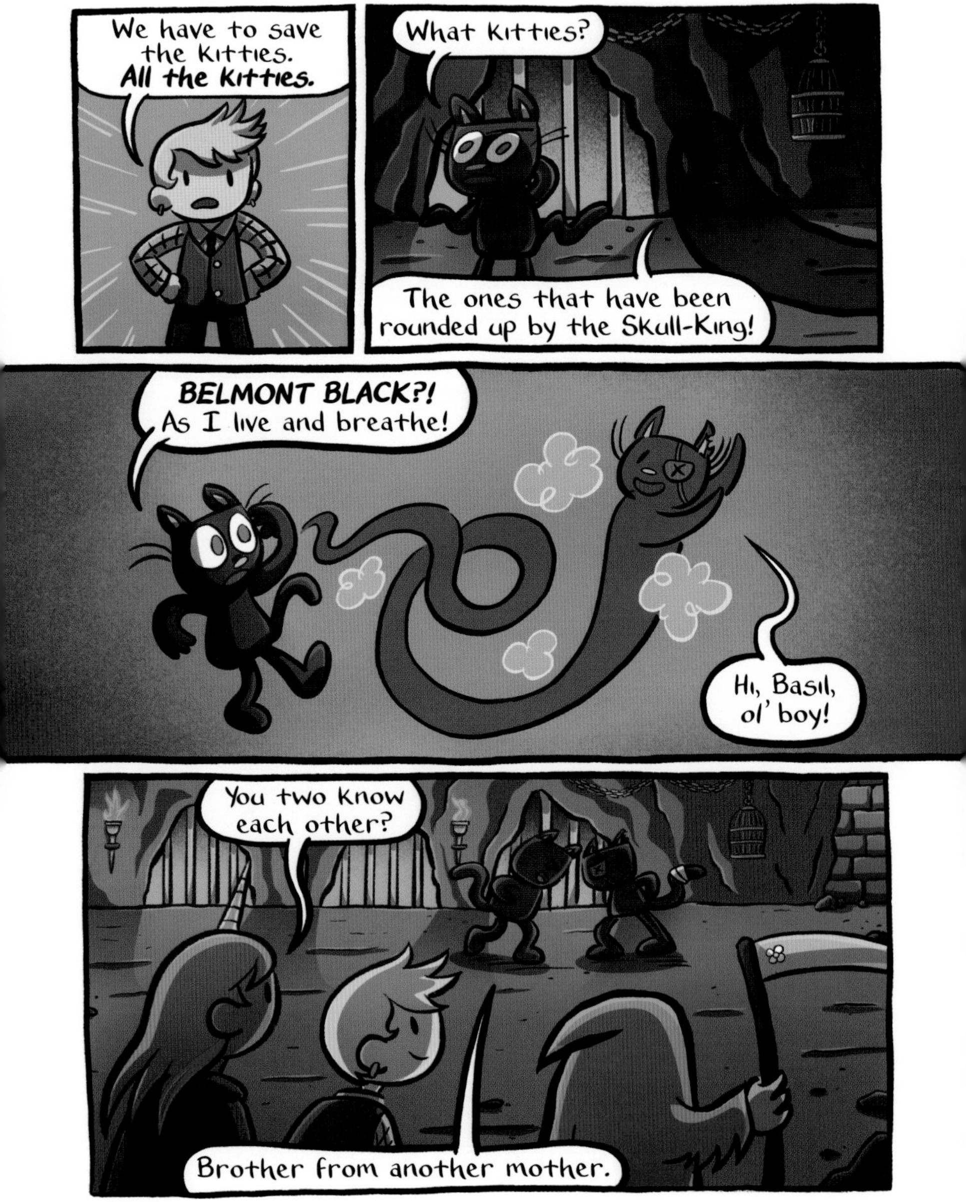
We have to save the kitties. **All the kitties.**
What kitties?
The ones that have been rounded up by the Skull-King!
BELMONT BLACK?! As I live and breathe!
Hi, Basil, ol' boy!
You two know each other?
Brother from another mother.

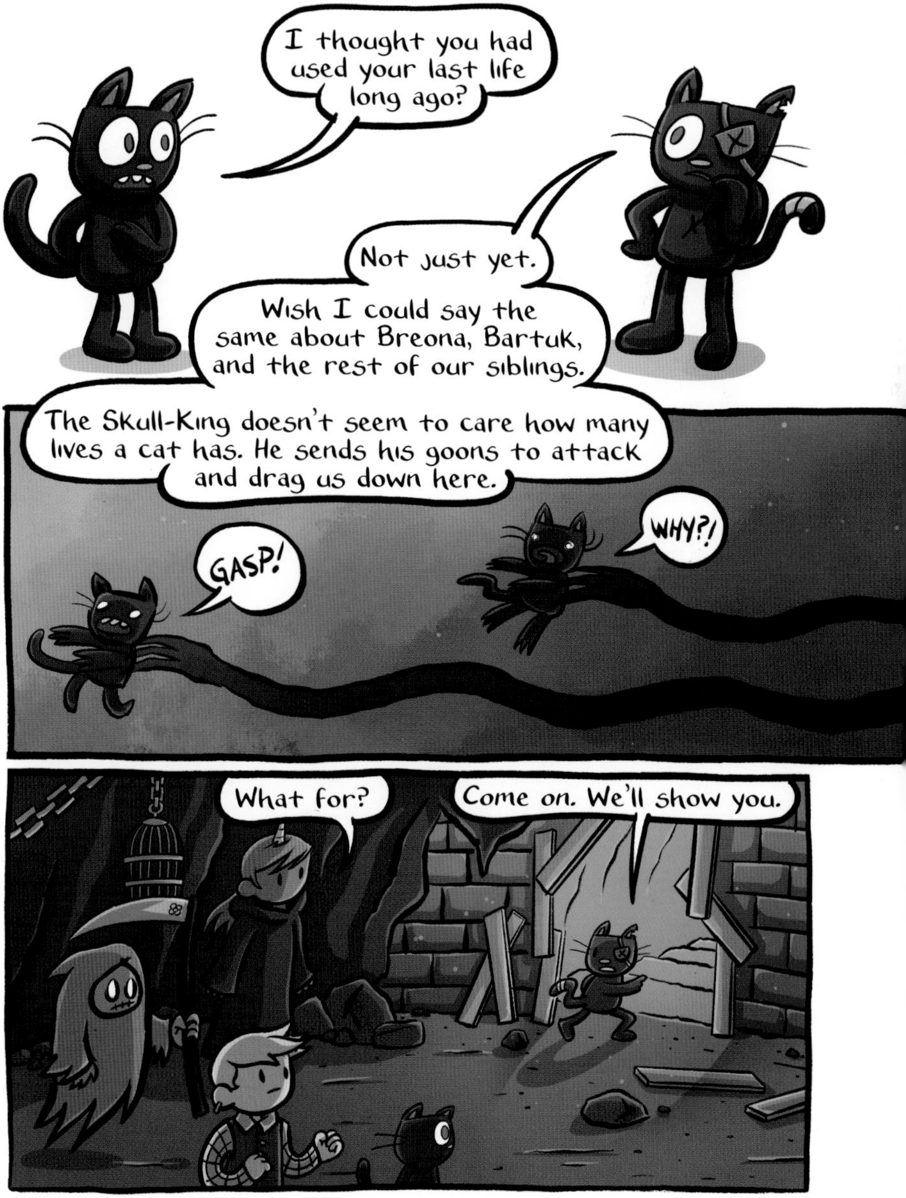
I thought you had used your last life long ago?
Not just yet.
Wish I could say the same about Breona, Bartuk, and the rest of our siblings.
The Skull-King doesn't seem to care how many lives a cat has. He sends his goons to attack and drag us down here.
GASP!
WHY?!
What for?
Come on. We'll show you.

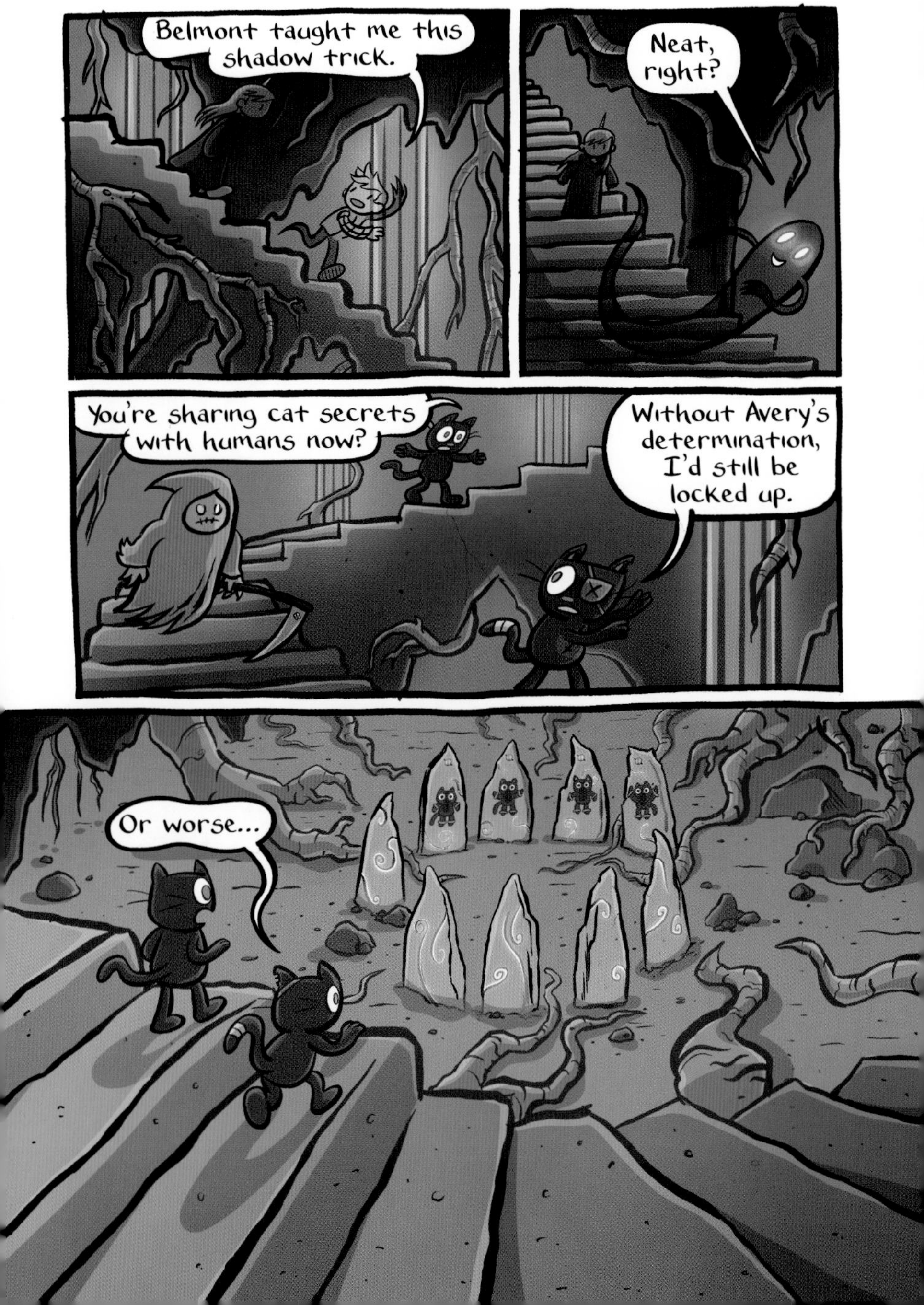
Belmont taught me this shadow trick.
Neat, right?
You're sharing cat secrets with humans now?
Without Avery's determination, I'd still be locked up.
Or worse...

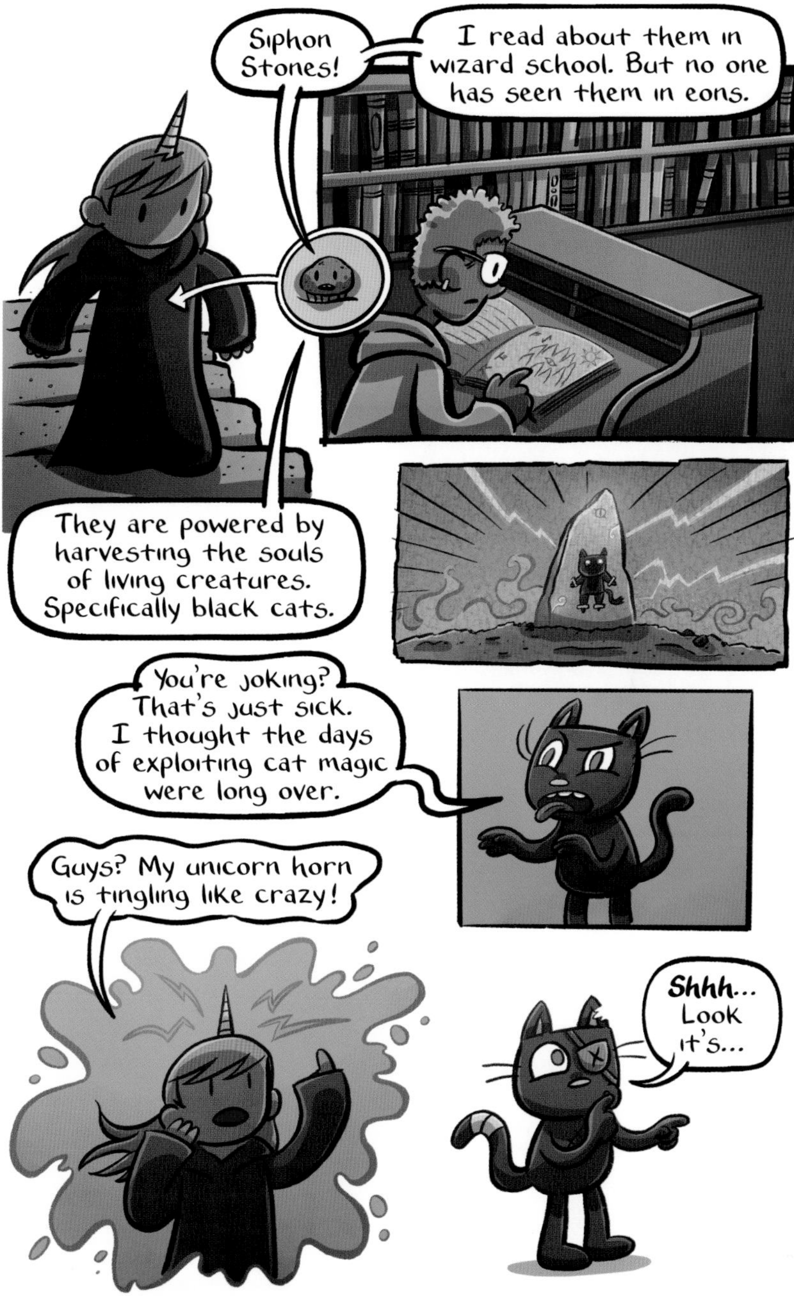
Siphon Stones!
I read about them in wizard school. But no one has seen them in eons.
They are powered by harvesting the souls of living creatures. Specifically black cats.
You're joking? That's just sick. I thought the days of exploiting cat magic were long over.
Guys? My unicorn horn is tingling like crazy!
Shhh... Look it's...

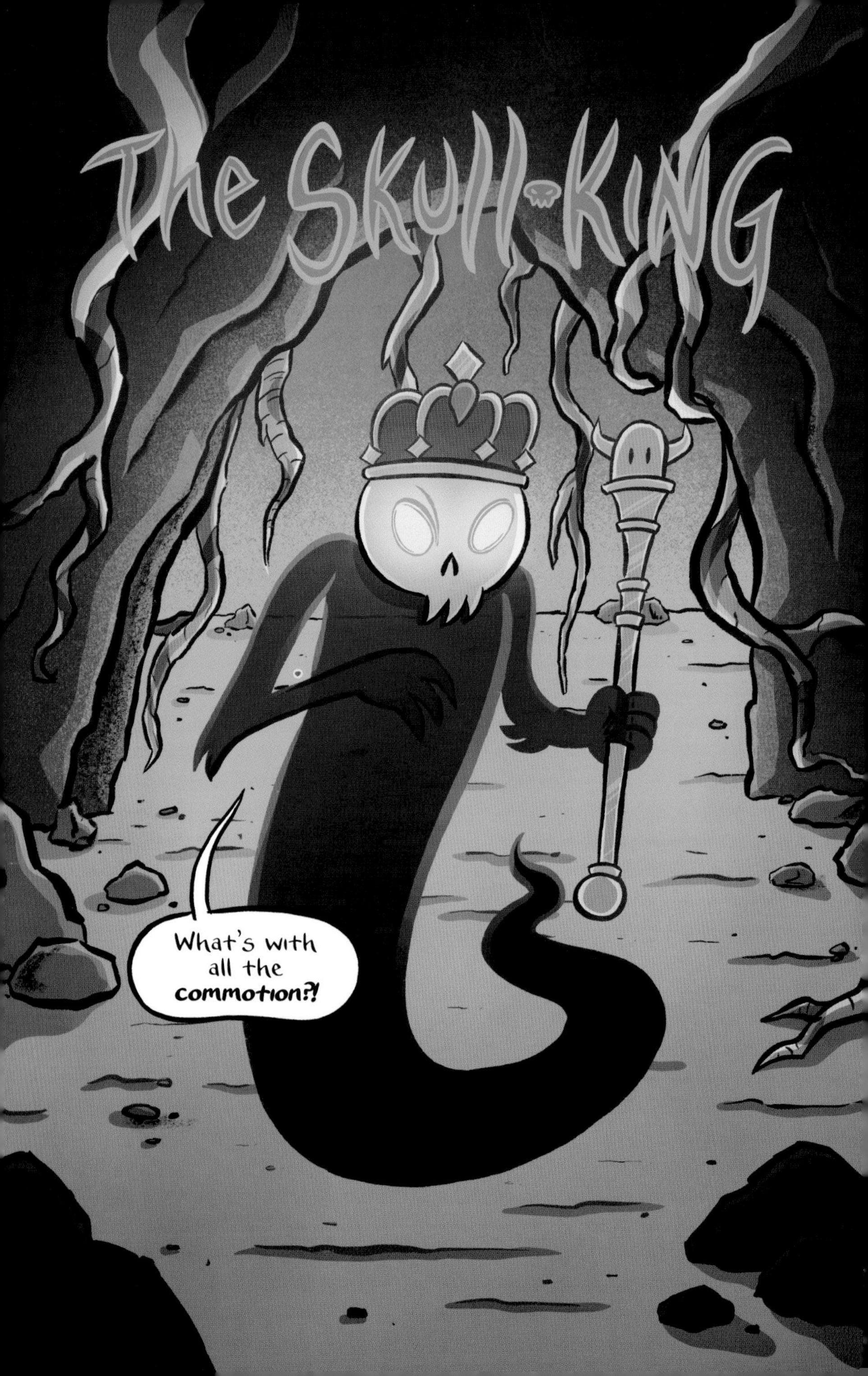
The Skull-King
What's with all the commotion?!

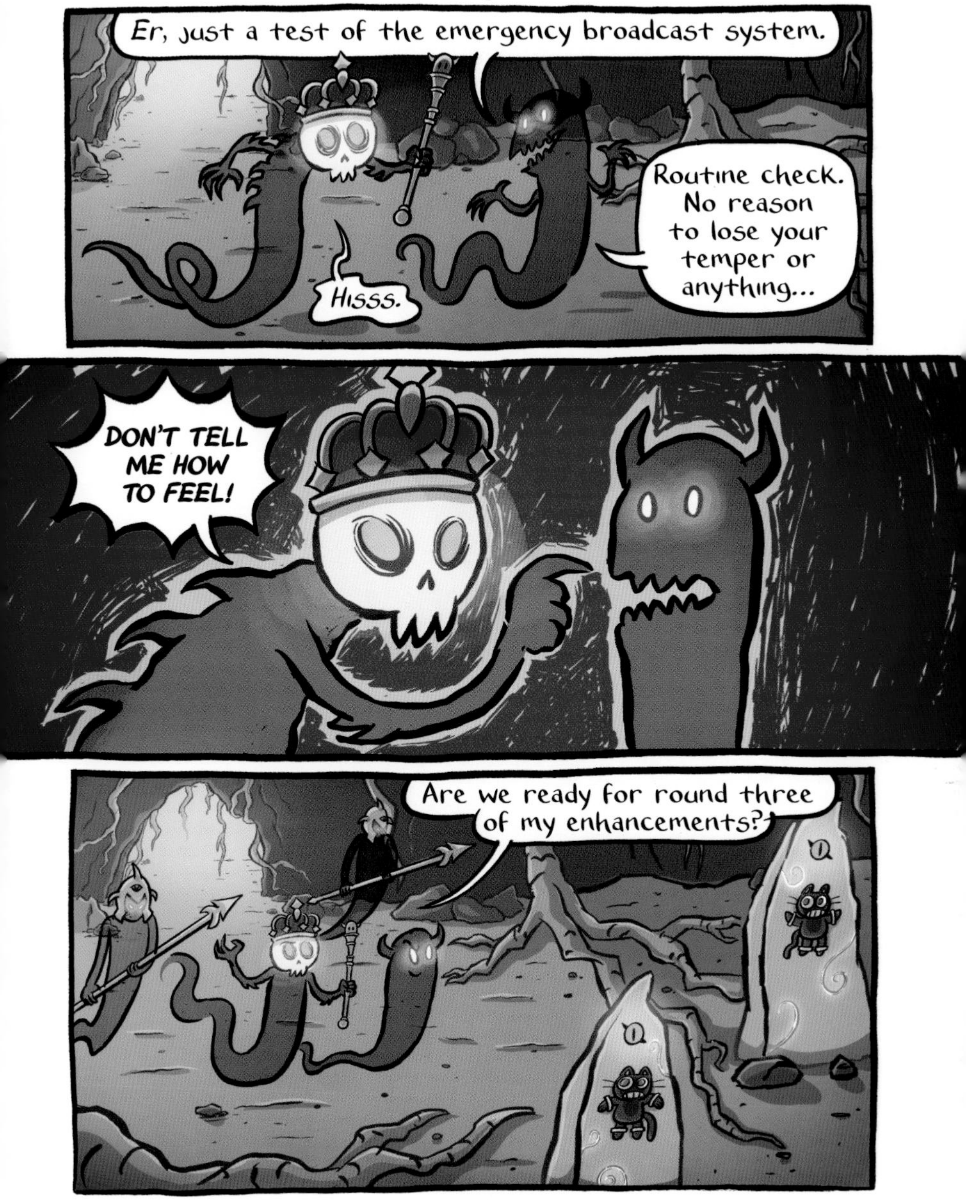
Er, just a test of the emergency broadcast system.
Hisss.
Routine check. No reason to lose your temper or anything...
DON'T TELL ME HOW TO FEEL!
Are we ready for round three of my enhancements?

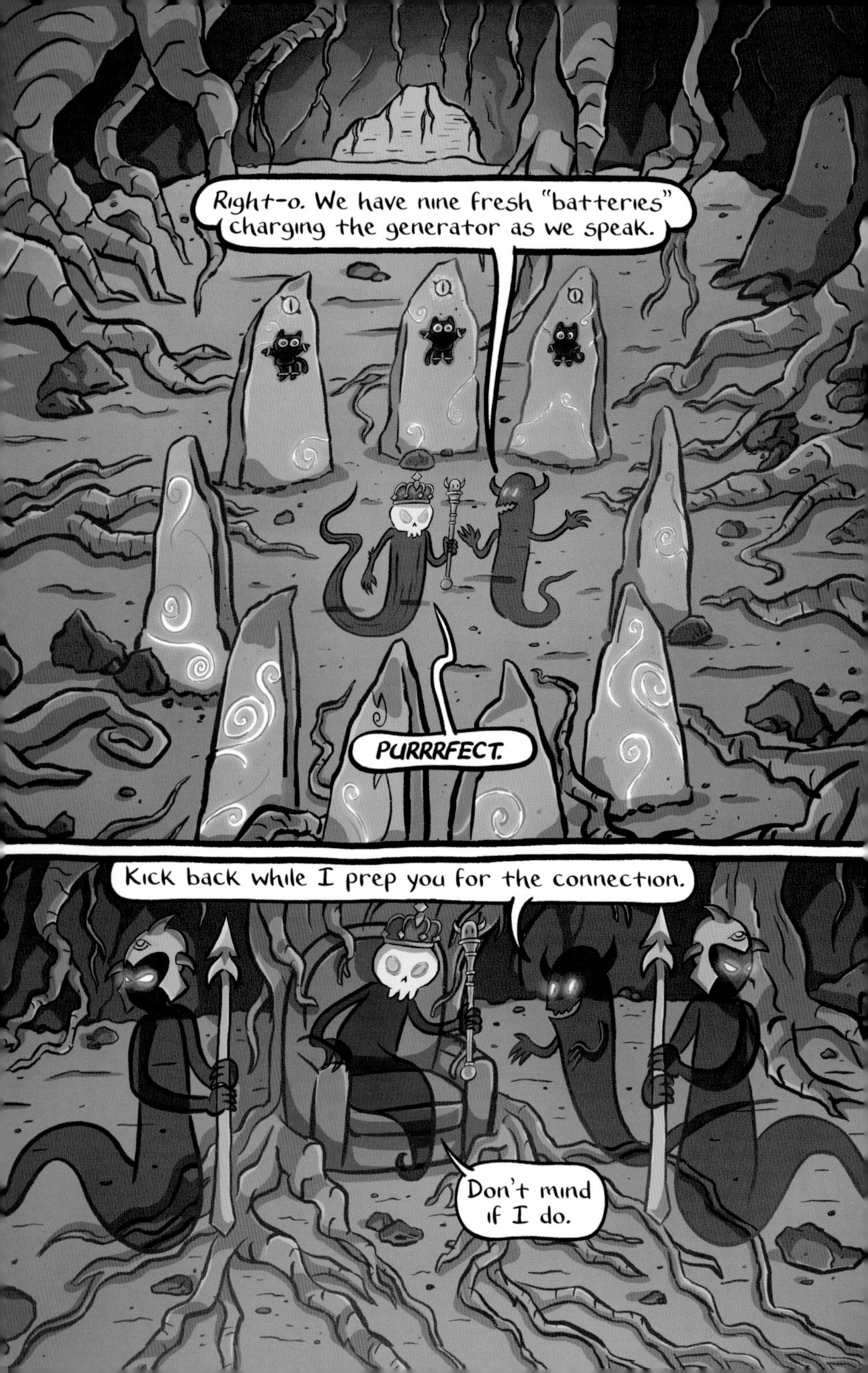
Right-o. We have nine fresh "batteries" charging the generator as we speak.
PURRRFECT.
Kick back while I prep you for the connection.
Don't mind if I do.

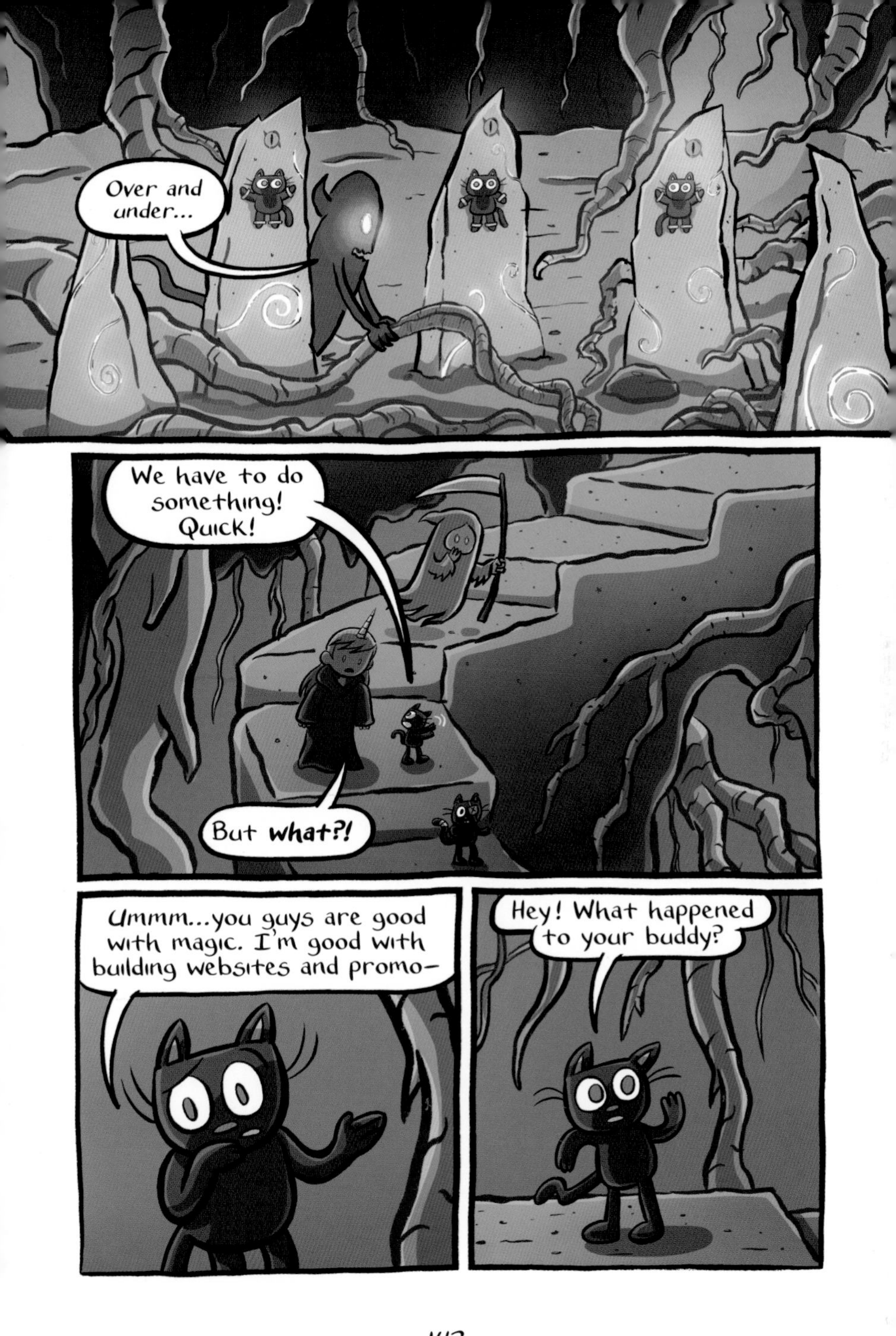
Over and under...
We have to do something! Quick!
But **what?!**
Ummm...you guys are good with magic. I'm good with building websites and promo—
Hey! What happened to your buddy?

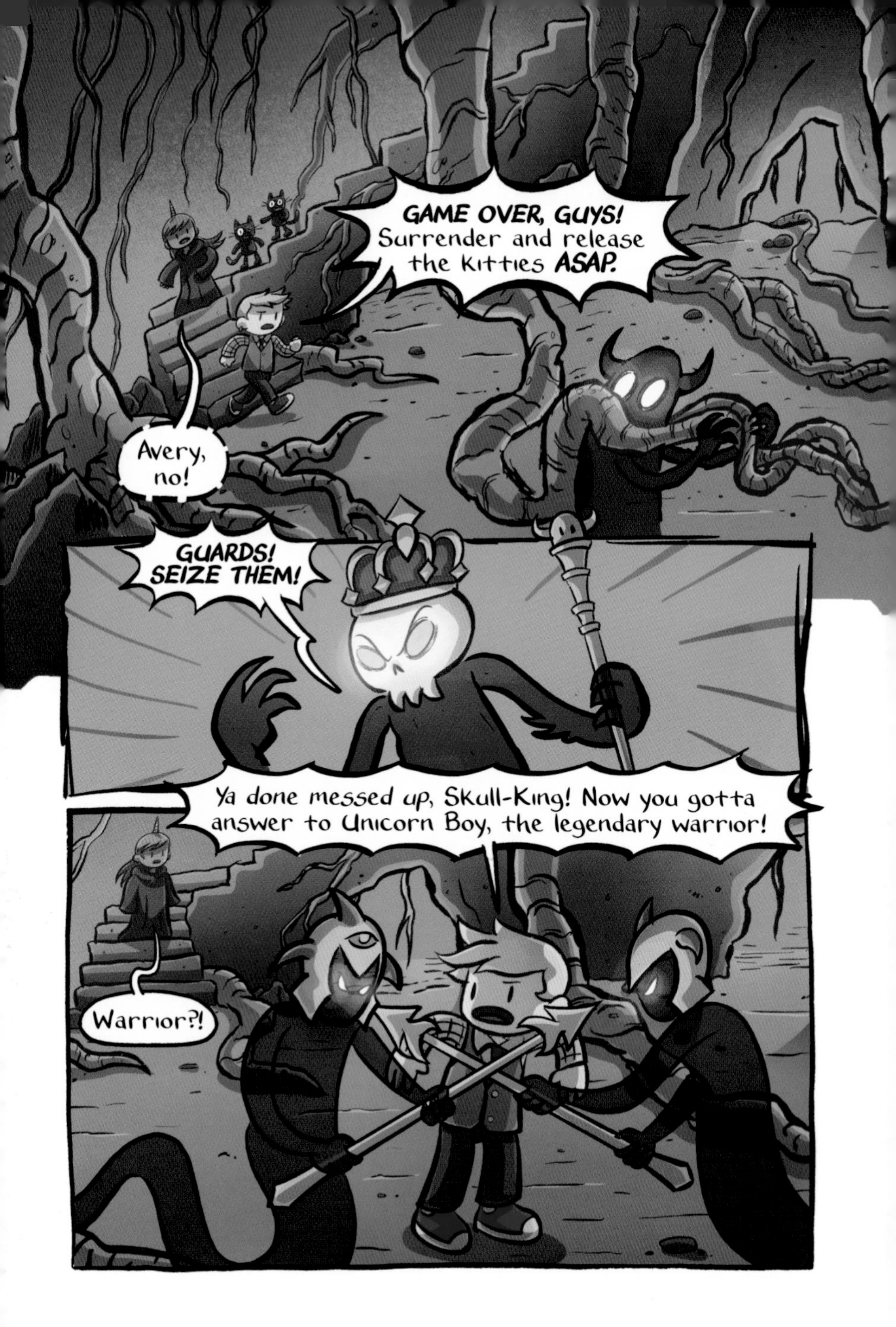
GAME OVER, GUYS! Surrender and release the kitties ASAP.
Avery, no!
GUARDS! SEIZE THEM!
Ya done messed up, Skull-King! Now you gotta answer to Unicorn Boy, the legendary warrior!
Warrior?!

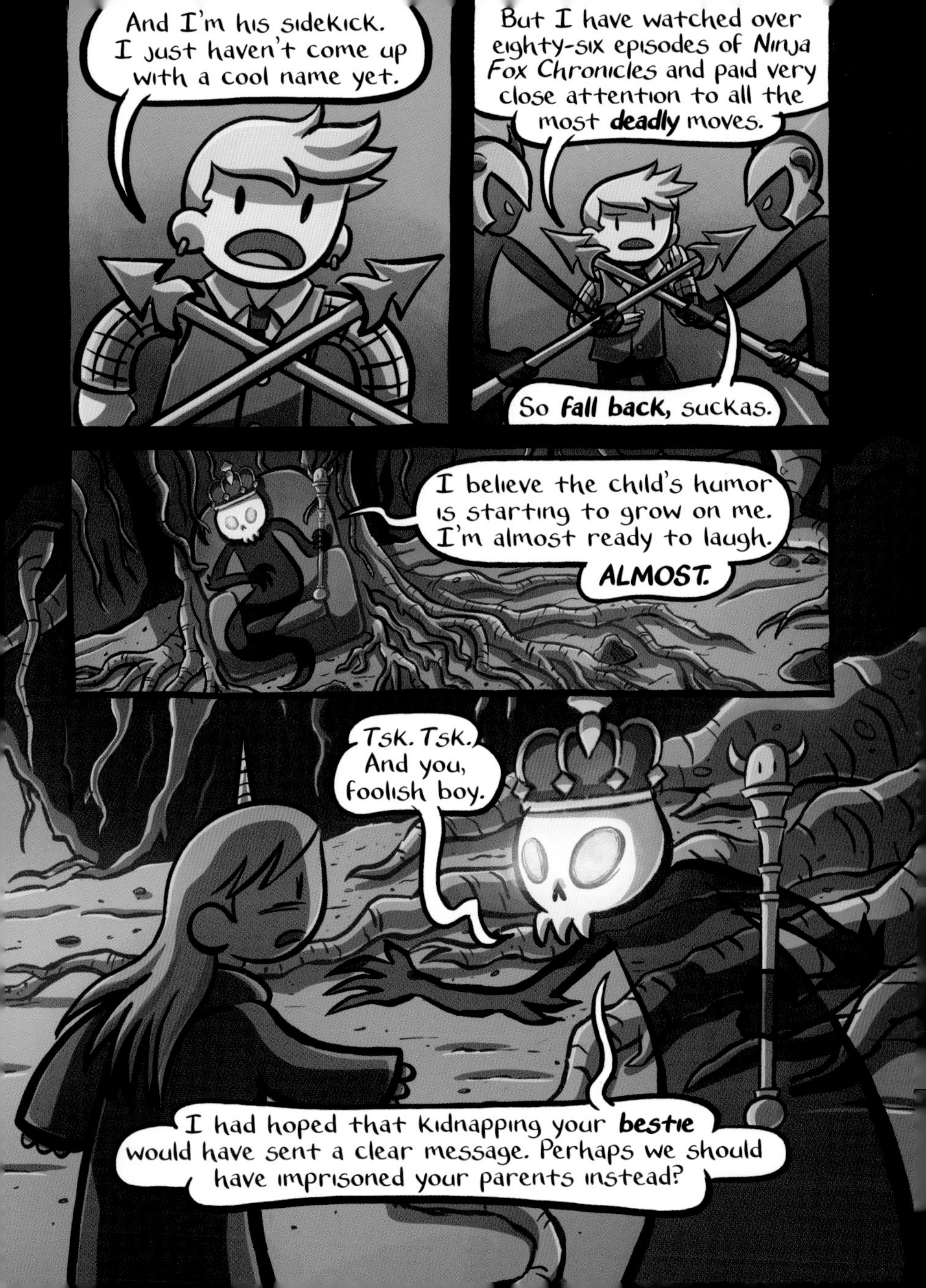
And I'm his sidekick. I just haven't come up with a cool name yet.
But I have watched over eighty-six episodes of *Ninja Fox Chronicles* and paid very close attention to all the most **deadly** moves.
So **fall back,** suckas.
I believe the child's humor is starting to grow on me. I'm almost ready to laugh.
ALMOST.
Tsk. Tsk. And you, foolish boy.
I had hoped that kidnapping your **bestie** would have sent a clear message. Perhaps we should have imprisoned your parents instead?

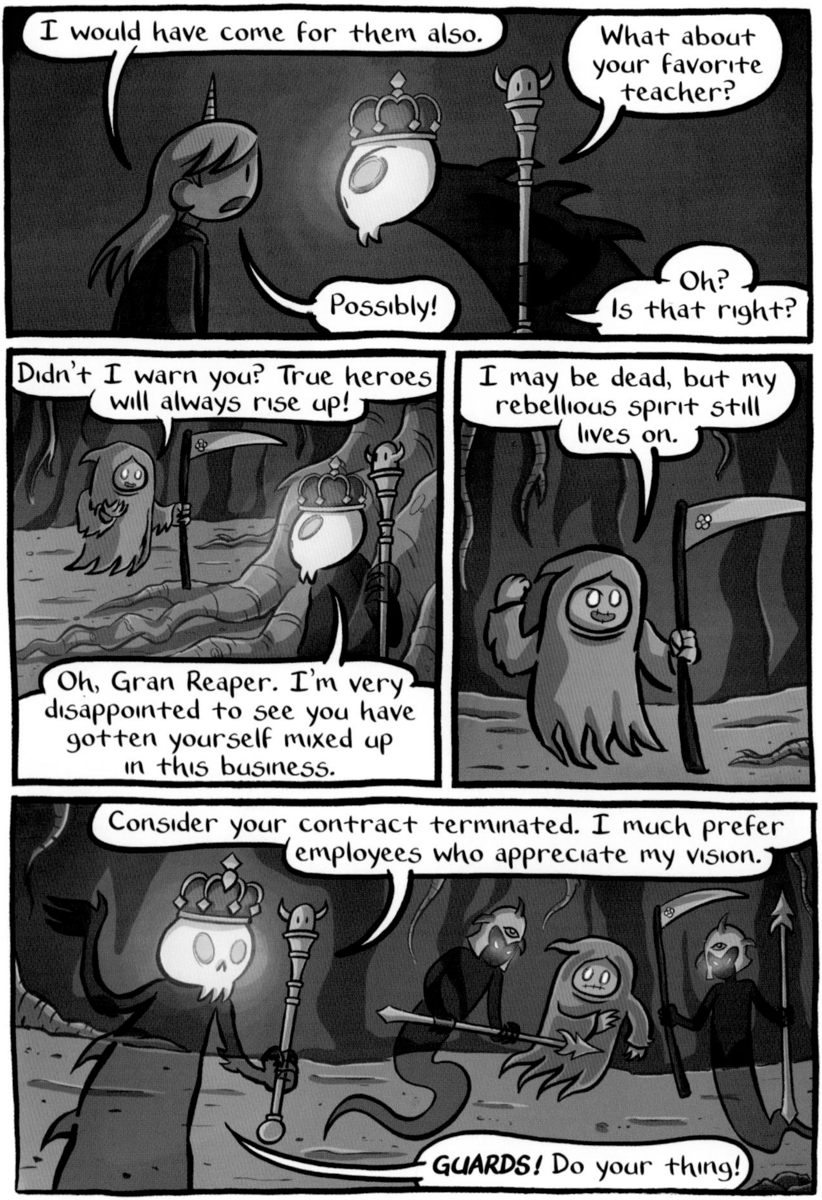
I would have come for them also.
What about your favorite teacher?
Possibly!
Oh? Is that right?
Didn't I warn you? True heroes will always rise up!
Oh, Gran Reaper. I'm very disappointed to see you have gotten yourself mixed up in this business.
I may be dead, but my rebellious spirit still lives on.
Consider your contract terminated. I much prefer employees who appreciate my vision.
GUARDS! Do your thing!

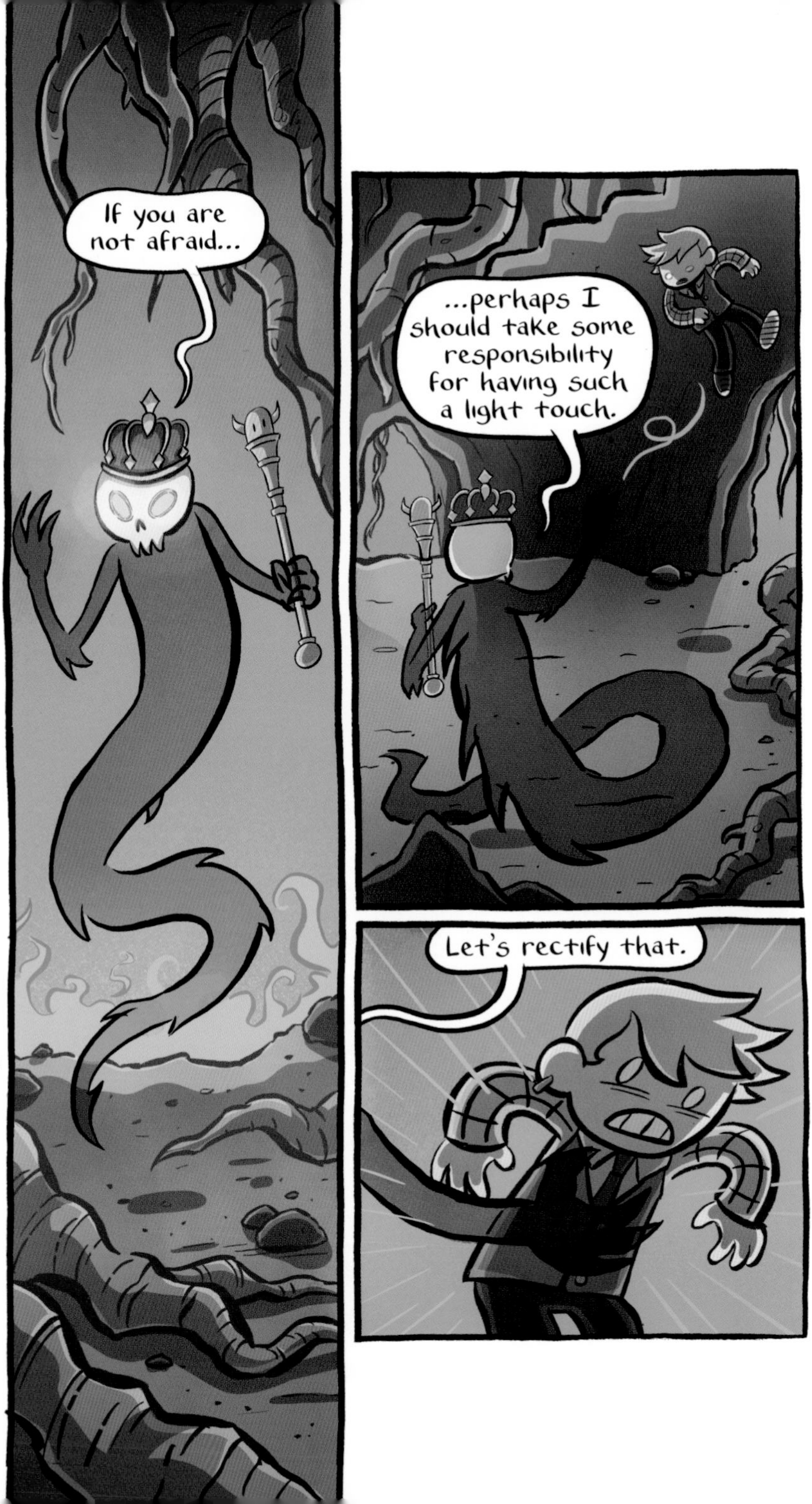
If you are not afraid...
...perhaps I should take some responsibility for having such a light touch.
Let's rectify that.

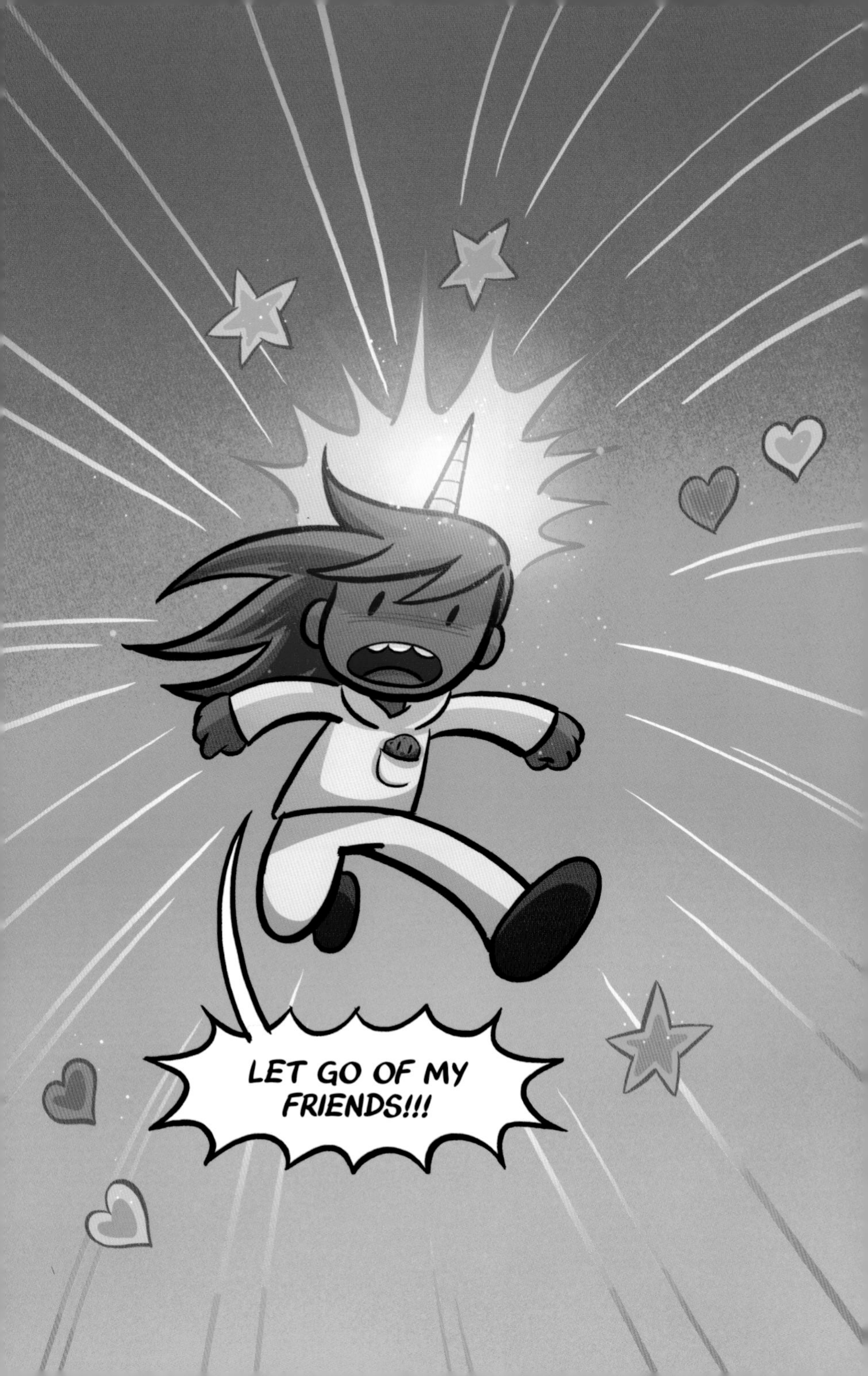
LET GO OF MY FRIENDS!!!

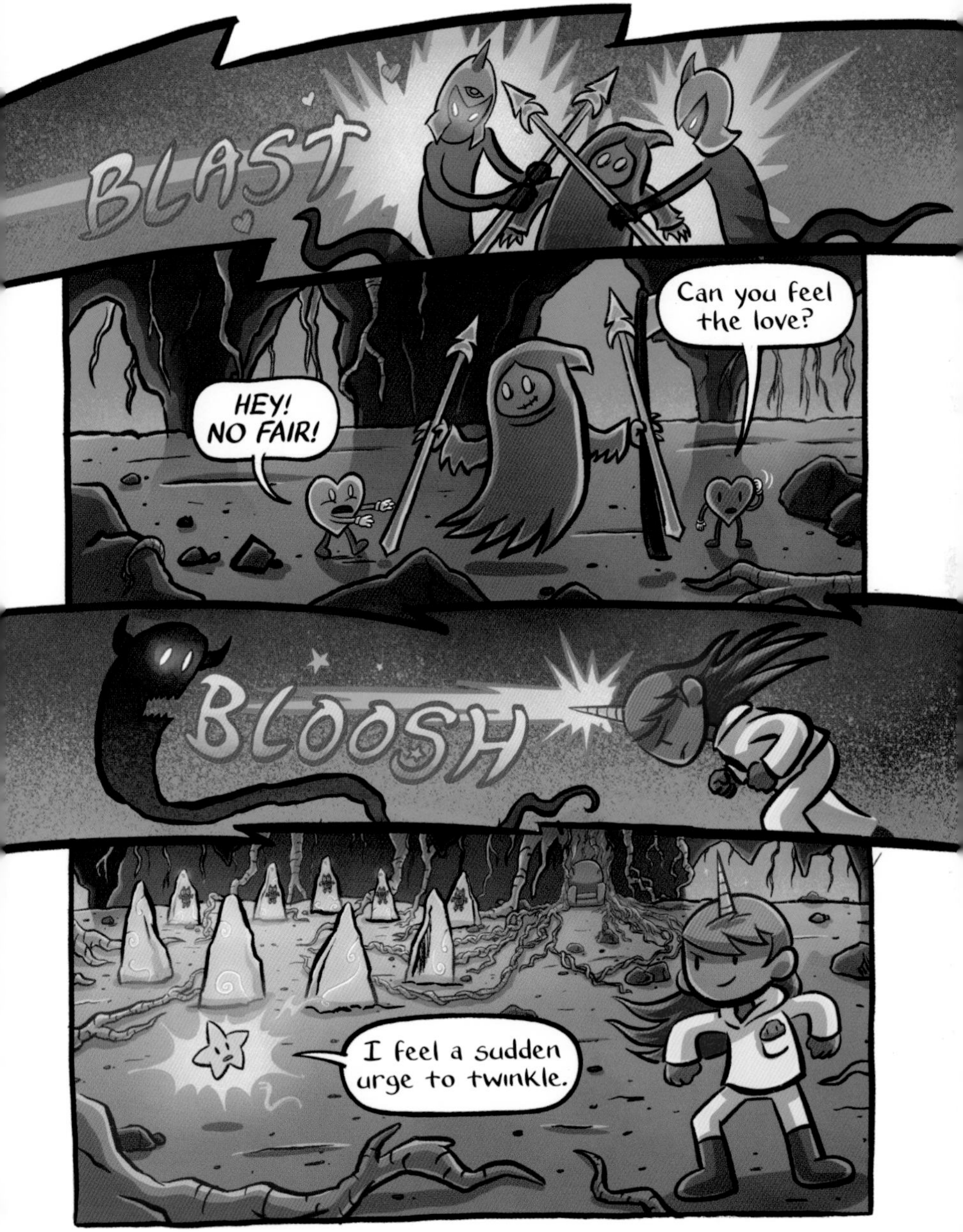
BLAST
HEY! NO FAIR!
Can you feel the love?
BLOOSH
I feel a sudden urge to twinkle.

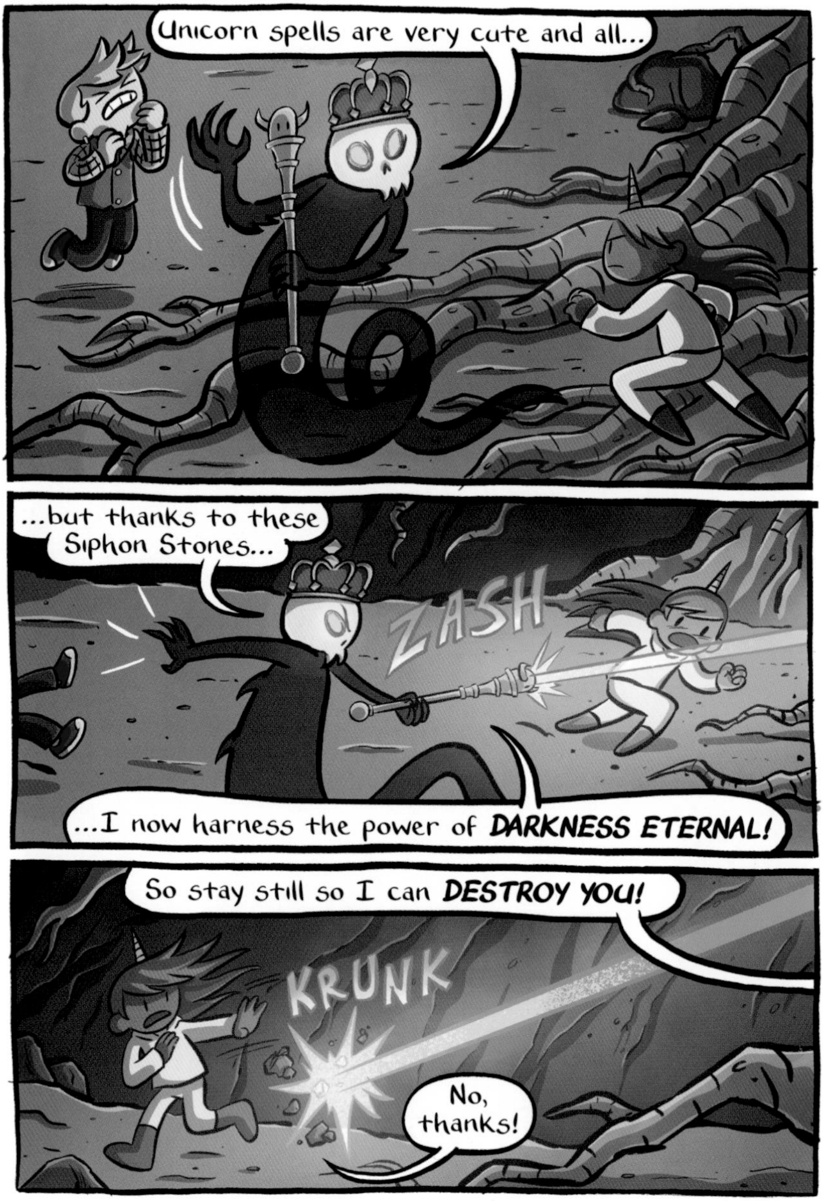
Unicorn spells are very cute and all...
...but thanks to these Siphon Stones...
ZASH
...I now harness the power of DARKNESS ETERNAL!
So stay still so I can DESTROY YOU!
KRUNK
No, thanks!

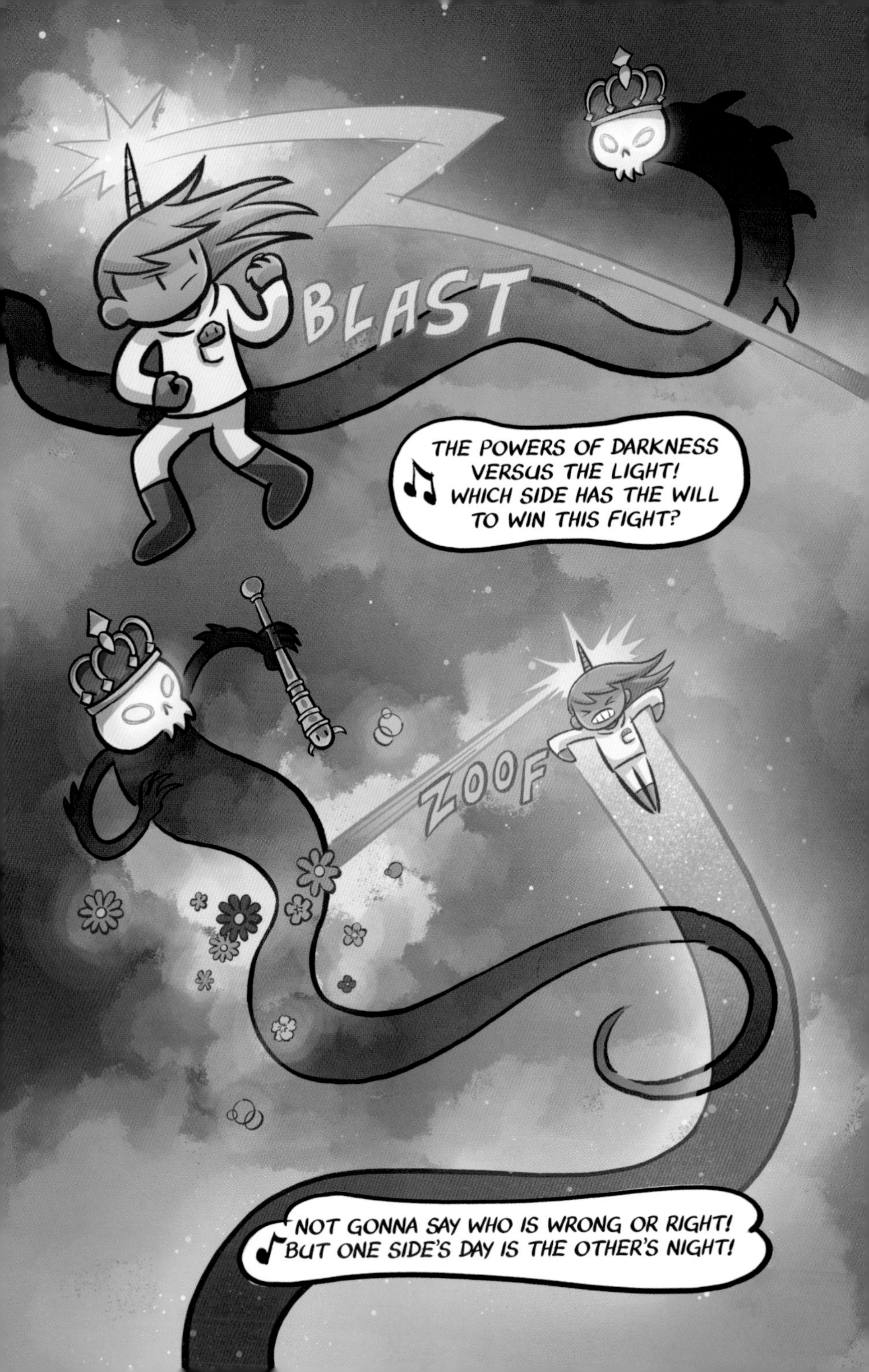
BLAST
THE POWERS OF DARKNESS VERSUS THE LIGHT! WHICH SIDE HAS THE WILL TO WIN THIS FIGHT?
ZOOF
NOT GONNA SAY WHO IS WRONG OR RIGHT! BUT ONE SIDE'S DAY IS THE OTHER'S NIGHT!

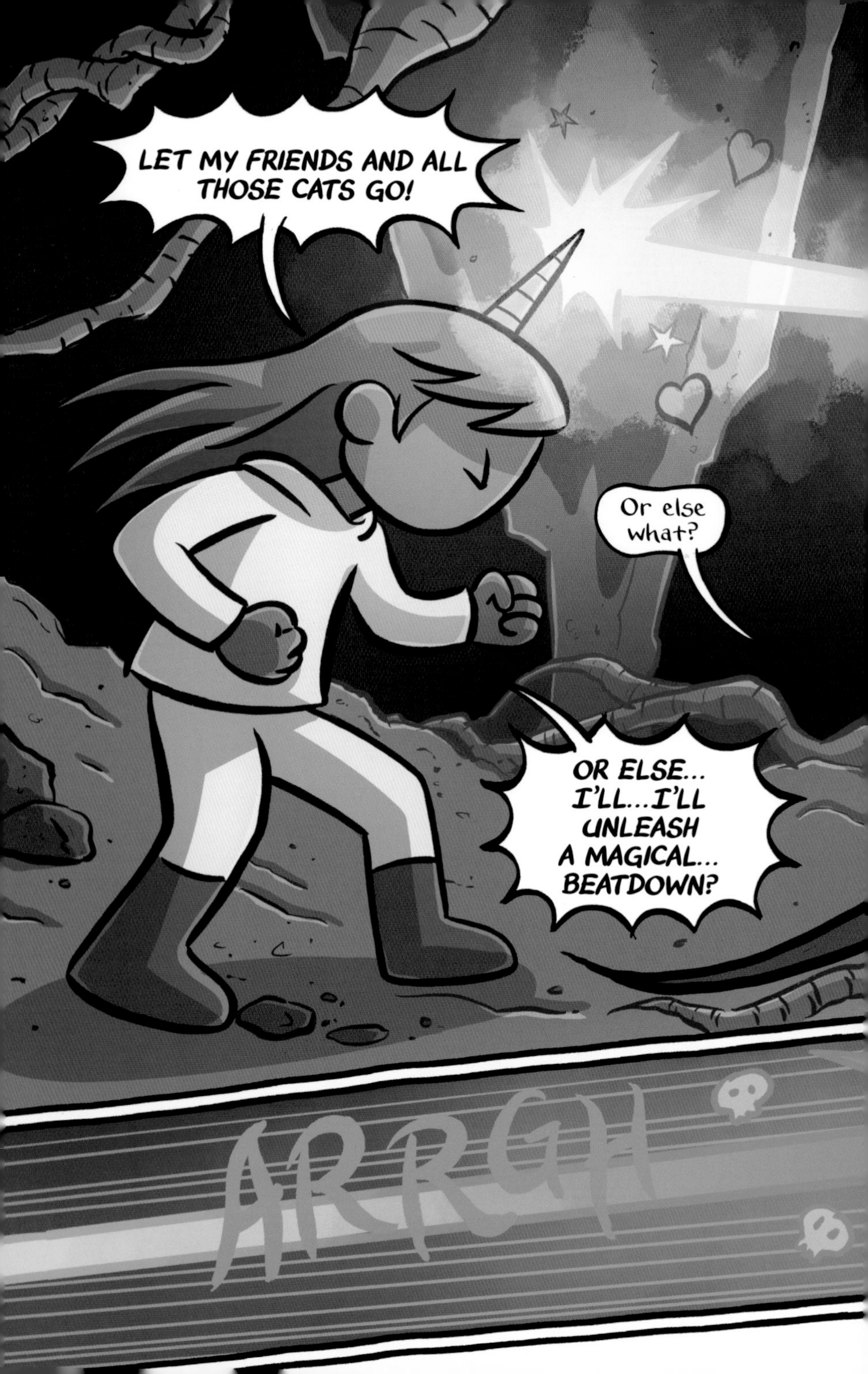
LET MY FRIENDS AND ALL THOSE CATS GO!
Or else what?
OR ELSE... I'LL...I'LL UNLEASH A MAGICAL... BEATDOWN?
ARRGH

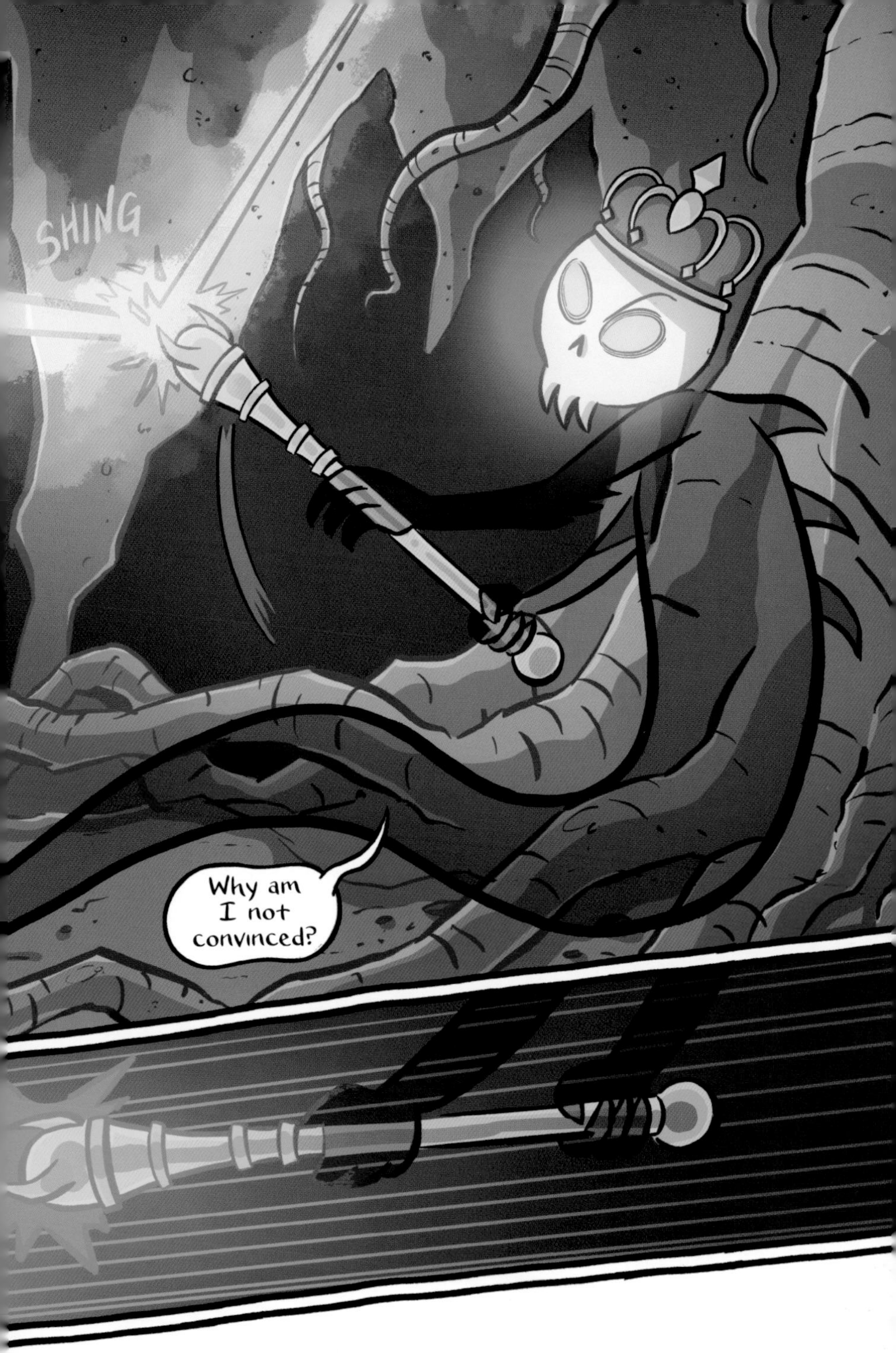
SHING
Why am I not convinced?

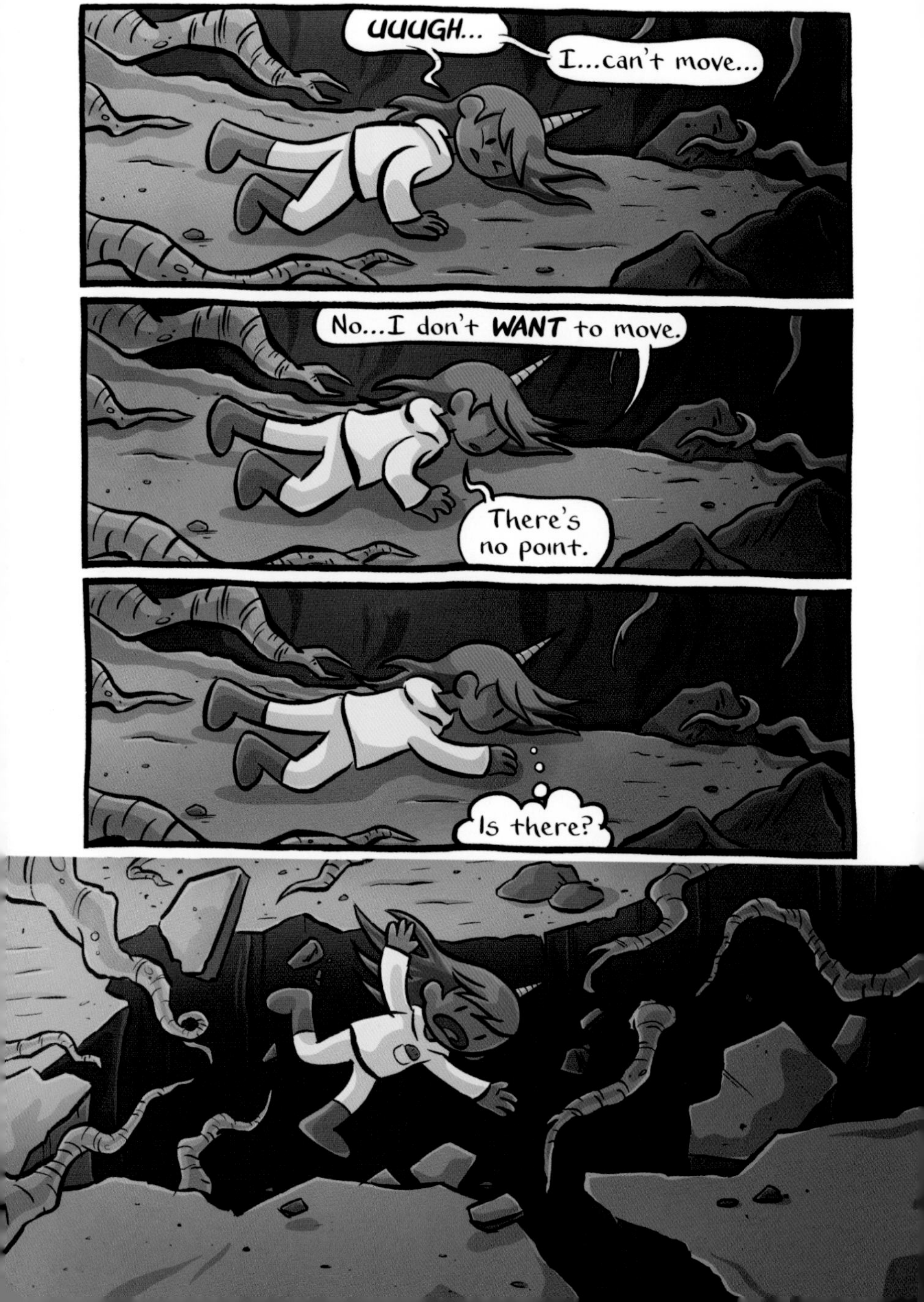
UUUGH...
I...can't move...
No...I don't WANT to move.
There's no point.
Is there?

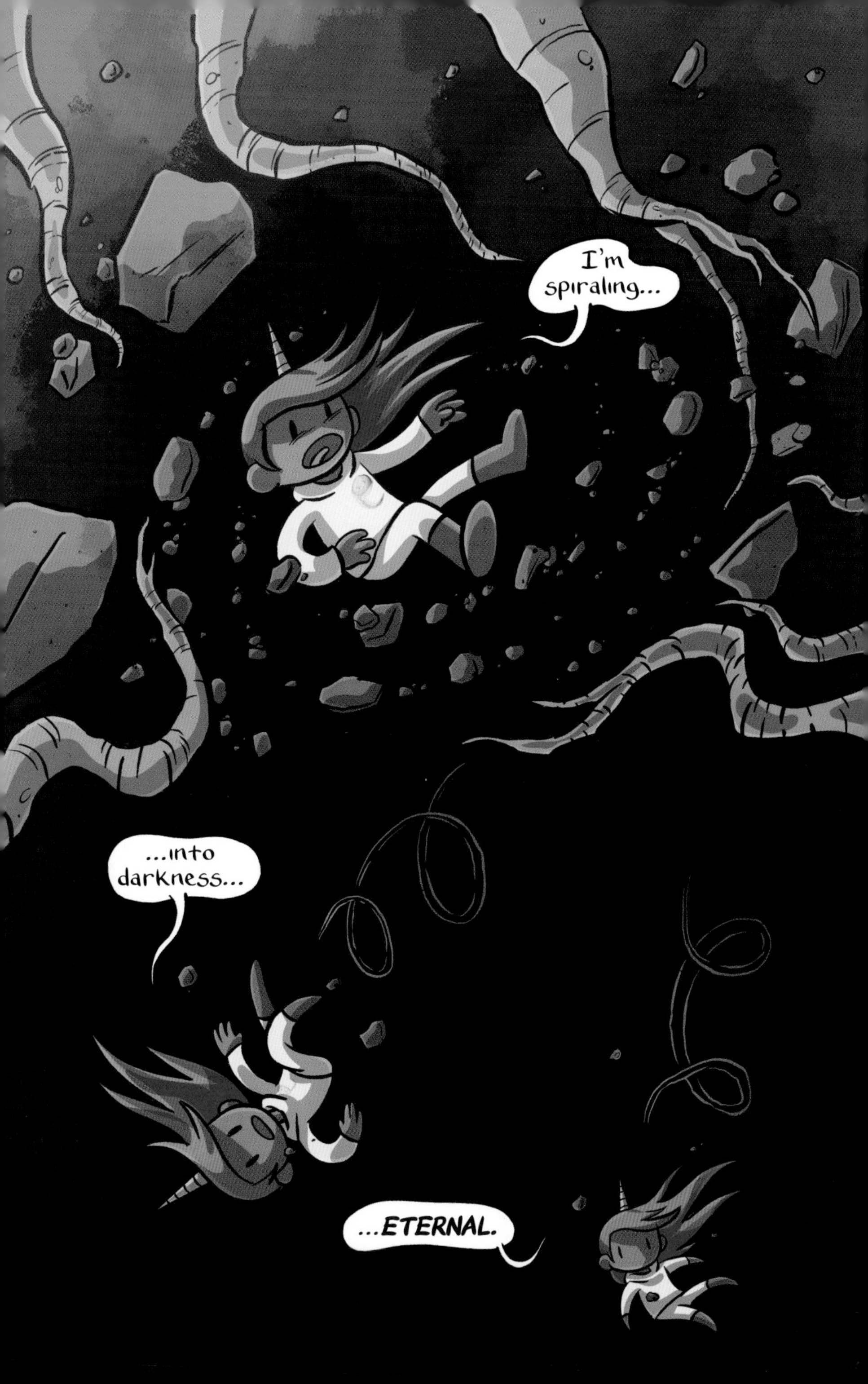
I'm spiraling...
...into darkness...
...ETERNAL.

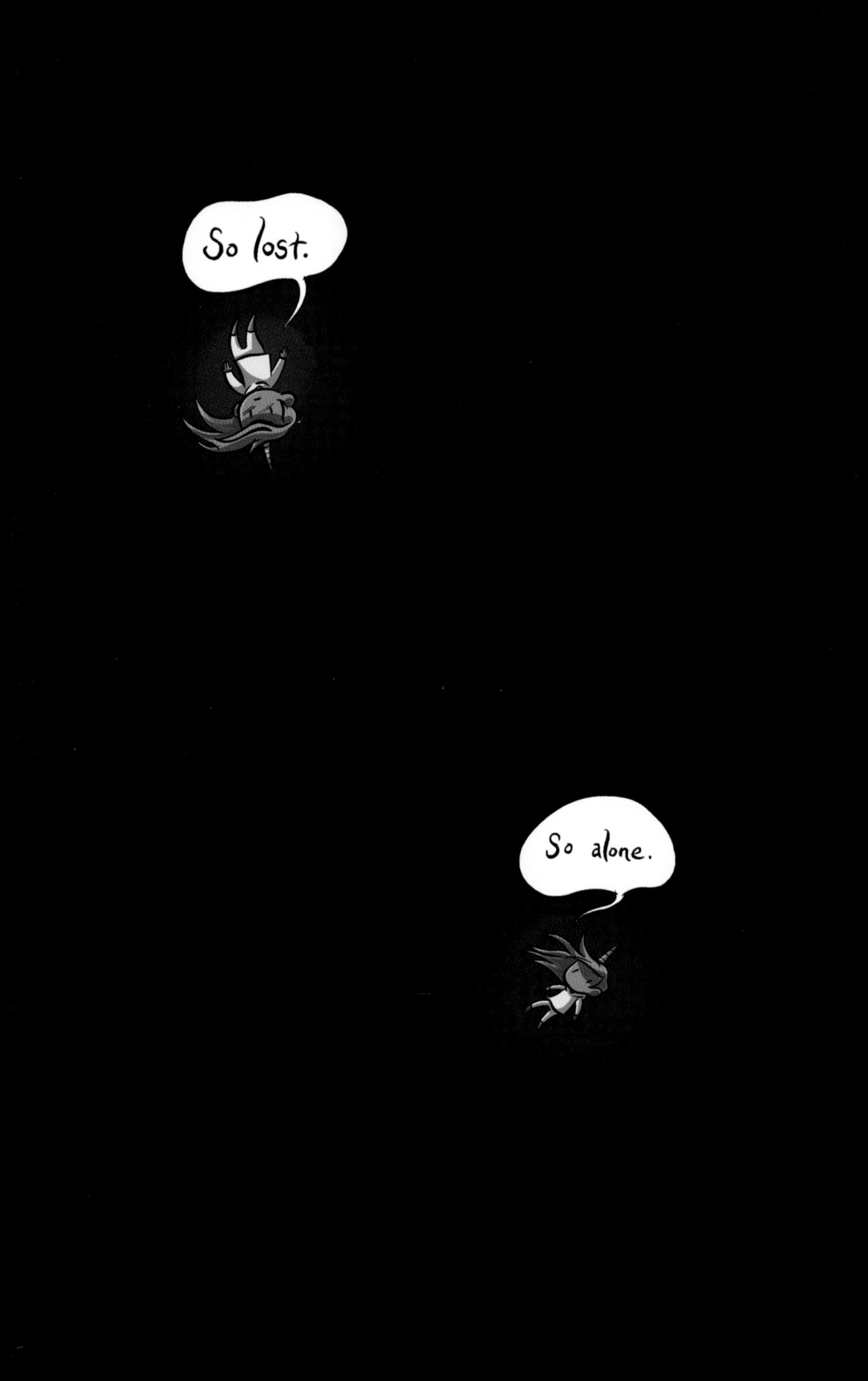
So lost.
So alone.

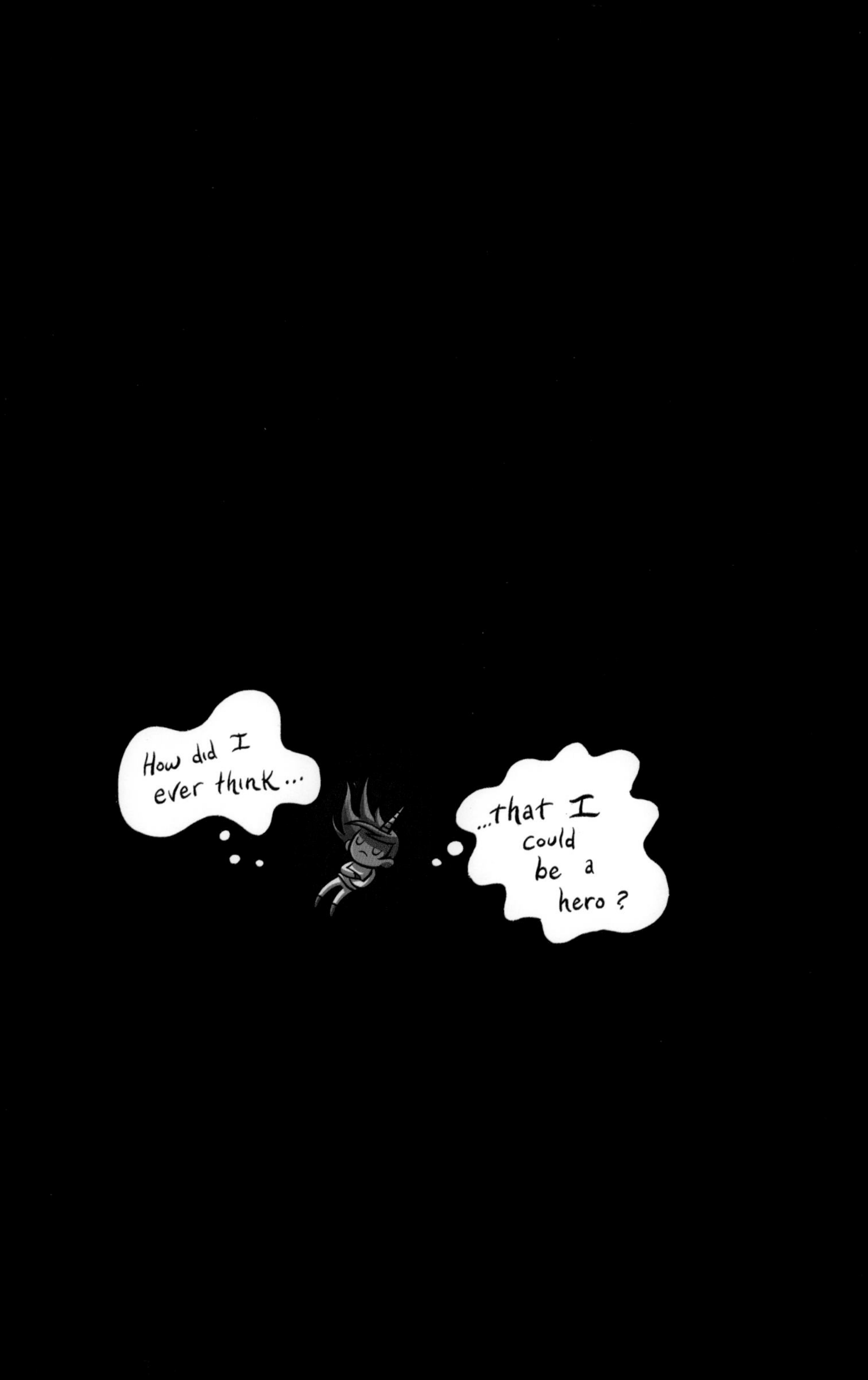
How did I ever think...
...that I could be a hero?

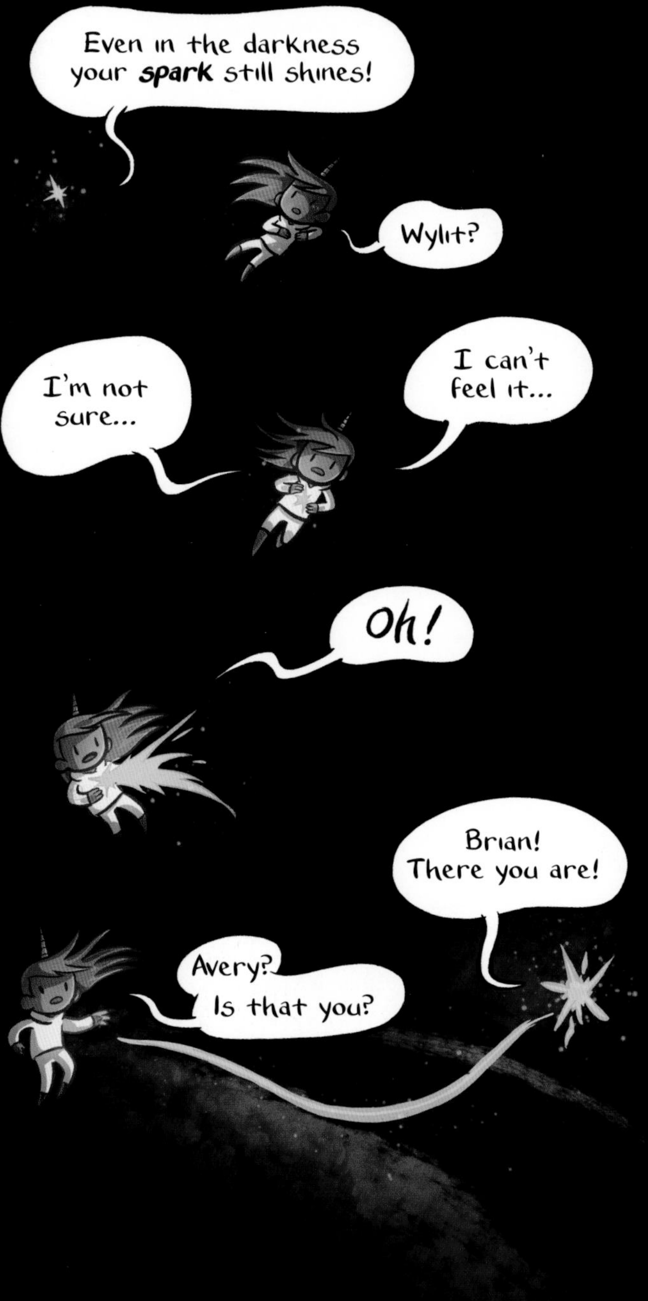
Even in the darkness your **spark** still shines!
Wylit?
I'm not sure...
I can't feel it...
Oh!
Brian! There you are!
Avery? Is that you?

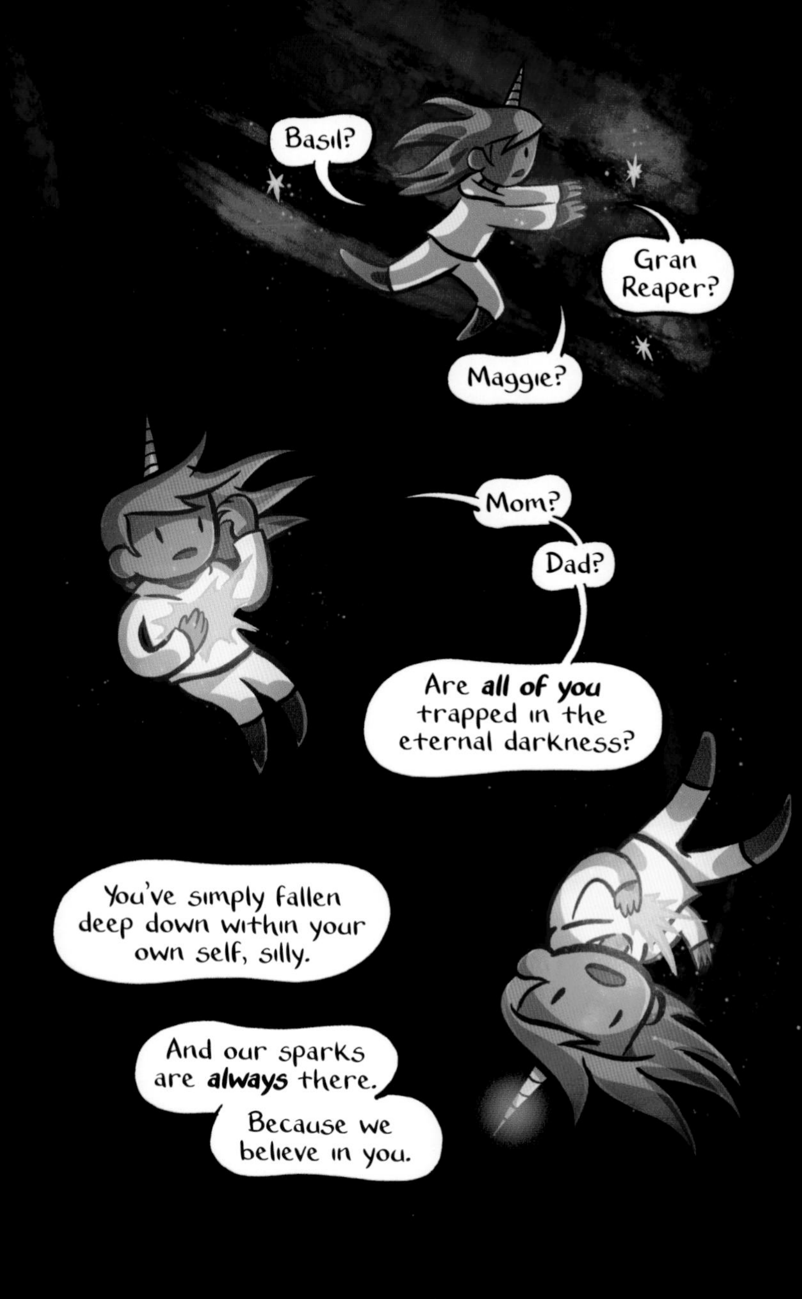
Basil?
Gran Reaper?
Maggie?
Mom?
Dad?
Are **all of you** trapped in the eternal darkness?
You've simply fallen deep down within your own self, silly.
And our sparks are **always** there.
Because we believe in you.

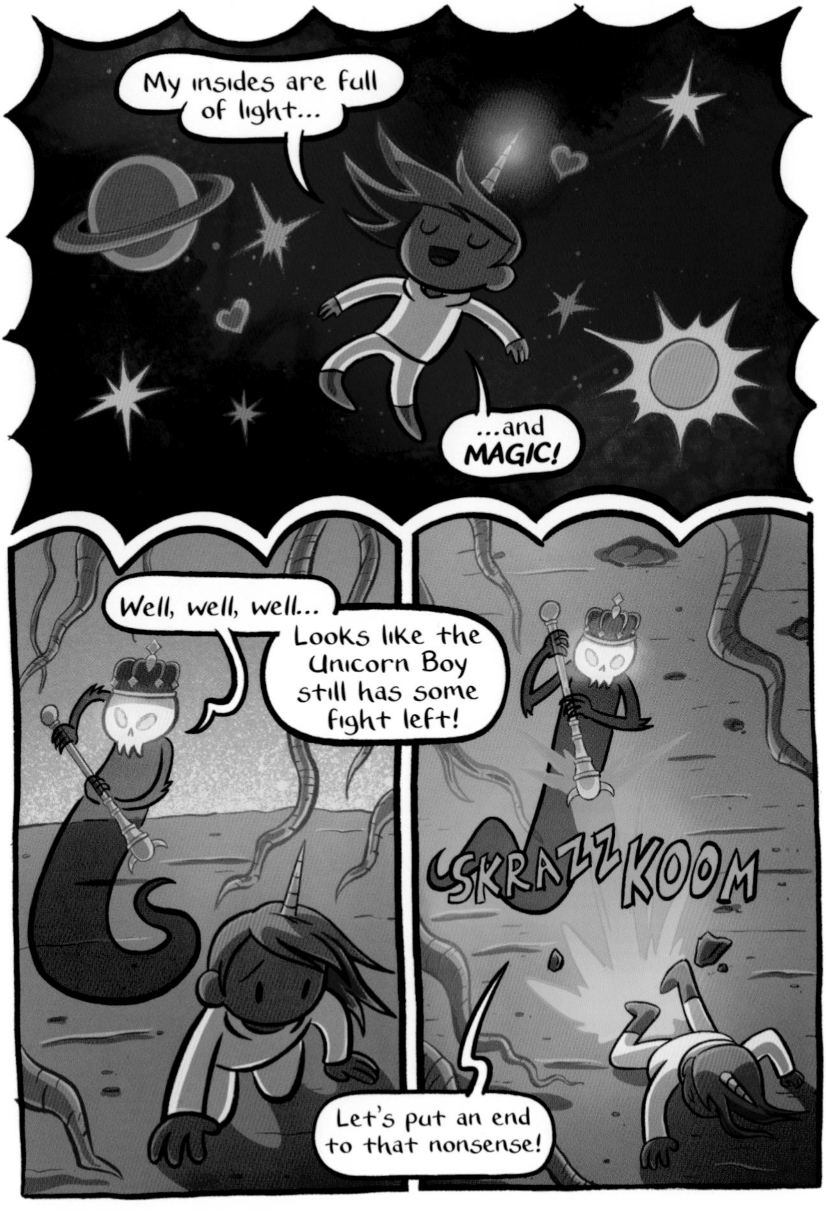
My insides are full of light...
...and MAGIC!
Well, well, well...
Looks like the Unicorn Boy still has some fight left!
SKRAZZKOOM
Let's put an end to that nonsense!

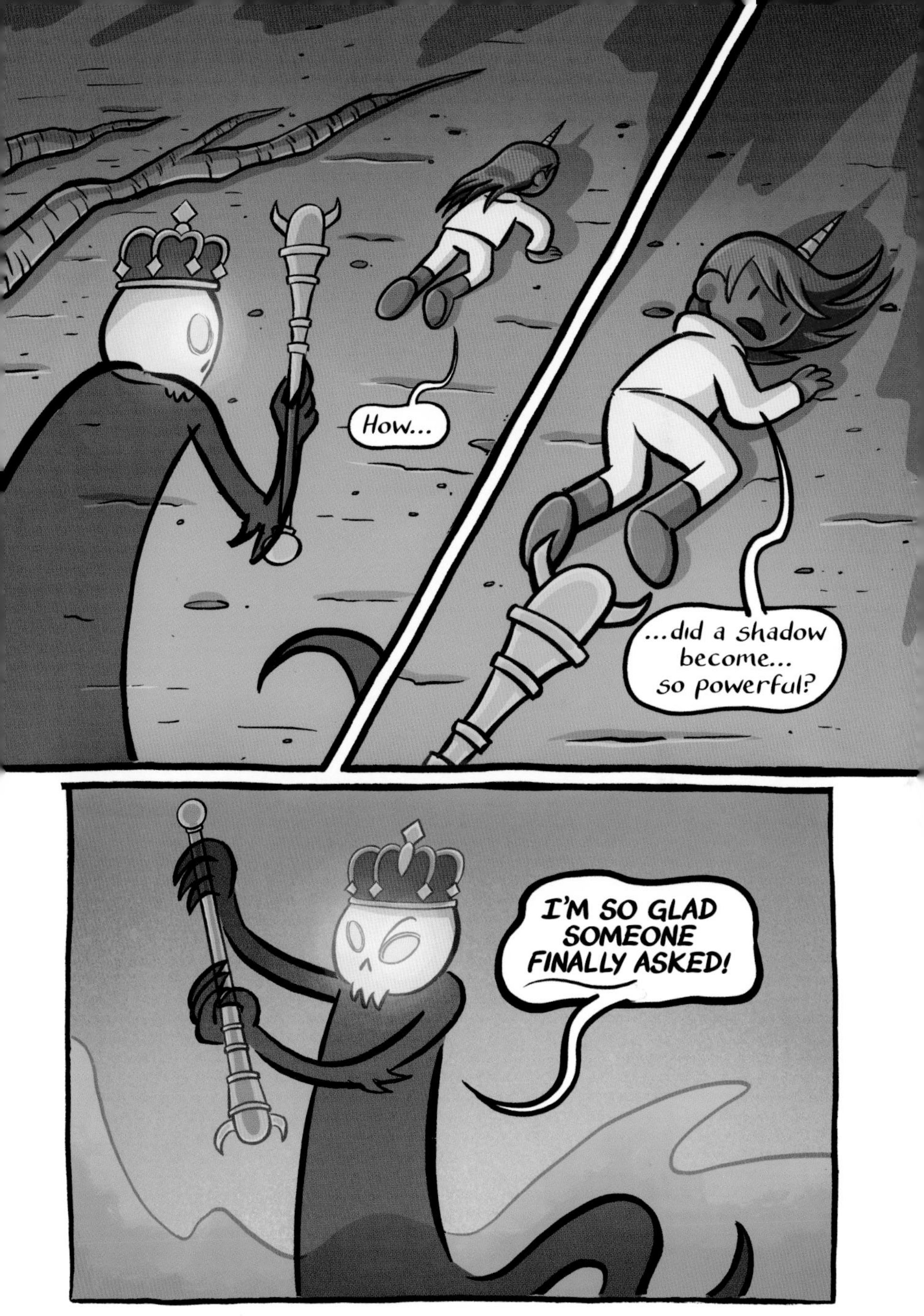
How...
...did a shadow become... so powerful?
I'M SO GLAD SOMEONE FINALLY ASKED!

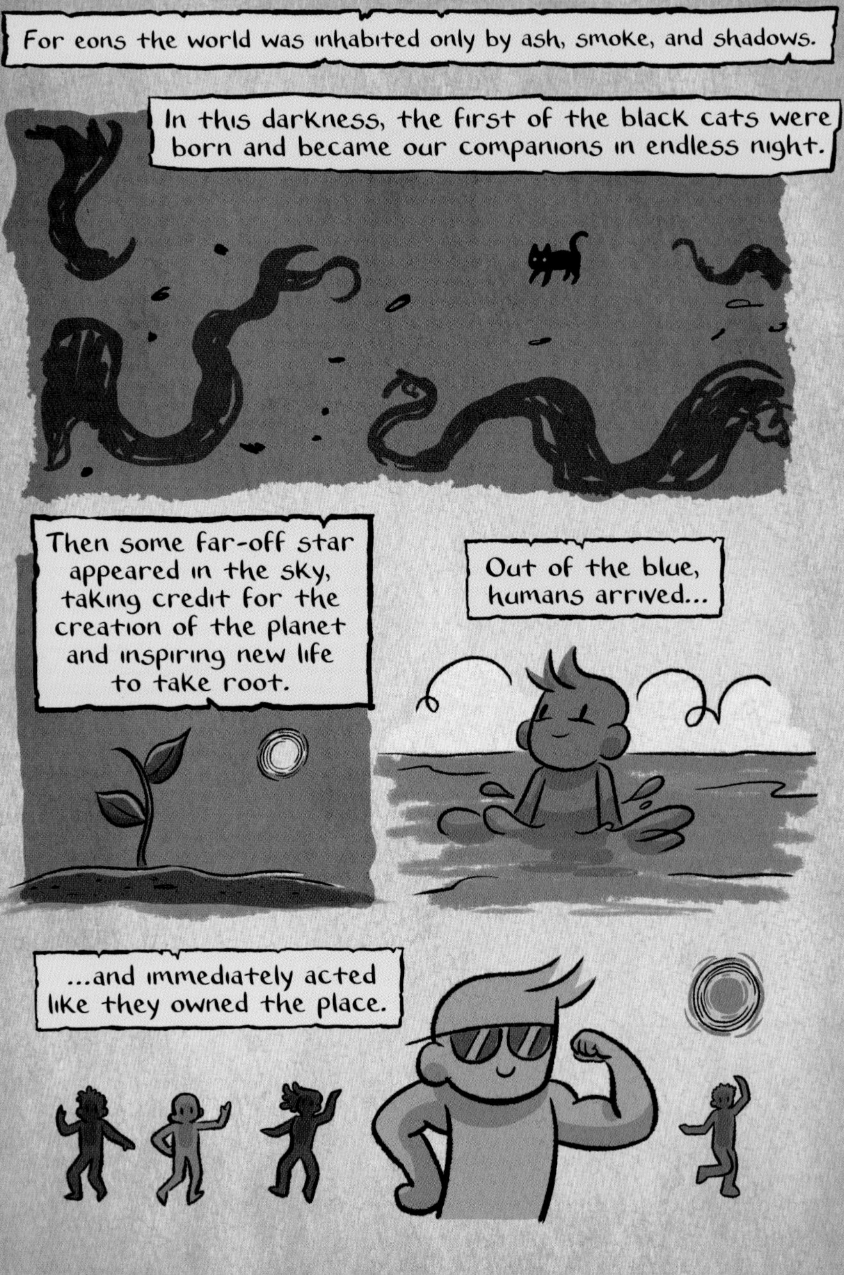
For eons the world was inhabited only by ash, smoke, and shadows.
In this darkness, the first of the black cats were born and became our companions in endless night.
Then some far-off star appeared in the sky, taking credit for the creation of the planet and inspiring new life to take root.
Out of the blue, humans arrived...
...and immediately acted like they owned the place.

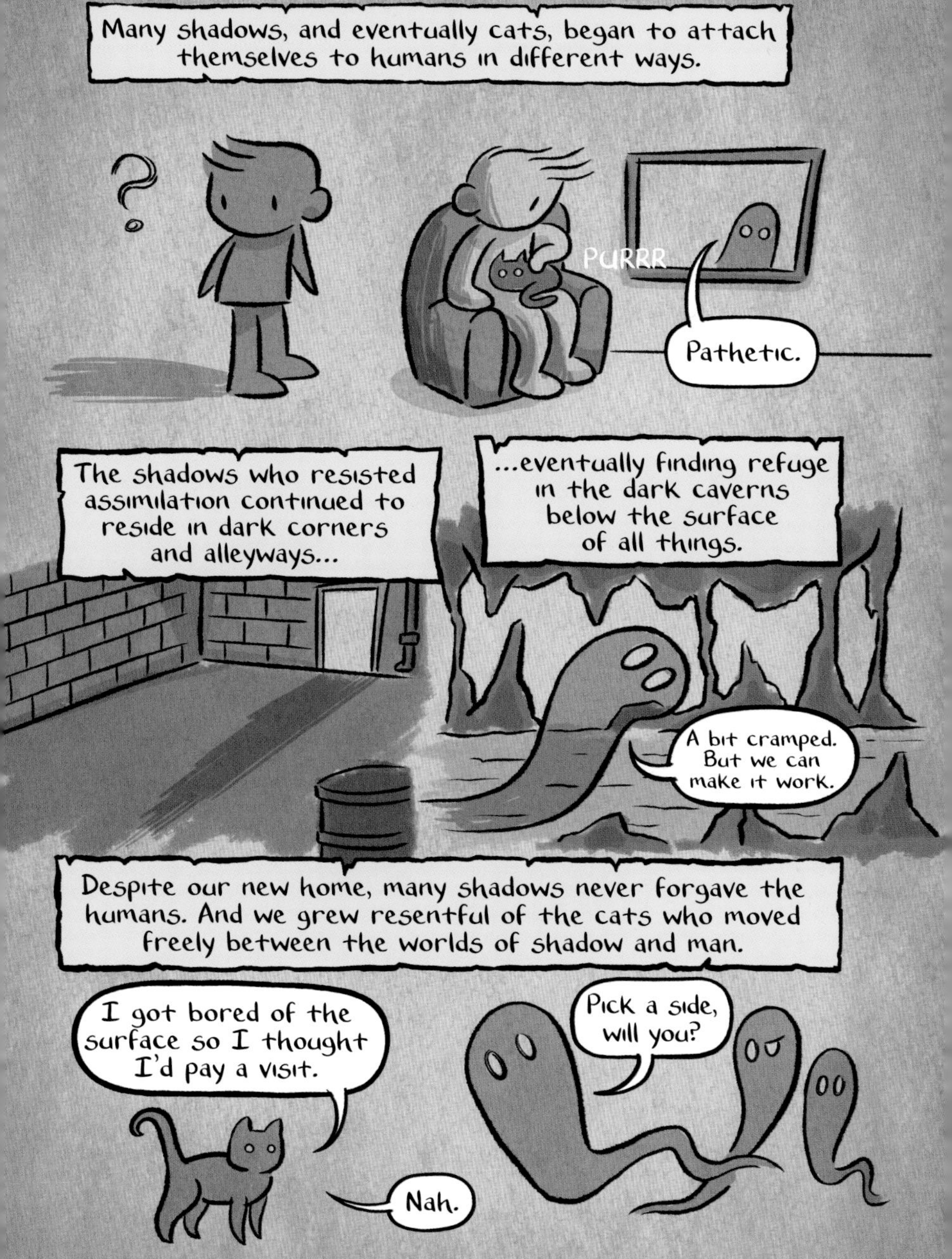
Many shadows, and eventually cats, began to attach themselves to humans in different ways.
?
PURRR
Pathetic.
The shadows who resisted assimilation continued to reside in dark corners and alleyways...
...eventually finding refuge in the dark caverns below the surface of all things.
A bit cramped. But we can make it work.
Despite our new home, many shadows never forgave the humans. And we grew resentful of the cats who moved freely between the worlds of shadow and man.
I got bored of the surface so I thought I'd pay a visit.
Pick a side, will you?
Nah.

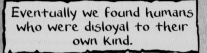

Eventually we found humans who were disloyal to their own kind.

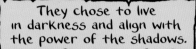

They chose to live in darkness and align with the power of the shadows.

I HATE EVERYONE!

These so-called dark-wizard alliances fought many battles to reclaim the surface world.

THE WORLD SHALL ENTER A NEW DARK AGE!

But much to our chagrin, it's always darkest before the dawn...

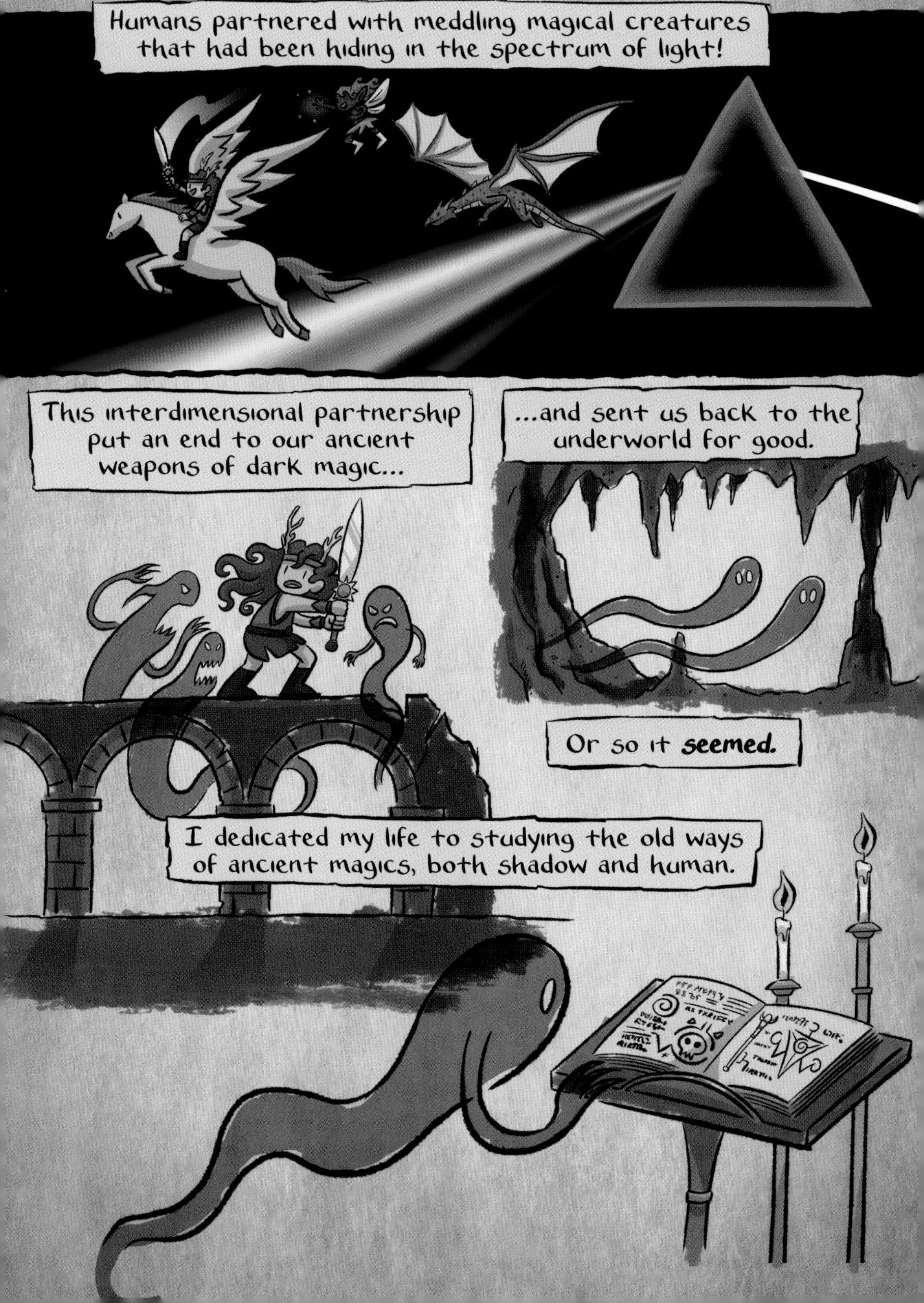
Humans partnered with meddling magical creatures that had been hiding in the spectrum of light!
This interdimensional partnership put an end to our ancient weapons of dark magic...
...and sent us back to the underworld for good.
Or so it **seemed.**
I dedicated my life to studying the old ways of ancient magics, both shadow and human.

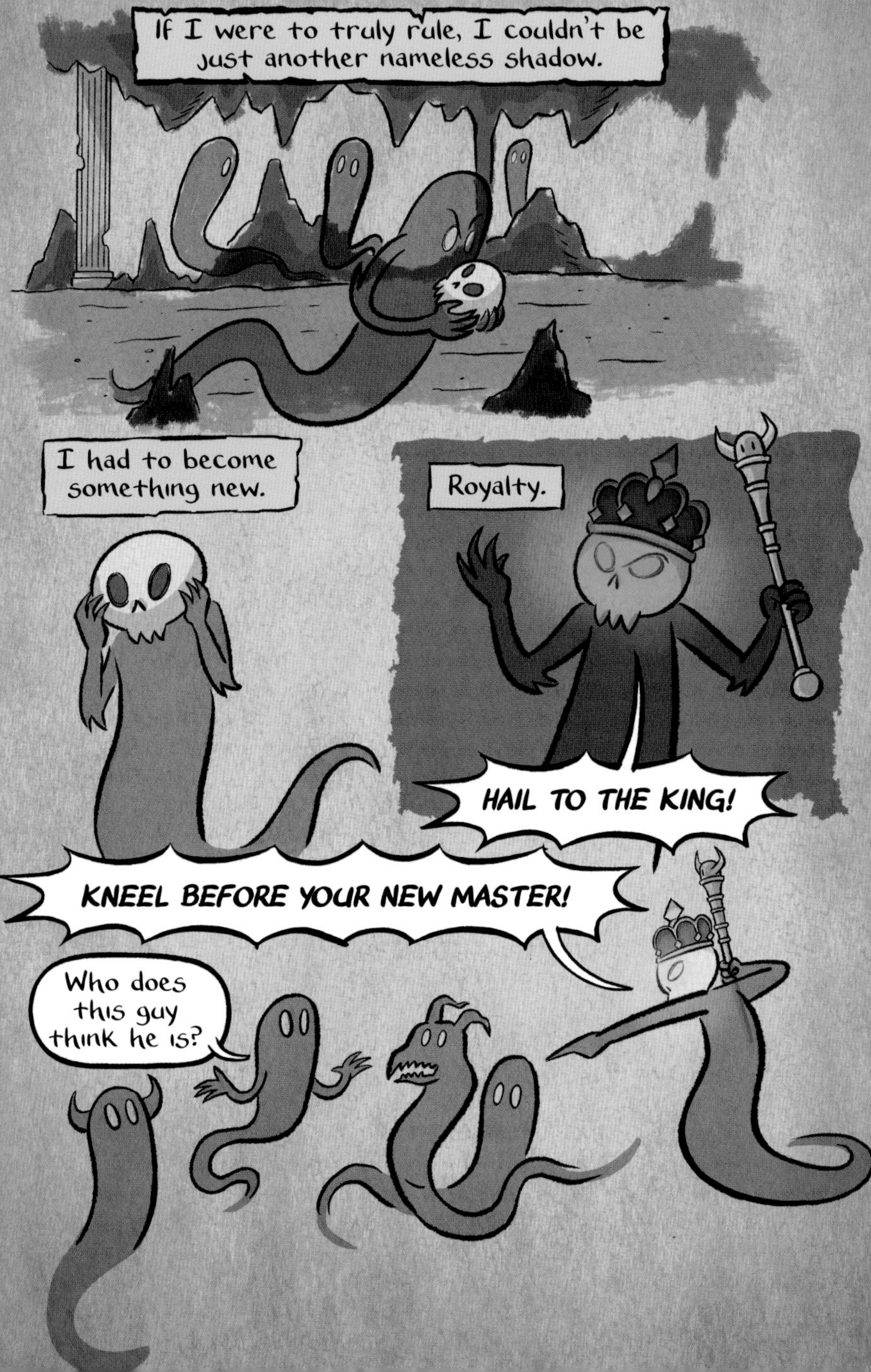
If I were to truly rule, I couldn't be just another nameless shadow.
I had to become something new.
Royalty.
HAIL TO THE KING!
KNEEL BEFORE YOUR NEW MASTER!
Who does this guy think he is?

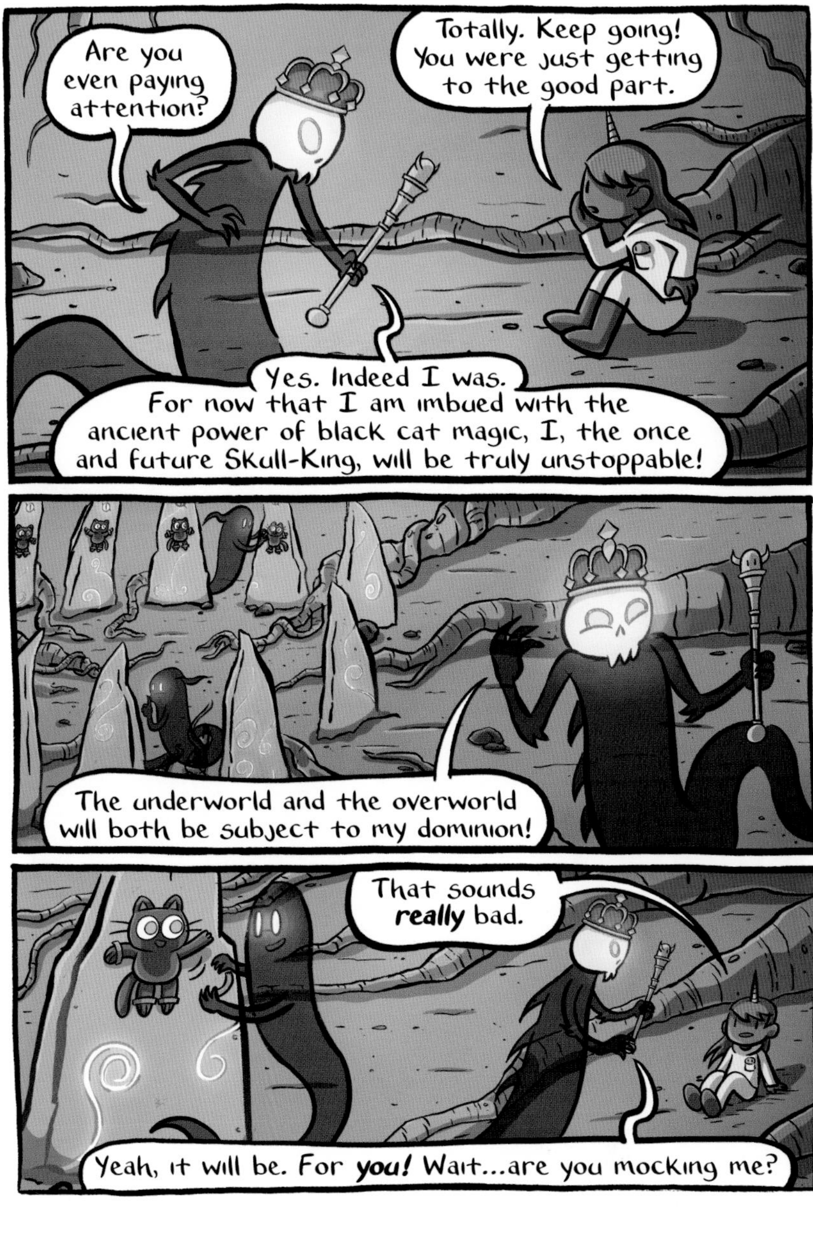
Are you even paying attention?
Totally. Keep going! You were just getting to the good part.
Yes. Indeed I was. For now that I am imbued with the ancient power of black cat magic, I, the once and future Skull-King, will be truly unstoppable!
The underworld and the overworld will both be subject to my dominion!
That sounds **really** bad.
Yeah, it will be. For ***you!*** Wait...are you mocking me?

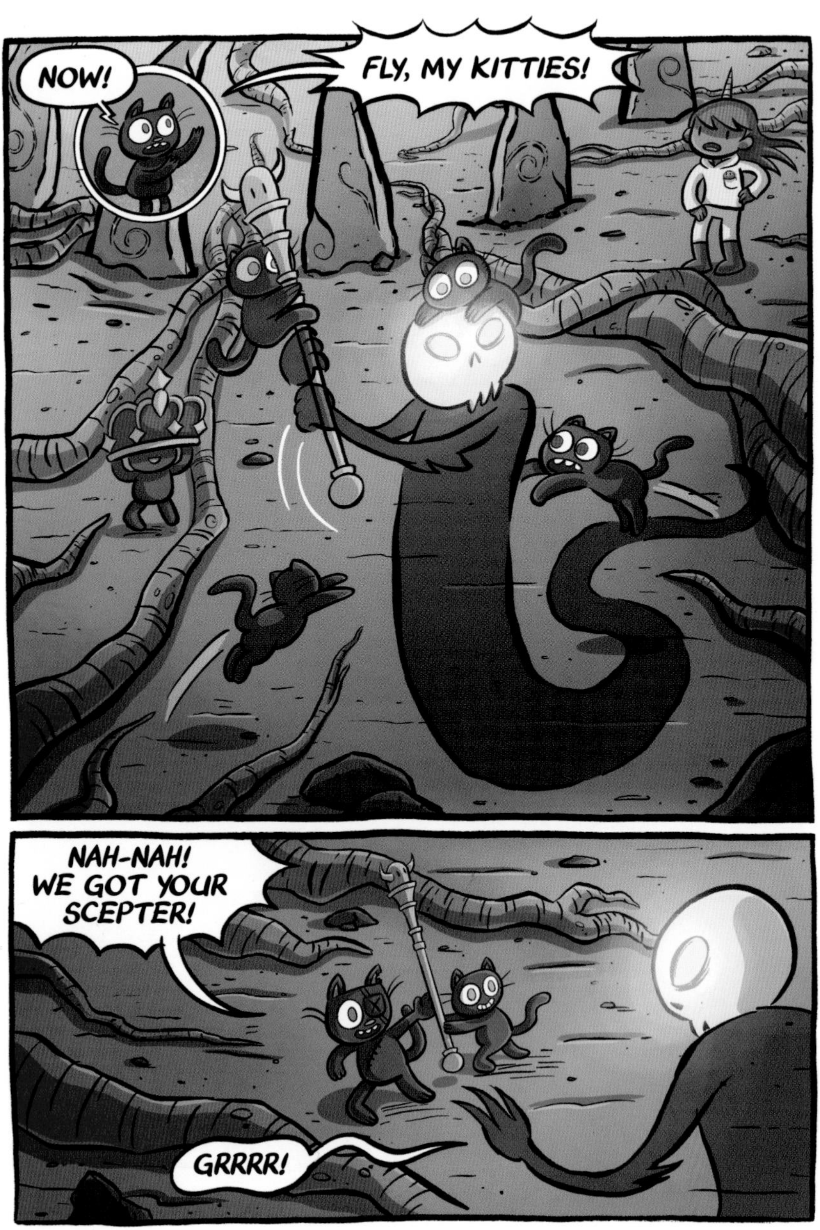
NOW!
FLY, MY KITTIES!
NAH-NAH! WE GOT YOUR SCEPTER!
GRRRR!

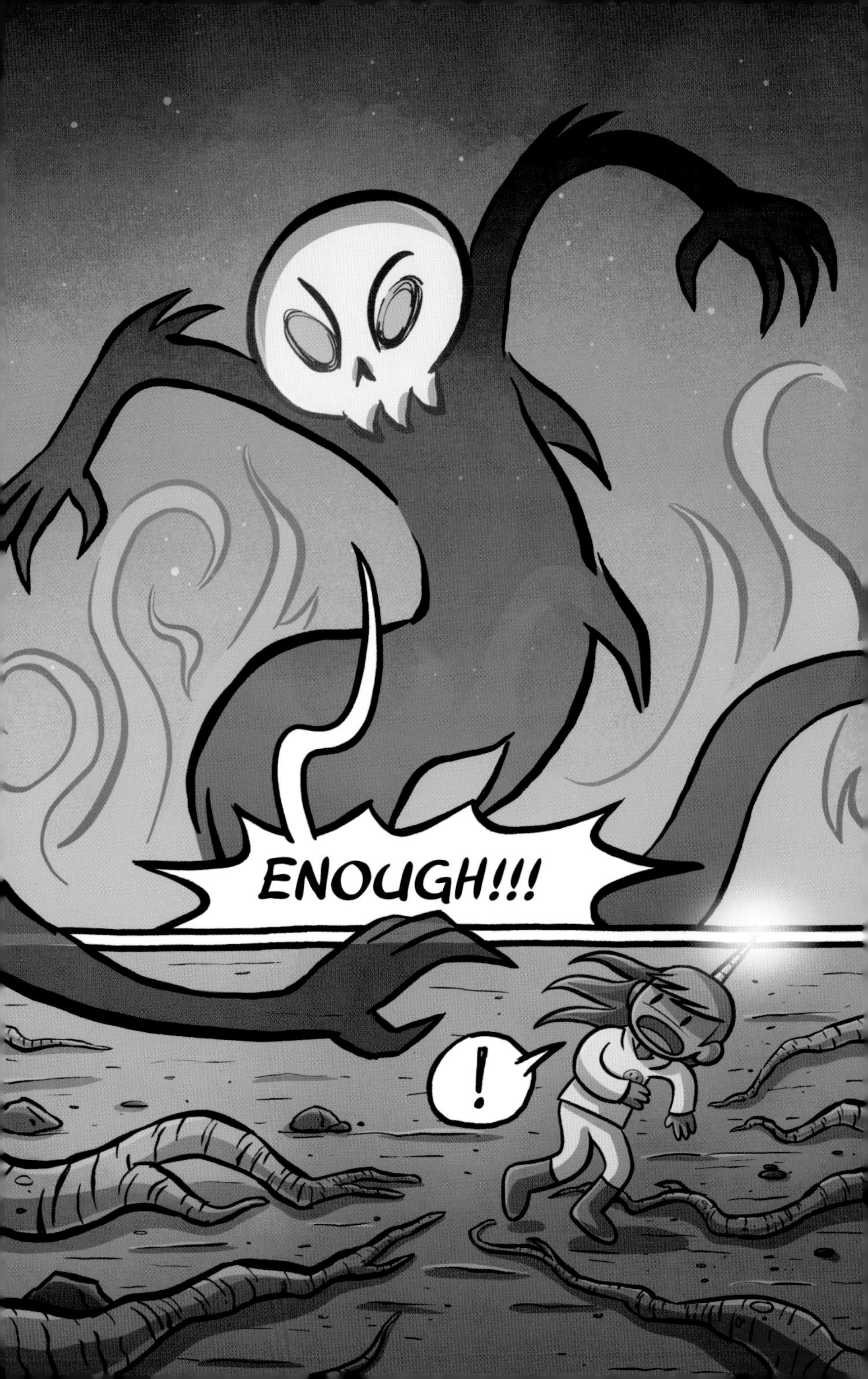
ENOUGH!!!
!

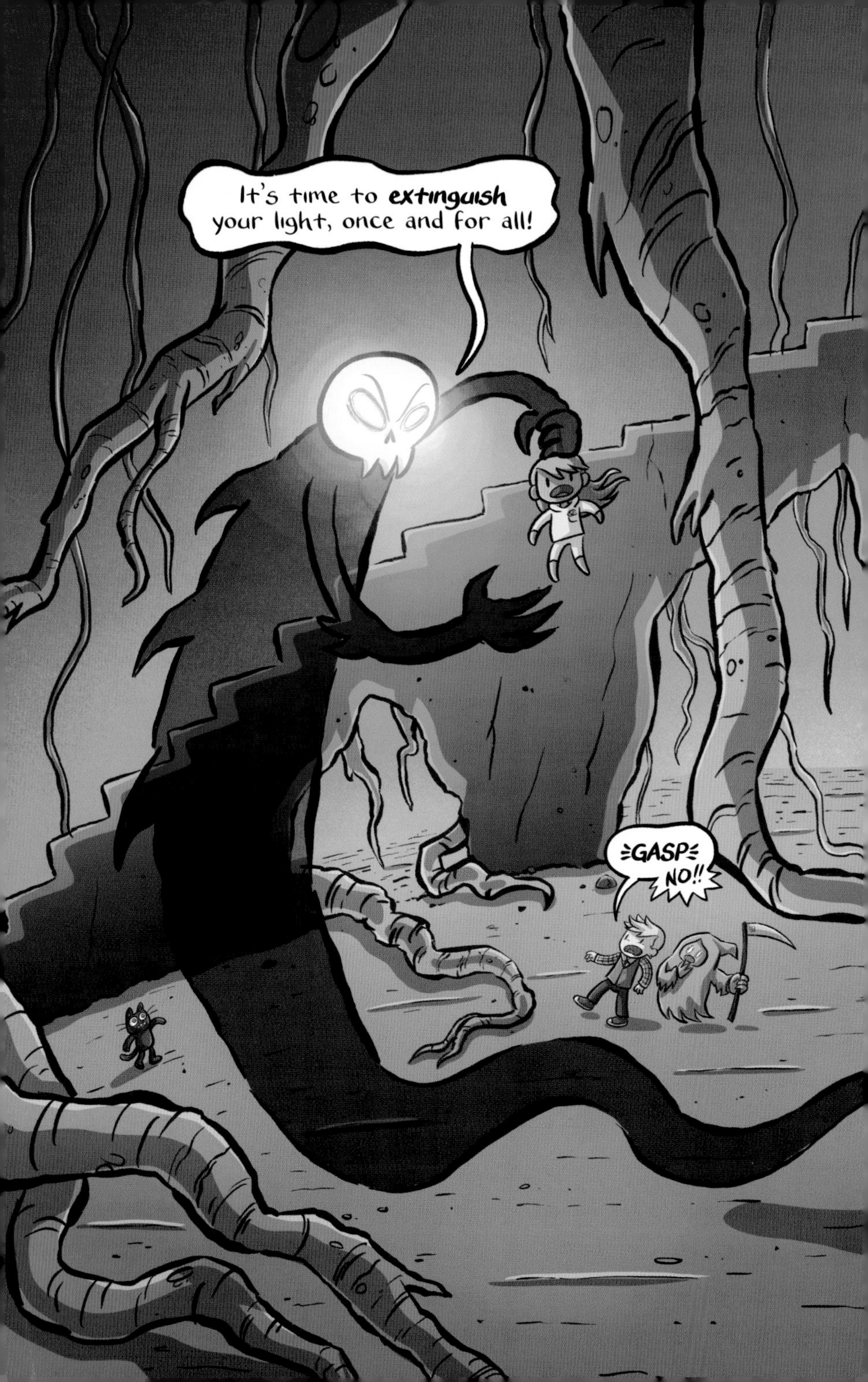
It's time to **extinguish** your light, once and for all!
GASP
NO!!

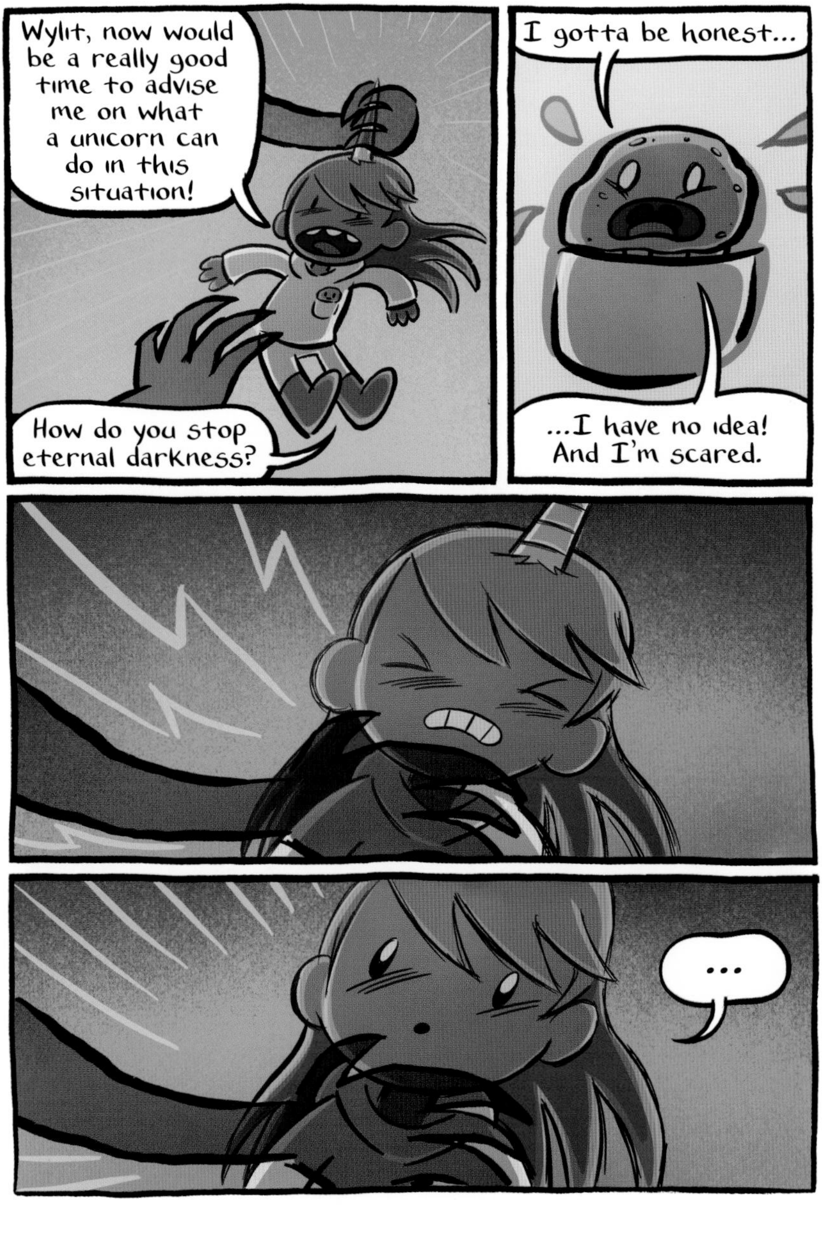
Wylit, now would be a really good time to advise me on what a unicorn can do in this situation!
How do you stop eternal darkness?
I gotta be honest...
...I have no idea! And I'm scared.
...

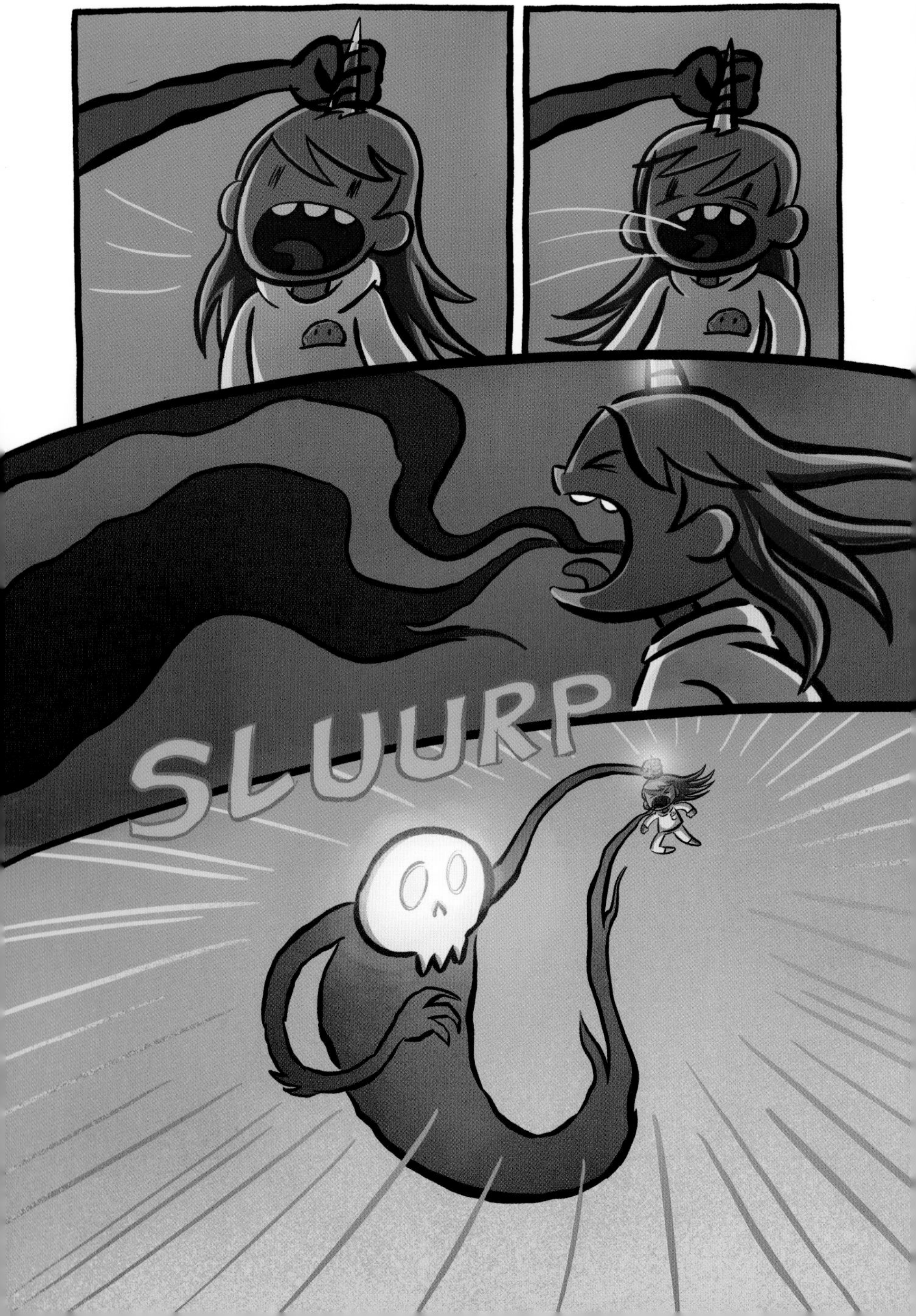
SLUURP

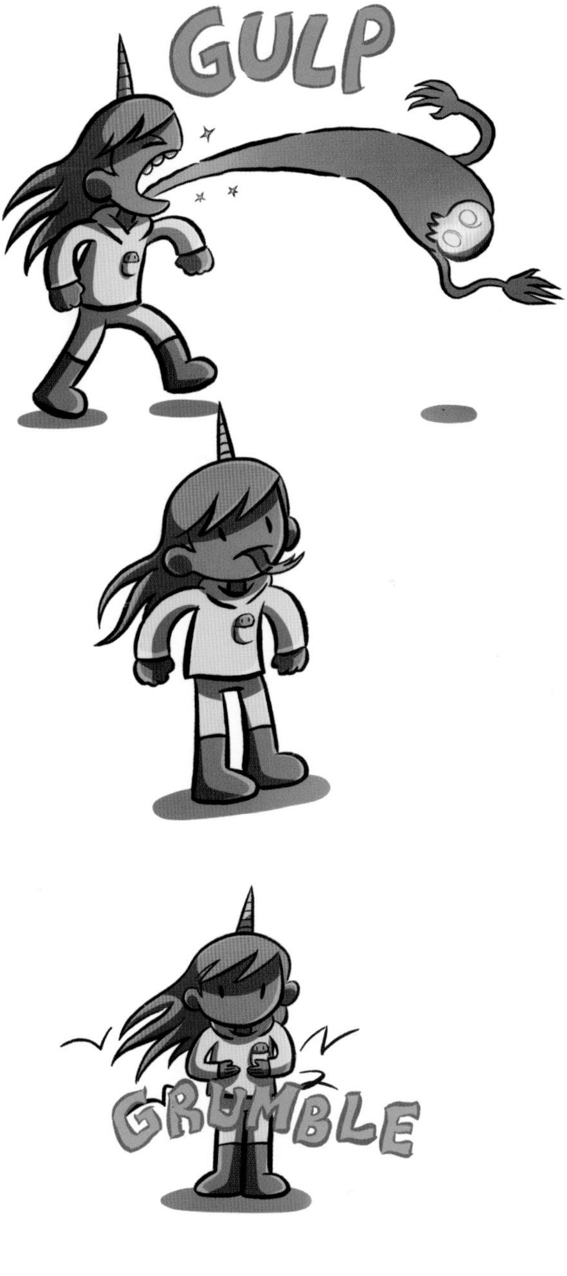
GULP
GRUMBLE

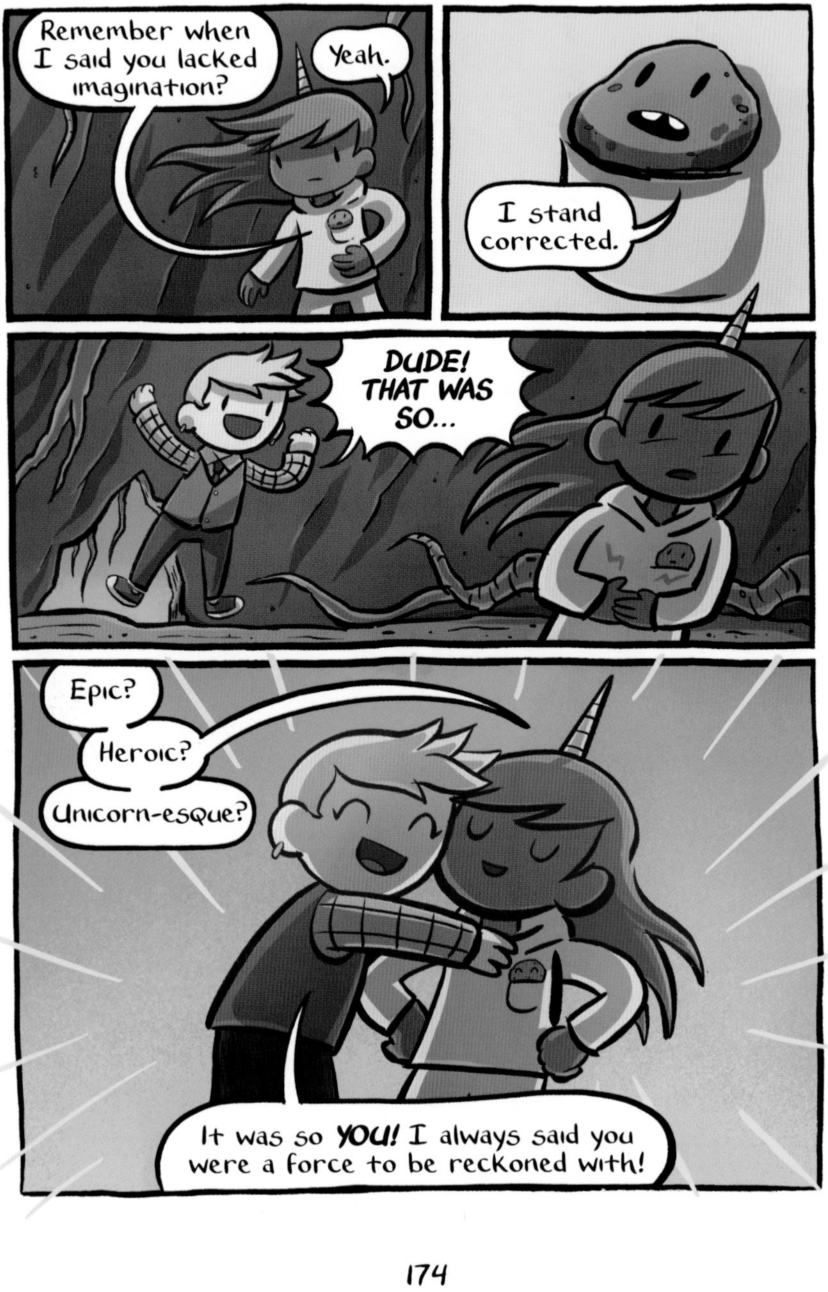
Remember when I said you lacked imagination?
Yeah.
I stand corrected.
DUDE! THAT WAS SO...
Epic?
Heroic?
Unicorn-esque?
It was so YOU! I always said you were a force to be reckoned with!

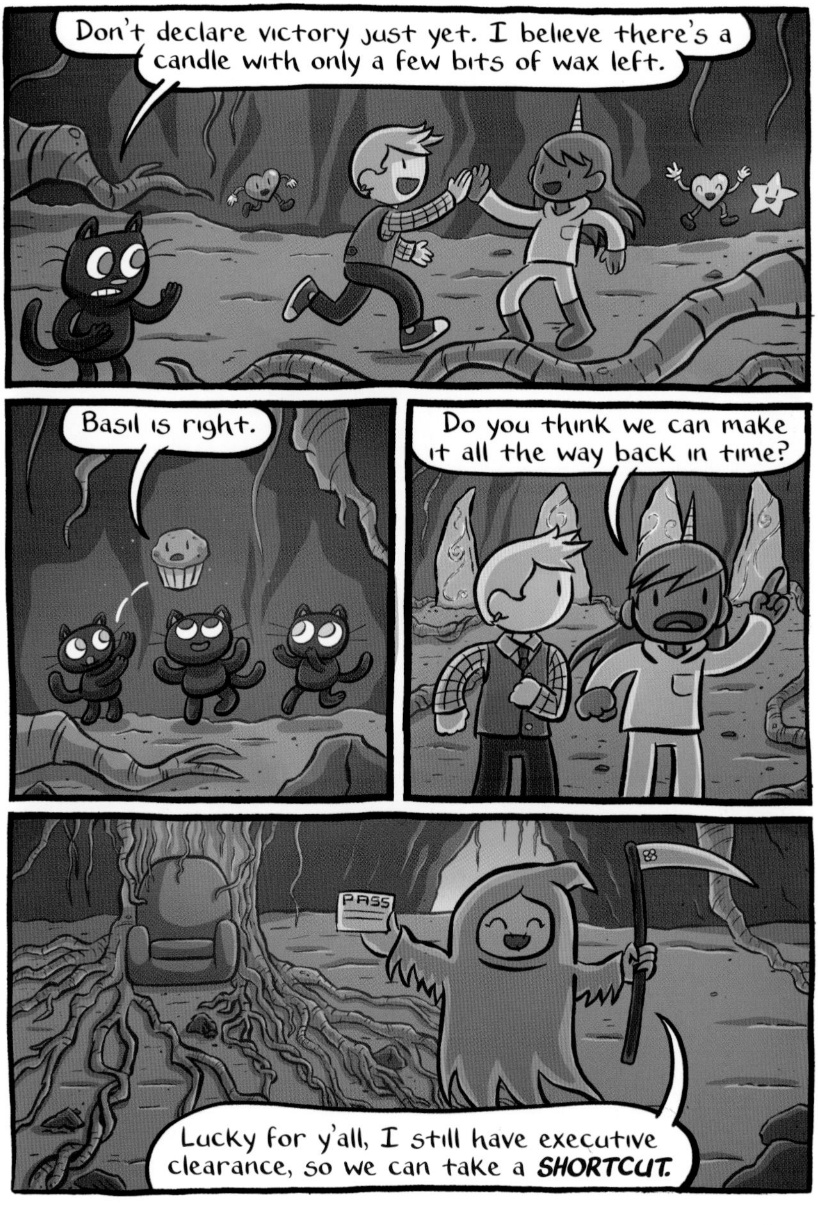
Don't declare victory just yet. I believe there's a candle with only a few bits of wax left.
Basil is right.
Do you think we can make it all the way back in time?
PASS
Lucky for y'all, I still have executive clearance, so we can take a SHORTCUT.

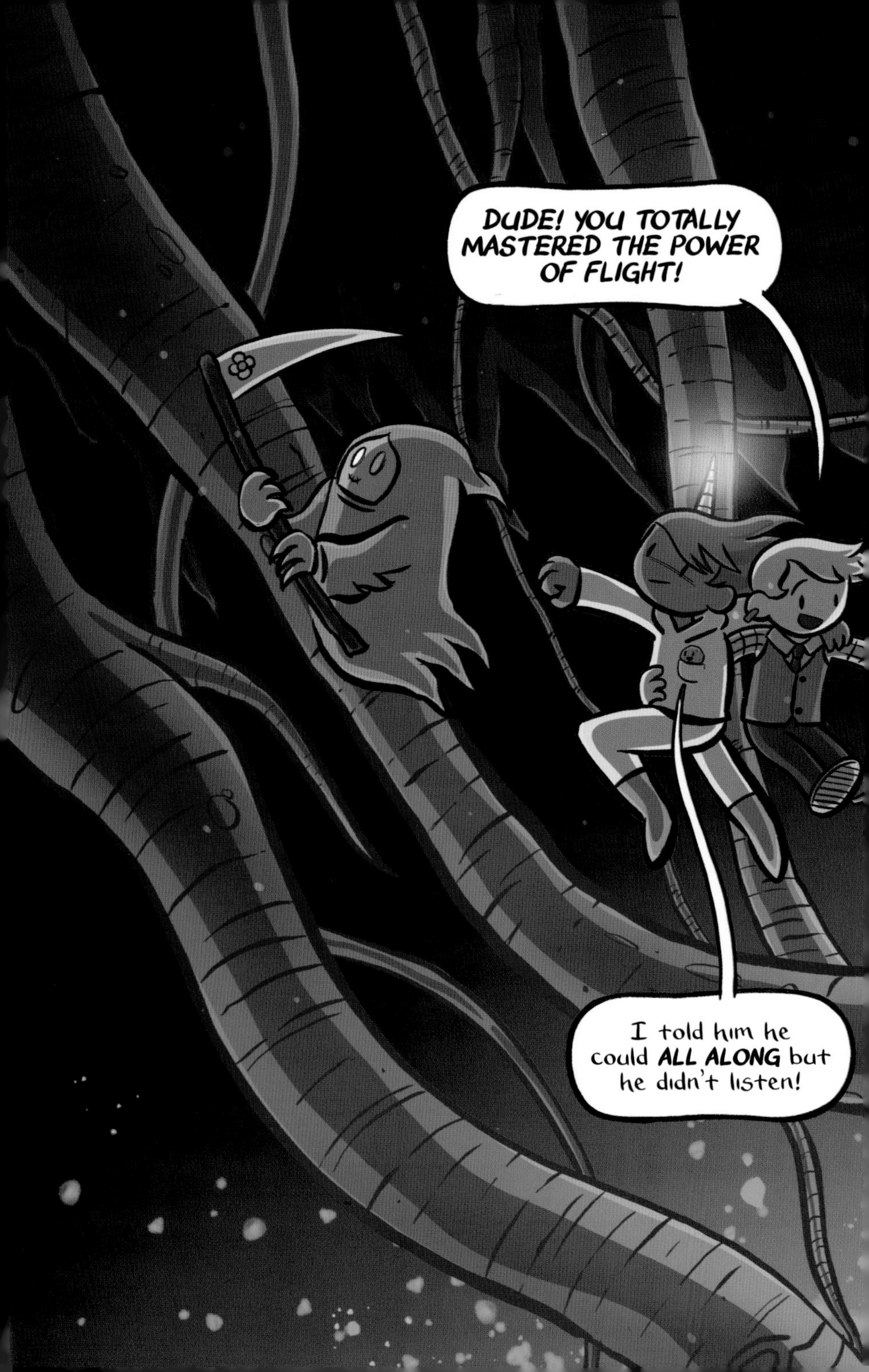
DUDE! YOU TOTALLY MASTERED THE POWER OF FLIGHT!
I told him he could ALL ALONG but he didn't listen!

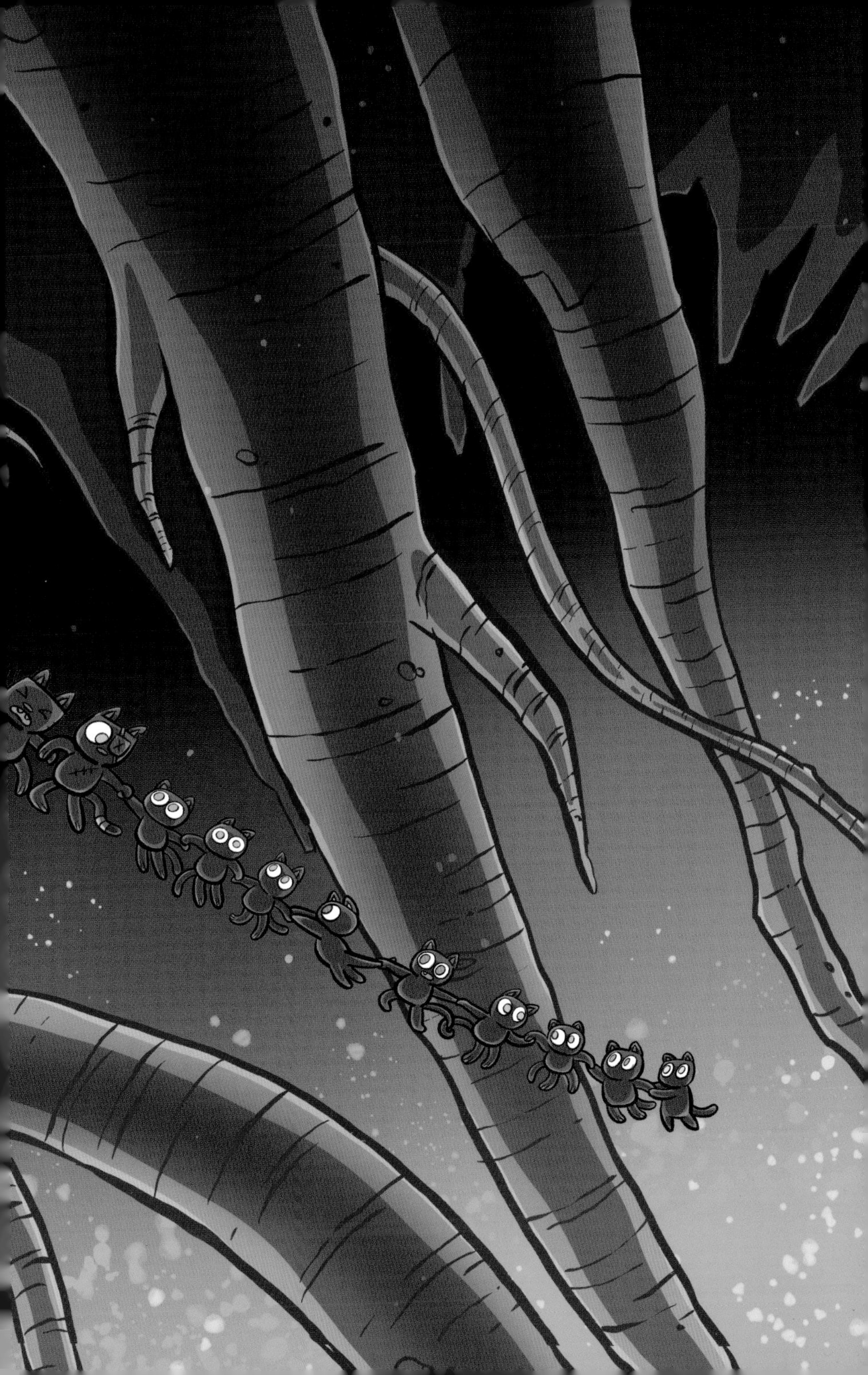

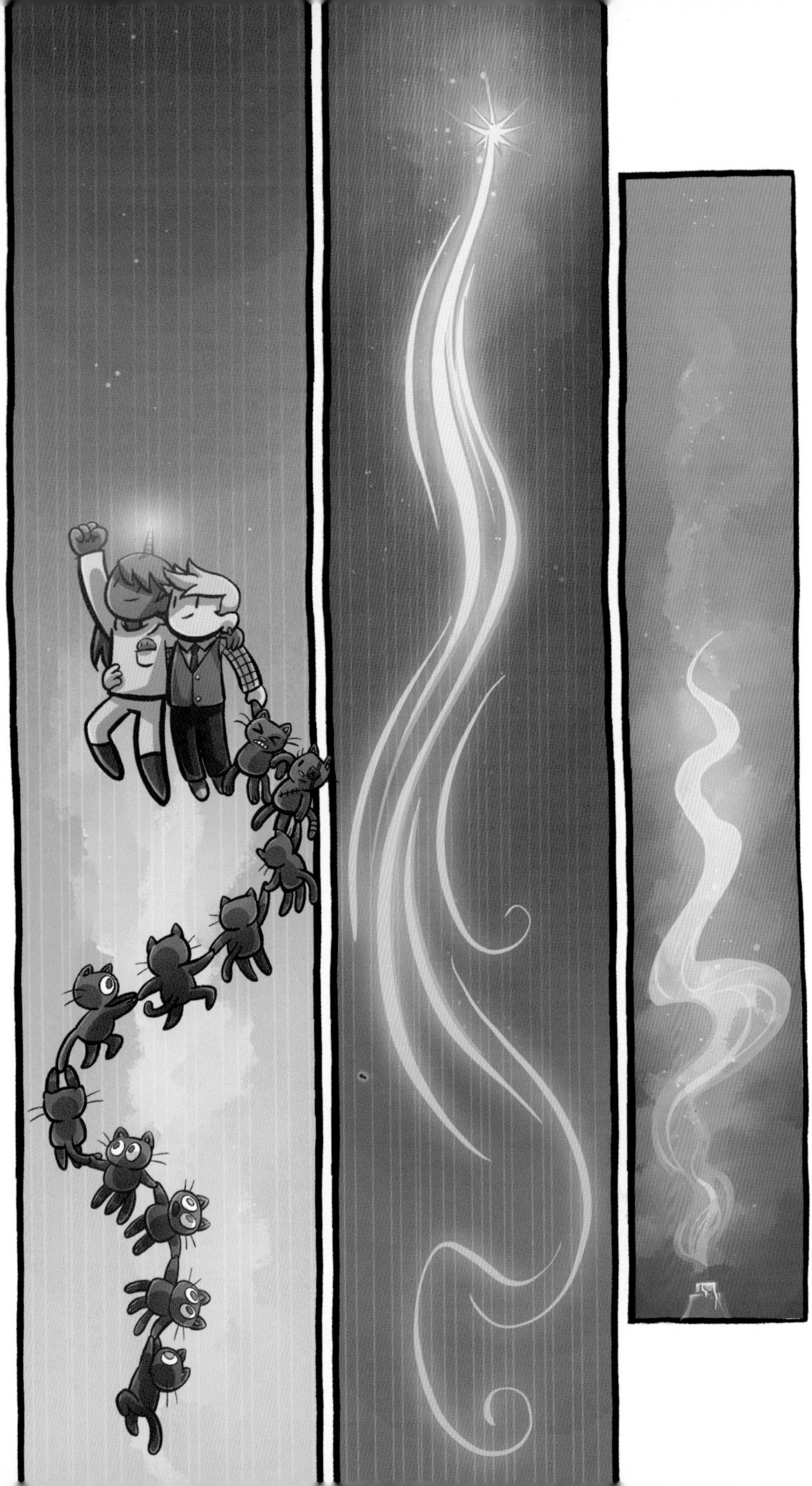

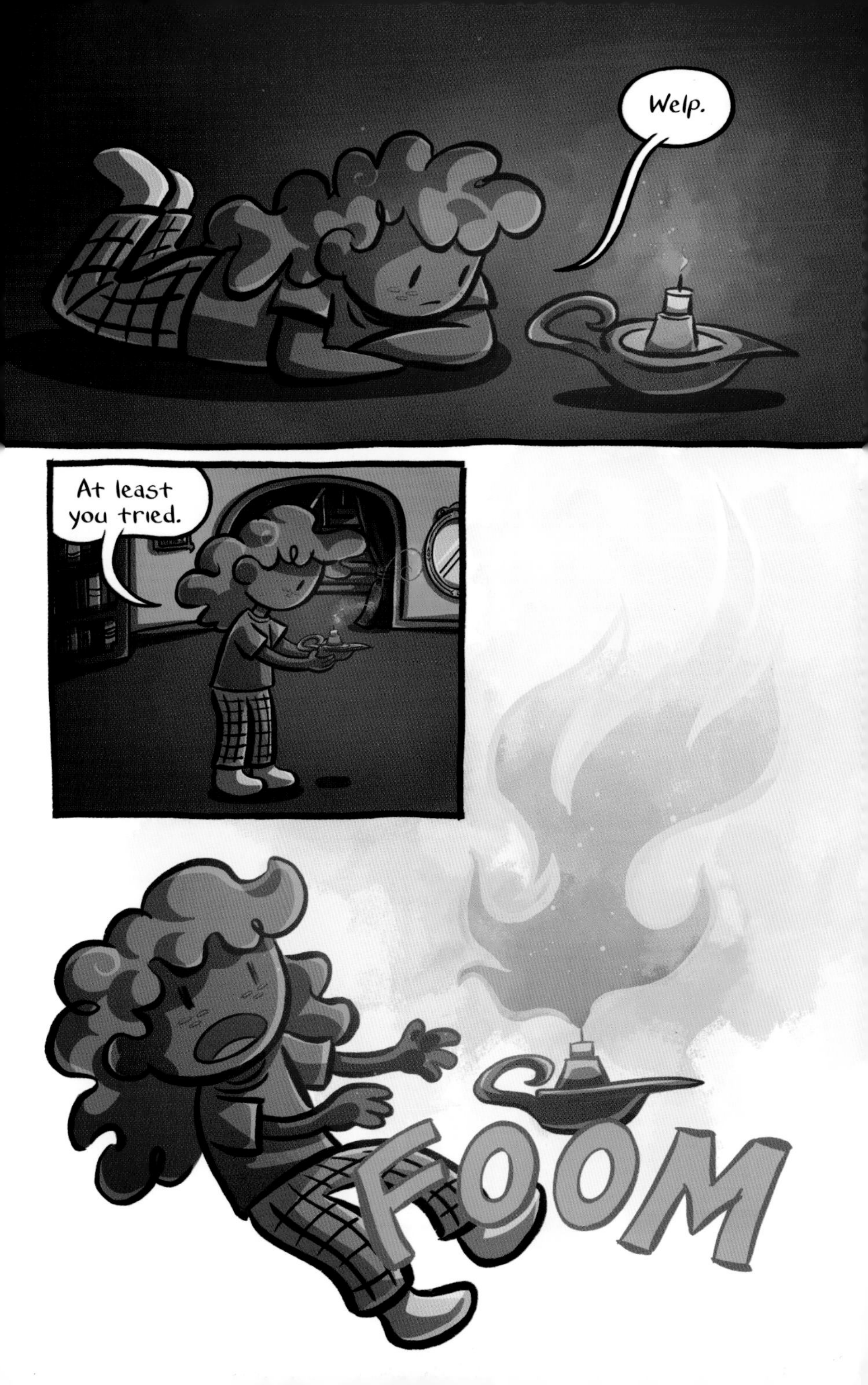
Welp.
At least you tried.
FOOM

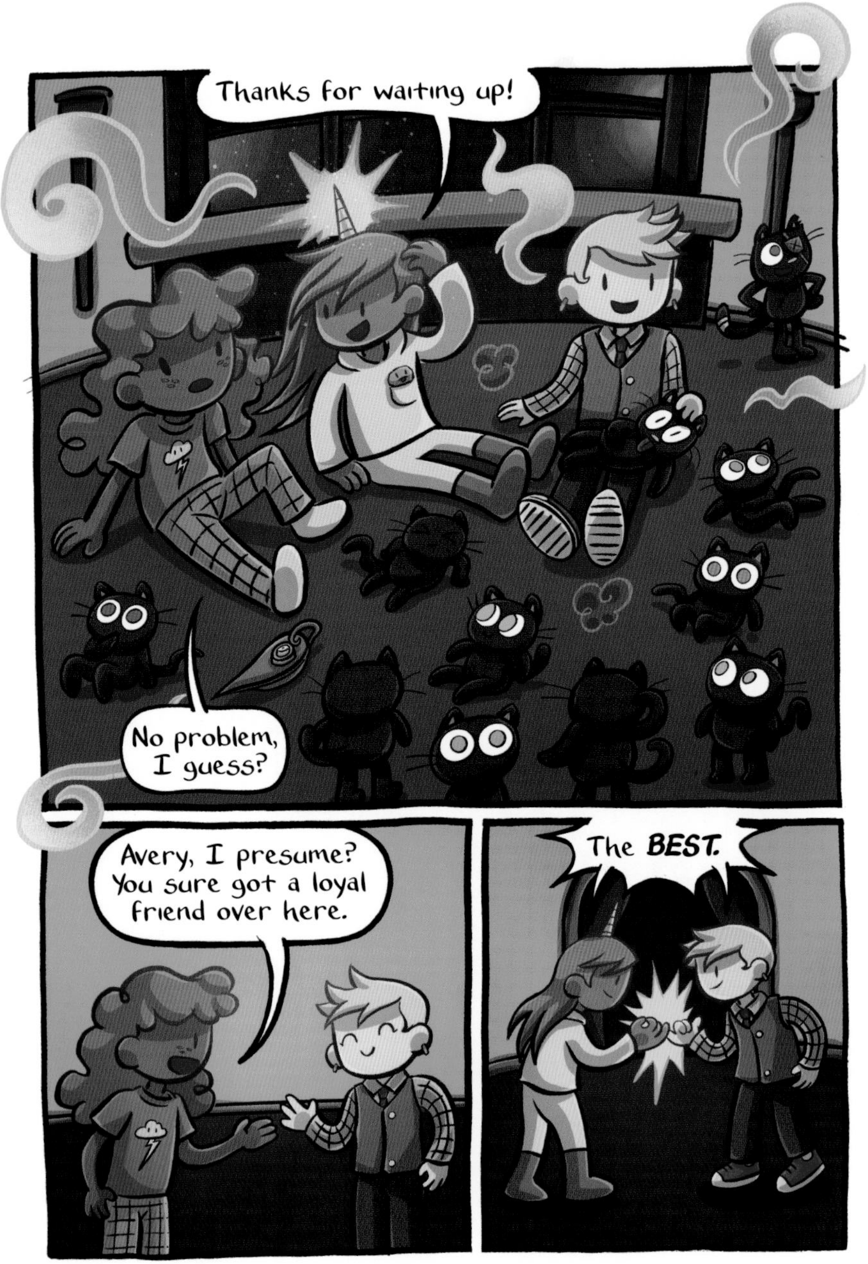
Thanks for waiting up!
No problem, I guess?
Avery, I presume? You sure got a loyal friend over here.
The **BEST.**

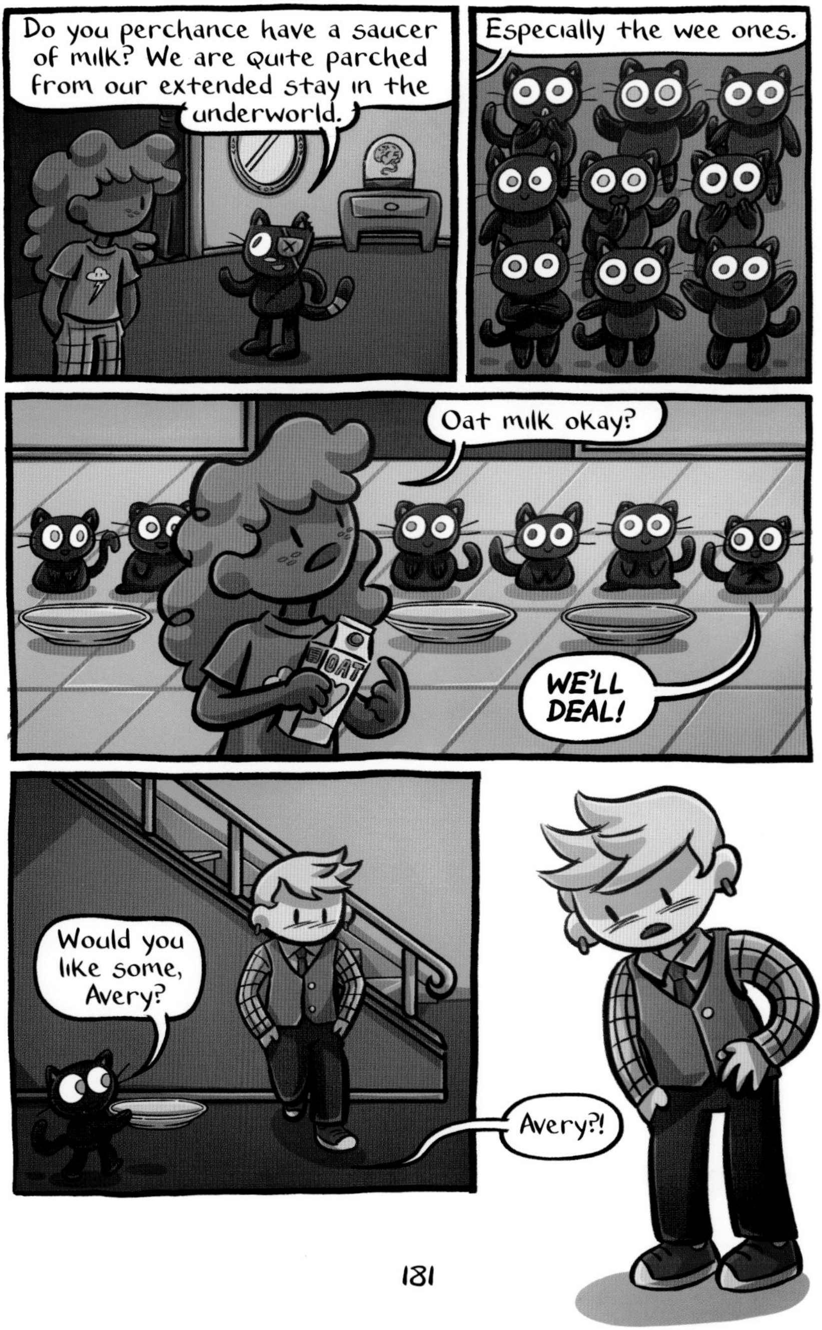
Do you perchance have a saucer of milk? We are quite parched from our extended stay in the underworld.
Especially the wee ones.
Oat milk okay?
OAT
WE'LL DEAL!
Would you like some, Avery?
Avery?!

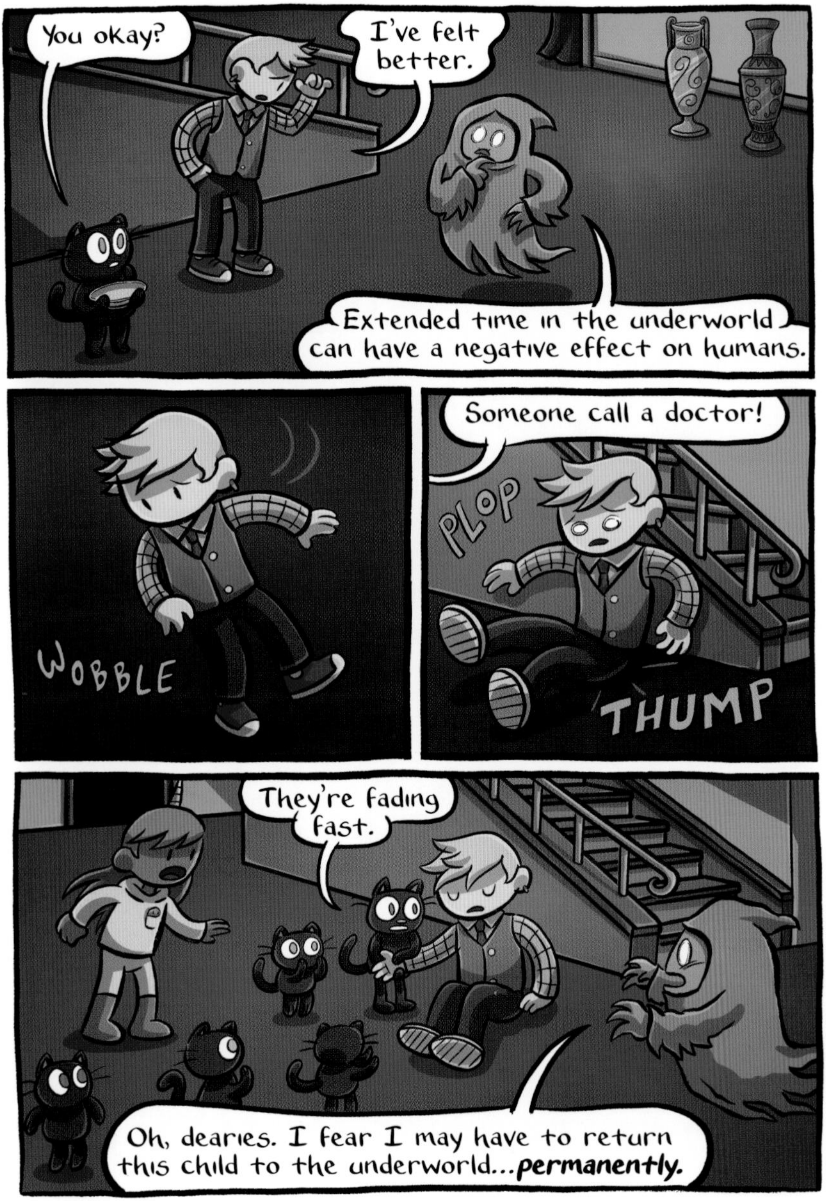
You okay?
I've felt better.
Extended time in the underworld can have a negative effect on humans.
WOBBLE
Someone call a doctor!
PLOP
THUMP
They're fading fast.
Oh, dearies. I fear I may have to return this child to the underworld...**permanently.**

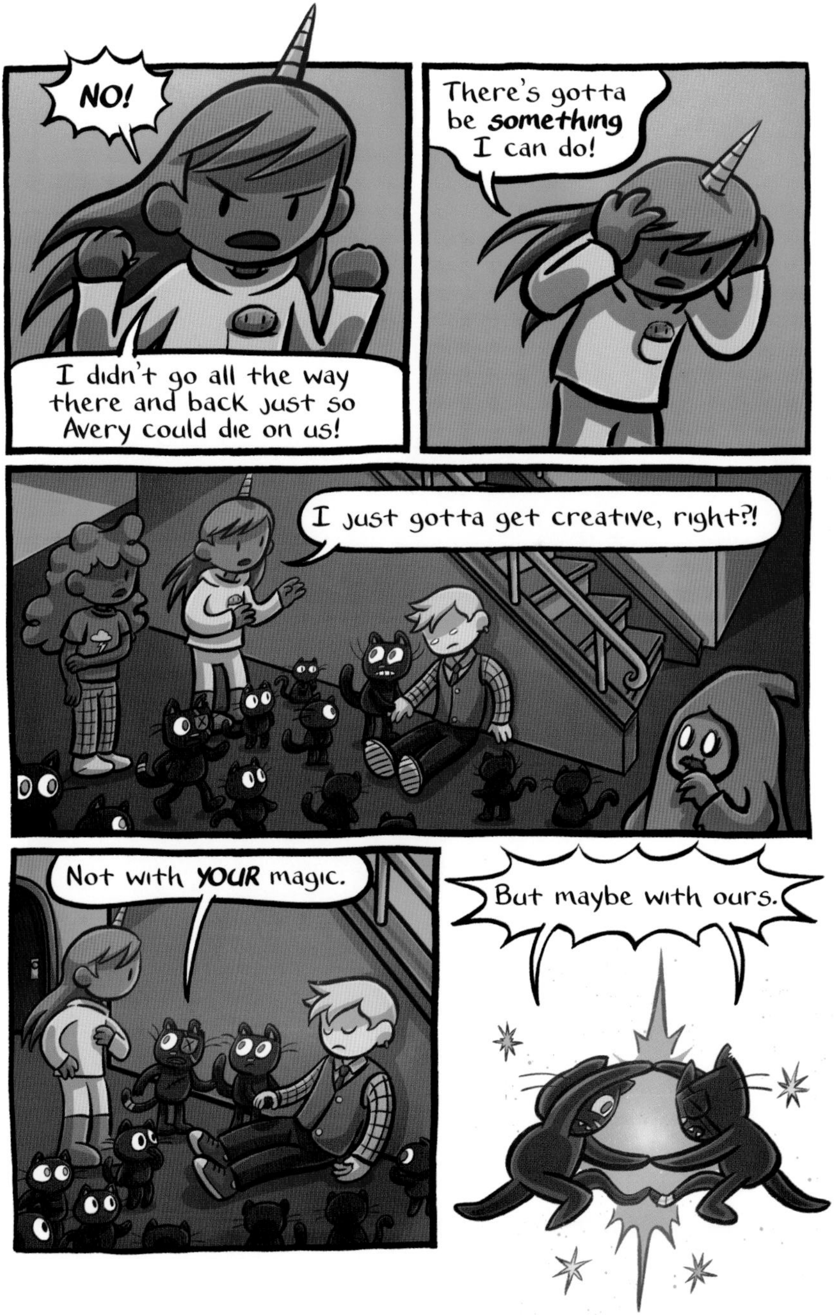
NO!
I didn't go all the way there and back just so Avery could die on us!
There's gotta be **something** I can do!
I just gotta get creative, right?!
Not with **YOUR** magic.
But maybe with ours.

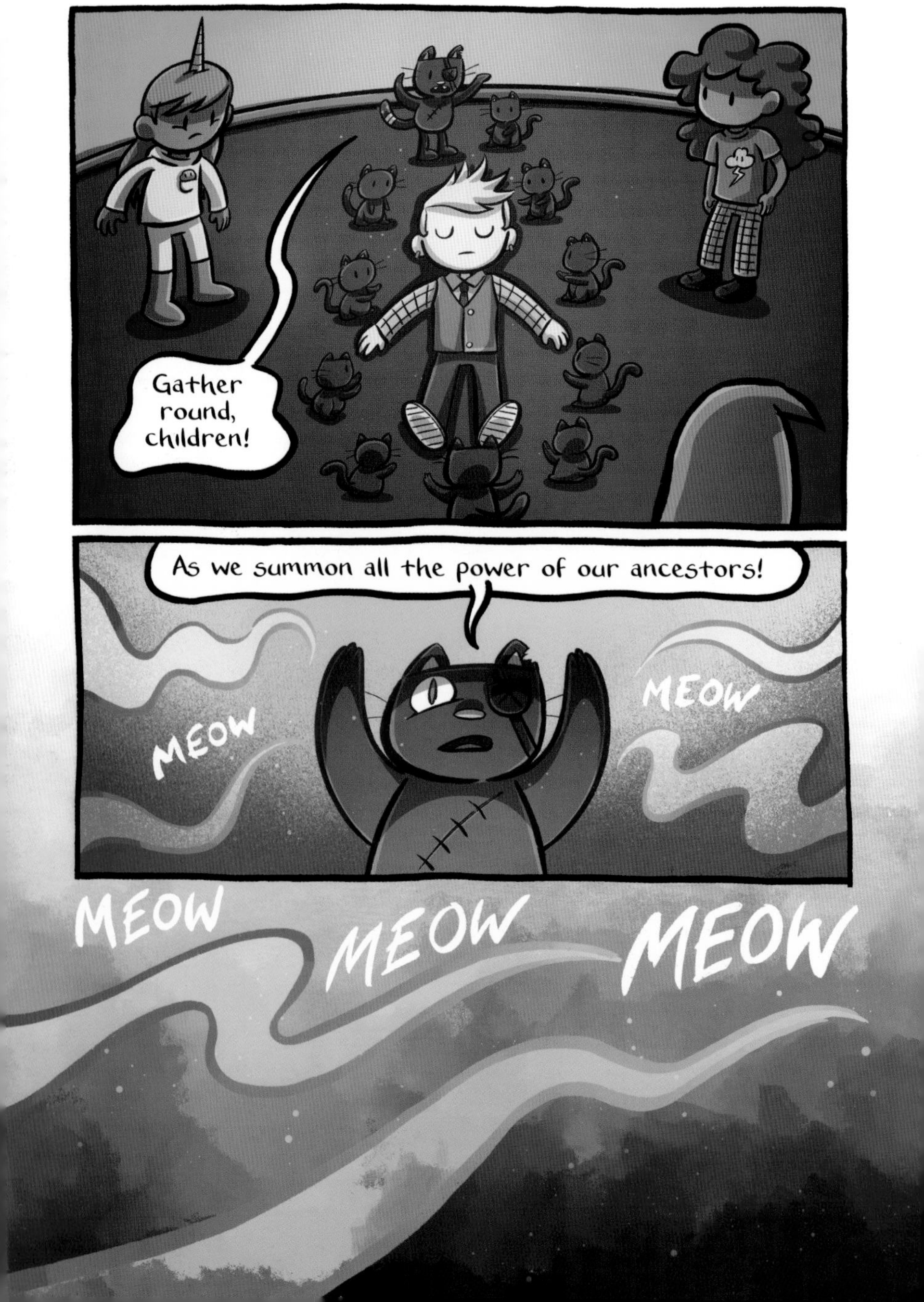
Gather round, children!
As we summon all the power of our ancestors!
MEOW
MEOW
MEOW
MEOW
MEOW

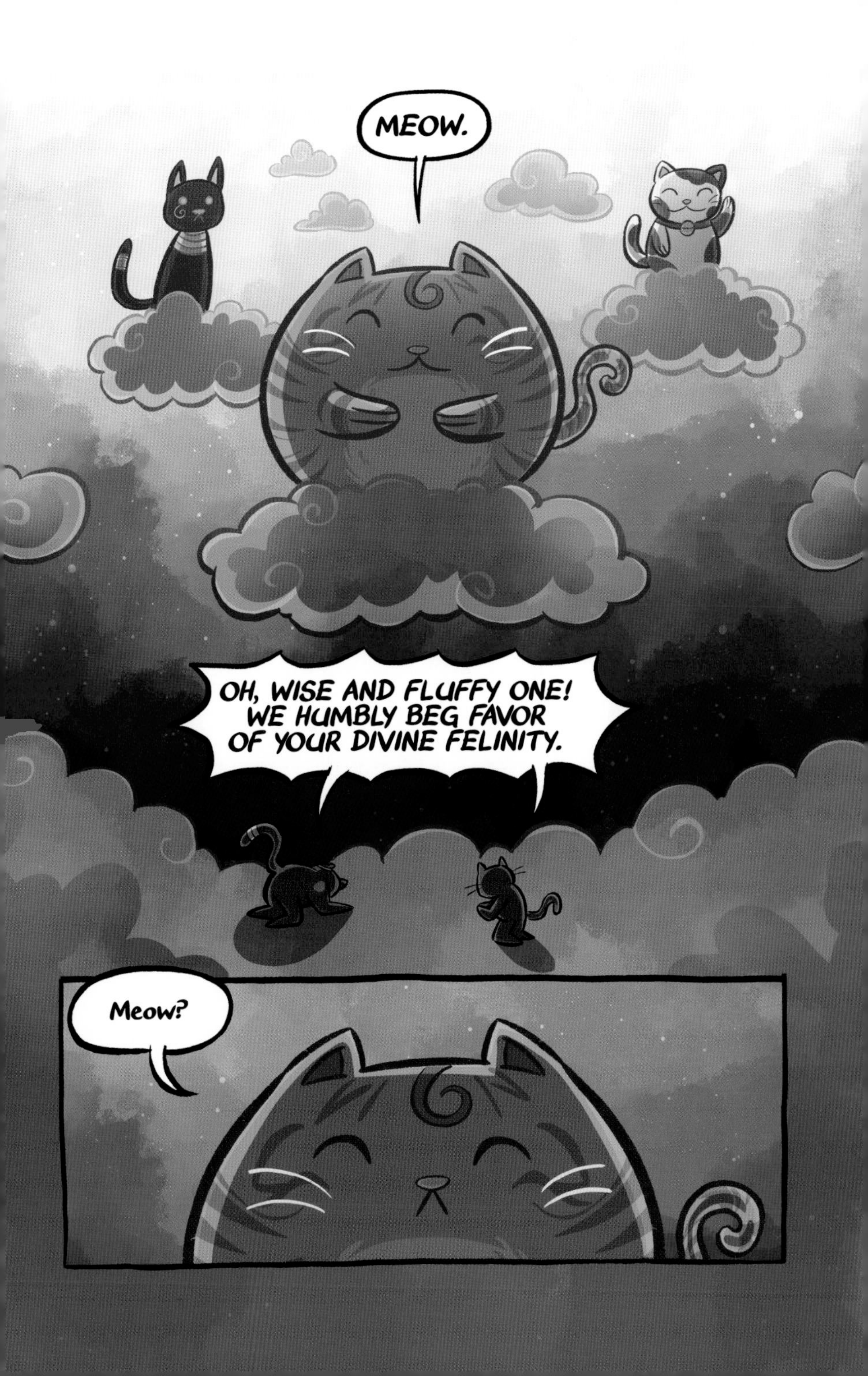
MEOW.
OH, WISE AND FLUFFY ONE! WE HUMBLY BEG FAVOR OF YOUR DIVINE FELINITY.
Meow?

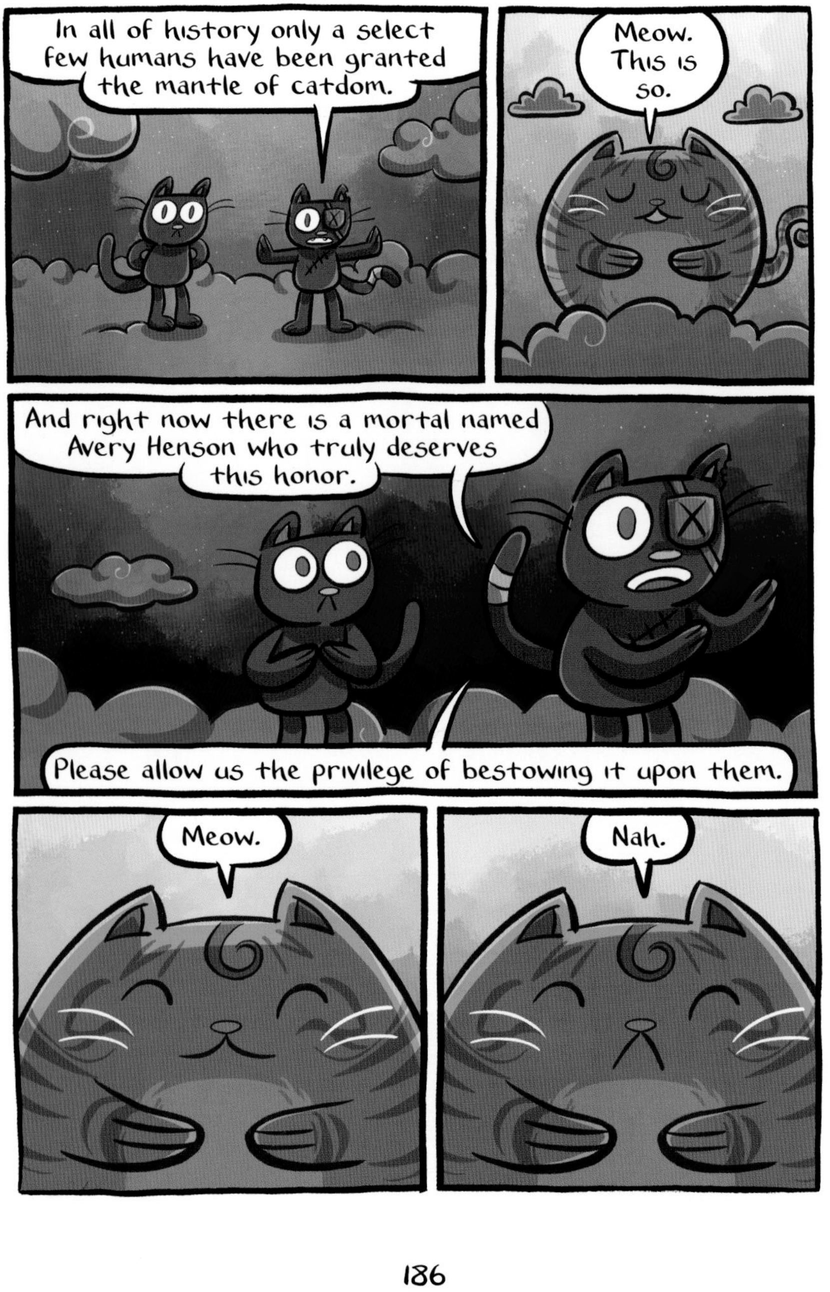
In all of history only a select few humans have been granted the mantle of catdom.
Meow. This is so.
And right now there is a mortal named Avery Henson who truly deserves this honor.
Please allow us the privilege of bestowing it upon them.
Meow.
Nah.

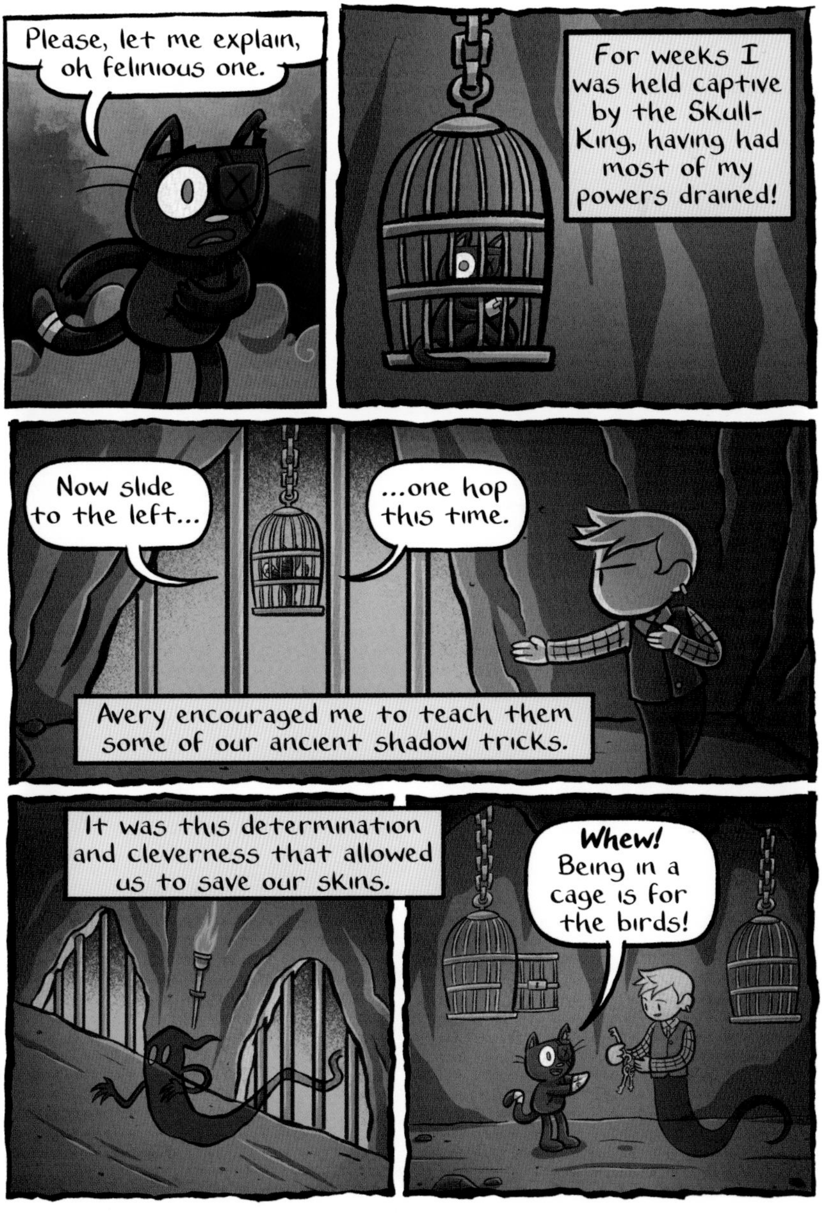
Please, let me explain, oh felinious one.
For weeks I was held captive by the Skull-King, having had most of my powers drained!
Now slide to the left...
...one hop this time.
Avery encouraged me to teach them some of our ancient shadow tricks.
It was this determination and cleverness that allowed us to save our skins.
Whew! Being in a cage is for the birds!

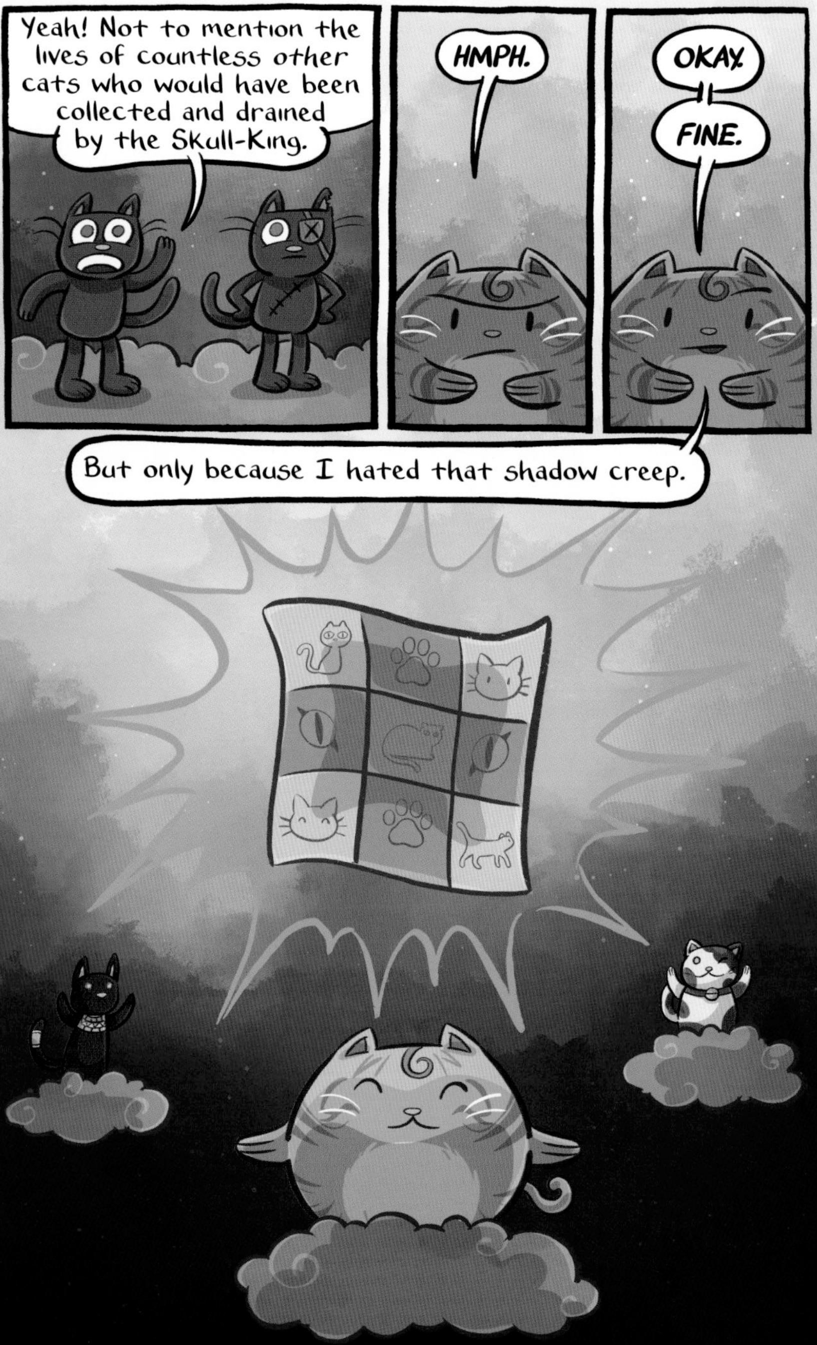
Yeah! Not to mention the lives of countless other cats who would have been collected and drained by the Skull-King.
HMPH.
OKAY.
FINE.
But only because I hated that shadow creep.

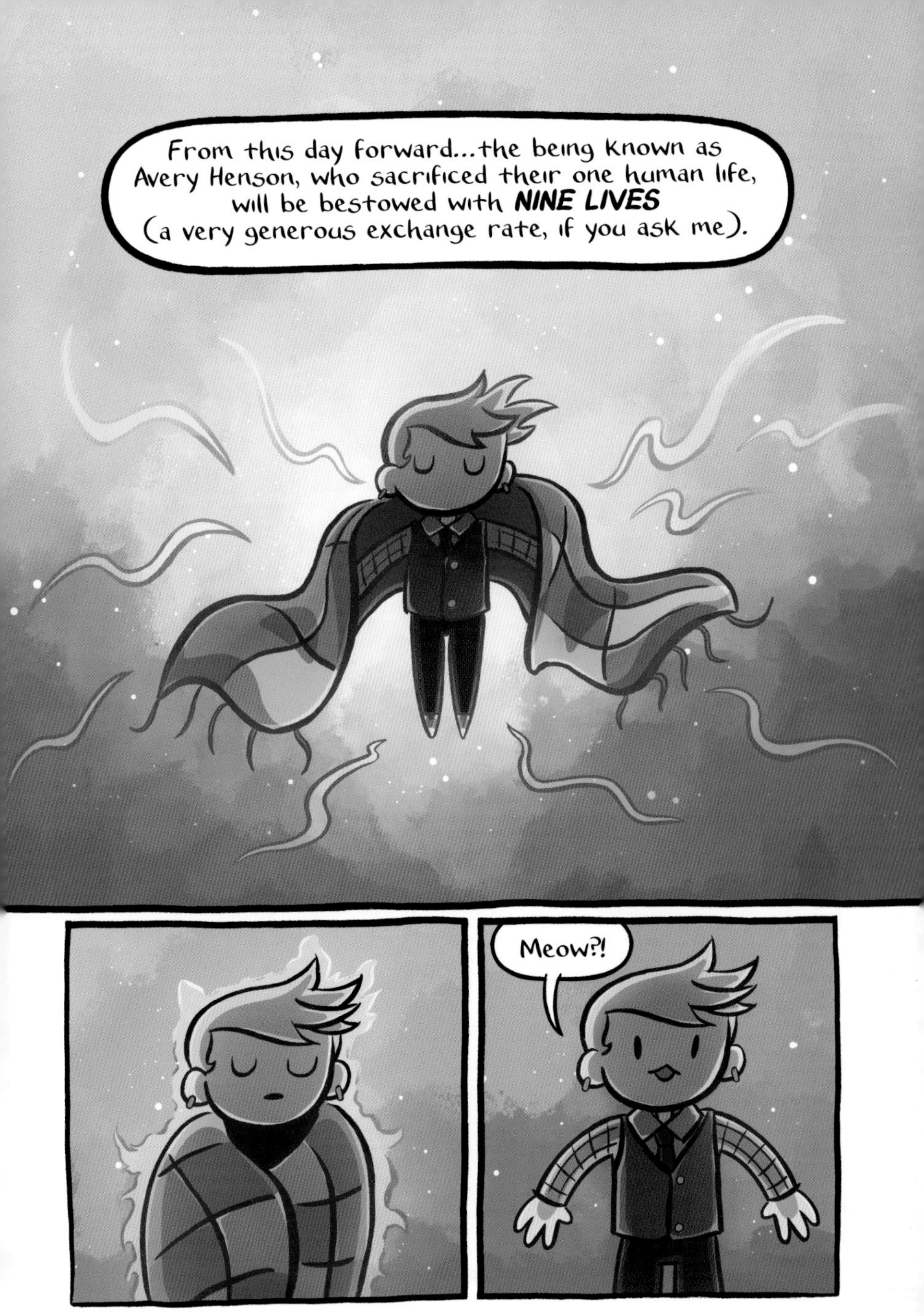
From this day forward...the being known as Avery Henson, who sacrificed their one human life, will be bestowed with **NINE LIVES** (a very generous exchange rate, if you ask me).
Meow?!

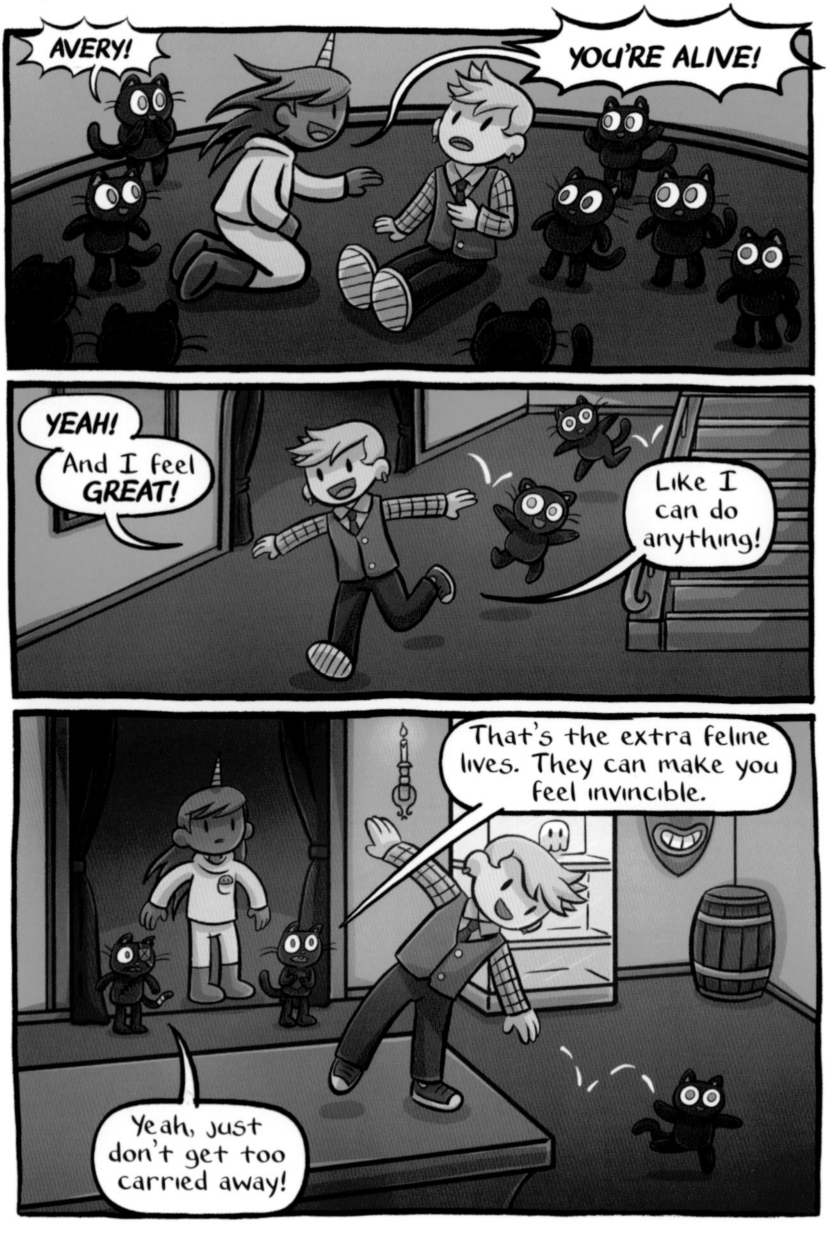
AVERY!
YOU'RE ALIVE!
YEAH!
And I feel GREAT!
Like I can do anything!
That's the extra feline lives. They can make you feel invincible.
Yeah, just don't get too carried away!

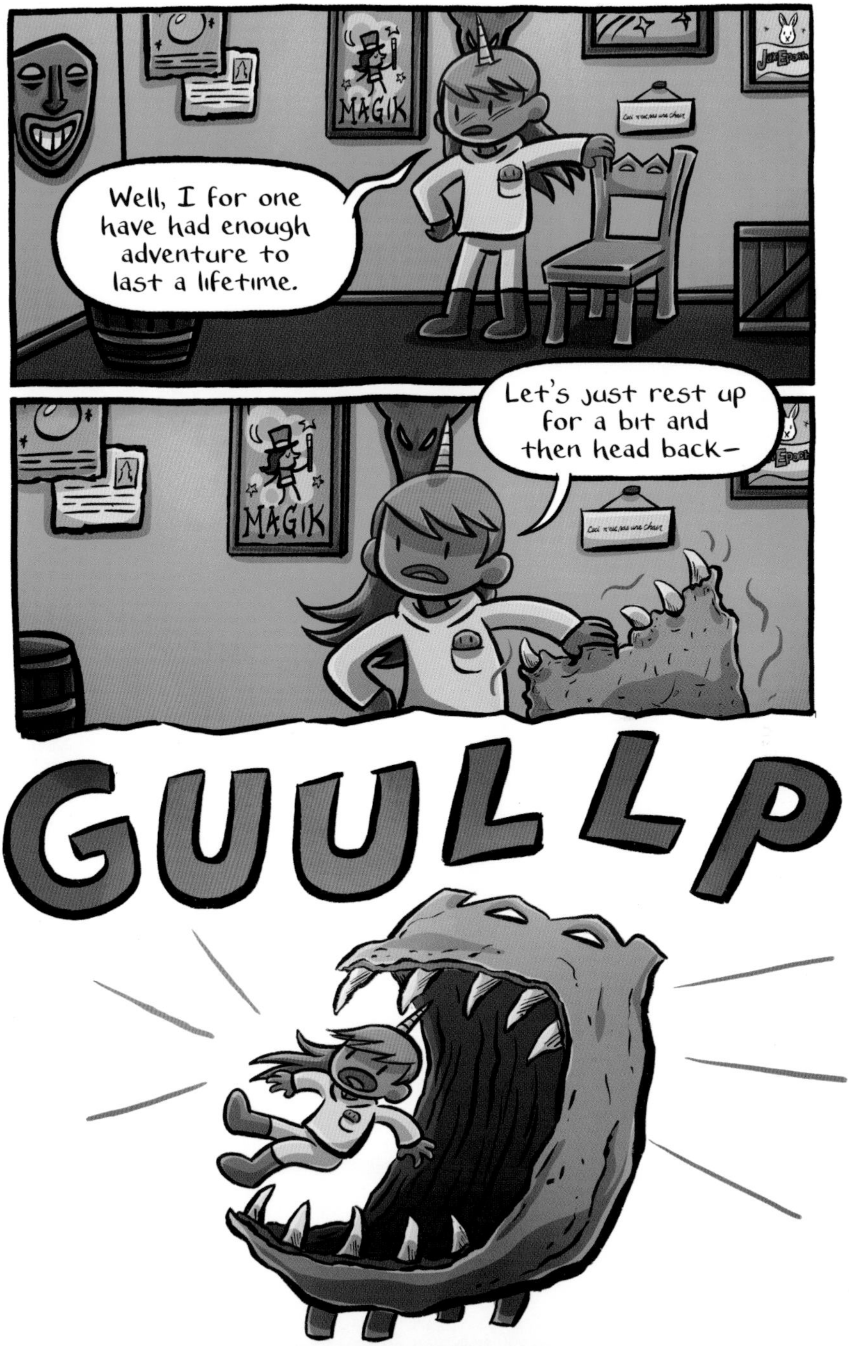
MAGIK
Well, I for one have had enough adventure to last a lifetime.
MAGIK
Let's just rest up for a bit and then head back—
GUULLP

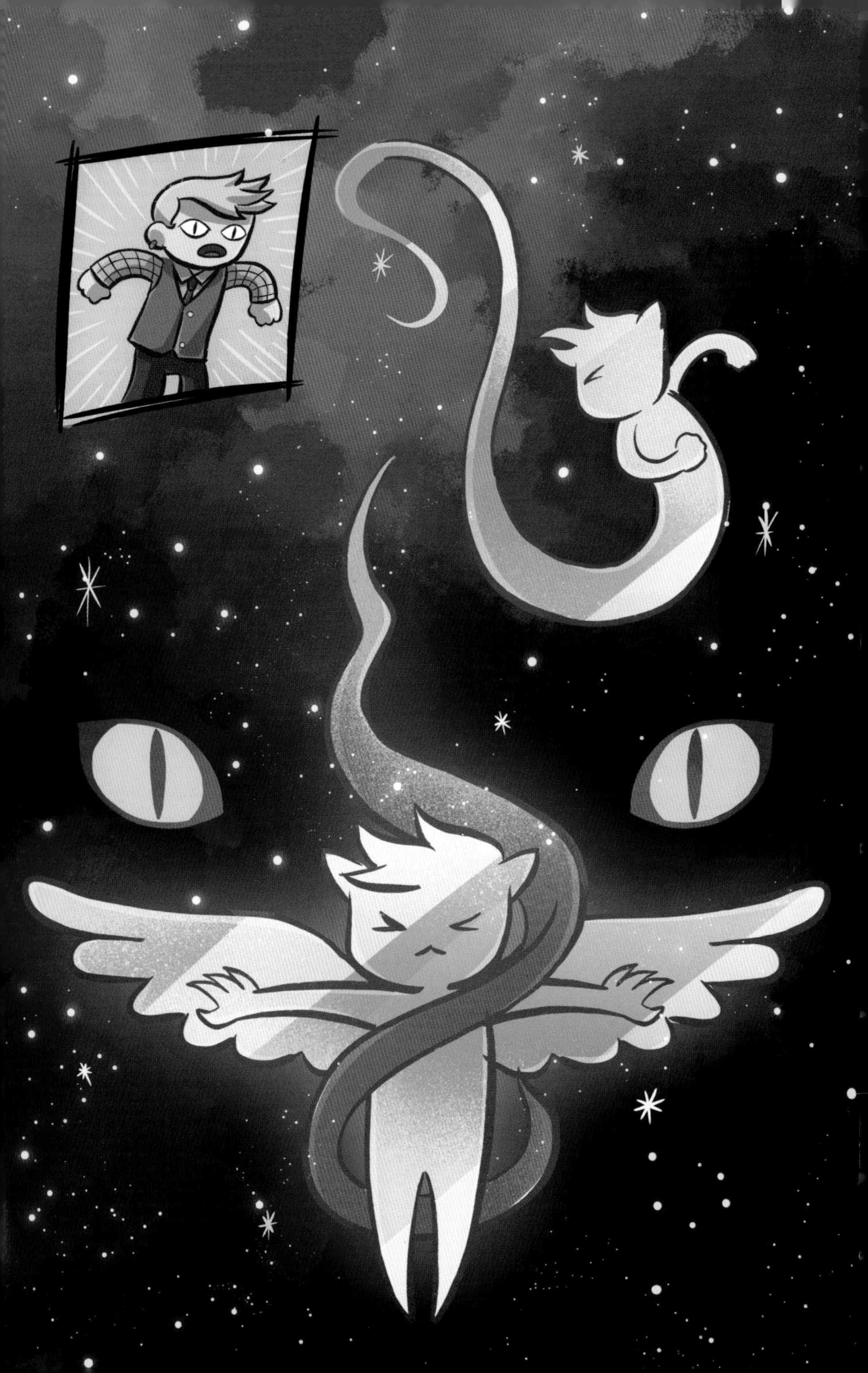

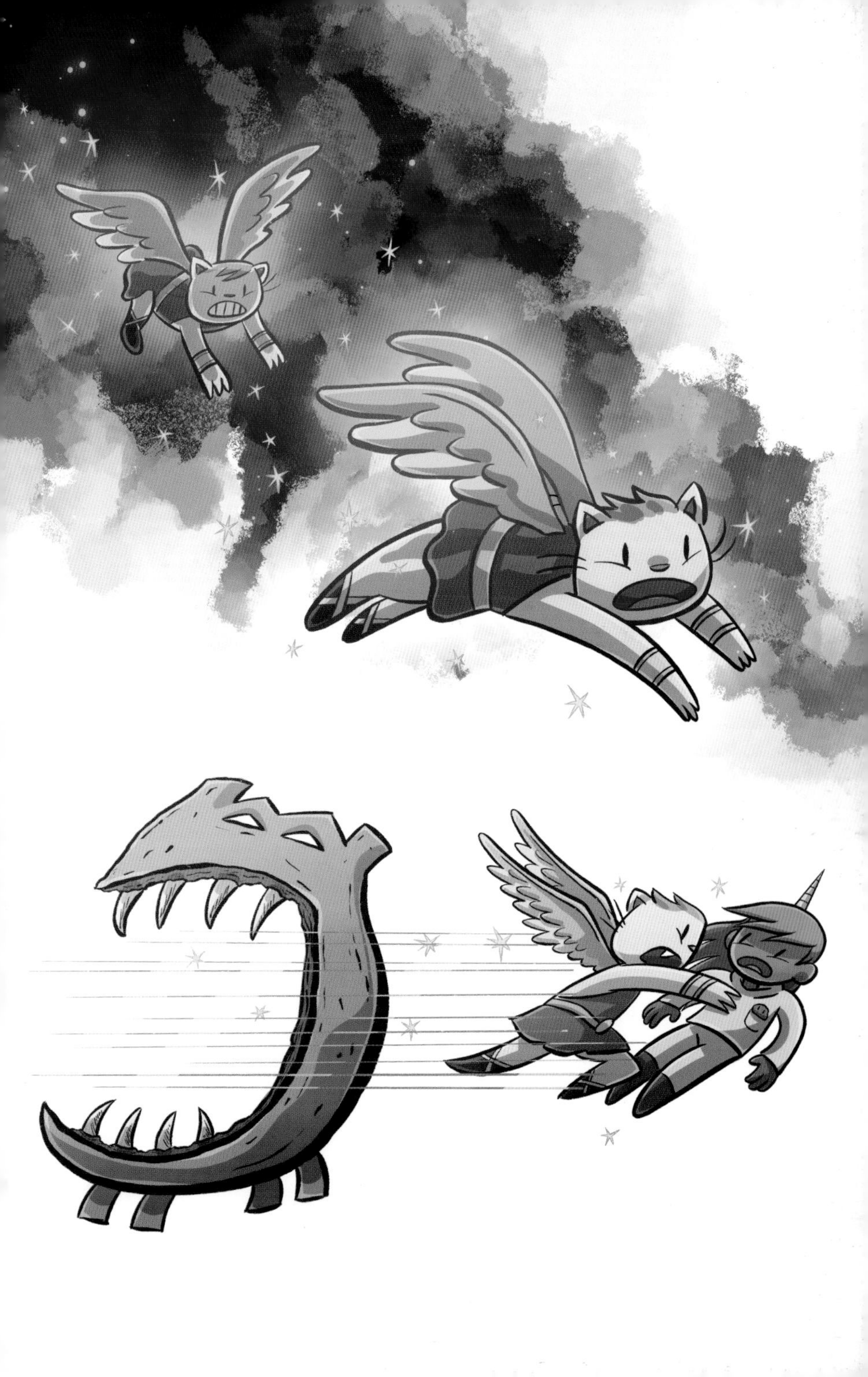

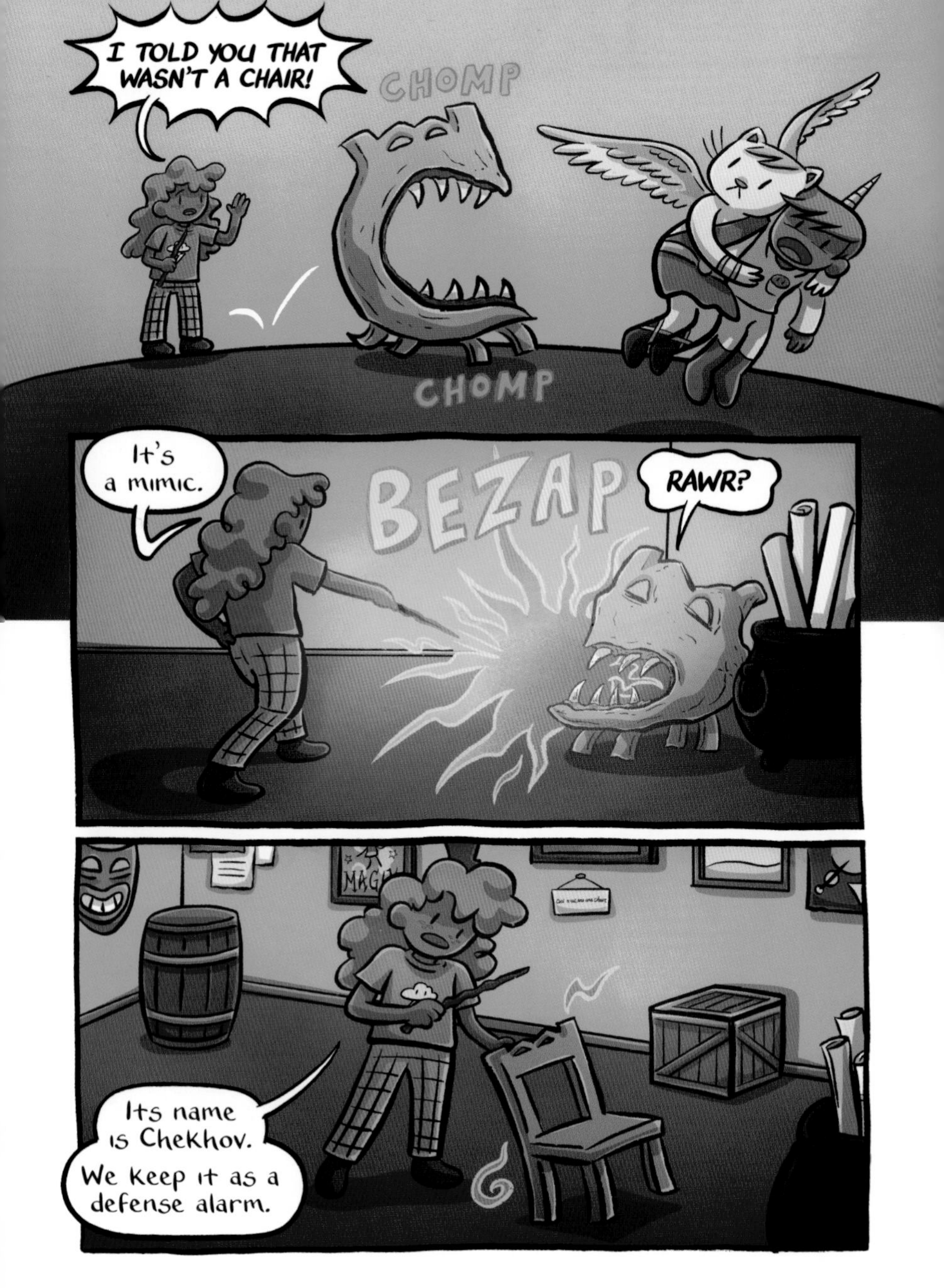
I TOLD YOU THAT WASN'T A CHAIR!
CHOMP
CHOMP
It's a mimic.
BEZAP
RAWR?
Its name is Chekhov.
We keep it as a defense alarm.

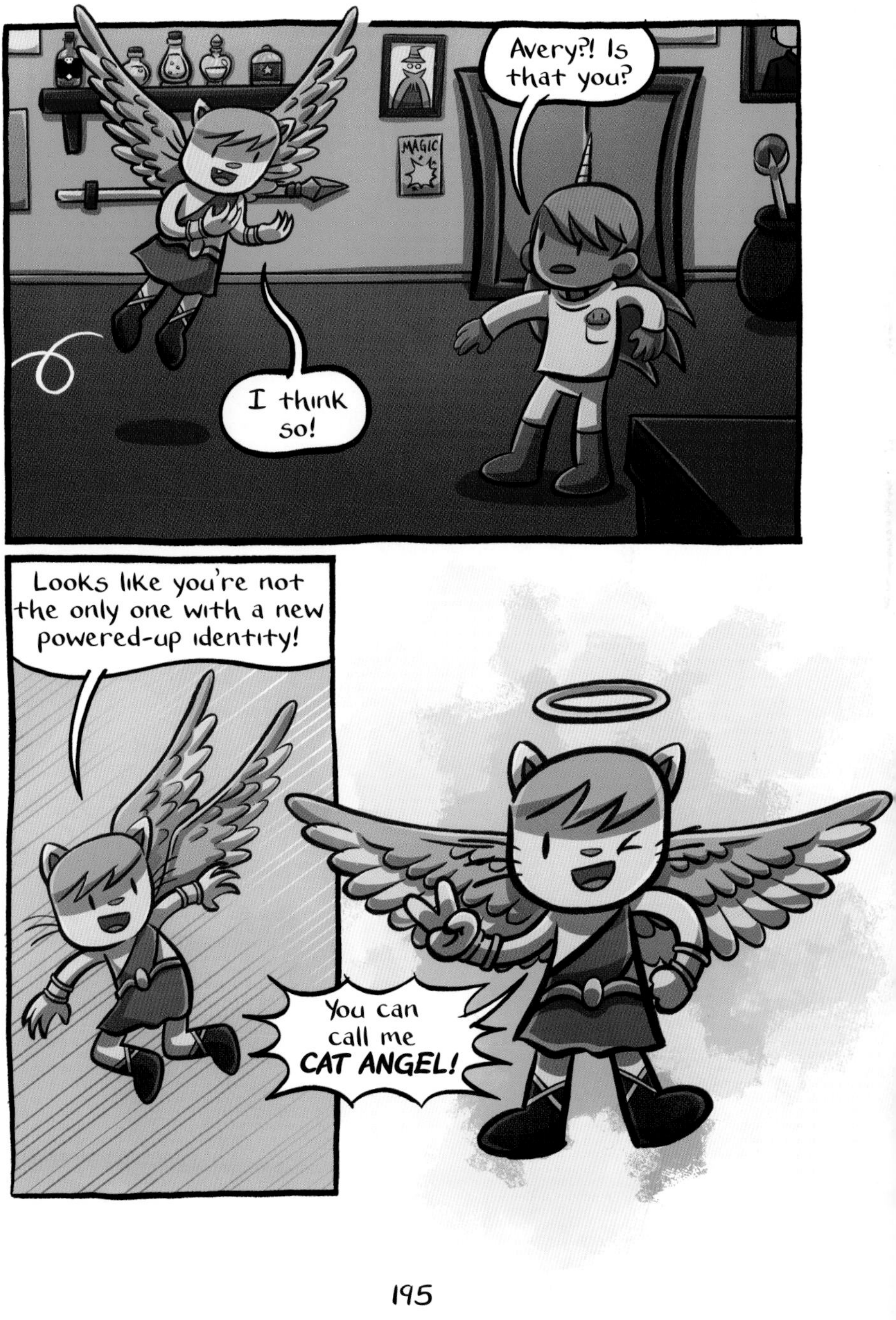

Avery?! Is that you?
I think so!
MAGIC
Looks like you're not the only one with a new powered-up identity!
You can call me **CAT ANGEL!**

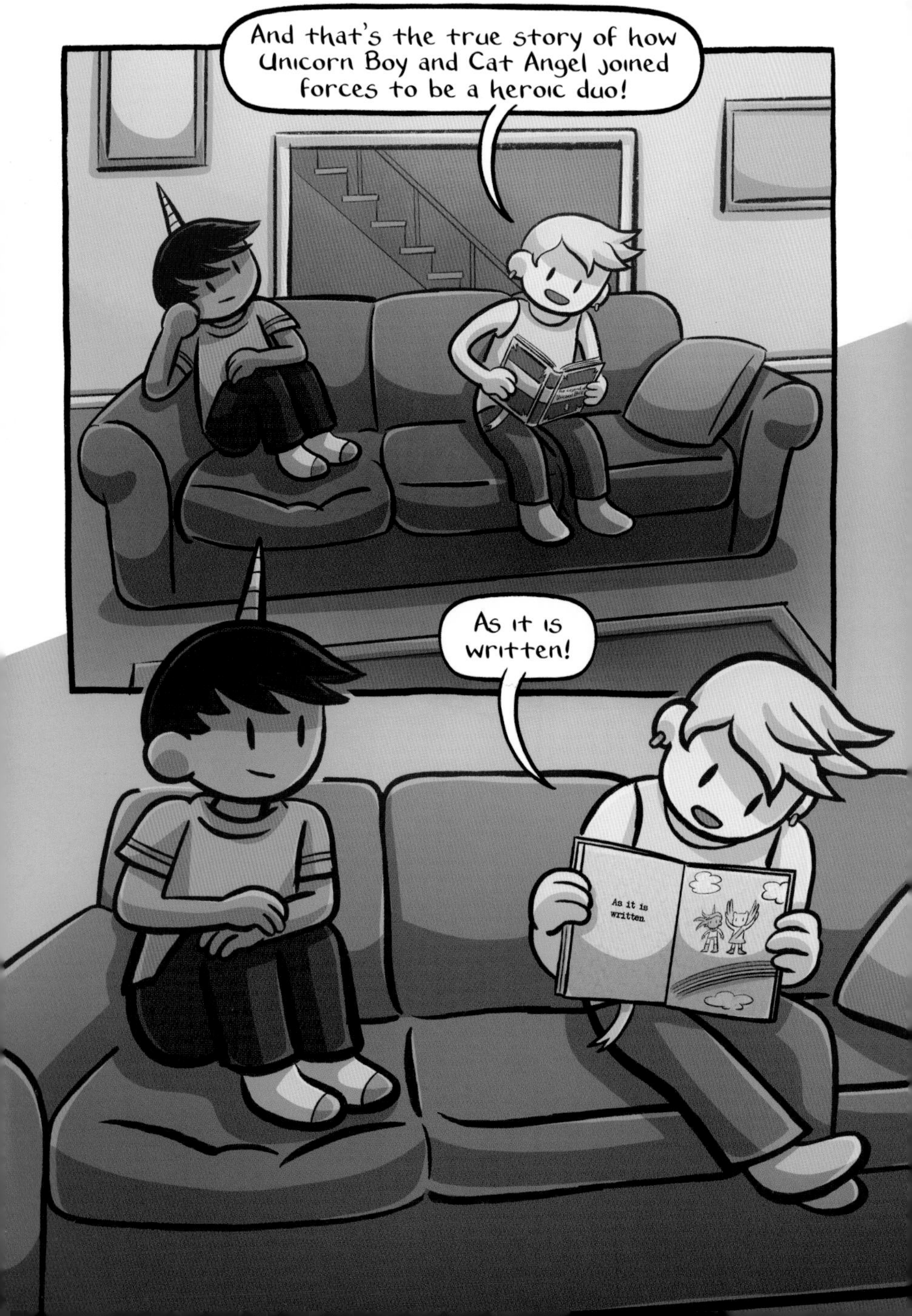
And that's the true story of how Unicorn Boy and Cat Angel joined forces to be a heroic duo!
As it is written!
As it is written.

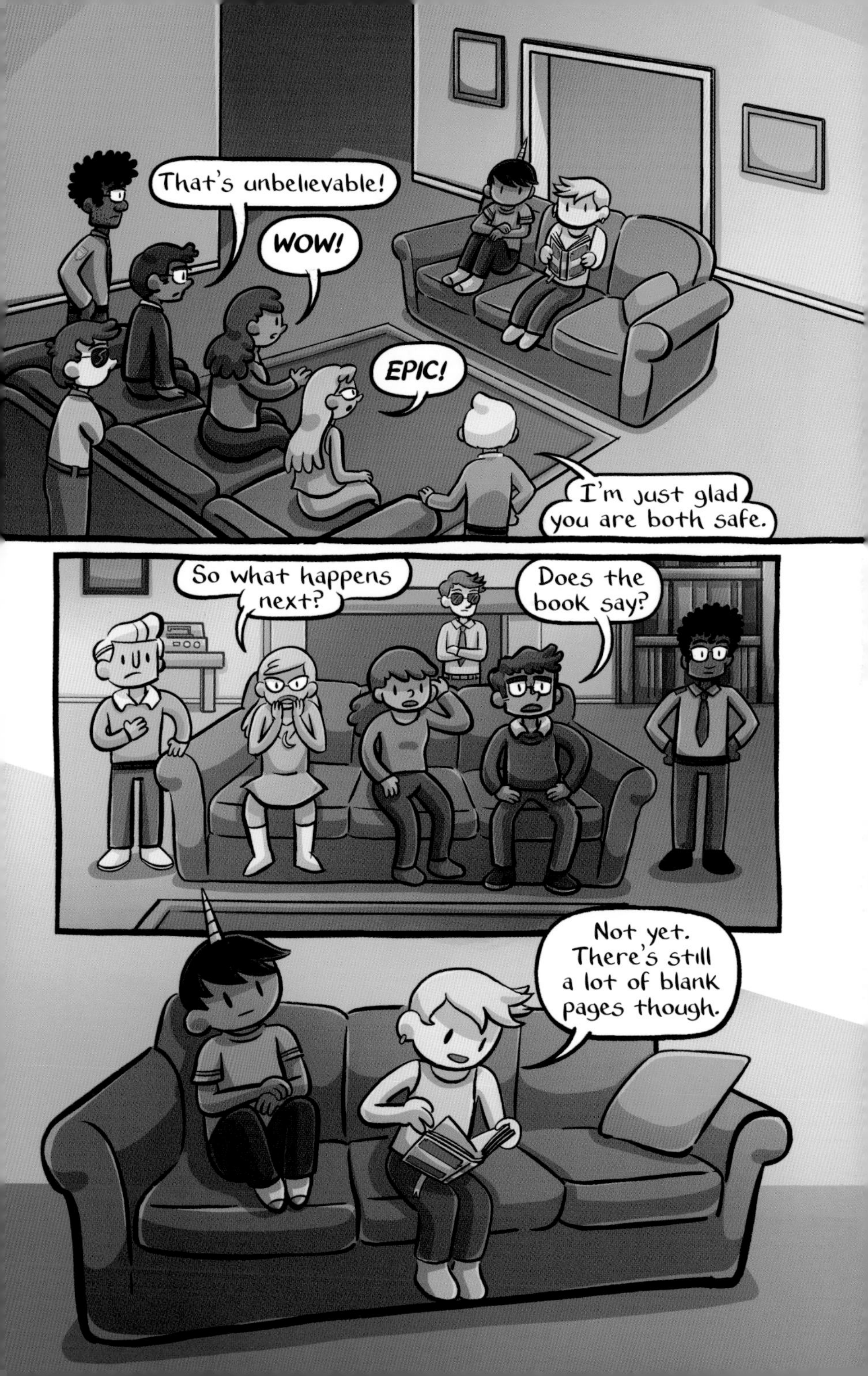

That's unbelievable!
WOW!
EPIC!
I'm just glad you are both safe.
So what happens next?
Does the book say?
Not yet. There's still a lot of blank pages though.

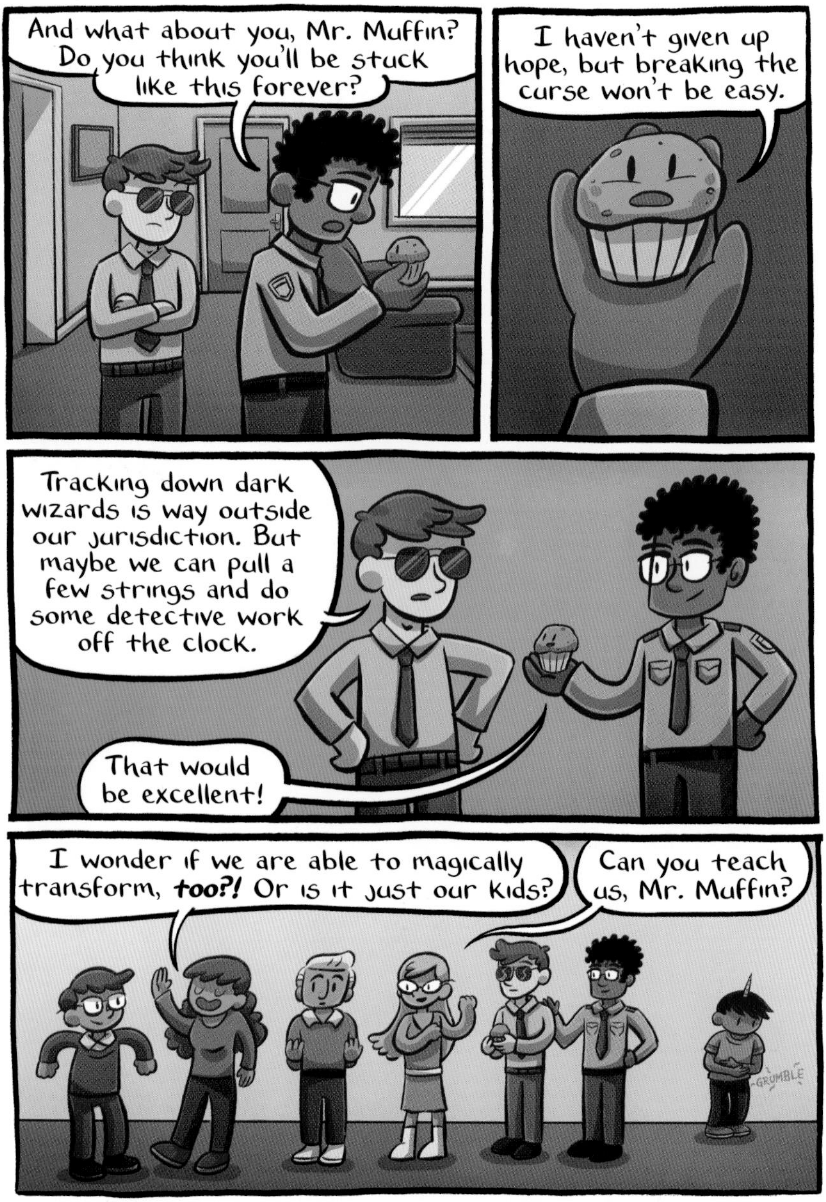
And what about you, Mr. Muffin? Do you think you'll be stuck like this forever?
I haven't given up hope, but breaking the curse won't be easy.
Tracking down dark wizards is way outside our jurisdiction. But maybe we can pull a few strings and do some detective work off the clock.
That would be excellent!
I wonder if we are able to magically transform, ***too?!*** Or is it just our kids?
Can you teach us, Mr. Muffin?
GRUMBLE

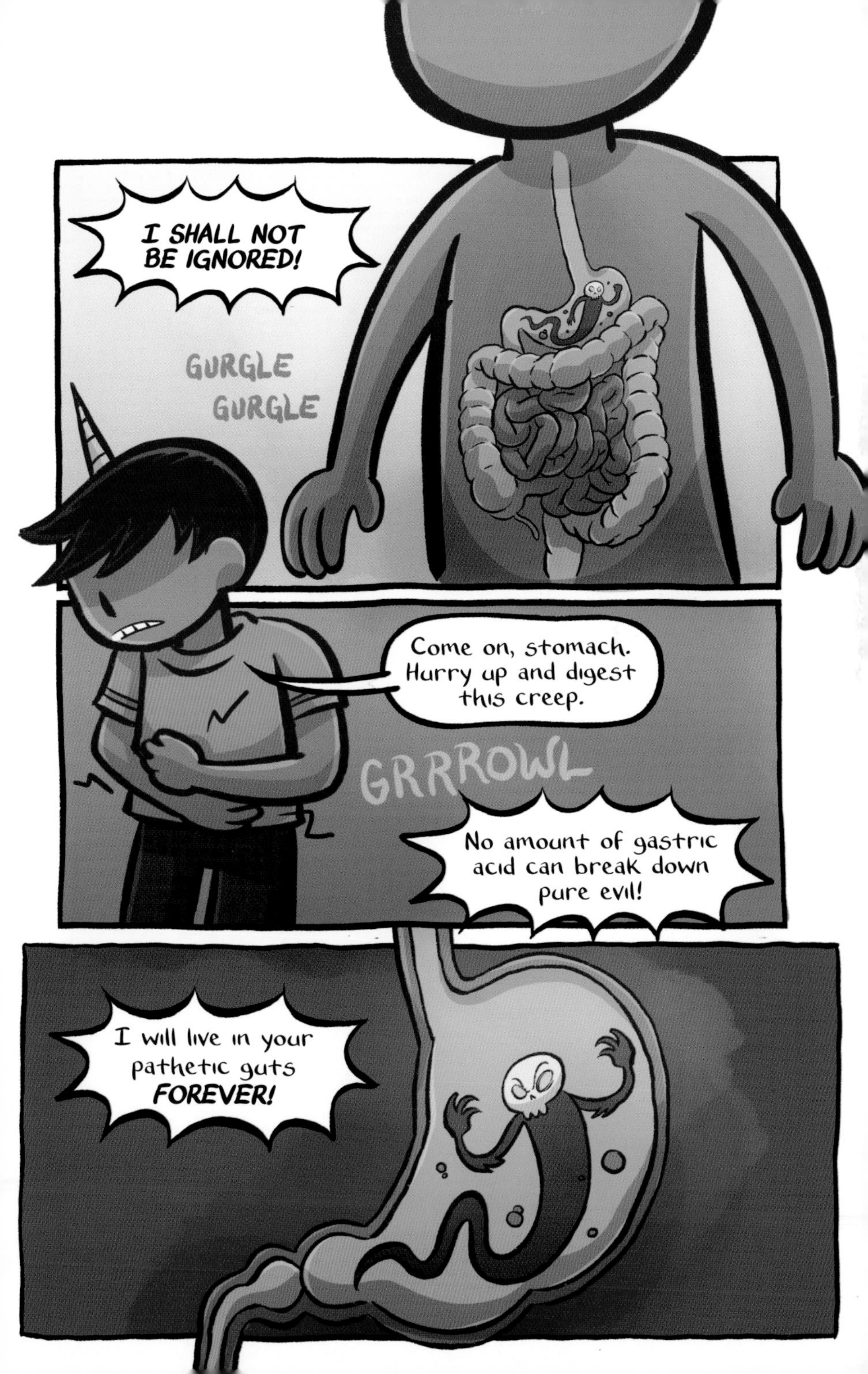
I SHALL NOT BE IGNORED!
GURGLE
GURGLE
Come on, stomach. Hurry up and digest this creep.
GRRROWL
No amount of gastric acid can break down pure evil!
I will live in your pathetic guts FOREVER!

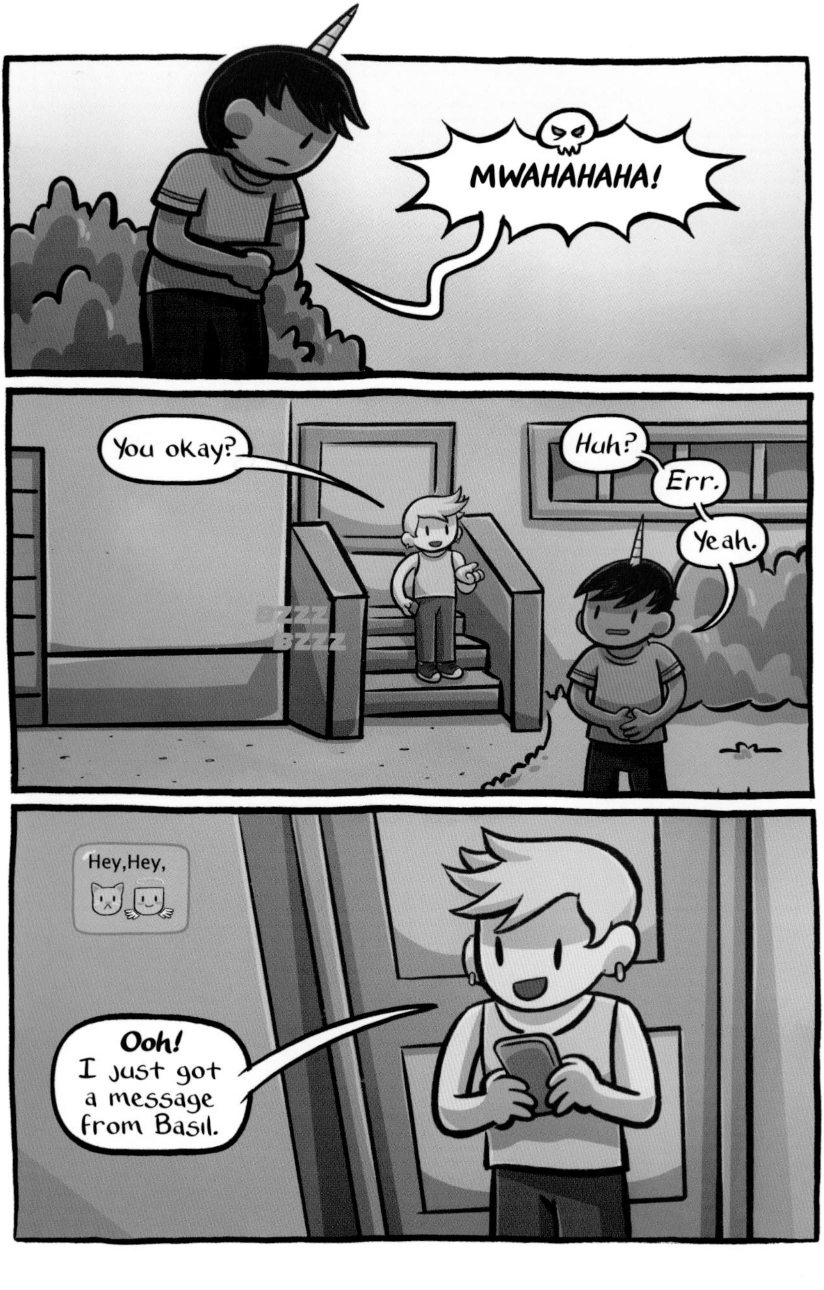
MWAHAHAHA!
You okay?
Huh?
Err.
Yeah.
BZZZ
BZZZ
Hey,Hey,
Ooh! I just got a message from Basil.

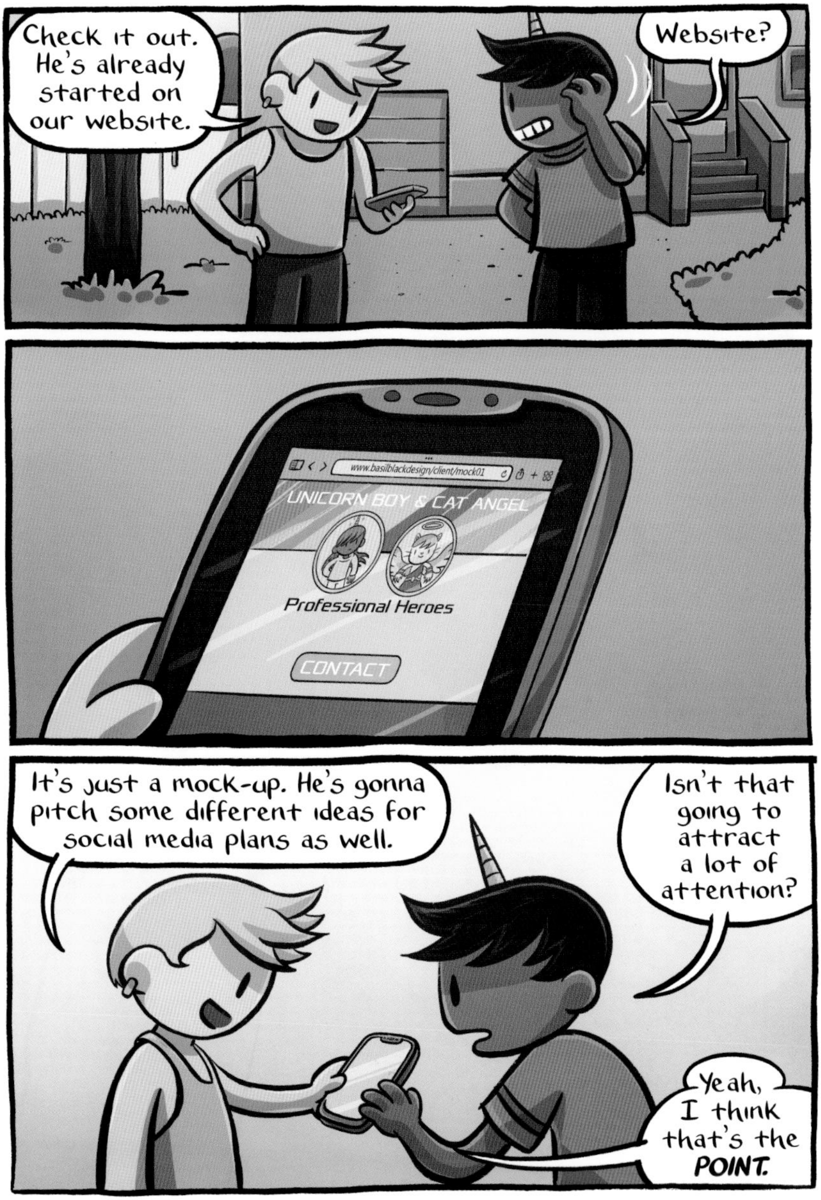
Check it out. He's already started on our website.
Website?
www.basilblackdesign/client/mock01
UNICORN BOY & CAT ANGEL
Professional Heroes
CONTACT
It's just a mock-up. He's gonna pitch some different ideas for social media plans as well.
Isn't that going to attract a lot of attention?
Yeah, I think that's the POINT.

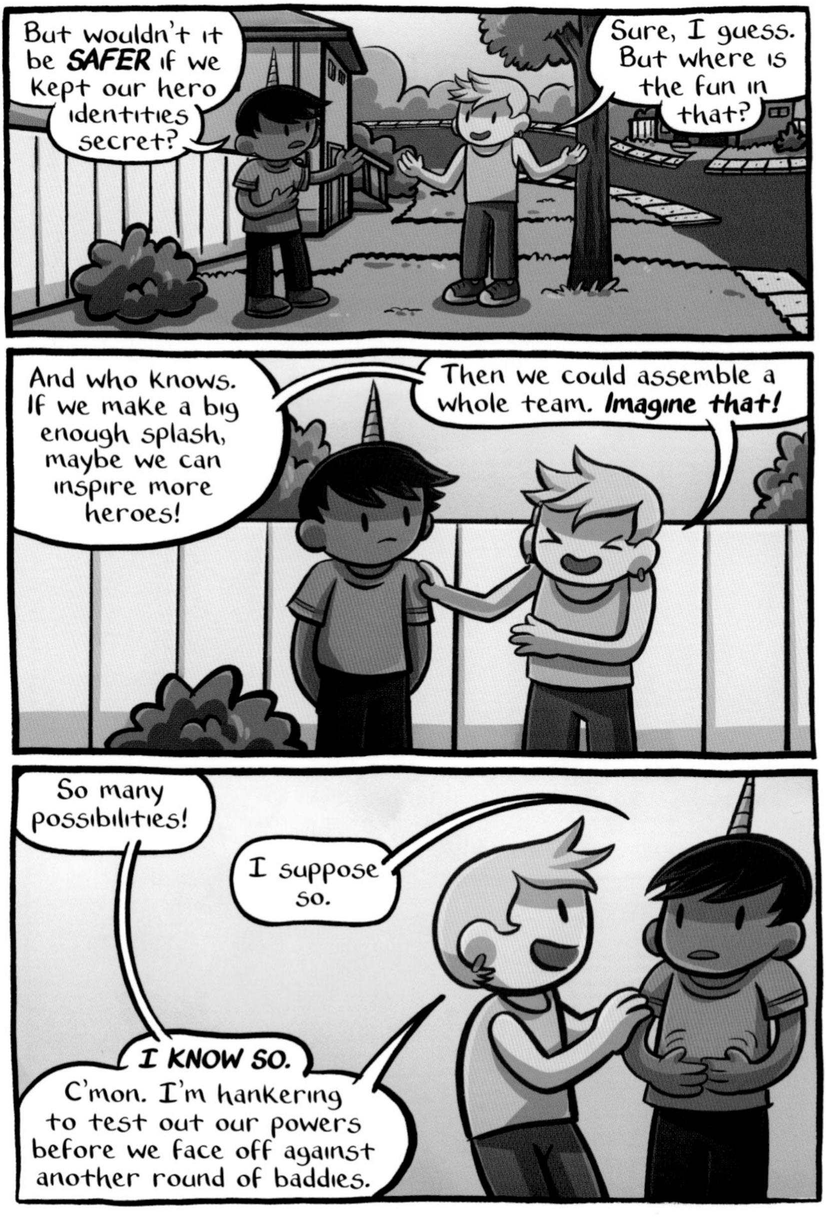
But wouldn't it be SAFER if we kept our hero identities secret?
Sure, I guess. But where is the fun in that?
And who knows. If we make a big enough splash, maybe we can inspire more heroes!
Then we could assemble a whole team. Imagine that!
So many possibilities!
I suppose so.
I KNOW SO.
C'mon. I'm hankering to test out our powers before we face off against another round of baddies.

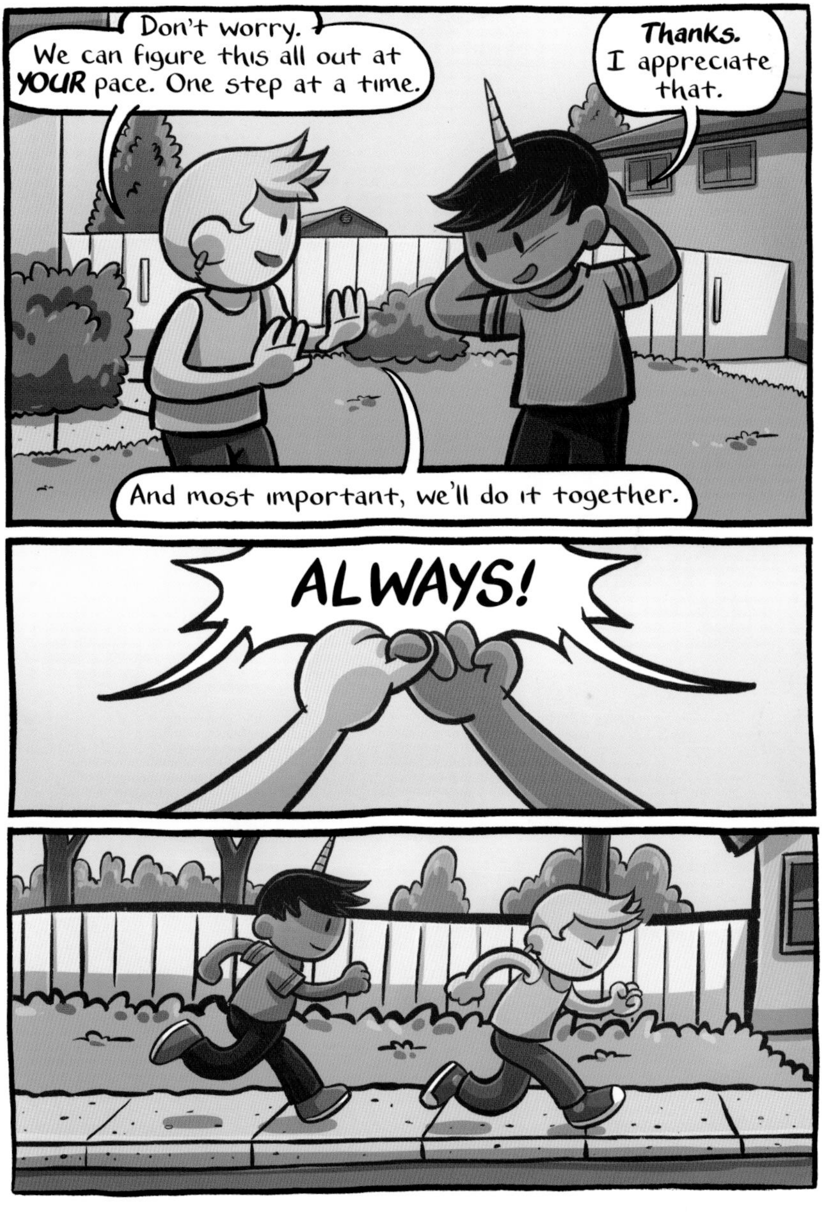
Don't worry.
We can figure this all out at **YOUR** pace. One step at a time.
Thanks.
I appreciate that.
And most important, we'll do it together.
ALWAYS!

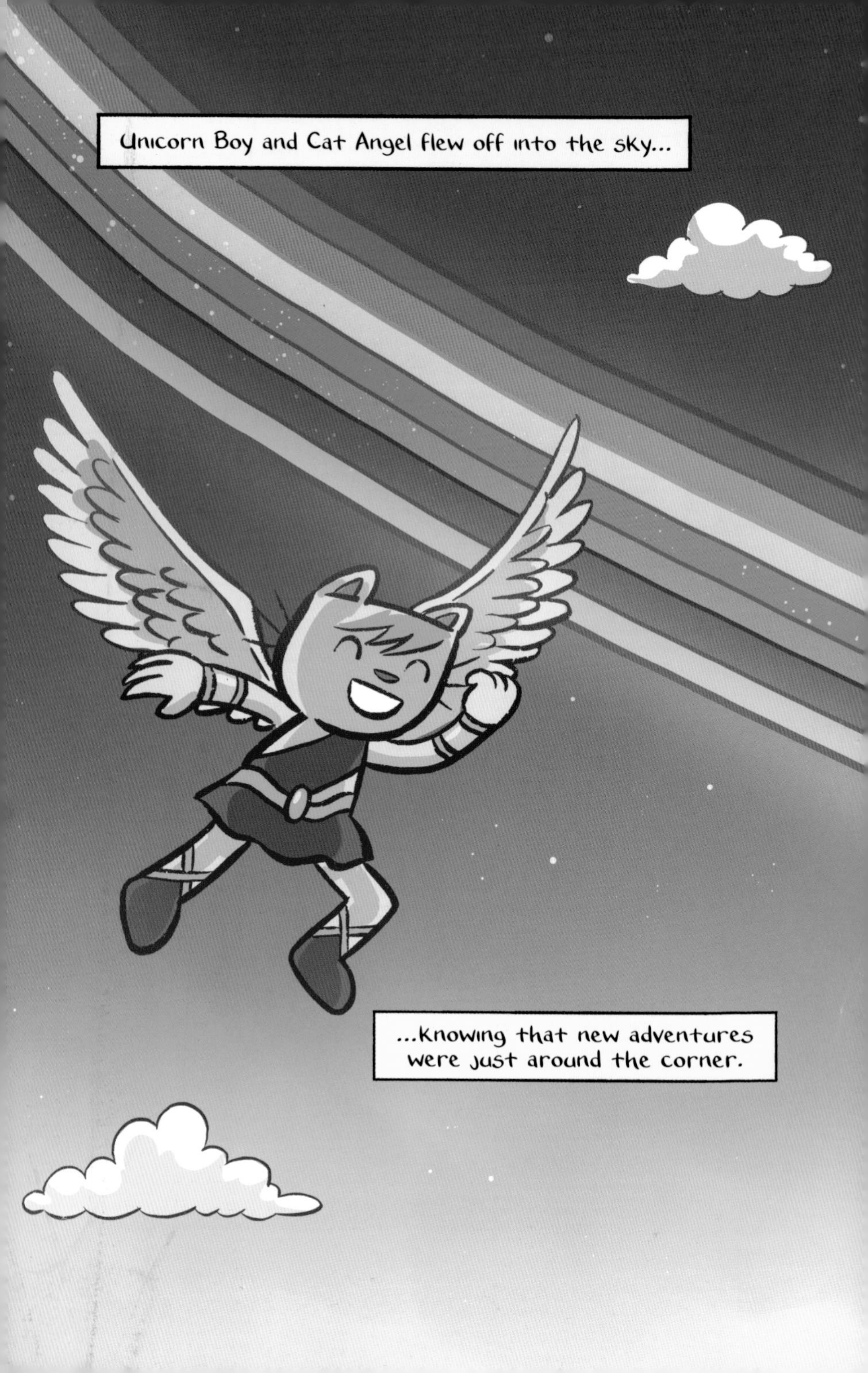
Unicorn Boy and Cat Angel flew off into the sky...
...knowing that new adventures were just around the corner.

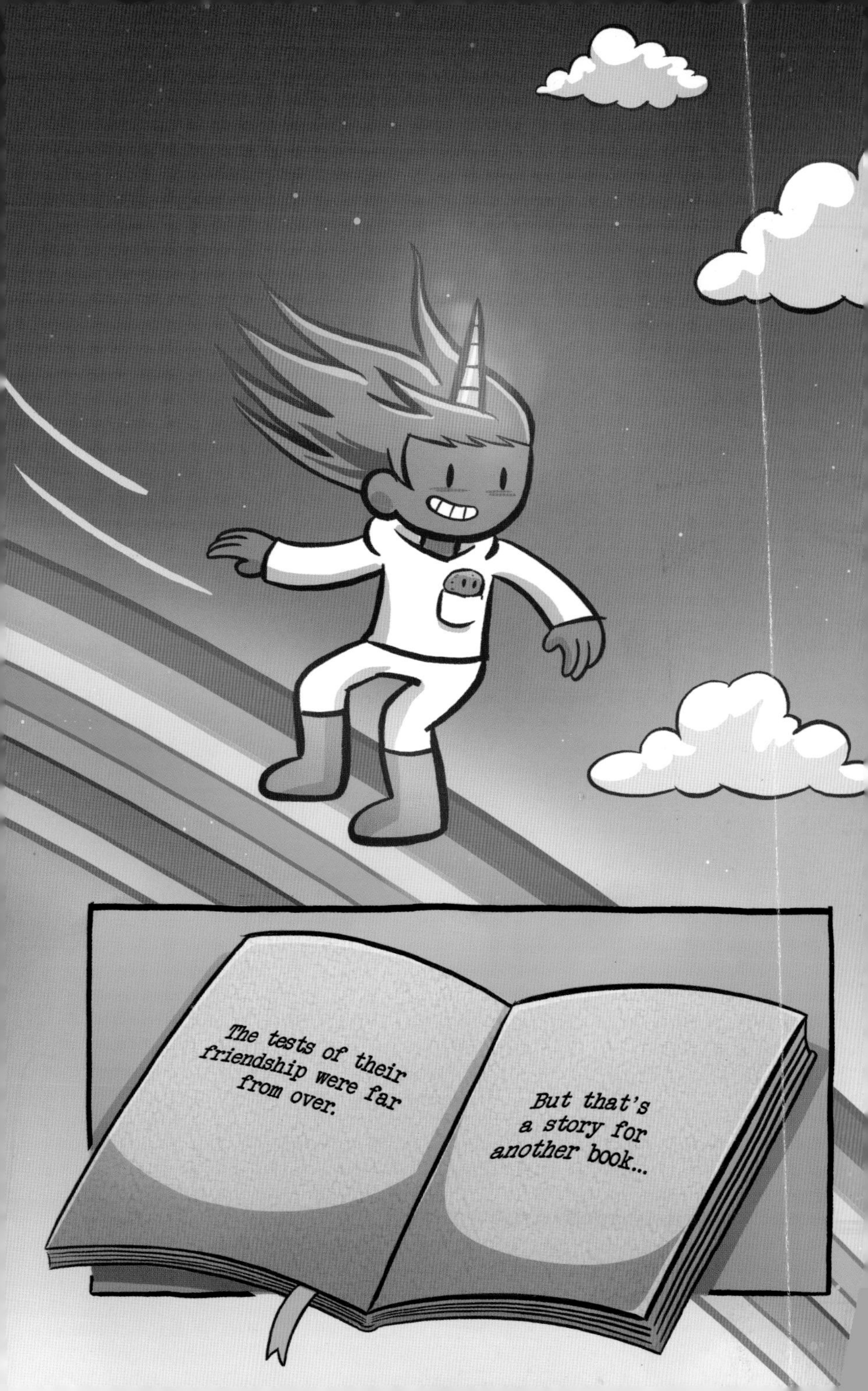
The tests of their friendship were far from over.
But that's a story for another book...

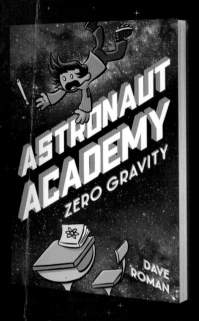

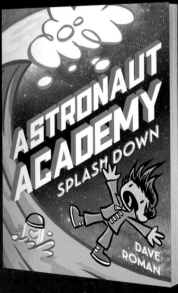